Exposure

Also by Talitha Stevenson

An Empty Room

Exposure

Talitha Stevenson

Virago

A *Virago* Book

First published in Great Britain by Virago in 2005

Copyright © Talitha Stevenson 2005

The moral right of the author has been asserted.

A CIP catalogue record for this book
is available from the British Library.

ISBN 1 86049 986 4

Typeset in Bembo by Palimpsest Book Production Limited,
Polmont, Stirlingshire
Printed and bound in Great Britain by
Mackays of Chatham plc, Chatham, Kent

Virago Press
An imprint of
Time Warner Book Group UK
Brettenham House
Lancaster Place
London WC2E 7EN

www.virago.co.uk

For Jonty Elkington

Acknowledgements

I would like to thank John Harwood-Stevenson for supplying me with essential information on the life of a London barrister. I am grateful to Michael Birnbaum QC, for allowing me to follow him about the Old Bailey. Thanks also to Dr Brian Kaplan, genius physician, who restored my health and then made clever suggestions about the early chapters of my novel, just to show off. I could not have written about Goran and Mila without the advice of Sergey M.

All our failures are, ultimately, failures in love
Iris Murdoch

Chapter 1

As if someone had come into the room and caused him to lose the thread of what he was saying, Alistair Langford had forgotten what he believed in. He had spent his life making ruthless compromises for the sake of his ideals and it had been a great surprise to find that they had just drifted off. The rest of humanity had continued to drive cars and carry babies and have lunch just the same. He gave the sky a wry smile because it was his sixty-third birthday and he had never expected to spend it standing on the edge of a cliff.

Sea spray blew up and fine chalk dust puffed over the drop as if in reply. He was not usually one for superfluous journeys, not one to leave the table for an ordinary sunset or moon. But now he looked down quietly at the grey sea, and the waves that rose and formed and broke in on themselves.

Nothing frightening had ever happened to him before. He had kept clear of all danger. He had cultivated interests rather than passions and had always presented his eyes with elegance rather than troublesome beauty. It was a discreet pleasure that he took in his nineteenth-century tables, his John Cafe candlesticks, his Chippendale chairs. These were all arrangements of lines and angles, essentially, prey to the laws of trigonometry.

The sea was very different. He looked at his shoes on the rough yellow grass. Behind him, two colourful girls came along the path. They were talking a language he couldn't understand and they laughed as they passed. For a moment, Alistair was afraid they were mocking his walking-stick, but he let the thought go with the sound of their voices and their shoes thudding on the soft chalk. What on earth was the point of worrying about his dignity now? Besides, it was too hot.

Beneath him the sea looked cold and fierce and he liked watching it hitting the bottom of the cliffs and spraying up in arcs against the chalk.

His leg had only been mobile for a week now and he knew the physiotherapist would not have encouraged him to drive or to walk this far. He was genuinely amazed at the way he had just grabbed the car keys and left. Why? He knew what had happened – he had been struck by a strong physical memory: the sensation of space, of the whole Channel in front of you. It had taken hold of his stomach like hunger. Next thing he knew he had walked out of his mother's old house – leaving his son packing up her holy china and brass relics, her lifetime's treasures – and made his way up here.

It was a warm wind and unusually hot even for August. As he drove through Dover, he had found it composed of white-hot, abandoned streets. There was a sense of what the hours after a nuclear disaster might be like in the dry, bleached lawns, the shrivelled geraniums swinging eerily in their baskets on Maison Dieu Road.

He had wound his way up the cliff road, left the car in the public car park and limped along the path in search of the view. And now here it was: the Channel, grey-green and empty all the way to Calais. A disembodied female voice drifted in from the vast ferry terminal on the right. It urged people in toneless French and German to get on or get off the boat. It all seemed rather pointless – but ultimately benign. There were seagull cries, which were always faintly exciting.

It was strange how this view still found its way into his dreams. As a boy, he had often spent whole afternoons hiding and plotting up here, but today he was exhausted after just ten minutes or so. He thudded his walking-stick against the ground, feeling obscurely disappointed. Still, he told himself, there was always the danger that excessive solitude might start him reliving the event. He was at least avoiding that.

In fact, there was no reason to be concerned about this, because his mind was clean of the recent past. Bizarre as it was, he was not haunted by the event at all, but by something his wife had said about it. At the hospital, holding his hand, Rosalind had turned her white face on him and said, 'But how could you not have *heard* them, Alistair? *How?* They must have been . . . silent as *dogs*.'

The sinister image was so foreign, so *film-noir* sophisticated somehow

2

on her neat, scrubbed mouth. It had made him feel oddly threatened. It was as if she had been hiding some part of herself from him all these years. Suddenly it occurred to him that she might have had an affair. *She* might have been duplicitous.

How could you tell with other people, even your wife? Was he sixty-three and still unable to feel certain of any of his instincts?

No, surely not. And it was ridiculous, the idea of Rosalind having an affair. In the complacent past he had almost wished she would, because sometimes he wanted her stripped of that inhuman faultlessness for which he had fallen in love with her. Now the idea felt dangerous, though. He needed her elegant conformity more than he ever had, as much as frightened children need stories at night. One act of violence had sent cracks through everything he touched.

Why had she used that odd phrase?

In fact, even though she had not actually been there at the time, it was a good description. The two men had been silent as dogs, padding under the street-lamps after him in their soft trainers. And when they stopped they were invisible too, except for a star of light that bounced off the buckle off the smaller one's belt. He noticed it and moved back a little, behind the phone box – and the star went out.

At exactly that moment, the front door opened four houses along, spilling light voluptuously down the white steps and through the shiny black railings. Bars of shadow grew over the London pavement. Piano music and that singing kind of laughter, which is not really laughter but civilized conspiracy, drifted out with a faint scent of cigar smoke. The host had his arm round the hostess and she raised her hand to hold it, her bracelet or watch-face playing the light back obliviously at the belt buckle. The host said: 'Well, you'll send Roz our love, won't you?'

'Yes, of course I will,' Alistair said.

The smaller man glanced at the other, larger one. Although it was too dark to see the recognition on his face, it was perceptible: yes, this was him. That barrister shit.

'Oh, *damn* it – the *card*!' Alistair said. 'Did I give you her card? *Damn* it! I bet I didn't give it to you – and she wrote you a bloody card especially . . .' He was rummaging in his pockets – patting them all twice.

To the figures in the darkness, it was as if he was playing for time. But he could have had no idea he might need to play for time – to him it was just the end of an evening.

3

'*Hon*estly,' he said, 'how typical of me. She wrote you a card – roses on the front, a window, a cat or something – she made me *promise* I wouldn't forget . . .'

'Well, you're utterly useless, Al. None of us ever understood why she married you,' the host said. He was a very tall, thin man, of the kind you imagine always got his glasses knocked off rather pathetically when he was younger and had arranged his life so it would never happen again. He laughed, just a little harder than was necessary. Then he slapped Alistair's shoulder. 'You just send her our love,' he said.

'I will, Julian.'

'And you're sure you don't want a cab? Last chance . . . you *must* be over the limit.'

The smaller man felt his heart leap, heard his friend's breath catch: after all this build-up, just to watch the bastard drive off in a cab, just to go on back to the flat with a couple of bags of Burger King . . .

'No, no – *really*, I'm OK to drive,' Alistair said, smiling.

The couple stood back in their doorway, framed by golden light, hands linked, a chandelier twinkling behind them. They looked wealthy and content while unseen faces wondered if they had ever been burgled.

The light from the door cut out behind Alistair's heels and he set off towards the new dark blue BMW the two men had identified when they walked that way earlier. They had both wanted to key it, but the larger one said they should save it up – save it *all* up for later.

Now that the time had come, they padded after Alistair, watching him search his pockets for his car keys. Eventually he brought them out of his jacket – along with something else. They heard the tut and groan he made as he recognized the card in his hand. He was coming up to a rubbish bin and he slowed down, his hand moving uncertainly towards it, questioned by his conscience. Should he throw away the card and let his wife assume he had given it to their friends? '*Suppressio veri* or *suggestio falsi*?' he asked himself mockingly, knowing he had told Rosalind many bare-faced lies.

It was then that two figures jumped on him and altered the rarefied quality of his perspective for ever.

They moved quickly: one held his arms back, and the other smashed the baseball bat into his right leg, hard, five or six times. Alistair heard the bone shatter and felt himself crumple. It was an odd, involuntary movement – a dive into the wave of pain. When they dropped him on the pavement, one of them must have stumbled back into a parked car, because the last thing he remembered was the whir of an alarm going off and the headlights pulsing, illuminating the running figures in heartbeats of time.

Now Alistair limped off the cliff path and spotted the car, which would be hot enough to bake cakes in: he had left it, unwisely, in the sunlight. He would not have been able to drive his own car, but this one, which belonged to his wife, was an automatic and just about manageable with his bad leg. He started it and looped his way back into Dover past boarding-house after boarding-house, each one like a long-lost maiden aunt to him, shabbily coquettish behind her busy-lizzies.

Time had really passed since he was last in Dover. The Igglesdon Square bakery, with its little tea-room – he could still taste the scones and jam, the sense of having been a good boy – was a sterile book-shop and stationer's now. The Café de Paris, whose name had conjured so much nonsense, in which he had sat dreaming with an ordinary cup of tea and a book the whole year before he went to Oxford, had been demolished and forgotten. Beach Street, his old friend Tommy's house, had been wiped out and replaced with a lorry park.

But all the old places had been there that morning in his mother's photograph albums. Tucked into the front of one of them there had been a picture of a little white-haired woman with a cat on her lap. Apparently this was his mother. He would not have recognized her. The woman he had known was one with chestnut hair and heavy hips and pretty eyes. Where was the glass of sweet sherry or the cigarette in her hand? On the back of the photograph it said, 'Dear June, thanks for a lovely day and a smashing lunch. October 2000.' He felt a pang of jealousy, of exclusion. This thin woman with the cat was the person who had died five weeks ago. It had not occurred to him to wonder what his mother had looked like when she died. It was so hard to believe other people existed when you didn't see them.

He and his mother had not spoken or touched each other in forty years. And yet there she had been, giving her friends lunch on an October afternoon. Her life had continued without him. She had owned a cat. Where was it? What had happened to her cat? he wondered.

When he and his son Luke arrived they had found the place in chaos. The hall ceiling had caved in and water had poured through it, ruining the carpet. He imagined the cat had probably run away in search of food. Had it watched its owner sleep tantalizingly through each mealtime, through three long days and nights, in a strange heap at the bottom of the stairs? It must have been a very quiet death, he thought, with only the cat for a witness.

It was not the way his mother's life should have ended. Suddenly he felt that passionately and the colour came into his cheeks and his eyes glittered. He knew he had no right to this indignation. The prodigal son had no right to grieve. He had recently discovered that all his emotions were in rather poor taste.

He pulled up outside the house. Two Iraqi Kurdish men walked past, one carrying a split bin-bag of clothes; the arm of a red jumper hanging down and flapping behind his legs. The man stopped and turned. His profile was gaunt and handsome, rough-shaven. When he sucked out the last of his cigarette, his cheeks hollowed. He threw the butt into the bushes and adjusted the weight of the bag, lifting it on to his hip. Then he nodded to his friend and they moved on. They were obviously practised at accommodating each other's checks and pauses. Perhaps they had done their long journey together. Was that bin-bag all they had brought?

The night before, he had seen news footage of a busload of asylum-seekers being deported from France. He remembered one man in the eye of the camera, twisted, crying, literally punching himself in the head, tearing out his hair. They had all been found squatting in a Parisian church and after several days of bureaucratic debate, of chanting crowds with homemade signs, of illuminated TV reporters and hunched cameramen, it was decided they had no right to be in Europe.

Alistair locked the car and walked towards his childhood home. He still expected to see the sign above it, 'The Queen Elizabeth Guesthouse. Vacancies', and the bright, flowery curtains in each window. But these things were as remote and obsolete as his childhood.

Apparently his mother had stopped running the guesthouse in 1980. She would then have been sixty-six. Just three years older than he was now. At one point, she had tried to sell the top half of the house as a flat, but no one had wanted to buy it. Dover was hardly a pleasure spot these days – just a place to be passed through, a place of temporary accommodation.

He had learnt these facts about the house from the legal documents he had been sent after his mother's death. She had probably thought of living on the ground floor because of the trouble with her hips, he thought. He had learnt about her hips from the medical report.

His mother's hips – the broad hips he had been carried about on, with his thumb in his mouth, feeling the folds of her cotton dress, the warmth of her soft waist and stomach, under his bare legs. At one time, he had not been himself but the most awkward part of her body. He could still remember the way she shifted him up more firmly as she leant towards the ashtray to tap her cigarette. She dealt with problems in twos always: you dusted with one hand, plumped the sofa cushions against your leg with the other. You swilled the old water out of the bedside carafes while you cleaned out the basin.

It startled him how often in his memory she was cleaning. Always cleaning. Turning down the beds, mopping the kitchen floor, reaching up for a cobweb with a pink feather duster. Or, most often, he saw her last thing of all on a Sunday afternoon, polishing the little ornaments in their own sitting room. He remembered a parrot on a swing from a trip to Bath (who knew why it had constituted a souvenir from *Bath*?), a silver cat licking its paw, a grinning shepherdess, thirty little painted china boxes. He still felt the poignancy of her satisfaction when the sideboard shone and she could settle down with her Sunday glass of sherry. In his memory, the radio was going in the background through a coil of cigarette smoke.

His mother came back to him intact – with her curlers, her fears. He had never appreciated her fortitude before. Now each of his memories seemed to embody her supernatural determination to get the job done. Her life had been brutally subdued to fulfil a cheery set of principles: if a job's worth doing, it's worth doing well; idle hands are the devil's playthings. He felt himself collapse inside with love and horror. The soul-destroying modesty of her expectations! This was what he had shaken off when he ran that last time for the train to London, slamming the window down as soon as he was on, taking huge gulps of air and listening to the wheels set off.

We don't really move very far at all in life, he thought.

But how could he be blamed for thinking he had, for thinking he had been reborn on another planet? The home he and Rosalind had made in Holland Park with the thick damask curtains, the walnut side-tables, the heavy, silver-framed photographs of their children playing tennis and of the place they often took in Italy – every aspect of their lives was a product of the taste his wife had inherited. And that was exactly how he had wanted it. He had wanted to forget where he grew up and to lose himself in another person's world. He had chosen a clean, ordered world with no smell of fried breakfasts or of large, unknown men.

'Luke?' he called, as he went into the cramped hallway. He could see his son through the back door, in the garden, smoking a cigarette and kicking at bits of loose turf. He watched Luke make a fist with his right hand and turn it over under his eyes as if he was calculating how powerful it might be. Alistair felt aware of violence stored up in people now. 'Luke? I'm back.'

His son let the fist slacken and blew out a jet of smoke. 'Just having a cig, Dad. Be there in a minute.'

'No hurry,' he called. Conversation was difficult with Luke. Always had been.

Alistair walked into his mother's sitting room and looked at all the dusty ornaments. He had not attempted to explain a single thing to his son – and, to his great relief, Luke appeared to be too distracted to ask. This was a surreal situation and could not possibly last – even if Luke had, as his mother put it, had his first heartbreak. Surely his son must be amazed by this past of his father's. After all, he had known precisely nothing about it, until the evening before, when they had arrived in Dover and shared a supper of beans on toast in a dead old lady's kitchen.

Alistair felt he would have to explain something – somehow. But in a bit.

His leg hurt a great deal after the walk and the drive and he sat down in the old armchair and breathed deeply. The quiet had the intensity of death. It was not unpleasant.

He was sitting where his mother had been sitting in the photograph. There were white cat hairs along the arm of the chair. Her chair – angled for the TV. What had she watched? he wondered. She had liked detective stories on the radio when he was little. Detective programmes, perhaps. He pulled a cat hair from the fabric and rolled it between his thumb and forefinger. Her cat.

That he must have shattered his wife's faith in the world in the past few months was another thing Alistair tried hard not to think about. This reality visited him occasionally in the form of a sharp contraction of his stomach and he would immediately pick up a biography or a newspaper in an attempt to prevent thought. He had developed a nervous habit of straightening his shirt cuffs.

It was a strange fact that, in a life often spent arguing the defence of drug-dealers and thieves in front of sceptical juries, he had never had to defend himself. He was literally lost for words now that he needed them most, when eye-contact with his demure wife was like

8

a blow to the face. He had never wondered before, in his whole career as a barrister, what the defendants told their wives, whether there were scenes in kitchens, in hallways. Whether there were tears.

Not that he had reached a state of humility now. In reality, the thought that made him throw down his book and pinch the bridge of his nose, as if he was holding the two sides of his head together, was that it could all so easily have gone undiscovered. A few altered details: if his attackers had been fitter and outrun the police, if he had genuinely drunk the awful wine Julian always served and had had to take a cab home, rather than emptying two glasses secretly into the sink and remaining almost sober. Or if Julian hadn't been quite so bloody *vigilant*. After all, how many Londoners came running out of their warm houses at the sound of a car alarm? They were just part of London's music.

But Julian's daughter had been brutally mugged only a few months before and any sound on the street would bounce him out of bed and over to the window tearing open the curtains, turning the bedroom pale orange with streetlight. His wife thought perhaps he should see someone about it, talk to someone. Alistair had heard Rosalind on the phone to her.

The alarm had gone off when one of the boys fell back into the car. To have heard it, Julian and Elise must have been seeing other guests into the hall. Out Julian had jogged. Having taken in what he had initially thought was two joy-riders holding a baseball bat near a neighbour's car window, he had called 999 on his mobile phone. It was only then that he saw his friend crumpled on the ground. He ran back into the house in fear.

If they had just disappeared off into the night, Alistair thought, the whole world would still hang together. He would still have his job, his reputation, the respect of his wife and children. Had he altered the course of history so minutely as to have stayed a few minutes longer and left *after* the other guests, by the time of the attack Julian and Elise might already have gone to the kitchen with the empty glasses. The sound of the car alarm might have been overwhelmed by the dishwasher.

A few touches here and there and Alistair might have suffered nothing more than a serious injury to his leg. He would have had sympathy.

But within the hour Michael Jensen and Anil Bandari had been signing their names in Chelsea police station and Julian was being complimented on his swift reaction. Three days later, the story was in the papers.

Alistair's daughter, Sophie, had not spoken to him since. She worked for the *Telegraph* and, of course, she had been forced to see her own father written about by her colleagues, who hunched, agonized, over their keyboards as she passed with her cup of coffee. He did not know it yet, and neither did she acknowledge it, but this had given Sophie the vocabulary she needed. She had been looking for a way to explain her desire to chuck in her dream job.

Alistair had no idea how lonely Sophie was. He loved his daughter in an awkward, passionate way. She was the fiercely intelligent girl he might have married. When his wife worried about why Sophie didn't have 'anyone special on the scene yet', he was disturbed by how repulsive he found the idea. He couldn't bear to discuss it. He had snapped his cufflink last time – when Rosalind had suggested they ask James Marsden over for dinner.

'*Anthony*'s son, you mean? He's an absolute *idiot*, darling. She'd argue him under the table,' he said.

'Oh. He's nice-looking, I thought. Friendly, polite. Perhaps you're right, though, darling. You probably are.'

As a teenager Sophie had been very ill with anorexia and Alistair was still mystified by this and deeply afraid of the sheer will she had shown – six and a half stone and silent at the table. Had he caused this weird illness? He had never referred to it in front of her. And, although she was outspoken about everything else, she had never brought it up with him. Instead, they had fierce arguments about current affairs and while they told themselves they enjoyed the discussions, there was always a subtext of betrayal implicit in the extreme positions they took. She was always the cynic in these arguments, always the one who sensed corruption, while he was the voice of conservative reason. Neither felt they represented themselves fairly in this after-dinner ritual. They would go through sadly to join the other two in front of the news.

'So, Dad,' Luke said, coming into the room with his hands in his pockets, 'do we take stuff back or what? I mean, what do you want to do with all the . . . *stuff*?' He had picked up one of the ornaments – a little china dog – and Alistair watched him for a moment, longing to remove it from his son's hand. He knew the judgements Luke would be making, thinking his unknown grandmother had been a tasteless, vulgar person. It was unbearable.

'Are you OK, Dad?'

'Me? Yes, fine. Just tired out.'

'You're not meant to walk, are you? Where did you go?'

Alistair stood up and stretched his leg again. Then he stretched his arms, rolled his head, rubbed the back of his neck, clicked his fingers. 'Oh – nowhere. Just a bit of fresh air. I suppose I'd better call Mummy and let her know what we're planning.'

'What *are* we planning?'

'I'm not sure . . .' Alistair's voice was uncharacteristically quiet. He glanced out of the window, through the net curtains. He felt an overwhelming urge to cry. For some reason, he remembered the letters his son used to write home from boarding-school, listing every goal he'd scored, every good mark he'd got. Sophie had never bothered to write. It ought to have been the other way round, really.

'Well, we'd better say soon, Dad, because Mum called earlier asking if we were going to come back for supper – you know, because it's your birthday and everything.'

Alistair's wife astonished him: her capacity to suppress the unwanted and lay the table was awe-inspiring. Luke turned away, almost as embarrassed as his father by this inappropriate birthday.

'Yes, better let her know,' Alistair said.

'Sorry I forgot, Dad.'

'Forgot?'

'About your birthday.'

'Oh, God – couldn't matter less.' He wanted desperately to share some kind of acknowledgement with his son. What would it have been like to turn to Luke cleanly and say: 'Look, we both know it's ridiculous to celebrate my birthday. I've spoilt your mother's life and my own and now here we are in the place I grew up and you can see perfectly well I've been pretending – lying, really, since before you were born.' But it was impossible. 'Couldn't matter less,' he said again. His son coughed. Alistair's eyes flickered to the lifeless TV. He imagined switching it on and filling up the silence of that room.

'So shall we go back tonight or what, then?' Luke said.

'Yes, I think we should. I just wanted to get an idea of how much there was to sort out.'

'A lot of it's left to people, isn't it?' Again, his son fingered the ornaments – he was probably wondering who on earth would be glad to inherit them. *Ghastly* things – that was what he must be thinking. Luke tipped the cat backwards and its mouth opened. He grimaced.

11

Alistair took it out of his son's hand. 'Yes, a lot of it's left to people. God only knows who would want all this rubbish, though, right?'

Luke smiled, barely conscious of what had been said, just glad to have an opportunity to look into his father's sad eyes with affection.

To Alistair, he seemed to be sharing the joke. He and his son were filthy conspirators in his mother's damp little sitting room.

Perfect, Alistair thought. You have made this son yourself; you have worked hard all your life to earn his prejudices for him. You bought him the ski-trips, the boarding-school friends with their country houses, the teenage girlfriends with their shiny blonde hair and pashmina shawls. And now you must stand here, he told himself, and laugh with him at your mother's possessions. This is how you finish the betrayal.

'Come on, let's head back to London,' he said, gently putting the ornament back in its place.

Chapter 2

Rosalind and Alistair had met when she was eighteen and he was in his last year at Oxford. It was 1958. Her cousin Philip had asked her along to a May Ball and her mother had insisted she go. She had not wanted to because Philip so obviously thought she was stupid. He was never actually rude to her, but if ever the conversation got on to something serious, like politics, he would worry that she was finding it 'boring' and change the subject. He would ask her about parties, who had been seen about together and so on. There was nothing she could do. Even if she had felt able to insist it wasn't boring, that she wanted to learn and be the sort of person who thought – well, *things*, she could not have risked contributing an opinion. But she would have liked to listen. She had a way of folding herself between her two white hands and looking out quietly. Sometimes people mistook this for smugness.

Her mother idolized Philip. Everyone did – but her mother particularly because she had lost her only son when he was two, and Philip had become her favourite nephew. They had an almost flirtatious relationship and when they were on the phone, discussing Rosalind's travel arrangements to Oxford, Rosalind thought it sounded as though it was her mother who was going, not her. Her mother laughed wildly at Philip's exaggerated descriptions of the chaos of preparation going on at his college, at the students' frantic taming of straggly hair and beards, which had seemed to lend them a philosophical air only the week before. Rosalind felt like the incidental component in an arrangement between two more vibrant personalities.

She often felt like that. She would have preferred to be more like her elder sister Suzannah, who told jokes and informed their father she was interested in Communism, or Buddhism. But when Rosalind listened to the rows Suzannah had with their mother, she buried her face in her pillow and thought how much nicer it was, really, just to be quiet.

'Cat got your tongue, Rozzy?' her father would say at lunch sometimes. And then he would ruffle her hair as if he was pleased with her for it.

'Sit up, darling,' her mother would remind her.

She got out her dress and laid it on the hotel bed. It was one of Suzannah's – a pale lilac, which went very well with her dark hair. She thought of herself as pretty, but not beautiful like her elder sister. Beauty seemed to be something that required more personality. Once, she had stared for a long time at a photograph in a magazine of Marilyn Monroe, her half-closed eyes fixed erotically on the lens. The image frightened her. She wondered what it would be like for a man to kiss Marilyn Monroe – the big breasts pressing on you, the plump arms round your neck. Was that what they wanted?

Again, she felt frightened. She got visits from this world of emotion she had not yet begun to understand. It was like seeing a ghost. The expression in Monroe's eyes belonged to it, and the time her sister had come home drunk and there was blood in her knickers and on her petticoat, leaves in her hair. Suzannah kept laughing, saying she couldn't believe *that* was all it was. She laughed all the way up the first flight of stairs, stopping outside their parents' bedroom to say, 'It's just so . . . *silly* – what you're expected to do. It's so . . . *silly*,' and Rosalind had had to put her hand over her sister's mouth. She'd had to undress her. The next morning Suzannah had slipped a gold bracelet she knew Rosalind liked under her door with a note that just said, 'Thanks.'

Rosalind put on the bracelet and tightened the clasps on her pearl earrings. She was pleased with the way she looked when she was all dressed up. She knew she fulfilled most of the criteria – slim, not too tall, even complexion, clear eyes. And she knew Philip was only half joking when they walked towards the college gates and he draped his arm over her and said she would do his reputation no end of good. It was a cool evening and the light rain pattered on the streamers and balloons. They got under cover as soon as possible, and Philip called out to a friend of his, who looked slightly comic in a dinner jacket several sizes too large for him. 'Al!' he shouted. The friend turned and grinned at them and they went in behind him in the queue. He had dark hair, blue eyes and very pale skin. He was so pale, in fact, that Rosalind wondered if he was all right. She watched his sharp eyes bounce from her face to the pavement to the church spire and back again.

'Al, this is Rozzy. Rozzy, this is Al.' They had not had a chance to shake hands before Philip was introducing her to someone else a few places along.

Alistair thought she was the shiniest, cleanest-looking person he had ever seen. How did a person get that clean and shining? You had to come that way, he thought. There was a dinginess about him you could never scrub off. He stared at the incredible symmetry of her curls. A lot of the girls he had passed on the way had flowers, ribbonish things, but she just had the shining dark curls. It was almost intimidating, so resolute was its simplicity. She was like a haiku, he thought – he had been reading some that afternoon with his tea. He would have liked to be able to pay her a compliment, but he had no idea what it was appropriate to say. When he arrived at Oxford, it had taken him only a few days to abandon his own voice for Philip's public-school one. He still found quite often, though, that he did not know what to say in the new voice.

He had felt increasingly insecure throughout the week – as he had each year – watching the college transformed into a playground of coloured lights, balloons and white marquees. He knew where he was with his books in his hand, walking back across the quad from a tutorial with Philip, patiently explaining whatever his friend hadn't understood. They were a good pair: Philip did the frivolity and Alistair did the more academically confident sarcasm, and together they believed in nothing at all. Philip relied on Alistair for help with his essays and in their first term began to take him out for lunch or dinner to say thank you. Soon Alistair helped with all Philip's essays and Philip paid for all Alistair's meals.

But now, in Philip's spare dinner jacket, aware that the sleeves were too long and that he did not know how to dance, oddly chastised by the irreproachable prettiness of this girl Philip had not even bothered to mention, Alistair wished he could just go back to his room. But he would have felt like a failure. This was the first ball he had come to – he had earned enough in the last holidays to buy himself a ticket and he had been determined not to leave Oxford without having been to a single one, no matter how awkward and unprepared he felt.

15

Philip handed him a glass of champagne. 'Drink up,' he said. He knocked back his own glass in one and Alistair felt panicky. Recklessness frightened him – because life took so much thought, so much control.

When Philip died in his early fifties, essentially of alcoholism, Alistair remembered those gestures of his, each one arriving in his mind like a drum beat. It was a strange funeral, full of flamboyantly dressed homosexual men with tragic faces. At the last minute Philip's partner had felt unable to do the reading and Alistair was asked to do it instead. He had felt frightened in case anyone imagined he was gay, too – and ashamed that this was how he thought when his old friend had died. There had been genuine love between them, even if they had drifted apart as Philip's lifestyle became less and less conventional and Alistair's more and more so. Philip always complimented Alistair on his clothes – and Alistair silently appreciated the depth of compassion from which this sprang. Philip had come to understand him in the early Rosalind days and he was someone who never judged or forgot the importance of what he had learnt about a person.

It had been Philip who suggested it in the first place: 'Why don't you ask her if she wants to be shown round?'

'Shown round?'

'Yes.'

'Is that OK?'

'What d'you mean?'

'I mean, wouldn't she think it was forward or something?'

'She's not as prim as she looks – I *hope*. Her mum's a scream anyway. She must have inherited *some* of it.' Philip elbowed Alistair in the ribs but he couldn't maintain the joke, faced with Alistair's frightened expression. 'It's perfectly acceptable to ask a girl something like that,' he said.

'Really?'

Rosalind was standing a little way off with a girl she had been to school with. Two nervous girls under a little galaxy of fairy-lights strung up in a tree. Was there anything less approachable?

'Come on, I'll distract the other one – she won't remember who I am but we won't let that matter.'

Somehow Alistair asked and somehow she accepted. It was an agonizing few moments, but Rosalind was unsophisticated enough to make it obvious that she was pleased, and this encouraged Alistair. He noticed the schoolfriend grin and raise her eyebrows, and saw Rosalind return a faint smile.

They walked away together towards the river where couples were going out in punts, the girls sitting on rugs, tilting their heads to look up at the sky as if they were drawn to do it by some irresistible romantic force. Everyone was putting on a beautiful show.

'You know, I'm sure Philip's never met Veronica,' Rosalind said, as they walked over a little footbridge. Philip had rushed up to the girl with his arms open wide and told her he'd missed her. Alistair looked at Rosalind and wondered if she was going to laugh about it, but instead, she visibly gathered the implication of Philip's pretence and blushed. She looked away towards the river, pulled her glove on more tightly. 'It's very beautiful, isn't it? The trees, I mean . . . with all the little lights,' she said.

He was impressed by her. He respected her capacity to regain her composure. She smiled at him as they got into the punt, and as he watched her smooth out her dress beneath her, he thought she was the neatest and most ordered person he could imagine. The river glistened and rocked the boat as they moved out into it. What would it be like to be around that neatness, to feel reassured by the action of those elegant hands? She was the opposite of his humiliating rehearsals in front of the mirror: Alistair smoking a cigarette, Alistair drinking a toast, Alistair reading a newspaper and looking up as someone brought him a cup of coffee *in his club*. The scenes he played out! She was the proof that he was nowhere near fooling anyone. She had been born into it all. She had lived the life he was piecing together from talks with Philip – of Sunday lunches followed by walks in Wellington boots, the opera at Glyndebourne in summer, drinks parties on crisp rainy evenings in London, quiet talks with your father over a glass of port. When he imagined Rosalind's life, he often forgot to include the fact that she was a girl. Sometimes this meant that as he sent her out into the dream a detail jarred. He would see her suddenly, and it made him feel oddly disappointed, so that he turned to dreaming about Philip's life instead, with which he could more closely identify, rather than wondering what Rosalind's might be like.

She did not have Philip's custodial air but she had his deeply impressive way of not being at all surprised that something delicious was waiting for her, so that when they got back from their punting she greeted a table covered with bottles of champagne, scattered with flowers, with a simple 'How nice to come back to,' and a quick smile. He wondered if he was in love already.

They had not talked about much as they punted along, past the other couples, sometimes close enough for Alistair to be embarrassed to hear the same male speech, 'And that's Magdalen Tower where they have the singing on May Day,' and so on. Mostly he had just told her about the different colleges and received the incredible reassurance of her nods and smiles. She seemed fascinated. She was so unlike the girls from Dover Grammar, who rolled their eyes if you 'harped on'. They thought he was dull and the books with which he had scrupulously characterized himself (often trying three different titles under his arm before he left the house) had made him unpopular with them. Books were a self-fulfilling prophecy – he saw that now.

For the first time, though, at Oxford, he had felt respected – because he was a scholar and because he spoke well in debates at the Union. But he knew that academic respect was as far as it went. He saw that the others felt they couldn't invite him for weekends at home, for holidays in the summer. They changed the subject, they avoided the issue. With his terrible capacity to accept the worst in human nature, he quietly acknowledged this and would never have suggested they include him. He understood; he even sympathized with them. He imagined they felt he did not 'know how to behave' – they said it often enough of other people. He would have hated to embarrass them or the good, highly cultured, loving parents he was certain they all had.

In fact, Philip was responsible for the situation. He was always tortured with concern that Alistair would not have enough money for holidays or even train fares for weekends away and that he would be humiliated by offers of loans. He made careful prior warnings to the others to stay off the subject of holidays or parties. So the combination of Philip's tact and Alistair's bleak and rigid view of humanity meant his life was confined to term-times and university gossip. When Michael and Sam started talking about people they knew in London or who was going where for Christmas, he would look away and wait quietly. He tried not to think about going home.

This habit, this hard-learnt ability to wait, offstage, philosophically observing other people's big performances, was what accounted for the sense of recognition between Alistair and Rosalind – even though they had come from different worlds. It's possible that the strongest connections between people are generated like this, by the odd coincidence of similar emotional histories, no matter how different the events that brought those emotions into being. They provided a neat solution for each other. He felt authenticated by Rosalind. Her conventional prettiness and the unfakeable accuracy of her good manners instantly included him in the world of colour that flared up so threateningly in his path each summer when the balls were on. He felt himself very discreetly let in – or, at least, that was how he interpreted it when Michael Richardson leant towards his ear and said, 'I didn't know you knew Rosalind Blunt. Lucky man. Lovely-looking girl.'

Rosalind thought Alistair was clever – obviously, indisputably clever. She noticed how his friends' eyes flashed to him when they told a joke or quoted something, to see if he approved. They said, 'Ask Al,' if something needed to be settled in a conversation.

They were both attracted to what the other brought to a crowded room. They did not think about being alone together. These were short-sighted, powerful reasons for vulnerable people to fall in love.

They stood near the punts, holding the new glasses of champagne. He said, 'Do you want to dance?'

She glanced at him and smiled, then lowered her eyes. With a sickening sense of dread he wondered if he had done something wrong and embarrassed himself. His mouth went dry. He thought he would rather break his leg, lose a finger, than embarrass himself in front of this girl. The abrupt violence of his imagination shocked him and he let his eyes close for a second as if to contain it. He must control himself.

'Maybe we should have a drink with the others for a bit?' Rosalind said.

'Yes – yes, of course. Sorry. Of course.'

At once the music seemed unbearably false, sinister as the hum of wasps, and the animal purpose behind all the ribbons and streamers and starched white shirts sweated through the artifice. This girl was too good for him. Who cared about the high esteem you were held in at the Ethical Debating Society if you did not 'know how to behave'?

And then she put her hand very gently, just for a second, on his arm – or his sleeve, really, the pressure was too light to make contact with his skin – and said, 'We could chat with them for a while and then we can ask if they'd like to dance too.'

Instinctively, he did not tell his mother about Rosalind when he went home after his finals. Not that there was much to tell: just a week after that night she had gone away for several months, first on holiday with her parents and then on a French course, staying with an aunt in Lyon. She had promised to send a postcard. Back in the damp hallway in Dover, with the cooked-cabbage smell and the snoring from room three, he thought he had been insane to think she could be a part of his life. That shining girl – here.

'D'you want scrambled or fried?' his mother said. She was doing the breakfasts. There were five staying.

'*Fried*,' he said, loading all his disappointment into that one word.

She moved over to the fridge for the eggs, her slippers flapping on the lino. 'God – what's the matter with you? Don't have them if you're not hungry – no point wasting it.'

'No – I am hungry, Mum,' he said. 'I'm really hungry.'

'I mean, I don't know what you're used to now. *Cereal* probably. *Orange juice*.' She almost shuddered.

'No. I want the eggs. I really want the eggs,' he told her.

She had decided they didn't eat proper English breakfast at university and that he had developed a hatred of this staple part of his upbringing. No amount of reassurance would convince her – particularly since he had come home underweight after the stresses of his finals.

She did eggs fried, scrambled, boiled or poached. An American man had once made the mistake of asking for an omelette. Bacon, kippers, sausage, tomato, mushrooms, he recited to himself. Tea, coffee, milk, sugar. Staring at the pattern on the plastic tablecloth, tracing his finger over it, he remembered that he was the person who had written the answer to question 14a in the jurisprudence paper, and his heart beat hard with excitement. He knew he had done well. It was like an electrical storm contained in his chest. He was going to be a barrister.

He watched his mother putting a row of tomatoes under the grill and slipping the toast into a rack with the other hand. He knew her movements by heart. It was always four steps between the fridge and the hob. Slap, slap, slap, slap – and then the thunk and clink of the fridge door opening.

'You're not drinking up your tea,' she said. She turned and put one hand on the sideboard, reaching for the cigarettes in the pocket of her apron.

'I *am*.'

'If you don't want it, Alistair, you don't have to. I don't want you thinking you have to.'

'I *don't*. What's the matter with you, Mum?'

20

She picked up the ashtray and slammed it down again. When she was angry you could literally see the rage jump into her eyes like a wild animal on a nature film. It filled the screen. 'Don't you talk to me like that!' she said. 'Don't you *ever* talk to me like that. You come here with your head full of ideas about yourself, thinking you're too good for the place you grew up in – not bringing one of your Oxford friends to visit the whole time *out of shame*. And now you talk to me like this!'

And this was his first morning home. All he could think of when he observed her was how different this angry, weathered woman was from Rosalind. How long had he hated her without admitting it to himself? Suddenly he could not separate her from the suffocating fug of her kitchen, the cooking-fat smell, the crazed sound of the kettle whistling. He stared at the veined hand splayed on the plump, aproned hip and wondered how often she had stood in that pose at the bottom of the stairs, calling him away from his desk – 'Come on, Al, you're supposed to be young. What do you want to waste a day like this for with those old books?' Always calling him away from his desk. He saw that now. It had taken Rosalind – the purity and order he imagined she would bring to him – to make him see it: his mother had been trying to sabotage his life!

She stubbed – or, rather, crushed – out her cigarette and looked right at him. 'Who do you think you are, Alistair?'

'I don't know, do I?'

'What do you mean "*I don't know*"?'

'I mean I don't know, Mum, because you won't tell me anything about my father, will you?' he said. And then he left the room, left the eggs, left the tea untouched, because he knew perfectly well he had said the unsayable.

'What are you thinking, Dad?' Luke said.

'Me?'

He always said that: 'Me?' Always the avoidance, the delay tactic, as if he hoped to find there was someone else in the room to whom the question was really addressed.

'You just looked funny for a minute.'

'Oh . . . I was just wondering what the traffic will be like on the A2. That's all.'

'Right,' Luke said. 'Look, you don't mind if I listen to my Walkman, do you?'

21

'No! By all means,' Alistair said. 'You listen.'

'Thanks.'

It was a relief to both of them not to have to make conversation. They had never had much to say to each other. Luke often dropped things or spilled his drink when his father came into the room. When his sister was around he felt like the odd one out and he couldn't understand why they bothered with their long, exhausting arguments when they were not going to change US foreign policy or President Mugabe's whatever it was, anyway. He loaded the dishwasher with his mother or had a look at what she had been doing to the garden while Sophie and his father stayed on at the table. In the past couple of years, since he had been earning a really good salary, he had gradually stopped feeling upset by it. He had stopped feeling so – stupid.

He believed in his mother's love in a way he could not believe in his father's. Not that this was because he and his mother 'really talked' the way some people did, going into details about their relationship problems and sex lives and so on. No – his mother parcelled out her love neatly and hygienically: she put flowers by his bed, remembered if he had a doctor's appointment, got him fluffy towels for the flat. That was her vocabulary: it was restricted, but it was sincere. He could never tell what his father was really thinking when he thumped him on the back and said, 'So, how *are* things, Luke?', looking as though he would rather get away to his study than suffer a long explanation. Sophie thought he imagined this. She said he should grow up and stop the childhood angst routine. The infuriating thing was, there was no 'routine' when he was away from home. He was cool and confident as far as his friends were concerned: he was the guy people called to find out what was happening . . . The 'routine' appeared as soon as he went through the front door. And his family thought it was the real him!

That Alistair had a background he had always kept hidden was the beginning of an explanation for the gap that lay between them. Luke did not know what to say about this, or about the scandal – though this was more out of concern for himself than for his father. It was almost impossible to contemplate what his father had done without a sense that the sky might fall in, let alone actually say something about it. A few times in the past week, he had realized Alistair suspected he was about to refer to it and seen fear, actual terror, in his eyes. He had never seen his father so much as unnerved before, not so much as taken aback.

Luke felt like a teenager again. It was terrible how quickly he had regressed in his two weeks at home. For a moment he felt embarrassed by the reflection of himself, sulky and slouched, headphones on, that the car window gave back at him. He was twenty-eight. But why be embarrassed anyway? Why go to all the effort? Both he and his sister had apparently stayed at around seventeen in their parents' minds, anyway. They were both openly amazed when he was up by midday. Normally he would have had to go out to the garden for regular ciga- rettes, gritting his teeth in anger, thinking did they not know he made £75,000 a year? Had they *seen* his flat? But it was not in his interests to emphasize his autonomy right now. He wanted to be a child again – just for a couple more weeks, until he got Arianne back.

He also felt deeply sorry for his mother and it seemed like no bad thing for her to have him around to worry about. He could see it was less complicated for her to look after him than his father, with whom each instinctive kindness triggered a reminder that all was not well, that he had spoiled everything. When he really thought about it, he was amazed that his mother was still in the same house. But he was prepared to believe things might work that differently when you were old and married. Actually, he wanted to believe it. His parents' marriage had to be unbreakable or he would fall apart.

A friend had said to him in a bar the week before, 'You keep saying that, Luke, but what d'you mean "fall apart"? What does falling apart look like? You just go on, don't you? Breathe in and out, go to work, eat a Big Mac, press "play". You'll find another girl, for Christ's sake. You're horribly good-looking, and Arianne was a nightmare, right? She was sexy, though, no doubt about that, mate . . .'

Luke thought about her waist, her breasts, the way she jutted out her chin to dismiss something boring or somebody 'weak'. 'Falling apart' looked like his flat when she left. It looked like him, on the sofa in his boxer shorts on a Friday morning, calling his mum. He was going to get Arianne back.

Luke and Alistair got home to find another car parked in the space on the driveway.

'Suzannah,' Luke said, with a sigh. 'Why's she here?' He glanced at his father's tense face.

'I'm not walking miles with this leg,' Alistair said. 'She'll just have to . . .' he scraped the gears '. . . get blocked in. I'll have to block her in.'

'God, d'you think she's come for supper? I'm not in a very Suzannah-ish mood, actually.'

'No. Neither am I,' he said. Why had Rosalind invited her? He and Suzannah had never got on – Alistair felt sure she had never forgiven him for being interested in her less beautiful sister. After everything that had happened, she would be pleased to see him and gloat. Why had Rosalind asked her over? But when he thought of his wife, of her pale eyes with their new, hunted expression, and of the world he had constructed and shattered for her, he thought, If this is a little revenge then just let her have it. 'Oh, Christ,' he said out loud. And then, for a second, Luke caught his eye. A spark of humour passed between them. Who knows why people laugh? The collapse of the last bridge of logical argument, perhaps – the discovery of shrugging humanity down there in the rubble beside you. There was nothing to do but submit to the good release in the chest and stomach and back. They sat there in the car, laughing together, Alistair shaking his head. It was something they had never done before.

Chapter 3

Suzannah was sitting on the arm of the sofa by the fire. She looked up with an expression of innocence on her face as Alistair and Luke came in. She had a book in her hand – Rosalind was checking the meat in the kitchen – and she plainly intended to appear to have been lost in the words rather than listening for the arrival of the car. She shook off the poetical vagueness and tossed the book on to the sofa.

'Hello, hello,' she said, kissing Alistair on both cheeks and squeezing his arm – to express her deep, her very deep, sympathy, he imagined. 'And hello, *Luke*, darling. How are things with you?'

'Not so good,' Luke said.

'Oh dear.'

'But I'm working on them. They'll get better.'

'Is it love? Or money?'

'Love.'

'Oh, I see. You must tell me all about it.'

The idea of continuing, in this frivolous way, to talk about the great tragedy of his life was impossible.

'Actually I should go and get changed and dump my bag upstairs,' he said. 'Where's Mum?'

'Your mother is in the kitchen.'

'OK.'

'Doing inspired things to the lamb or the potatoes or something. I forget which. It could have been the apple crumble . . .' She looked portentously at him, then grinned.

Suzannah had a way of mocking his mother that made him angry.

25

'Oh, has she made apple crumble? She makes the best apple crumble I've ever tasted,' he said. 'She's a totally amazing cook.'

Suzannah was looking for her drink now, and muttered vaguely, 'Yes . . . yes, she is.' She found the glass of vodka-tonic on the mantelpiece.

Luke went to get changed. Alistair walked towards the window and drew the curtains, tugging them sharply, watching the thick red fabric cut out the last sliver of the street.

'So, how are you?' Suzannah said. He listened to the ice chink in her glass. 'I was so sorry to hear about your mother.'

'Thank you.'

'What a — I hope you don't mind me saying, but what a shame you never got a chance to make it up.'

'Yes.'

'I mean, what a peculiar thing that must be.'

'Yes,' Alistair said, 'it is.'

'Dad and I argued a great deal, of course, all the way through, but particularly at the end. It's odd — you expect the end of life to bring harmony, don't you?'

'Do you?'

'You expect it to bring resolution. The urge to tie up the loose ends.'

'Depends how many loose ends there are, I suppose. Sometimes everything frays uncontrollably.' How bizarre, he thought, that he should have dreaded this so much, and then be continuing the conversation himself when she was so unexpectedly moving off the subject. He was addicted to self-sabotage these days. Or had she engineered it? He was becoming paranoid. 'Would you like a drink?' he said.

She held up her glass. 'Got one, thanks.'

'Oh, yes — of course. You've got one. *I* need one.'

'Yes,' she said pensively. 'I feel more and more the urge to make peace with people.'

'You do?'

'Yes.' She laughed. 'What's that supposed to mean? You've always thought I was polemical, Alistair. I'm really not.'

'No, no. I just . . . I just — need a drink, that's all.'

'So you keep saying. Do you need *me* to make it for you?'

'What? Oh — no,' he said. He had not moved towards the drinks tray and she was looking at him. 'Sorry. I'm on another planet.'

He went over and picked up the bottle of whisky. It was a wonderful single malt Sophie had given him last time she came over. He poured

26

some, took a mouthful and felt the heat going down his throat. He let the perfume fill his nose and tipped a handful of salted almonds into his mouth, crunching them, feeling consoled by the delicious flavours, by the simple act of eating and drinking. This was life too, he told himself. He could smell the lamb cooking down the hallway – the rosemary and the garlic roasting.

'Yes, I want to make peace with people,' Suzannah was saying, 'with Andrew, with Michael and even with Stefan, my first ex – the one nobody ever met.'

He turned and faced into the room. 'So how will you do it?'

'How? I don't know. Maybe I'll write letters. You have to pay attention to letters, don't you? Actual handwriting looks so poignant, these days.'

She sighed. 'Why don't you write a letter to Rosalind?'

'Write her a – because we live in the same house, Suzannah.'

'I just thought it might be a way of . . .'

'It's kind of you.'

They heard Rosalind's footsteps coming up the hall.

'You know, Alistair, I'm really not as dreadful as you think.'

'Oh, probably not,' he said.

She laughed heartily. It was the kind of comment that appealed to her sense of humour. 'Cheers?'

'Yes,' he said. 'Why not?' He closed his eyes as the whisky went down.

Rosalind stood in the doorway, holding an empty wine-glass.

'Hello, darling,' Alistair said. He went to her and gave her a kiss on each cheek. A casual observer would not have known there was anything wrong between them. Suzannah, whose observations of other people were never casual, felt shocked and thrilled by her sister's coldness. Alistair pointed at Rosalind's glass. 'Can I fill that for you?'

'I put a bottle of Chablis on the drinks tray.'

'So you did.' He carried the glass away.

She was wearing her pale pink silk shirt and a pair of cream trousers. Her hair, which she still dyed dark, was curled and shining as it always was. Unlike Suzannah, Rosalind had kept her looks. Where Suzannah's beauty had taken risks – the sharp cheekbones and the plump red mouth – Rosalind's was essentially the result of balance. And it had remained undisturbed through childbirth, through her children's illnesses, through summer holidays and supermarket trips and traffic jams and school sports days. She had a neat mouth, neither full nor thin, pale blue eyes and a softly curving forehead. It was a placid prettiness — but there it was, still quietly making its point. She was not wearing the pearl necklace he had given her for her birthday.

The wine felt cold through the glass as he carried it towards her.

'Thank you,' she said.

'Thank you for cooking for me. What a treat.'

She stared into her glass.

'God — it's your birthday, isn't it? I totally forgot to say anything,' Suzannah said. 'Many happy returns.'

They listened to Rosalind plumping up a cushion and sitting down on the sofa. 'Where's Luke?' she asked.

'He's upstairs, darling, getting changed.'

'Have you brought things back?'

'Not really. Actually — not.'

'But that was half the point, wasn't it?'

'Yes.'

She looked at him desperately for a second. 'Well, was everything all right? Is there much to sort out?'

'I've got rather a lot of papers to go through. It's a bit of a mess because she hadn't made a detailed will. There's no executor. I'm what's called the administrator because I'm her only living relative. The local authority track you down. You don't get a choice.'

'But you don't know anyone . . . connected with her. How are you going to decide what to do with it all?'

'I'll have to go back, darling. I'll be more efficient next time.'

For a second, Rosalind felt sorry for him. On top of everything else, his mother had died. Even though she had been under the impression it had happened years ago, she still wanted to comfort him. She was a gentle person and she found her own anger painfully distorting.

Luke came in, dressed in a clean pair of jeans and a shirt. His hair was wet from the shower. He looked very young and healthy with the last of the tan from his summer holiday still on his face. The room felt simpler with him in it. He kissed Rosalind. 'Delicious smells, Mum,' he said. 'When are we eating?'

'Are you starving?' Her own voice surprised her. Her remarks just arrived on her lips and she wondered if that was the way it had always been — only now she could hear them. They did not seem to take any thought at all.

'Well, I can't say Dad and I exactly feasted while we were away. It's not the culinary centre of the world, Dover.'

'God, I can imagine,' said Suzannah. 'What is it? All "pub grub" and fish and chips? Actually, it's McDonald's now, probably, isn't it? Bright pink milk shakes.'

'We were fine,' Alistair said.

'Greasy plastic burgers.'

'We did all right.'

His father looked humiliated. Again, Luke felt a jolt of compassion for him. 'Of course we did all right. It's just lovely to come back to something you've made, Mum, that's all.'

'Yes, indeed. We're very lucky,' said Suzannah.

'I do wish you'd all stop making such a fuss about supper,' Rosalind said. 'It's only roast lamb, for God's sake. You just put it in the oven and take it out again.' She blushed and her eyes were slightly wet with tears for a moment.

'Well, I think I'll grab a glass of that wine,' said Luke.

'You can get your venerable aunt one too – I've finished my vodka-tonic.'

Rosalind felt as though the world was going on in another room. It was like a song playing quietly downstairs on a radio, which you think you recognize to the point where you can pick out the words, until the rhythm starts to seem wrong somehow.

She felt too shocked by what had happened to know what to do with herself. She got up in the mornings and had her bath and put on her face cream and curled her hair and did her powder and her mascara and her lipstick. She chose a pair of trousers and a linen shirt or a cotton blouse – because it was still hot in London – and she went off to the showroom where she and two friends had a furniture and interior design business. There, she sat down at the huge table with a cup of coffee and studied the new catalogue they had put together. Rattan baskets, embroidered cushions, bamboo coffee-tables, *faux*-wolf throws. The pictures, the words, went past her eyes. She sifted piles of invoices while she ate her salad at lunch.

Carol and Jocelyn had been wonderful. They had become really close over the three years they had been running Home From Home. On the day after it had all been in the papers, she went into the showroom for fear of spending another day watching Alistair watch her. Carol had got her a bag of bubble-bath and creams to spoil herself with and Jocelyn had taken them all out for lunch.

'Will you leave him?' Jocelyn asked, when the waitress brought their water.

'Don't ask that now. It's too soon, isn't it?' Carol said. She put her hand over Rosalind's and smiled. 'You're in shock.'

'Look, all I really wanted to say was, you've got a place to stay – any time – with me,' Jocelyn said.

'Or me,' Carol said. 'Of course. It goes without saying.'

'Thanks. Thank you.'

'It's nothing. We're your friends. There's been a disaster. Have some water.'

'What are you feeling?' Jocelyn asked.

They waited. Rosalind gazed into her lap.

'Don't ask that. This is all too much for her. Of course it is. What would you like to eat, Roz? The salmon fishcakes look good. Let's think about that.'

'I don't agree with you, Carol. You don't get anywhere by skirting round the issue. Not that this is the same thing at all, but when Tom had his little dalliance I was straight on to him and I've no doubt it's the only reason we survived.'

The business – Home From Home – was essentially Jocelyn's. It had been her idea and she owned most of it. The other two were shareholders and paid a salary. She had not told them but the money she had used to start it was guilt money – the guilt her husband felt for cheating on her had made him write the cheque. She knew this and it didn't matter to her. She could accept the genuine apology at the core of it because she saw herself as a realist about the scope of emotional transactions. She had more than paid it back now anyway. She owed nobody anything – least of all him.

'I think you're right,' Rosalind said. 'You don't get anywhere by ignoring things.' She was staring at Jocelyn. Unusually for her, Jocelyn felt unnerved by the scrutiny. It was as if, finally, this was what she had set herself up for with all her sassy remarks. 'I think you're right,' Rosalind said again.

Carol looked at her. 'You mean you *do* want to leave him?'

'I still love him,' she said. And then she started to cry.

She had carved the lamb herself and she put it down on the table. With a casualness she did not usually exhibit, she threw the oven gloves across the kitchen and on to the sideboard. Alistair noticed it all. 'What can we get? What can we bring over?' he said.

'Everything else, I suppose. Potatoes in the oven, green stuff on the side.'

'Right,' Alistair said. The oven gloves had fallen on to the floor and he picked them up and put them in their place on the oven door. The others sat down.

'Rather fascinating place at the moment, Dover,' Suzannah said. 'Did you think so, Luke?'

'You mean all the stuff in the news?'

'Yes. Exactly.'

'Places never feel like the news, though. I remember when they did a thing on Eton and we all watched it and thought how great it would be if it was really that weird and exciting. They made it into a story with, like, a beginning, middle and end when it was really just a big mess. It was just ordinary bullies and teasing and spraining your ankle at rugby and not concentrating in history. A mess – you know, not like a book or a film where things fit together and *mean* something.'

'But there have been demonstrations in Dover, haven't there? Riots? Pretty dramatic stuff.'

'There were St George crosses up in people's windows.'

'Were there really? How strange. But how strange that our own flag should be so conspicuous to us, so embarrassing somehow. Why?'

'It wasn't like there were actual fights in the street.'

'But there are, Luke. On the news. An Albanian man got stabbed there the other day, stabbed in the street by two skinheads.'

'What does it all mean – "skinheads"?' Rosalind said. 'These weird descriptions and you're meant to know what it means. Why do they shave their heads?'

'I don't know, Mum. It's just a sign, isn't it? Membership.'

'Like your pearl earrings,' said Suzannah. 'It's sort of monastic, I suppose – shaving your head like that. Paring yourself down. You refine yourself, show you mean business. Then off out to stab a couple of asylum-seekers and down the pub for a few gallons of beer to celebrate.'

'No, Suzannah. It's exaggerated. It's all exaggerated in the press,' Alistair said.

'You can't argue with photographs.'

'Suzannah, that's ridiculous. Photographs tell incredible lies.'

'Like propaganda,' Luke said. 'The Nazis.'

'Not in England, for God's sake.'

'Why not?' said Rosalind. 'Probably they con us all the time and we just think it's the truth.' She pulled out her chair and sat down. They all watched her unfold her napkin and lay it on her lap.

'No, I see,' said Suzannah.

'Can we start, Mum?'

'Of course. I'm not stopping anyone.'

'It looks delicious, darling. Such a—'

Rosalind scraped her chair out suddenly and said, 'Salt and pepper.'

As a gesture towards acknowledging the incredible tactlessness of starting a conversation about newspapers, Suzannah lowered her voice to a stage whisper and carried on: 'You can't argue with the fact of a death, though, Alistair. The man got stabbed.'

'You can argue with why it happened. The press interprets things.'

'You're telling me there's no racial tension in places like Dover and Folkestone?'

'I'm saying it's hard to know how much of it is exaggerated – or caused – by the press.'

'Dad, I saw a woman spit out of a car at this Albanian guy. It was pretty bad.'

'I'm not saying there's nothing. I'm saying—'

'And the b & b on the corner of your road had a sign saying, "Asylum scum not welcome". That was pretty bad, too.'

'They're threatened, Alistair. It's not surprising. We all are. We have no sense of national identity any more. You try living on the edge of a country – a weird outpost – with people passing through all the time, never staying. Ferries coming and going. Europe coming to get you. That'll only make it harder to know who you are. Like a constant tide wearing you down – in both directions.'

'I grew up there, actually.'

'Oh, yes. I keep forgetting,' Suzannah said.

After supper they went into the drawing room while Rosalind and Luke made coffee. The Chopin CD was still playing quietly, on repeat. Alistair turned it off. There was something exhausting about it, the piano going on and on.

'Why have you been so secretive about your past? It wouldn't have mattered, you know,' Suzannah said.

He laughed. 'Wouldn't it?'

'*I* certainly wouldn't have cared.'

You would have been disgusted, he thought. You're the worst snob of them all. He smiled at her. 'You would have found it funny because it would have upset your father,' he said. So, he still had the capacity to humour them, to prettify their disgusting prejudices, making them sound playful – exuberant. 'Them', he thought. Still 'me' and 'them' after thirty years.

'Would I? Oh, God. You might be right. Maybe I am as terrible as you think.' She took off her shoes and lay back on the sofa. 'Am I allowed a whisky anyway?'

'You are.'

It was strange. They had never got on so well. Not that he trusted her for a second. She still smiled at nothing in particular, in her secretive way, as if she knew all about him.

But you can forget all that, he told himself – she does know now. You can stop being afraid. He gave her the whisky and noticed how the wilted leaves hung off the tree outside the window onto the garden. It tapped a spiny branch on the glass as if it was asking to be let in. He went over and drew the curtains.

'What are you going to do?' she said.

'I don't know.'

'You can't work any more, I suppose.'

'No. Not after this – no.'

'Perhaps you should move to France or something. Spain.'

'Perhaps. Perhaps I should just move away.'

As he said this, he felt a deep cleft of regret and confusion open inside him. He was falling into it, falling into himself.

Had he done this deliberately? After a life of exercising such intense control, it was as if he had suddenly indulged the part of himself that told him, 'Stand up! Shout! Spit!' in the middle of the stalls at the latest play. He might still have been a respectable member of the audience.

Late that night, as he shut the door of the spare bedroom and switched on the bedside lamp, he remembered saying his prayers once with his mother. It was the first occasion on which he had realized that she did not know all the answers. '*Why* do you, though?' he had asked her.

'Because that's what you do at night.'

'But *why*?'

'What do you mean "why"? *Because everyone does*. Do you want to be the only little boy who doesn't say his prayers before bed?' She looked at him with pantomime horror on her face.

He had thought about it for a moment, kneeling by the bed in his pyjamas, holding his favourite toy soldier. He opened his mouth to argue.

'Oh, just say them, Al, there's a good boy. I'm tired out.'

What a lot of trouble he had been to her. He could not bear to think how tired out she must really have been.

Chapter 4

The first time Luke saw Arianne she was standing on a table at a bar called Noise. She was holding up one of her stiletto-heeled boots and laughing at the man on the floor beneath her. He seemed to be talking to her through gritted teeth, his hunched shoulders jerking with each word, and he pushed his hands into his pockets with a violent kind of casualness. Just then, a glass by the girl's foot tipped over, rolled off the edge of the table and smashed. She noticed this and kicked another one after it.

When the second glass smashed, the scene responded – as if that was the signal it had been waiting for. It was as if the car-chase music had begun. There was a flurry of movement; a man jumped up unexpectedly from the shadows of the leather banquette behind the table. Now that he looked Luke could see that, incredibly, three people were just sitting there, still drinking, while all this was going on. The new man shouted above the music, 'OK, why don't you leave her alone now, Dan? I really think that's enough, don't you?' He took off his jacket with enough difficulty to suggest that he was very drunk. The sleeves got pulled inside-out and he had to tug his hands free; one of his arms flicked back with a jerk and put him off balance. In his T-shirt, he provided a reference by which you could judge the incredible height and width of the other man. One of the girls from their banquette stood up now. No one paid any attention to her. She eased her way round the two men as apathetically as if they had been large rocks and made her way over to the bar for another drink.

'Leave her *alone*?' the larger man shouted back incredulously. 'She's gone completely fucking *mental*. Look at her. She's standing on a

34

fucking *table*, Andy. What do you mean, leave her alone? To what? Smash the fucking place up?'

'Um – hello?' the girl shouted. Her voice was piercing, furious.

'You're just upsetting her more. That's all I'm saying, man.'

'So what? She's been a little *bitch* this evening. Do we care if she's getting upset? She's having a tantrum. Oh, poor baby.'

'Hello? I am actually *here*, you know?'

'*Are* you, Arianne? Are you here – on the same *planet* as the rest of us?'

'Oh, fuck you.'

'Fuck *you*. What makes you think it's OK for you to stand on a table and kick glasses on the floor? When did you get a letter from fucking *God* saying it was OK for you to do that? No one else did. *I* never got that letter.'

He sounded Dutch. It was an Americanized Euro voice. His sense of the dramatic had obviously been acquired from action films: it was lead-weighted with portentousness that no real-life circumstances could have fulfilled. His posture was studied, dumb-bell refined. But you could have had nothing but respect for the breadth of his shoulders.

Luke turned abruptly to the friend he was standing with at the bar. 'Is that Andy Jones?' he said.

The DJ let one tune recede and another take over, and the dancing became faster in the background.

'Who? Where?'

'That guy. By the table behind us – with the girl on it. Andy Jones.'

'Andy Jones . . .'

'*That* guy. The one on the right, in front of the door. You must be able to see him.'

'I can *see* him, Luke, I just can't remember who the fuck Andy Jones is. Do I know him? Is he famous?'

'We were at fucking school with him. Didn't he, like, act or something? Something artistic and vaguely poncy. Was it the choir? You did all that stuff. I *know* you remember Andy Jones.'

What was Andy Jones doing with that incredible girl? It was against nature somehow. Not that he was with her – just near her, really. She was an independent figure in the scene.

Arianne would always give him that impression – even much later, when she angled the mirror so they could see themselves making love on the bedroom floor. He watched her watching herself, analysing

35

her own performance. He felt fascinated and lonely. Was Narcissus drawn to his own reflection as much out of fear of others as love of himself?

In spite of her beauty there was little genuine conceit in Arianne. Her self-obsession was born of alienation, of the early disappointment of realizing her parents had an 'open marriage' and that the word 'love' was liable to interpretation by sophisticated minds. Her consultations of all reflective surfaces were made with the intention of reinforcing self-sufficiency. Arianne feared that she could not surrender herself to dependence on another person, no matter what superficial trappings of it she allowed to exist. In fact, she was increasingly aware that the superficial trappings – financial, practical – were merely conjuror's diversions she had developed over the years. These were ultimately destined to fail in convincing both her and the men she chose.

'So, I think I'll go over,' Luke said.

'You think you'll go over. Right. What for, exactly?'

'To say hi to Andy Jones.'

'Oh, I *see*.'

'So, back in a minute, OK?'

'Luke?'

'Yes?'

'I'll bet you a million quid that big one's her boyfriend.'

Luke grinned and finished his drink. 'Look, this is Andy Jones we're talking about. I can't miss an opportunity like this.'

'Yes. What you can't do is chat up girls who are plainly insane and who are obviously *with other men*.'

'I know that. I do know that,' he said.

He put down his glass and turned to move off towards the table, but before he could, something else was said – something quiet between the two men – and the big man knocked Andy Jones off his feet.

It was a perfectly timed right hook to the jaw; a punch Dan had always affectionately termed his 'classic'. The atmosphere in the bar changed immediately. It liquefied. A wave of bar staff crashed at the edge of the bar and the distinction between dancers and drinkers dissolved as people stopped moving. 'Where? Where?' they said to one another as they strained to see what had happened. They wanted a bit of blood, a bit of human drama to mark out this evening among all the others. The strobe light was more apparent, slower and more

36

sinister without the dancing. For a moment it was like cold, flashing moonlight, bouncing off all the hard surfaces – the glasses and table edges, the geometric aluminium chairs. The small act of violence had changed the room into a store of weapons.

To Luke, it seemed that the whole scene had spun out from the girl on the table, that she had effortlessly choreographed everyone around her. An entire bar full of people. He would have liked to make this observation to his friend James, but James laughed at him for the grandiose things he said about girls. James thought girls were for sex and men were for friendship, and it amazed Luke how many women his friend had to brush off.

Arianne got off the table. Now that he no longer had an opportunity to introduce himself to her, Luke felt invisible and drifted over towards her with the little crowd of people who had been near the bar. They stood less than a metre away. People were using the word 'ambulance'. He heard the girl say, 'Oh, for fuck's sake, why do you *do* this shit, Dan?'

She was tall, about five eleven, so the large man – Dan – did not tower over her in her high heels. Somehow she managed to look impressed while she put her boot back on; she kept her eyes fixed on Dan's while she pulled it into place. She had an accent, too – it might have been French.

'Really, why are you such a total wanker?'

'Why? Because that's what you fucking *turn people into*,' Dan said.

Luke remembered that exchange – often. He remembered the unexpected pulse of anxiety across the girl's face and the instant softening of her manner. 'Hey, come on,' she said. 'I'm wasted. Let's stop fighting, baby. I want to go home. Let's go to your place, shall we?'

Luke was astonished by her voice. In a matter of seconds it had gone from searing anger to honeyed fragility. He couldn't help imagining that such range might have other applications.

All of the others in the little crowd were trying to catch sight of Andy, but Luke just watched the girl. They were separated by less than a metre – but there was no reason in the world for her to notice him. She put her hand on Dan's face. 'Oh, Daniel, you *hurt* him. What have you gone and done now?' she said. The big man slumped for her like a circus elephant. Then she turned to Andy, who was being comforted by the other girls from the banquette. His nose was bleeding and he was sitting on the floor. She leant down to him: 'Andy, honey, are you badly hurt?'

Following her, Dan shook Andy's knee back and forth in a vigorous, playful way. 'Hey, look, I'm sorry, man,' he said. 'I totally lost it there.' Then he raised his arm to give Andy a genial slap on the shoulder.

Arianne caught his wrist. 'Dan's *sorry*,' she said. 'He's very sorry and he's a *total wanker*. I will call you tomorrow, Andy. We *will* speak about this, sweetie. Don't worry.'

She made it sound as though this unforgivable act would not go unrecorded. And then she looked around for her handbag and left – with the perpetrator.

This was not so much a sense of justice as one of composition.

Luke walked back to the bar and picked up his drink. He felt as though he had been dancing right by the speakers for hours but, of course, he was not deafened and it was not sound that had affected him. His mind was reverberating with longing, as if it was a bell, struck by lust. Behind a vacant stare, his imagination laboured shamelessly. James was speaking about something, but all Luke could picture was the girl stopping, as she just might have done, half-way up the stairs to the exit. The boyfriend went on up to wait for her outside while she ran back down to the loo. Before she got to the doorway on to the corridor, she caught Luke's eye. A nod: yes, you.

He was not used to playing this submissive role, because he could get any girl he wanted, you could ask any of his friends, but he found it strangely sexy – in thought, anyway, where it was secret.

By the time he got out into the corridor, where it was cool and dark and muffled, the very long girl was hitching up her very short skirt. There was a store cupboard with a lock and she slammed the door behind them and the light burned round the edges in a dazzling line. He got his fingers all deliciously confused in her suspender belt and she tore them away impatiently, kicking and wriggling, her heel spiking her knickers into the carpet. He had never met a girl more desperate to give him a blow-job. She couldn't wait: she licked her lips and pulled down his boxer shorts with her teeth. But, on the other hand, Luke thought, was this wise? Maybe, he decided, he just pushed her away and she looked slightly disappointed for a second until he thudded her up and back against the wall and she was forced to sink her teeth into his neck to stop herself screaming.

'Luke?' said James. 'Am I interrupting something? I can come back if this is a bad time for you. *Luke?*'

'Sorry. What?'

Just then the bouncer came running down the stairs, looking angry.

He had been up the road buying some cigarettes. One of the bar-girls had texted him to come back right away. He went over to the bar and Luke heard the bar-girl tell him they wanted to see him upstairs in the office immediately. 'Babe, you might have really fucked it this time,' she said.

'Why? What the fuck? Was there an incident?' The bouncer peered around the room frantically – as though he might still catch the last moments of it. 'I *knew* there was an incident. I'm gone for two fucking minutes and there's an incident.'

An incident. It was the right way to describe a story without a beginning or an end. Just the middle was there, the comical climax – the girl on the table, holding up her boot as if she was going to take out that big man's eye with the heel of it. Luke wondered what had made her so angry. He was surprised by how exciting he found the thought of her anger – and by how reluctant he was to acknowledge the false note in the scene. The truth was that when he watched her walk away up the stairs, hand in hand with her enormous boyfriend, it occurred to him that it might all have been an exciting game before bed. The jealousy this inspired was unbearable, directly proportionate to his lust.

Arianne had long, muscular legs and he watched them climb the stairs, imagining the feel of her skin, picturing her standing above him in killer heels, letting him do whatever he wanted to her inner thighs.

When he lay in his bed that night, blushing and exhausted after he had done full and appropriate justice to their time in the store cupboard, he thought about Arianne kicking the glass off the table. He smiled to himself. Smash. He loved these sassy, violent women. You envisioned their gratifying orgasms – you *heard* their gratifying orgasms; you conjured up the gorgeous shame of passing the neighbours on the stairs the next day. His girlfriend Lucy favoured pastel colours; she reminded him about dry-cleaning; she said, 'Oh, that was so lovely, darling,' after sex.

And he was *very lucky* to have her, given the long hours he worked. He mustn't forget that, he told himself. No, Lucy was great. She was very pretty and she loved him and these qualities brought a lot of satisfaction – even if the subject of marriage had become more and more of an unspoken issue since her best friend had got engaged. How many times had he heard about the darling Tiffany diamond ring? But at least she was forgiving – even when she cooked for him and he fell asleep, too tired to eat at eleven thirty when he got home from work.

Would he prefer to be *alone*? This was a rhetorical question he asked himself from time to time. He considered the idea of being alone with horror, with the sensation of free-falling through darkness. Like many English boys, he had, at great expense, been expelled from the home at an early age and sent to a boarding-school. 'Alone' was a sensation never more perfectly represented than by sitting in his school bedroom on the first day of term, the last traces of his glossy, silk-scarfed mother on the air, knowing he must just *get on with it* and unpack his trunk.

All that week at the ad agency where he worked, he had played a recently invented game. It involved a vastly complex set of rules, which were just confusing enough to mean he could almost always win without being absolutely certain he was cheating. For the third time in a row, he got the balled-up chocolate wrapper into the ten-point zone between the computer monitor and the phone. That, added to the work-experience boy's four trips to the photocopier before the clock read a quarter to, and to his colleague Hamish's three sniffs in three minutes, meant the score was now high enough to allow Luke to alter history.

What had actually happened now was that he had walked over to the table and said hi to Andy Jones. And Andy, of course, had remembered him perfectly because Luke had been a big figure at school – captain of rugby and cricket and tennis. (He had actually been the first person in school history – other than a vast-jawed, bovine-looking boy named Dorian Anderson who featured in ancient crackly photos from the 1960s – to be captain of three sports at once.)

Andy said: 'Shit, how *amazing* to bump into you like this!'

Luke lit a cigarette distractedly. 'Yeah, it's good to see you again, too, Andy.'

'*Fuck*. I mean – *Luke Langford*!' Andy slapped his forehead and laughed. At this point Luke raised his hand at a girl he happened to know. (This girl was beautiful and fashionably dressed in maybe a miniskirt or hot pants. She looked as though she would like to come over but was afraid to interrupt – she assumed he was talking business, perhaps.)

Andy was still staring at him. 'Sorry, I'm really blown away,' he said. 'It's been, what – ten years? Listen, let me introduce you to everyone. I mean, d'you want to meet my friends?'

'Well . . . sure – OK. But, listen, I can't stay long, Andy.'

'No, of course. Of *course*. Just quickly.' He put his arm round Luke's shoulder. 'Everyone? This is Luke Langford. This is the school fucking hero!'

And it was then that Arianne had looked down from her pedestal and smiled at him, with a kind of recognition in her eyes.

It was really hard to concentrate on the Calmaderm shampoo account. He knew he would have to do better that afternoon because, in an ad agency full of neurotic creatives, he was the one who held it all together. Everybody relied on him. Just the day before there had been a scene between Adrian Sand, one of the creatives, and the head of marketing at Calmaderm. Adrian had presented an idea that had been deemed, with a sarcastic smile, 'Just a bit too way out,' and he had thrown up his hands and said what the hell was he supposed to do, this shampoo was just like every other fucking shampoo and he might as well shoot himself in the heart. There had been a stunned silence.

It was only a shampoo, for Christ's sake, Luke thought. But it was his job as account executive to liaise between the warring factions and – as his boss, Sebastian, said, with a hand on Luke's shoulder – to help get the fucking money in. Luke was renowned as a 'people person'. He knew perfectly well that he had been so successful by the age of twenty-eight because of his sportsman's calm in a crisis, because of his placid, unifying smile and because of his cufflinks.

He had been left a whole box of cufflinks by his maternal grand-father and one day, to please his mother whom he was meeting for lunch, he had worn a pair to work. With an uncharacteristic sense of self-parody, Luke had noticed that, along with his public-school accent and floppy hair, the cufflinks conveyed to his colleagues a note of patrician authority, which did him no harm at all.

When he walked out for his sandwich at lunchtime he looked up at the icy blue sky over Hoxton. The wind pulled his trouser legs taut round his ankles and tugged his hair back straight. The weather was abrasive, at odds with his reflective frame of mind. Movements around him seemed staged, menacingly interconnected. A can of the drink he was about to buy bounced in the gutter beside him. A woman rushed out into the road and a hairbrush fell out of her handbag; as she bent down to get it a motorbike passed, whipping up her long hair, which caught the eye of a window-cleaner, who dropped his sponge. Behind the soapy glass, a row of blow-up sex dolls mouthed their obscene 'O' and just as Luke wondered what on earth this had to do with selling neat racks of footwear, someone threw a cigarette butt on to the pavement – at the exact moment he lowered his new shoe. He crushed it out.

When had life started feeling like this, like a steady-cam shot with him as the walking figure?

He sat down under a tree in a nearby square with his can of Lilt and his smoked-duck wrap. He was not hungry: he had bought his lunch out of habit, standing numbly in the line at the deli, distantly reassured by the familiar rows of sandwiches and cartons of juice, by the bright signs asserting the magic words 'healthy' and 'fresh' to some half-dormant part of his consciousness. A crisps packet skimmed across the grass and was caught against the railings. He put the lunch in his shoulder-bag and lit a cigarette.

What had begun as an odd game had become a preoccupation with how easily he might have altered the story of his life. His mind ticked over the endless range of improbabilities, the minute coincidences, that had brought his current existence into being. He had found out about the company he worked for from an ad in a newspaper that someone had left on the tube. Who? And hadn't he been on the wrong tube, drunk, on his way from one party to another? He had folded the page into his pocket. Hadn't he met a girl that night and slept with her? What was her name? He had left his jacket at her flat – and had to go back for it because of the ad, pretending he had also forgotten to ask for her phone number.

She didn't believe him about the number, he remembered. He had done a big, broad smile at her and asked her for it and she had pulled her dressing-gown round her very tightly and blushed. She handed the jacket to him on the doorstep and scribbled the number in tiny handwriting on a piece of notepaper with 'THINGS TO DO TODAY!!' printed at the top. He remembered the smell of toast behind her, the traffic rushing by behind his back as she wrote.

What was her *name*? He could recall oddly pendulous breasts . . . but not her name.

And into this void went the missed opportunity of meeting Arianne.

Was it TV that made you think the world was smaller than it was? He had worked in advertising for six years now and he was sure he ought to know better. He would never see Arianne again, no matter how similar their bio-active yoghurt purchases or their taste in music, no matter how inclusive 'youth culture' seemed to be in magazines or cable documentaries about twenty-somethings.

His mobile phone was going in his pocket and he knew it would be Lucy. Everything about his relationship with her had been consciously planned. It was formulaic, designed to challenge the terrible sensation he was scarcely allowing himself to feel, even now. What was the sensation, exactly? It came between heartbeats; it was like clicking on the wrong link, being launched involuntarily towards web addresses you hadn't typed in, pop-ups bursting on to the screen advertising humiliating products that must yet appeal to someone (but *who*? *Where*?), telltale cookies accumulating faster than you could press 'Escape', 'Escape', 'Escape' . . .

He and Lucy had been introduced at a dinner party as two nice-looking single people, aged twenty-six. They were a good match. He diverted her call.

Luke felt breathless. He looked around at the offices and the people he could see through the lit windows, all doing their jobs. Mothers, fathers, boyfriends, wives. Betrayals, longings, grief, pride, heartbreak, ambition. Two girls passed by eating chips from the same bag. The smell of vinegar made him salivate.

'What – like Buddhism, you mean?' one of them said.

He felt crushed by detail, by the equal importance of other people's lives and the contingency of all his accomplishments. His heart went fast as he tried to think of an aspect of his life that existed independently of his blind faith in it.

It occurred to him that he could just *not go back to work* – ever. And would it matter to the stars in his gap-year shots of Tanzania? Would it disturb for one minute the thick-set horses in his book on the Mongolian planes?

Worse than the content of all these thoughts, though, was the suspicion that, as ever, he was the last person to have them. He had a desire to cover his ears – as if people were laughing at him for his slowness – but he lowered his arms in time and lit another cigarette.

It was just three weeks later that he got into his friend Ludo's car and discovered Arianne on the back seat. Ludo had said he was going for a drink with a few friends and that his 'mad cousin' would be there.

Ludo's family was a sophisticated mess, spread out in the most picturesque-sounding cities in Europe. Luke had imagined a Eurotrashy cousin called Philippe or Sasha, who smoked Gauloises Légères; someone with a manicure, a ski-tan, a cashmere jumper. But instead there was Arianne.

She had bleached her hair blonde. She slouched sulkily in a cloud of honey and jasmine scent, her worn-denim-clad knees resting on the back of the driver's seat. She moved them over a little to give Luke room.

'Cheers,' he said.

'Cheers'? He never said 'cheers'. It was a depressing, flat beer and stale smoke word. Darts competitions and rain. Cheers? That was not him. It was not even anyone he knew.

They set off and he thought about introducing himself. What was called for was an ordinary exchange. He must simply tell her his name and ask her what hers was. This was what people did – ordinarily. But how could it be an ordinary exchange when he already knew her name?

Arianne . . . Just the name filled him with dreams, with adolescent nostalgia. There in his mind were all the unattainable French girls of his early teens. Unchanged in his imagination, they sprawled out like kittens on the white beaches of Cap d'Antibes; they wriggled off their bikini straps and flipped expertly on to their fronts. He remembered the agony of watching them flip-flopping at high speed through the beach bar where he languished podgily with his bottle of Coke. They had an edible smell of coconut oil and you wanted to lick it off, but you knew they would smack or scratch you if you tried. They cried out in delectable fury, '*Oui, j'arrive! J'arrive!*' to friends, who waved by the pedaloes a little way off.

Arianne was a holiday name, which made his mouth water for the taste of pear juice and croissants, for the flavour of every breakfast he had ever sleepily consumed on sand-dusted hotel terraces while his parents consulted maps. His memory had preserved a deep blue sea just beyond the edge of a terrace, blinding white tables chequering a lawn, a sense of complete faith in the world.

He watched Arianne's face out of the corner of his right eye. She was busy sending a text message and paid him no attention. Again, he felt condemned to invisibility as he had in the bar. And again he let himself enjoy it, like a peeping Tom – or a plump boy at the beach club. It was so odd to return to this adolescent role! Particularly given that now, of course, he could get any girl he wanted.

Arianne had milky-coffee-coloured skin, and the new blonde hair looked almost metallic against it. It had been cut in a 1920s-style bob and it swung into her face as they turned a corner. She pushed a supernaturally gleaming strand behind her ear. In profile her mouth

44

protruded, forming a sharp little curve at the top of her lips; her upturned nose seemed gently to echo the shape. But then, as if to save her face from bland, girlish prettiness, the jaw was strong – almost masculine. She had long, muscular legs; to Luke they suggested sport, tennis matches in the sunshine on red clay courts in southern Italy. He saw lemon trees, he heard cicadas. He could imagine her devastating serve.

His mind was full of faraway pictures as he sat there beside her in the car.

It was not a precise, photographable beauty. In fact, it was brought together by strength of personality. Later it would seem to Luke that her face was a manifestation of her mind, or rather that an artist had wanted to depict the polarities at war within it and had set the strong jaw and the little girl's nose against each other. She gave over her whole physiognomy to whatever emotion she was feeling. At that moment it was to abject exasperation, which increased with each text message she received. Luke decided her impatience had a distinctly sexual quality – and then wondered guiltily if he might be imagining it.

He decided to wait until she was free to introduce himself. He looked out of the window and saw his friend Jessica waving outside South Kensington tube station. Ludo pulled up and she got into the front beside him.

Jessica was a friend of theirs from university and Luke was always glad to see her. She had been a sort of big-sister figure when the three of them lived together in their second and third years, even though she was actually the same age. She had prepared meals for them, since Luke had always been cooked for and Ludo had always eaten out or ordered in, neither was much use in the kitchen, and they consumed her miraculous shepherd's pies and pasta bakes like starving children. They had also left her in charge of all the bills, merely scrawling cheques absentmindedly when she asked for them. Both he and Ludo felt embarrassed and confused by all this when they remembered it. Luke had found out recently that Jessica had been working secretly at a Pizza Hut in a nearby town to supplement her student grant and pay the bills. Her two flatmates, on the other hand, had idled away their three years in hangovers and come-downs, leaving on lights and hot water and blow-heaters, carelessly squandering their parents' money.

Jessica leant right back between the seats and kissed Arianne, whom she had obviously met before, then gave Luke a big hug. She was one of those people who always insisted on proper hugs and kisses, even if it meant climbing over a restaurant table. Her hair smelt cold and Christmassy; it felt icy against Luke's face. She smiled at him. 'Are you well, sweetheart?' He nodded and smiled back, and she began to adjust the car stereo, looking for a song she liked while she waited for the lighter to pop out. She glanced at Arianne in the vanity mirror. 'Are you *still* texting? She was texting all last night. Have you had a break?'

'Done it,' Arianne said. 'Finished. I shall never send another text message ever, ever, ever again.' She dropped the phone casually into her handbag. Arianne was fond of absolute statements.

They set off again and Luke felt increasingly awkward. They turned corners fast and three times his leg almost touched hers as he slid around on the seat. Why did Ludo not say *anything*? Suddenly he felt exasperated by his friend, who was just sitting there, steering with his knees, singing along to David Bowie with a cigarette hanging out of his mouth. It was absurd. It was Ludo's *job* to introduce them.

Luke clenched his fist and turned towards Arianne, wearing his best smile. Unfortunately, though, before he could say anything, a gun-metal blue jeep came out of a side street on to the King's Road and slammed into the passenger side of the car.

The road was icy and they spun a hundred and eighty degrees through the bright, cold air and smashed into a tree.

The first hit had taken them all by surprise, but the second came with a calm inevitability. The tree trunk loomed larger and larger in the side window until it filled the view. It felt like dancing, as if London itself had swung them out, out, out – and then snatched them back in again from the other side.

The side windows cracked on impact. And then came the gentle shower of glass on the pavement, the standstill, the car creaking in its new shape, and the two girls crying quietly. There was a strange, starlit quiet as the scene took shape around them. A few passers-by came up and stared, dumb and curious as cattle.

If it hadn't been for that tree, they would have gone right through the window of the Indian restaurant. The winter sun bounced off the huge pane of glass in front of all the tables. It remained intact; a sparkling miracle. They were all alive.

And that was how, twenty minutes later, the incredible girl came to be crying in Luke's arms in the back of an ambulance – before he had even told her his name.

★   ★   ★

46

Arianne didn't have a French accent any more. Luke discovered later that it came and went according to her mood. Her mother was French, but Arianne had only ever been to France on holiday herself. She wanted to be an actress and she expected acceptance of this and other small insincerities as part of her vibrant performance. In fact, acceptance was not enough: she found it hard to forgive the sin of literal-mindedness in any of her friends.

Thankfully, none of them was seriously injured. The other driver was unhurt and had given Ludo his details, looking guilty and afraid. A gaudy blonde girlfriend came to collect him. She eyed the dishev-elled opposition, tightening her fuchsia lips, anticipating litigation.

Ludo and Luke had mild whiplash and Jessica, whose whole weight had been caught by her seatbelt as they spun towards the tree, had bruised her hip badly. Arianne had broken two bones in her foot. It struck Luke that she barely complained about the pain. She merely referred to the shock of what had happened as if it had been full of sinister import – like a terrible noise in an empty house at night.

Arianne had a deep-rooted pessimism to which her imagination gave lurid expression. It was not uncommon to see her wince – while she brushed her hair or put on her clothes – at the potential injuries and betrayals that ran through her mind. She sensed a forest fire of disaster raging just over the horizon, and if she came too close to it her reac-tion was always to fall asleep, as if she had been drugged by the smoke.

They spent the whole afternoon in the hospital, having X-rays and waiting for the promised doctor to come and see them after the initial examination and filling in of forms. After a while they were asked to wait in a cubicle. They felt demoted, ushered offstage on their big day, but there was no protest in them. They had waited so long that nurses had ceased to be a source of information and passed them by holding peculiar objects, entirely without significance. Arianne slept peacefully on the trolley while the others sat on plastic chairs. They were too tired to relive the accident any more so they stopped talking and listened to the comings and goings of other patients. It was with an increasing sense of contamination that they realized this was a world of bad luck that usually they had no cause to acknowledge.

Stories could be pieced together around them. The woman in the cubicle next to theirs had somehow spilt a kettle of boiling water over her neck and chest. Her husband refused to leave her alone with the nurse. 'We'd just like to ask her a few *questions*, Mr McPherson,' the nurse repeated. 'That's all.'

'What questions? There are no questions which I can't answer,' Mr McPherson said.

Opposite them an old woman lay on a trolley and a young man held her hand. She slept placidly, her small head sunk deep in the pillows. Every so often, he would say, 'Mum? *Mum?*' with a note of panic in his voice. The old woman would smile and raise her free hand as if she was too tired to answer him in words. And the man would rub his eyes under his glasses as if he was trying to wake up. Up and down the hallway, two children wearing surgical masks ran back and forth squeaking, '*Peow! Peow!*' at each other, their fingers pointed like guns.

The doctor was only a year or so older than they were. Her name was Dr Bandari. She gave them prescriptions for painkillers and told them to go to the hospital dispensary. She said, 'Look, you really shouldn't drink with these,' and smiled. She wore the Muslim *hijab* and they were glad to escape from her purity, from the correct assumptions she seemed to be making about their lives.

When they got out on to the street, the traffic looked fast and dangerous. The darkness had gathered itself without their knowledge while they sat in the windowless hospital, and the headlights and glaring shop windows were threatening. They felt a need to stay together. They were connected by an important experience and were not yet ready to allow others in.

'Let's go back to my place,' Luke suggested.

'Cool. Perfect, actually,' Ludo said. 'You've got DVDs and shit. We can chill out there.'

'Yeah, we'll hide out.'

'Exactly. We won't even answer our phones,' Jessica said.

This made sense to all of them. They hailed a cab.

Luke was glad he had suggested they go to his place. He wanted Arianne to see his flat. He wanted her to take in the way it looked, what it said about him. His father had given him and Sophie a hundred thousand pounds each to start themselves off and he had bought his first place at twenty-two. He had sold it for a good profit in the London housing boom and put everything into this new one. It was in Notting Hill. It was open-plan. You had a power-shower then walked serenely, barefoot, across the polished wood floor. Your guests drank martinis on the suede sofa. That was the look. He had recently had a thirty-two-inch plasma-screen TV delivered – one of the white ones, which were a limited edition, if she cared about that kind of thing. Irritatingly, most girls didn't and he knew Lucy faked it, saying obvious things, like, 'Oooh. Is it surround sound?' which of course it bloody was.

In the taxi on the way there, they drove past Ludo's car. It was more wrecked than they had realized. The bonnet was crushed and the passenger side was buckled in just between the front and the back seat; it had missed Jessica and Luke by inches. They both squinted, picturing their body shapes on either side of the dent, experiencing a completely abstracted form of pain, the idea of pain. Someone had put a bunch of flowers on the roof, assuming everyone had been killed.

'It's like being at the scene of your own death,' Arianne said. They were all quiet for a moment.

'We should drink champagne or something,' said Luke. 'We're fucking lucky to be alive. Let's stop and buy a couple of bottles of champagne and celebrate.'

Arianne rested her head on his shoulder. He had said something that pleased her. It was an immediately addictive sensation. He found himself looking out of the window as if to find space for the deluge of pride. She could move him from despair to elation by the slightest sign of her approval. Just a few weeks later he would have bankrupted himself for her, left his job, sold all his possessions. Her personality destroyed all sense of proportion, the way the height and velocity of an aeroplane can make the whole canopy of a forest look like moss held close to the face. Luke felt his mind's eye spiral back into his imagination in search of a scale by which to measure the importance of her remarks. Her head tattooed its shape on his shoulder.

What accounted for this effect she had? He was not the first man to feel it.

In fact the explanation, when accompanied by her unquestionable physical beauty, was surprisingly simple. There are few examples of unqualified achievement in a lifetime. Success is generally tainted by all the failures that came before it, or diminished by a prologue of endurance and compromise. Naturally, people are driven to seek out the indubitable. Some climb mountains – after all, who can argue with a boot on a rock at the whistling summit? Some jump out of heli-copters, some swim with sharks. For those who cared to face it, Arianne presented a similar challenge. She came with an insoluble problem: a gap in her heart, which, she would explain, could never, never, never be filled. It had been made long ago and she dared each of her boyfriends to do their best, each time genuinely hoping that if they did hurl themselves in, they would not simply be lost like the one before.

She was, essentially, desperately lonely and in need of reassurance and, having received a long tutelage from a serially unfaithful and narcissistic father (with silver hair and a brow lift), she was dangerously knowing about the male ego. She could tempt men to leap off cliffs just to prove the strength of their dive, but their suicides went only a little way to making her feel better. And then, of course, she was left alone.

'Oh, that is *such* a great idea, Luke,' she said. 'We should get magnums.'

They carried the champagne, the Chinese takeaway and the extra DVDs up the stairs to Luke's flat. The cleaner had been that day and every surface glistened. The amazing TV shone like a portal to another universe. The stereo was sleek and minute – miraculous. These were his hi-tech possessions and he was glad she was seeing them. He put on a film but no one was really watching it. They were all slightly hysterical.

'Were you knocked out, Luke? I wish *one* of you cared enough to remember how long I was out for. I have so definitely got concussion,' Ludo said. 'There was no fucking way I was staying at that hospital for observation, though.'

'You don't want observation, you want an audience, darling,' Arianne said. 'No rock-and-roll death tonight. Next time.'

'*Next* time? I'm never getting into a car again. I'm going to walk everywhere and never cross roads,' Ludo said.

'Which means you can't go anywhere.'

'I shall wave at friends when I get to the end of my street. I'll order in. I'll get fitness equipment.'

'You just went in a taxi,' Luke said. 'You already went in a car.'

'What? Oh – don't be strict with me. I'll cry.'

Luke laughed and passed him a bottle. 'Here, have a drink.'

'Oh, I hate opening these.'

'I'll do it, then.'

Jessica threw the magazine she had been flicking through on to the floor. 'Fuck. Fuck. *Fuck*. We could all have been fucking *killed*,' she said – in the blood-drained voice they had all reverted to from time to time throughout the day. This observation had been made hundreds of times already, but on each occasion it arrived with the force of the unexpected. The bang of the champagne cork startled

50

them and they all laughed. Jessica held out glasses one by one, speaking more brightly, more philosophically: 'We *could*, though. We could all have been dead now.'

'Perhaps we are,' Ludo told her. He made his eyes comically wide.

'Well, perhaps we *are*.'

'Oh, don't. You're scaring me and I'm fragile. Why does no one ever recognize this?'

Jessica flapped her hand at him and turned away. 'Are you scared of dying, Luke?'

'Me? I . . . I don't really think about it.'

'No. Me neither. Why is that?'

Ludo said, 'Because we're young. Isn't it? We have a false sense of invincibility. I'm completely happy with that.'

'Are you really?'

'Oh, *why not*, Jessica?'

'Just because it's self-deception. Yeah – *yawn, yawn*. Look, I know you think I'm being morbid . . .'

'Which you are.'

'. . . but we *could* get killed any minute. No reason why not, just because we're in our twenties.'

'It's chance. Chaos,' Arianne said. 'Isn't it? I mean – oh, you know what I'm talking about.'

'Look, I'm just going to keep fit, have my wheatgrass juice, avoid sugar and fat and intravenous opiates, except when I've been very, very good – and I think I'll be fine.'

'But you won't, Ludo. You will die – one day.'

'Thanks, Jessica. This I already knew.'

'What I mean is, we don't let ourselves think about *actual death*, do we? That's why this is all such a shock. Look at us. Are we prepared?'

'What do you want – Bibles? *Wills?* OK – Luke, you can have my Asian-babes collection, all right, mate? I have nothing else of significant value. Jessica, we're *exhausted*, for God's sake.'

'No, it's more than that,' Arianne said. 'She's right.'

'*There* – your own cousin agrees with me. I'm just saying it's like we think about getting older instead these days. It's true – that's what we do. We worry about wrinkles, about sagging.'

'But it's all death,' Arianne said. 'It's all fear of death. That's what all those face creams are for. So you don't see the signs of death.'

'Why are you telling me?'

'Not just you, Ludo.'

'Tell him then. Have you ever seen anyone look more complacent than Luke? Look at those broad, dependable shoulders. Bastard. Anyway, I do not go to the gym or look after my skin because I'm afraid of dying.'

'Are you absolutely sure?'

'No, Arianne. Change the subject. Who do you get this from? Aunt Marie? Not my side anyway.'

'You *can't* change the subject,' she said. 'We nearly died. We've got death on us – in our hair and our clothes, stinky like cigarette smoke when you come home from a club.'

Ludo had found Luke's panama hat on the back of the bedroom door with his dressing-gown. He put them on and drank out of the champagne bottle. Somehow he always found a clown's outfit.

'Look, we *survived*, darling. This is the important and, moreover, this is the *scientific* fact. The rest is speculation.'

'Science is like that too, now,' Arianne said, 'isn't it? I don't think it is just facts any more. I mean – I get that impression. Don't you?'

'Fuck knows. But I'll tell you one thing that *is* a fucking fact. I'm going to sue that bastard for all he's worth and go away somewhere nice. Anywhere in the whole wide world. Where shall I go?'

No one said anything.

'Will you come to Chile with me, Luke? Start over?'

'*Definitely*,' Luke said. He grinned and looked down at his hands.

He and Ludo were growing less and less like each other. Luke had started to feel embarrassed by what he saw as his friend's immaturity, his reluctance to discuss anything that might lead him to question himself, his money, his holidays. Ludo's performances had always seemed joyous before, but now they were hollow and revealing. His hairline was starting to recede.

Ludo had no job. He had a trust fund and really didn't need the money. He had been a species of assistant for a while at his father's property firm, but the work had gradually faded out – or been forgotten. Luke found it impossible to understand how his friend could have so little ambition, even though he took it for granted that Ludo could drop by and see him for lunch on weekdays and was hurt if ever he said he was busy. For a long time Luke had passionately envied Ludo his three-day weekends in Paris or Rome, and had sat near that high sheen of leisure-wealth in a state of longing and admiration. But at that moment he found he desperately did not want the girls to think they were alike. He needed to separate himself.

'It is true, though, Ludo,' he said, feeling treacherous. 'It was just chance that we survived.' The two girls angled themselves towards him, acknowledging he was on their side. It felt wonderful.

'Exactly,' Jessica said. 'How can you *not* think about what happened? If I'd forgotten to wear my seatbelt, say, *which I very often do*, I could have gone right through the fucking windscreen and broken my back on the road. I could have smashed my *skull* open.'

The word 'skull' was shocking – it contained something of the sight of that first dead pet, that first imperfect adult explanation that Grandpa had gone somewhere in the sky to rest, and that, well, no, it was not possible to visit. They glanced at one another uneasily and Jessica said, 'But, hey, it didn't happen.' She shuddered. 'OK, maybe you're right, Ludo.'

'I am. Thank you and goodnight.'

They listened to Arianne sending a text message, turning off her mobile phone and – again – dropping it casually into her handbag. Jessica took a bag of weed out of her coat pocket. 'Yes, enough of this *thinking* palaver. Have you got any Rizla, Luke? I'm out.'

'Anyway, we do think about death,' Ludo said, unexpectedly, 'all the time. What about the *news*? *Terrorism, famine, earthquakes?* Incredible horror stories all fucking day long!'

'Yeah, but it's almost like we can take it that way, don't you think?' Jessica said. 'If it's *amazing* or *terrible*. Or if it's in *another country*. Or if it's unnatural – if it's cigarettes or radiation from your microwave that's killing you. Or an evil disease – AIDS, cancer. Better still an *amazing and terrible evil disease caused by something unnatural from another country*. We just can't handle the fact that it simply is *happening* in a totally ordinary way to all of us. Even in our fucking twenties.'

'You're telling me that looking at, like, hundreds of people dead from an earthquake on TV isn't thinking about death?'

'Not from your sitting room in Portobello it isn't. Not like looking at your dead uncle. Not like being in a car crash.'

'I might be wrong,' Luke said, glancing at Jessica for reassurance, 'but in a funny way it's like it makes you feel better watching the news – the people starving in Africa and so on. You get to see just how far off it is, just how much it wouldn't fit into your lifestyle.'

'*Lifestyle?* Thanks Mr Ad Man,' said Ludo. 'What does that have to do with it?'

Arianne said, 'You shouldn't laugh at him – he's got a point. You're always laughing, aren't you? You know it's a sign of insecurity never to be able to take anything seriously?'

'Is it? My God, that explains everything!' Ludo said. He looked slightly hurt, beneath his smile.

Arianne spoke patiently to him: 'What Luke means is it's comforting in a kind of horrible way. Like scary films about mad, demonic psychopaths. Because all anyone says when they see the *real* serial killer in the paper is "But he looks so . . . *normal*." Normal – like dying in your friend's car on the way out for a drink.'

Her eyes were fixed on some object on the coffee-table, her fists clenched in her lap. A horrifying thought appeared to pass through her mind; she shook it out of her hair and looked up again. 'So I remember at school we had this talk on chaos theory. They showed us patterns on a projector.'

'Fractals,' Luke said, feeling confident now, feeling authenticated.

'Fractals. Exactly. I can't remember what they were, though. Can you remember?'

'Just that it's something to do with chaos. Sorry.' Immediately he wished he hadn't spoken.

'Who knows about the pictures? Anyway, the big idea is about how a tiny little thing you would never have noticed can change *everything*. In the atmosphere it could be the movement of one particle. Just change one particle and you can affect the entire world. Gradually the air flow changes, a wind builds, the sea gets rough,' you saw her mind leap behind her eyes, '*sharks* move inland towards children.' She lit a cigarette and took a deep drag on it. 'Let's say there's a couple who were going to the beach that day. They're listening to the radio in the kitchen.' She did the radio voice: ' "Sharks are reported near the Summer Beach area." They decide to stay at home. They'll spend the day in the garden – he's just put in a new water feature for them to enjoy and, hey, she's got home-made lemonade in the fridge.' She smiled, to illustrate peaceful resolution. Then she dropped the expression abruptly. 'Somewhere else, ten minutes later, a small aeroplane is struggling in the high wind. The pilot isn't experienced – he only got his licence a week ago. The lessons were a birthday present from his girlfriend. Anyway, he loses control and the plane starts heading inland.' She turned to the dark window, took another drag on her cigarette and drew her hand through the air in an arc, making twinkling, raining motions with her fingertips. 'Falling, falling, falling,' she said. Her voice was gentle and kind, just as the world could seem to be.

'Anyway, after the crash, when all the TV reporters are jamming up the street, because this is a *big human-interest* story – a plane crashing into a house in a quiet little cul-de-sac like that – there's only one neighbour who's prepared to do an interview. She tells the anchorman how sad it was that God chose Mr and Mrs Jones because they were a sweet couple and they loved that garden of theirs – and they'd only just put in the water feature, after all.'

They all stared at her. Arianne's sense of disaster showed connoisseurship: she had left sharks near children, she had sent planes crashing into people quietly holding glasses of lemonade. She was laughing at herself as she stubbed out the cigarette. 'So my imagination is weird. Whatever. The big fat scientific discovery is that it's literally impossible to predict what will happen.'

'Is that right?' Ludo said. 'That can't be right. That sounds wrong.'

'I think it is right,' Luke said. 'I saw a TV thing about it. The butterfly flaps its wing and causes a hurricane.'

'Yes – yes, that's an example,' Arianne told him. 'We all know this stuff. You hear it all the time.'

Or you, Luke thought, what you have already done to my mind, my life. Suddenly it struck him that meeting Arianne again after the wasted miracle of her being at a bar with Andy Jones might be some kind of sign or message.

'What do the *pictures* mean, though? Something about snowflakes and computers,' Arianne said, oblivious to his thoughts.

He felt his heart going, just as it had on that icy afternoon when he had thought he would never see the incredible girl again.

'I mean, how does it all connect? People say all this stuff about infinite possibilities, randomness, chance,' she said, letting the words excite her with their remoteness, their obscure poetry, 'about parallel universes . . . *black holes* . . .'

She was frightening him.

'I might never have met you again,' Luke said. He stared at her passionately, his face flushed.

There was a silence. Jessica tried to make a lighter work, scraping the flint a few times. Then came the sound of the flame burning the end of a cigarette. Arianne turned her face to him. 'How do you mean "again", Luke? We've never met before, have we?'

'No – I know. I mean. It was just a figure of . . . I just – I thought I saw you somewhere before, that's all. Not *met*. Just *saw* . . .'

He stood up and searched around for the Rizla Jessica needed, feeling his own heartbeat swelling through him as if it was actually distorting his shape. When he felt able to turn round again, he saw she was smiling obscurely, pulling an invisible hair off her sweater.

Jessica laughed to fill the awkward gap. 'So,' she said, 'maybe we'll all go to Chile with you, Ludo. Probably fewer black holes there – what with all the sunshine.'

Jessica felt sorry for Luke, who often embarrassed himself in front of girls. There was no need for him to be nervous – she imagined he was exactly what most women were after: he was tall and friendly; he had the broad shoulders and so on. At any rate, he was the best-looking guy she knew. He was phenomenally insecure about his intellect, though. Sadly, this was understandable, given the brilliant, neurotic sister and the closed-off tragic dad, who dismissed all his son's observations as trifling and spoilt.

Why did he do that? Why give your child privileges only to hate him for accepting them when they were all he knew? Jessica felt she had rarely seen anyone more at war with himself than Mr Langford, who appeared constantly to be in a state of adoration and loathing of his own wealth. He luxuriated – sometimes almost vulgarly, which made her like him – in his fine clothes, his good wine, but when he was challenged by the predictably left-wing outspokenness of his daughter, he was prone to moments of searing shame. The daughter plainly knew this and she was the one member of the family who could exert power over her father's mood if she chose to. This game of chess was beyond Luke, who seemed only to have a relationship with his mother. Mrs Langford was a lovely, intuitive person who, like too many women of that generation in Jessica's opinion, devalued her worth altogether by presenting herself with an apology, as if she was a consolation prize for those who weren't lucky enough to win the attention of her husband.

'Oh, all right,' Ludo told her, 'girls can come to Chile too. At least now you're talking sense. Hey, Luke, doesn't Davina's mother have a house out there?'

'Davina's mother? Where?'

'In *Chile*.'

'OK, OK. Can I ask you people something?' Jessica said. 'How come everyone you know has, like, five houses?' She licked the Rizla and raised her eyebrows.

'They do not,' Ludo said.

'Yes, they do.'

'What are you saying? Are you implying that we're spoilt rich kids with a limited social circle? So what? You went to public school too, darling.'

'I had a scholarship,' she said, winking, 'so it really doesn't count.'

'Did you? I never knew that,' Luke said. He wished he could find Jessica attractive, but she was too plain for him. She was such a cool, clever girl. 'What are you doing hanging out with us? You should be at the Socialist Workers' meeting or something.'

'Oh, shut up.'

'Drinking beer. With *actual poor people*.'

'Here, have a beautifully rolled joint, Ludo,' she said.

'Bless you. You are a highly accomplished young lady and will one day make someone a lovely wife.'

'Yeah, right.' She snorted contemptuously.

Arianne propped her leg on the sofa and held out her glass to Ludo. 'I hate snobs. My dad's a fucking snob.' She pulled her face into a frantic caricature. '"Why don't you go out for dinner with the Honourable Fuckwit, darling?" I can't respect it. It's such a bullshit attitude. He's always pimping me, that bastard.'

'Pimping your daughter sounds like a bullshit attitude,' Jessica said. '*Jesus*.'

Ludo pointed the champagne bottle at Arianne as if it was a microphone – or a gun. 'Hang on just one second there, Miss Tate. Have you, of your own free will, ever been out with a man who was not stinking rich?'

Jessica giggled and Arianne looked at her. For a second, Luke wondered if there was hostility between them. He thought Jessica might be jealous of the prettier girl.

But then Arianne did her breathy laughter, her Sunday-morning-in-bed laughter – she seemed to have no other kind. 'OK, so you got me there,' she said.

'Oh, that is *so* fucking outrageous,' Jessica gasped, 'I assumed he was *jo*king!'

'I know. It is outrageous. I'm just not independent like you.'

'Independent? What do you mean? You know I'm not rich.'

'I don't mean in that way. I mean in the important ways.'

This natural revelation of her vulnerability was disarming. The beautiful girl, so honest about her failings, was hard to resist. Jessica wondered if she knew it.

Arianne shrugged. 'Look, rich boys have this kind of *authority* that makes you . . . I don't know, it makes you feel *safe.*'

'Yes, it comes of being *waited* on, always getting the best *table*. A gold watch for Christmas, a ski-trip, a new car. It's totally superficial,' Jessica said. 'No offence, guys.'

Luke wanted to tell her he wasn't given money by his parents any more.

'Look, I know it's bullshit. Like anything, I suppose it fools you if you want it to, for as long as it can,' she said.

Without question, Arianne was the main character in the room. The recklessness of her honesty made for compelling viewing. She risked her dignity in a way that was beyond the nerve of the others, beyond their sense of style. She pulled off high-dive spectaculars and emerged from the water absolutely herself.

'Yes, it's all fascinating, of course, darling,' Ludo said, 'but what about that brute Dan, though? I mean, really. *Really.*'

'Dan? He's a poppet.' She looked away, embarrassed for a moment by her own insincerity, because she and Dan had exchanged thirty-six angry text messages that day. He exhausted her. She didn't find him sexy any more and had to grit her teeth when he forced himself inside her. He had made a fool of himself because of her and she had already decided it was time to move on.

Ludo sighed. 'Arianne, Dan is a meat-head who completely misunderstands everything you say. It's impossible to have a conversation with him about anything other than protein shakes or the best way to target your abs. He's *not* mixing in our gene pool.'

'"*Safe*", though? That's what I want to talk about,' Jessica said. 'He couldn't protect you today, could he? What does "safe" mean, for fuck's sake? Don't you get bored with your meat-head?'

'Oh, I've asked her this before. She says boredom is better than fear.'

'That's *crazy*! Boredom is total alienation from what's going on around you. It's as lonely and frightening as it gets,' Jessica said. 'It must be awful to be with someone who bores you. I could never go to bed with someone who bored me. It would be less emotionally significant than *masturbation.*'

'Jesus, Jessica,' Ludo said.

She blew out a mouthful of smoke. 'What?'

'Just . . . what you said . .' he told her. For a second he felt a flash of insecurity – as if a photograph had been taken when he wasn't expecting it. He wondered if she would have gone out with him

58

anyway — if he had found her pretty enough to ask. He studied her face and thought maybe she had lost weight and the features were standing out more. Then he picked up the cover of a CD, worried that after his last comment everyone would think he was a prude in bed, which, in fact, he was.

'You're such a romantic, Jessica,' Arianne said.

'OK. That is definitely *not* something I've been called before.' She filled Arianne's glass and they smiled at each other.

'Do you really want to sit on the floor? Come and sit up here, if you like.' Jessica got up and Arianne patted the sofa beside her. When she sat down, Arianne lay back across her lap. 'Is that OK?'

'Yes. Yes, it's fine,' Jessica said quietly.

For a while, the music from the film filled the room. The two boys had been used to these faintly erotic displays of female solidarity at university. But somehow this was not like the usual titillating perform-ance of hair-plaiting and neck rubs. Conspicuously absent was the standard repertoire of mmms and oh-yeses plainly designed to convey erotic promise to the men in the room. Here instead were two women who liked each other and were engaged in some kind of private understanding. Both boys tried to think of a way to interrupt it, but could not.

Arianne lit another cigarette and blew out the smoke above her head. The little cloud that hung over them added to their separate-ness: it located them in their own atmosphere. Ludo took off the hat and dressing-gown and poured some champagne into a glass.

Luke watched Jessica move a little to accommodate Arianne's shoulder. He felt more lost and unsure of himself and more excited than he ever had in his life. He could feel his phone going in his pocket and he knew it would be Lucy again. Nothing in the world would have made him answer it now. His intense curiosity about Arianne was tinged with horror, deep fear of what she might tell him and of just how unreachable she might turn out to be. She was plainly beyond his usual small-talk, and yet her brand of spontaneous heady intimacy was alarmingly foreign to him. He felt himself at a loss for the right words, the right *approach* to conversation. He wanted to ask her something about herself, but instead he said, 'Arianne, you seem to have a seriously low opinion of men.'

She held out her hand to Ludo for the bottle of champagne. 'The doctor said not to drink, didn't she? Did she? Are we worried?'

'No, we're not worried. We've all done far worse and survived. Hey

59

– what's the matter with us men, though? Why the low opinion?' Ludo said.

'Oh, I'm just a silly billy,' Arianne giggled. Then she smiled softly at Luke and held his gaze for a second, 'so never mind what I think.'

It was an end of all conversation, but it seemed to Luke that it had been cut short, that he had been fobbed off in some way and was expected not to notice. He felt indignant, but he was also sufficiently concerned that he might not have understood a single thing this girl had said to stay quiet. Instead, he hoped he looked as good in his red T-shirt as Lucy always said, and with the light from the TV noticeably modelling his biceps, he suspected he probably did.

They all concentrated on smoking joints and watching the trite happy ending of the film. Luke handed out the boxes of Chinese takeaway, some plates and cutlery and the room was filled with the smell of hot and sour soup and fried noodles. They listened to Ludo crunching the cashew nuts in his sauce. The couple in the film had their child. The father stood holding the newborn baby by the window of the hospital, gazing down on the frenzy of New York. It was autumn. The music was strong, passionate, resolved.

By three a.m. they had all fallen asleep – except Luke. He was feeling uneasy. He got up and walked around his flat, leaving the others sprawled on sofa cushions and beanbags, the blue planet of the TV flickering over them.

First he went into his kitchen and opened the fridge. He took a long look at all the jars and beautiful packages, the things he threw out and repurchased regularly. He never ate in but he liked to have a full fridge. He liked it full of tropical fruit, papaya, pineapple, kiwi, and exotic continental deli items, gravadlax, caperberries, and Serrano ham. He adored that collective expensive smell.

What he looked for unconsciously when he opened the door of his fridge was travel, or rather transportation of a more intimate kind. His fridge contained the essence of his aspirations – props from the photographic images that arrived in his mind when he wondered about his lifestyle and whether he fulfilled its criteria. His fridge helped him arrive at himself.

He ran his fingers over the buttons on the microwave as he walked towards the centrepiece of the kitchen, the eight-burner gas hob which he had never turned on. Not even to light a cigarette. He had bought it because of the fabulous dinner-party photograph in the brochure. He had seen himself in there, flame-grilling lamb, laughing

60

girls in the background holding oversized glasses of Cab Sauv. But there was never the time: time to shop, to call people, to reschedule because of unforeseen circumstances.

What did he spend all his time doing? Working, travelling across the city, absorbing the delays and the jams and the cancellations into the tension he stored between his shoulder-blades. He checked email; he missed calls and listened to messages on his mobile phone. There were friends he had not seen for a year.

Only two years before, days had seemed long, resilient to failures of planning, flirtatiously responsive to unplanned gestures. Time had been mysterious and plentiful, a natural resource. He had splashed around in it. But now it seemed to be an idea in his own mind. He himself decided its properties, its texture; whether he experienced it in the surreal little jerks of phone calls and meetings, as office quanta, or in undulating lunar stretches in front of his computer at the weekend, his mouth chewing fuel when his alarm reminded it to. This was a new sense of responsibility, of artistic control. But he did not want time to feel like art, he wanted it to feel like science.

He studied the dates on a couple of jars of cornichons, some sun-dried tomatoes, olives stuffed with almonds. They were beautiful glass jars: fantastic packaging. He threw them into the big, cylindrical silver bin, feeling blasphemous.

He went into his bedroom and opened his wardrobe. He looked at the racks of shoes he never wore, the casualwear he was never casual enough for. If he was honest, all he really made use of was the row of work shirts neatly ironed by his cleaning lady. And yet he regularly ordered sweatshirts and chunky sweaters online – like posthumously acquired souvenirs of his leisurely early twenties. Just three years before he had not needed to plan a four-day ski-trip six months in advance. He would have crammed those chunky sweaters into an overnight bag, chucked in some Rizla, a bottle of vodka – and then off.

Now the days passed quickly between lifting off the duvet and folding the duvet over himself again. He was beginning to see why people wanted a family. You could want a family solely because it was something that wouldn't go off or go out of fashion before you had time to notice it.

He ran his hands over the shelf of T-shirts and pulled out one that he had worn during his gap-year. It had a picture of a spliff on the front. He remembered standing under the clock at Waterloo, while he waited for his father to collect him, holding his surfboard, vowing never to shave off his beard, never to get stuck in a normal job. Ludo laughed about this lost idealism, but he, like most of his friends, was still embarrassed to have proved so ordinary, and quickly changed the subject if ever it came up.

But he did not really think for a moment that he could have acted differently. How else could you afford to live in London, be a member of a good gym, have a decent car? He wondered why his sister, Sophie, still dreamt of going back to India, to the places she had visited at eighteen. Surely they would not be the same now. Backpacking was dirty, European hotels were nice; these were axioms of adult reasoning.

But he had still not shaken off the belief that Sophie's excellent grades, her grade-eight violin and piano, meant she had a firmer grip on reality than he did. Where he suspected her of sentimentality or nostalgia, he found his judgement encroached on by a sense that he might simply have missed the point. She was always saying that to him, after all: 'You're missing the point, Lulu. You're not hearing what I'm telling you. You hear clichés.'

Normally, having remembered this crushing observation, he would have been tempted to brood, but just then his mind could not stay still: it felt pursued and aggravated. He slapped his hand against his forehead and wondered if he had ever actually felt physical desire before, because this, what he felt now, was close to humiliating. Again and again he thought of going into the sitting room, waking Arianne and offering her his car, his salary, *anything,* if she would let him take off her clothes – just her *jeans,* even – and run his mouth up between her legs. It didn't matter if she did anything to him really – not right away. First he just wanted to kneel down in front of the sofa with the weight of those beautiful legs over his shoulders, those thighs cushioning his cheeks, his lips and tongue lost to her taste and smell – and to watch her face, to watch what *he* could do to her face.

But why on earth would she let him? And why had he never wanted to do this to Lucy?

He looked at the T-shirt in his hands, unsure how long it had been since he had touched it. *Two years?* We don't have time to touch the things we own, he thought. And then he felt close to tears.

'Hey? Is it making you feel funny, too?' Arianne said. She was leaning on the wall by the doorway. 'The painkillers are making me feel funny. Maybe it's because of the champagne. She said not to drink, didn't she – the doctor?'

He imagined she had caught him looking through her clothes,

rather than his own, and hurriedly put back the incriminating T-shirt. 'What is it? Do you feel sick?' he said.

'Sick? No – no. Not that kind of funny . . .' It was never 'that kind of funny' with her. She could profoundly understate herself at the least expected moment. She used words associated with mild physical sensation to describe deep emotional change.

'Does your head hurt?'

'No . . . not that kind of funny at all. No, it was just . . . I dreamt I saw God.' She walked over to his bed and climbed on to it.

He felt this intimate contact in his own body. 'That – that's pretty full on,' he said.

She pulled a pillow half-way down the mattress and rested her head on it. But almost immediately she sat up again, drawing her legs under her with a jolt. 'I'll tell you about it if you like. Want to know about God?'

'Um – OK.'

'Well, it was the whole "bright light" thing people talk about,' she said. 'You know? On talk-shows or whatever, where people say things like that.'

He nodded.

'But it wasn't a nice "bright light". It was this burning, devouring light like a nuclear explosion and I knew if I looked I'd go blind. It was like my skin would *blister* from the exposure. You'd get cancer instantly if you got near it – your cells would all *die*. It was like being killed with light – only I knew I was already dying or I wouldn't be allowed to see it.' She looked at him, horrified. 'It makes no sense,' she said.

Then she started smiling and shaking her head as if she couldn't believe how silly she was – and then she burst into tears. They were long sobs, painful to listen to. She covered her face and he went over and put his arms round her – instinctively at first, feeling only a desire to stop a girl crying. 'Hey, hey – you're not dying. Nothing's going to kill you,' he said.

'I just get so *scared* . . .'

'I know, I know . . .' he said. He knew.

'So incredibly scared.'

'Yes, I know, I know . . . *Hey*, I know, I know . . .'

But his words quickly became a meaningless repetition, their delicate sincerity heavied out by lust. Moments later he found himself kissing her salty mouth – or was she kissing his?

Her ribcage jerked with her sharp, convulsive breaths. Again, according to the artist's design, her body was a kind of conundrum. The adult muscular legs were at war with the fragility of her upper body. Physically, Arianne seemed to be rising above herself, leaving the earthly legs behind, becoming less worldly with every inch she grew towards the sky.

A police car passed under the window, its siren going, and Luke wished it would be quiet, just shut up, in case it broke the spell and she told him to get off. At that very moment she pulled away from him and looked him fiercely in the eye.

With a plummeting heart, he began to prepare an apology. But the next thing he knew she was undoing her shirt, pushing his fingers softly into her bra and whispering, 'So, are you going to make me feel better, Luke?'

Perhaps suffering always precedes style, both in its origins within a personality and in each of its subsequent manifestations. Without pain behind it, strength of personality has no depth, no poignant darkness by which it is thrown into luminous relief.

Luke had never known anyone so desolate or so powerful by turns. Nor had he ever been subject to an aesthetic instinct by which, occasionally, even his own dominance seemed somehow to have been requested. Having raised a sceptical eyebrow at him, Arianne suddenly became a feast of softness and pliancy: she let the strap of her bra submit to his fingers in one joyous burst and he remembered nectarines, which Sophie had picked for them all as a surprise in Portugal. She had come running in from the garden in her sundress, giggling, her skirt full of something, and sent three million nectarines bouncing and rolling all over the lunch table.

With amazement he looked down at the pile of clothes and then at the hot expanse of femininity, a full-bodied and slightly terrifying responsibility, in his arms.

Arianne sat up smiling gently and turned him over. Her face lowered towards him until it was all dark and smelt only of her perfume and her sweat and the wine on her breath. She brought about a total eclipse – then she popped his jeans undone with a practised flick. Her hot palms pressed his wrists back into the duvet, and Luke thought quite clearly that this, right now, was all the French girls in Cap d'Antibes that he could possibly ever have wanted.

Even so, his upbringing told him he ought to *say* something! He knew he ought to halt proceedings because she was a girl, because being a girl meant you felt things in special ways and he really ought to tell her that they needn't rush into anything if she wasn't sure — if she didn't know him well enough, which of course she didn't.

But he was terrified that this might really stop her taking off her knickers. So he said nothing — except her name a few times — and in due course she threw the knickers over a photograph of his rowing four (who were grinning victoriously after the school championships) saying, 'Lucky boys!' and giggling.

And then, with a serious expression, she wriggled away from him up the bed and lay back against the pillows. She observed him anxiously as if she was wondering what was meant to happen next and was afraid that he was going to show her. He clambered after her, grabbing her ankle to hold her still, concerned that if she did tell him to stop now, he would actually have a heart-attack from the frustration. But she let him continue and when he was safely inside her he felt dangerous and exceptional. Or was it desperate and ordinary? It was strangely impossible to say which, but it didn't seem to matter very much. In fact, nothing mattered at all, as long as he was able to match the violent movement of her hips and to stop the bed frame collapsing, without for a moment suggesting that he ever, ever wanted her to stop.

Anticipating him at the vital moment (with what seemed later to have been a supernatural sense of timing), she put her hand over his mouth to prevent him waking the others. He found himself licking her fingers like a grateful dog.

Chapter 5

When they woke up the others had already left. Ludo and Jessica had obviously pieced together a simple story and closed the door quietly behind them. It was around eleven on Saturday morning. Luke and Arianne lay staring at each other on the pillows.

'Don't go back today,' Luke said, not knowing where 'back' was. 'Do you have to?' She smiled and said no, she didn't have to go anywhere. She turned her back to him, and moved in against him wrapping his arm over her, covering his hand with kisses.

Why did he feel such intense joy? He was smiling into her hair. Grinning into that shiny, white-blonde bob. She was beautiful, of course, but it was far more than that. He had never met anyone before who seemed to hum with that high voltage of personality, that super-charge of stored passions. She made him feel he was on the verge of something incredibly exciting. Life had been a dark plain, barely visible against a black sky and Arianne was the impending flash of lightning.

Until Sunday evening, they did nothing but sleep and wake and make love again. They were no more than the sum total of their mouths and hands, their lust, hunger, thirst. Lust came before every-thing else, though. A few times they felt hungry and ordered food. But having thrown coins and notes at the delivery boy and torn open the boxes frantically, they left it almost untouched. It was as if their senses were already promised elsewhere, to a physical desire that left them laughing at its excesses. It left them prey to comical impulses – to biting a wrist as it reached out for a bottle of water; to appetites so sudden that lamps were knocked off tables and upended glasses sent ice skidding across the floor.

They put on clothes for the first time when Ludo dropped by on the Sunday evening, curious to have heard that Arianne was still there. 'Hello, *you*,' he said, in his camp, cynical voice, when she opened the door. 'This is an interesting development, isn't it?'

When the buzzer went Luke had gone into the kitchen to get drinks. A small part of him knew that what he was really doing was hiding. He dreaded seeing his friend laugh at the idea of him and Arianne together. Ludo – everyone, probably – would think he was just old Lulu: reliable, but not bright or sophisticated enough for a girl like her. He needed to collect himself for a performance of virile indifference. He also felt guilty – as if he had hurt Ludo personally – and was not sure why.

He wondered if he was just vulnerable from physical exhaustion and lack of sleep. As he took out three glasses, he remembered having jet-lag after watching a rugby Test match in Australia a few years back and how difficult it had been to talk to his parents over dinner when he got home. The food had tasted bizarre and alien, somehow. Onions were like plastic, green beans squeaked like rubber against his teeth. He felt just as disoriented now.

He and Ludo hugged without making eye-contact and Arianne opened the bottle of wine. Luke sipped his, but it was like drinking wine at that strange dinner and he put it down again. He pushed his fingers into the back of Arianne's jeans, letting them sit against the soft skin, which was still hot and flushed from sex, feeling an ache in the palm of his hand to touch more of her. Her body was the only real thing in the room.

'So I basically wanted to go to Blue Monkey, but they were all, like, "Come to Noise, Bas is DJ-ing, Bas is DJ-ing",' Ludo said, rolling his eyes. 'So there was this huge mission out there – four taxis – and it was really pretty crap. Not crap, but you know – just one of those nothing nights.'

'Nothing nights,' Arianne repeated. 'Was Bas rude about me?'

'No. Why? Oh, God, I'd forgotten all about *that*. No, he was perfectly dignified. Anyway, he was busy. We said hi. He's pretty good, isn't he? But – *fuck* – it's like you spend so much of the evening deciding where to go you haven't got it in you to enjoy yourself when you get there. Texting, phoning, listening to fucking whiny voicemail from Saskia: "Ludo, man, where are you? Have you got any coke because I'm a silly tart and I can't get anything done without you." You know what she's fucking like. *Devastatingly bovine*. God, I think I danced, like, twice, maybe. Actually, I think I might still have concussion. I can't believe I let you all talk me out of staying at the hospital for observation. I should probably be on a ward and shit. With, like, monitors on me.'

While she and Ludo talked, Luke remembered visiting the little gallery his aunt Suzannah had run for a while. He must have been about seven because he had been carrying a cap, which was part of his pre-prep-school uniform. He clearly recalled standing there in his duffel coat, in an agony of frustrated sensuality, beside a marble sculpture he had been told not to touch. The sculpture had been polished to smooth perfection; it was curved and heavy – as if explicitly to please the hand. But his mother had caught his wrist as it reached out.

What was the point of making things so lovely for touching if you were just going to stop anyone doing it, he had wanted to know. He had wanted to know it very much and right that minute – even if Aunt Suzannah was crying. (She was *always* crying, after all.) But his mother just shook her head firmly and said there were yummy biscuits in the car if he was good, but otherwise not. Adults had once been full of weird formulas like this.

Luke smiled privately on the sofa. He felt certain that Arianne was helping him return to lost truths about himself.

At that moment she laughed buoyantly at some nonsense of Ludo's and wriggled back against Luke's fingers, catching them behind the elastic of her knickers. Her face was perfectly composed and he glanced at his unsuspecting friend and was exhilarated by her dishonesty.

But this feeling was soon followed by deep apprehension. He was, after all, in the presence of an aspiring actress and, unlike Lucy, she could cover up whatever she was feeling. With Lucy there were tears, there were flushed cheeks in spite of her efforts to appear calm – and if anyone had faked things, it had always been him, pretending he hadn't noticed so they could just get on with it and have dinner, have sex and go to sleep.

His deceptiveness had always been pragmatic. But for Arianne it seemed to have become a pleasure in itself. She concealed, but then she went further than this, as if for the sheer fun of it, simulating the exact opposite of whatever she was feeling. When he had reason to know this was the case, her talent astonished and frightened Luke. At times he sat beside her and it was as if she had crept out of the room, stifling giggles with her hand, leaving a counterfeit girl in her place.

68

Actresses were dangerous. Even Arianne's arms and legs could act: her fingers would tap in turn against her thumb, to imply consideration of what she had already decided; her legs would stretch out nonchalantly while her heart contracted with rage; she could do 'person daydreaming out of window' when she was breathless with anticipation, or have her shoulders and neck wilt in lily-like despair at some practical concern she knew Luke would soon disregard.

Much later, Luke came to suspect she could even tell lies in sleep. He listened to her nestle and sigh with soft femininity, and wondered what polemical resolve this obscured.

When Ludo left, she leant back against the door and pushed it shut with her bottom. Luke pulled her jeans down, laughing at the wonderful ripple of buttons. Inanimate objects were drawn irresistibly into the music of their long afternoons: the mattress thumped under the fall of their joint weight, the bed legs scraped on the wooden floor, the headboard high-fived the wall, and the water splashed joyously out of the bath and giggled all over the tiles.

Arianne's strong right leg kicked off her jeans and then she leant down, saying, 'Careful, *careful* of my bad foot, silly,' over Luke's hurrying fingers. She stood there in her T-shirt – the word 'genetic' in faded yellow letters across her breasts – and then he took that off too. All this before they had even heard the outer door bang closed and Ludo walking down the steps!

Arianne had simply assumed she would move in. Even the assumption was communicated obliquely, by hints too subtle or organic to single out afterwards. Luke just realized he had arrived at a conclusion – and because he adored it, he found no need to ask questions.

'Living together' had been an issue between himself and Lucy for months now. Her poignantly restrained statements had made him wince: the pink toothbrush she had placed neatly beside his, the bottle of cleanser in the cupboard a discreet but purposeful *one inch* in front of his razors. Somehow none of her tactics had worked.

But Arianne's sense of fate was consistently weightier than that of anyone else with whom she came into contact: it heavied outsiders into mystified passivity. To Luke, this passivity was just one more mode of sensual abandonment, closely related to the fall of his eyelids when her fingers undid his belt.

Quietly, quietly, he removed all the little signs of Lucy from around the flat, storing them all in a plastic bag under the sink, which seemed slightly less appalling than throwing them out. He was relieved to hide them away – it was as if they were loud, or hot, or dazzling. He found a novel called *Oh, Serena!*, a bottle of pink nail varnish, a rare photo of himself and Lucy with his mother in which, oddly, he was also holding a camera and squinting into the sun. He found a pale blue hairband by the kettle. He read the last lines of the novel:

'Well, that's lucky, isn't it?' Gus said. 'Because I've got a plane ticket here. You see, I thought you might like to come with me.'

He wondered if you could actually die from guilt and threw the book into the plastic bag.

Later that morning he discovered Arianne using Lucy's cleanser and his heart palpitated with fear. He stood in the doorway unable to speak until she smiled at him with cotton wool held over one eye and said, 'Just be a second,' as if it had not occurred to her that this bottle might belong to some other girl.

But she required no explanations – as if they, too, were superfluous to the requirements of her performance, to her own suspension of disbelief. Arianne consumed without question or conscience in every area of her life. When she was hungry she unwrapped things from the fridge, sniffed or picked at them absentmindedly, then left them out on the sideboard to go off.

Luke couldn't help finding this beautiful. Unlike his own culpable wastage, his shamefaced fiddlings with clingfilm, this was high-spirited; this was the decadence of kings. It implied a joyous consciousness of her worth and he was not going to argue with that.

He found an oozing packet of Cornish butter; a crusted slab of *foie gras*; a flat bottle of elderflower pressé from which she had only removed the lid, before being seduced by some other treat. And he threw them into the bin as if he was scoring a goal. The fridge had ceased to be a focus for anxiety because even though these 'luxury goods' were the physical evidence of his ambition, his aspirations, it felt good to waste them on her. It felt *luxurious* to waste them on her. She transfigured the guilt he felt, drawing the waste, the hours spent in bed ignoring his work ethic, into the realm of self-expression.

Maybe important people really do arrive in your life at crucial moments, he thought. She had come at a point when he was increasingly conscious that he was working for a cause in which he no longer believed. He could not even think, then, what this cause had been, though he could remember how fervently he had believed in it just weeks ago. He remembered early mornings, late nights, weekends spent in prayer. He remembered penitential cereal for supper while the printer ran.

But in reality this loss of faith in his work was only a tiny scatter of stones and did not account for the dreadful rumbling sound. There were other questions in his mind.

One evening, a month before, an old lady had got on to the tube and stood beside him. By making a practised Londoner's dive (eyes dead straight, arms tight against the body and *go*) he had secured a seat. There he was, dishevelled but victorious. Of course, he knew he ought now to stand up, but he didn't seem to be doing it and instinctively he hugged his briefcase to his chest as a shield from mob judgement.

Quite suddenly, a troubling thought occurred: what if it just *didn't matter* whether he offered the old lady his seat or not? Would he be shot? Would he go to prison, for God's sake? Gradually, defiantly, he found himself lowering his shield.

There she stood –

1. *old*
2. a *lady*

– holding on to the rail with her arthritis-thickened fingers. He took her in: the grey comfort-sole shoes, the tan tights, the hem of the tartan coat, and all he felt was . . . irritation. Why did they *all* wear that hideous stuff anyway? The train moved off and she grabbed the sleeve of the man beside her, apologizing in her wobbly voice.

What he would have liked was for everyone to know that he had mustered the energy to work right through for twenty-four hours for the sake of a *threatened shampoo brand*, and that even his toes were tired, his hair was tired. Did he have no right to the seat himself? Yes, he was young, but he was a *tired, tax-paying* young person. And, most important of all, his parents DID NOT GIVE HIM MONEY ANY MORE.

In the bottom right-hand corner of his field of vision, hallucinated email boxes kept levitating with sinister import.

He glanced around at the downturned faces: girls whose earrings swung as the train moved; men with loosened ties, reading the sports pages; two schoolchildren with orange, skull-shaped ice lollies hunched over a mobile phone. Far from stoning him to death, the mob was entirely self-absorbed.

And even if one of them should happen to look up and think he was a horrible person who stole seats from old ladies, why exactly did he imagine they would ever give him another thought after that day? It was as if he felt people were keeping score.

But he didn't keep score himself: he saw angry tracksuited women thwack sticky-faced, anaemic toddlers, he saw schoolkids pocketing Mars bars in pitiful corner shops, he saw teenage boys dive past exasperated ushers at the cinema, and he tutted, perhaps, but that was all. Then he forgot. And in the same way, all memory of him would be wiped out as soon as the tube doors hissed closed behind his back.

Why did anyone care what total strangers thought, anyway, even for an instant? The fact that his parents did had always maddened his sister – only slightly more so than her own brother's capacity to humour them. He knew he had always scandalized Sophie with his casual shrugs, his ability to put on the little suit at Christmas feeling no obvious loss of personal identity.

Just then, the Christmas suit concerned him, too. He had simply *put it on*, hadn't he, because his parents would be more likely to let him stay up or go out or to buy him something? He had simply understood early on that this was how the world worked. But underneath he was his own person. Wasn't he? He made his own rules. Or had there always been more to it than this? Perhaps the immaculate family image had appealed to him just as much as it did to his parents. It was possible that he had liked the idea of being the spotless boy at church, pegged by all (he had proudly hoped) to be a fighter pilot and tennis superstar one day.

It had made a good picture: well-groomed, prematurely muscular young Luke Langford, with the beautiful mummy and the important father on either side. But then there was Sophie, spoiling the view. She dyed her hair blue, tore up her tartan Christmas dress in protest, sat two feet away on the pew beside him unable to speak with rage. Consequently she was sent to bed early. And although he hated to recollect it now, he had once stood in her bedroom and patiently explained (before her hairbrush took a chip out of his left incisor) that he considered his parents more than fair to her in this respect.

Another phantom email rose up in the corner of his eye.

He took a newspaper out of his bag and flicked it open. At this point the old woman went so far as to drop her glasses, without which she was probably *blind* and *defenceless*, on to the dirty floor. A girl reached down for them, losing her balance as the train lurched, and there ensued an agonizing pantomime of altruism as one kind person helped another kind person to balance until eventually the glasses were put back in the trembly hand. 'Thank you, dear, thank you. *So* kind,' the old woman said – in her stupid trembly voice.

Luke was too paralysed with unexamined aggression to read the newspaper on his knee. He surveyed the downturned faces and a question kept running through his mind: *What if being good doesn't matter?* It had never occurred to him before.

It was certainly not that Arianne provided an answer to this; but she did provide an alternative anxiety. A compelling, all-consuming anxiety. She sat with the ash dangling off her cigarette, occasionally seasoning the carpet, looking distracted or bored or depressed, and Luke watched her, ransacking his heart and soul and body for ways to amuse her.

He had still not returned Lucy's calls. Sex with Arianne conquered his guilt every time. Sex with her conquered guilt and fear and ambition and inadequacy. He lost them all with his hands on her hips, his head pressed back into the pillow.

'Look, I'll have to get my stuff from Dan's place,' she said, at around three a.m. that Monday morning. 'You can drive me over tomorrow. OK?' She laid her head on his chest and sighed. 'And then the day after won't belong to anyone else at all.'

He stared out of the window, at the bare branches against the sky, and he smiled. The day after wouldn't belong to anyone else at all . . .

How could he disappoint her romanticism? He saw he would need to take the week off work. He had taken no holidays that year. He hadn't dared to, because, unlike the creatives, his job at the agency was secured by physical dependability rather than ethereal talent. Unflattering as it was, he knew he simply had to *be there*.

But life seemed so unbearably short! Twenty-eight years wasted already. He rolled towards Arianne with his eyes closed. She wrapped her legs round him and, after an astonishingly deft movement of her bottom and hips, she had swallowed him up.

Every time – literally every time – he felt as though he had burst garden doors open on to glorious summer. And she was so long-limbed and so – elastic! She dragged her nails up the back of his thighs, her tongue licked the inside of his elbows, his earlobes, his armpits, the palms of his hands, his nipples, his lips. She was a searchlight of eroticism and his senses were caught in it like boys after lights-out.

At first he was stricken with fear and nervous hilarity. These responses were all that held him back from a hot, golden, long-legged, jasmine-scented future. They belonged to his past, to Lucy whispering, 'Is that not very nice, darling? Oh, sorry, why didn't you say? I'll do it a bit harder then, shall I?' He cast them off. This proved to be a mutually gratifying decision.

Invariably, having wrung the last out of both of them, Arianne would drop down hot and shivering against him, her face turned away, her hair covering her eyes. For a short time, his existence was irrelevant to her and he blinked behind the lovely blonde haze and enjoyed the feel of her heart thudding against his. She was everywhere and she contained everything – at least all that was of any interest in the world to him. Arianne was her own weather system with a million volatile seasons and the world outside it was just so . . . slow and so quiet.

That evening they drove over to Dan's flat. Luke waited in the car while she unlocked the door. She ran up the stairs under a bare light-bulb, past builders' equipment and cans of paint. The door swung shut.

It had become clear to him gradually that breaking up with Dan meant Arianne had nowhere to live. He was overwhelmed by this – and also powerfully attracted by it. She had no money: her family gave her none because her father drifted in and out of contact according to whether or not he had a girlfriend, and her mother was too involved in her own love affairs and legal proceedings to show any concern for her daughter. They were selfish in the way that only people who were once very rich can be. They had lost all their inherited money in a series of investments risky enough to appeal only to those convinced by the benevolent sparkling of their own chandeliers that they had a divine right to wealth. As a consequence, they had become fiercely vigilant, always suspecting that they had not received their fair share, whether it was of money or respect or roast potatoes. Mr and Mrs Tate had divorced, but they were subsequently united more fiercely than ever, not in love but in joint litigation. And from the age of eight, in place of a more rounded moral education, Arianne was raised on bitter sermons about the dishonesty of the world in general and of stockbrokers in particular.

This had distorted her values somewhat and occasionally she found herself twiddling her hair and wondering, aware that it made no bloody sense, whether it mattered if you were happy as long as you were rich. Then she would burst into tears.

In spite of her charisma, Arianne was actually quite unpopular. She had no female friends because she inspired envy in other women, who felt their complacent relationships rocked when she danced into the room. And she made all her male friends untrustworthy. When she rejected their advances – with a combination of tact and searing guilt apparent on her face – they punished her with demonstrations of power. As soon as she said she didn't think about them in 'that way' she knew what was coming. She gritted her teeth.

And in due course they left her alone at restaurants, waiting for them. They texted blunt cancellations to her dinner parties, then arrived, looking stormily resentful, at the last minute. They were only too glad to put her on hold for another call. They made sure she missed the start of plays, films, concerts to which they had generously bought her tickets. They told her how fabulous small brunette women were. She waited outside a lot – she smoked cigarettes to appear occupied, she blew on her hands to stay warm. And when finally they turned up, she made no protest because she understood that, on some level, this was justice: payback for the blonde hair, the crazy legs and their disproportionate power.

The way Luke saw it, to all intents and purposes, Arianne was an orphan. She simply lived with whichever boyfriend she was seeing at the time, knowing that when love or lust was replaced by possessiveness and jealousy, it would be time to find new accommodation. He felt a pain in his heart for her, an actual pain in his heart. Thank God she had found him now. Thank God she could put all that behind her.

He glanced up and saw her in the lit window, talking to Dan. They had hoped he would be out, either at work or 'training' at the gym where he went twice a day. What did the idiot think he was 'training' *for*? Luke watched the clichéd performance of argument: hands held out imploringly, palm upwards, faces covered, heads shaking. Then he looked away and lit a cigarette.

He did not want to think about Dan's feelings. He wanted to remember him as a stock character – a fool in a club, mouthing off, a person in whom Arianne could never have instilled any *serious* expectations. This had more to do with his guilt about Lucy than it did with any sympathy he felt for Dan. If he pretended he and Arianne had met with no attachments at all, he did not have to think about Lucy – or to return her calls. Just then he felt his phone vibrating in his pocket and could not believe the ugly coincidence. Sweat broke out on his back, but when he took the phone out he saw he had imagined it was ringing.

Reprieved, he wondered again if it mattered anyway. In the huge long history of the world, what did it matter if he was a bastard to

Lucy? After all, no one knew because they had few mutual friends – and, anyway, *no one was keeping score.*

Ten minutes later, Arianne was limping across the road towards him, holding a large sports bag and a box. Oddly, her hair was wet.

'He threw a bottle of water over me,' she explained. 'It was instead of punching.'

'Jesus *Christ.*'

'What?'

'It just hadn't occurred to me he might *hit* you.'

She put her things on the back seat. In the box he saw there was a hairdryer and a few framed photographs, a jewellery box, a fluffy rabbit with a chewed-looking red ribbon round its neck. Again . . . oh, the pain in his heart.

'Well, I'm lucky because he hardly got me at all. Only a bit on my ribs,' she said. She lifted her sweatshirt and showed the red mark where Dan's huge hand had slapped out at her. She had no bra on, he noticed. She said, 'Look, give me a cigarette, will you? Calm my nerves.'

Luke found that he was shaking now – incomprehensibly, since it was all over. 'I can't believe he hit you. That *bastard* . . .' he said. He thought about the big hands, which, not so long ago, had been licensed to riot and scrabble all over her. He dropped the cigarettes on to the floor of the car and banged his head as he leant down for them.

'Oh, God. Don't get into all that, Luke. He'd *kill* you – in about two and a half *seconds.*'

He handed her a cigarette with his eyes fixed on the road, jaw clenched. He was offended. He was not that much smaller than Dan – he had let his pectorals go a little, it was true, but he still had good biceps. Dan was simply a beast of a man and probably schizophrenic with steroid abuse. And to think that she had once actually wanted that gorilla's hands on her, in her, she had let him come inside her – and even now he thought he could leave his pawprint across her ribs!

They said nothing for a few moments as he worked himself into a frenzy of pain and then she leant across, put her hand down his trousers and said softly, 'Come on, let's go back to your place and do what we're good at.'

Arianne knew how to restore male ego, just as she knew how to destroy it.

As a final gesture of love and support before Arianne was sent out into the filthy world to scratch and fight for her life, her parents had promised to pay her drama-school fees. Neither of them had actually sent the cheque yet, because there was debate as to whether this was a paternal or maternal responsibility, but Arianne was genuinely talented and the principal allowed her to attend in the meantime.

She called her teacher to explain why she had not come in. Their relationship sounded peculiar to Luke, but he reassured himself that he knew nothing about drama school and, anyway, he was thrilled by the idea of having access to multicoloured, eccentric characters. Vibrant, artistic people – for dinner parties! He had not had anyone worth flame-grilling lamb for anyway. Now he foresaw a candlelit future in which people came to the golden couple for exquisite dinners. At the end of the evening guests would reluctantly accept their coats and return to colder, darker lives, all too painfully aware that they were neither Luke nor Arianne.

'Hi, Jon darling,' Arianne said, twisting the phone cord. 'I can't make it into class this week because I was nearly killed in a horrific car crash.' Luke watched her take a drag on her cigarette, a sip of coffee while she listened to the histrionic response. 'I know, I know,' she said. 'I'm in a lot of pain. So much *pain*, Jon.' Lilting sympathy followed. Then she said, 'And I saw God in a dream.'

Her voice became a musical instrument when she wanted it to. It sang out from the depths of her diaphragm and thrilled the ear. She was an actress and would one day be famous! Luke sighed at the thought of how she would stand centre-stage, receiving bouquets – and then she would run wholeheartedly to him.

It was true that she was in a lot of pain. It had increased very suddenly. She could not put her weight on the foot at all now – except momentarily, as she walked. In fact, when they had arrived at the outer door of the flat with her things, Luke noticed the terrible limp as if for the first time. He couldn't believe his self-absorption. He suggested he carry her up the stairs to the door. She laughed – it would be ridiculous, she was *far* too heavy, she said. But she agreed none the less. And then she lay back heavily in his arms, like a woman being carried unconscious from a burning building. He took her up to the door with a devastating sense of occasion. Then he ran back down for her bag and her box, and for her heart-, lung- and gut-rending fluffy bunny.

Imperceptibly this became their habit. Soon he carried her up and down the stairs. Sometimes he lifted her into bed. And when he went back to work the week after, she called down to him as he was opening the outer door and said she needed a few things from the shop. He was already late after she had wanted to make love elaborately while, from the bedside table, his alarm clock nagged and chased them. There was a chemist across the road. He looked at his watch. 'I'll go quickly,' he said. 'Tell me what you need.'

'Oh, no, look – forget it. I'll cope.' She leant down to rub her poor bad foot. 'They're things I have to choose, Luke. You know, *girl's* stuff. Cream and things. You don't know what to get.'

He checked his watch again and then smiled with a sigh, dropping his briefcase on the floor. She giggled as he ran back up the stairs for her, two steps at a time, his arms outstretched like a sportsday daddy.

That afternoon, he got an email from Lucy.

From: Lucy, Whittome <lucy.whittome@hddl.com>
Sent: Monday, April 18th, 2002 13:00:46
To: Luke, Langford <cool_hand68@hotmail.com>
Subject: Hello!
Dear Luke,
It's been funny not hearing from you. I hope everything's OK. I know you had your big presentation to prepare for on the 17th, so I suppose that's been taking up all your time. Of course, I understand. I'm really well. The cold has gone – finally!!! No awful cough to drive you mad any more, you'll be glad to hear. I went home last weekend and Mum and Daddy send their love. Mum gave me three more jars of her jam for you. Your favourite – raspberry. Hope to hear from you – maybe today? I love you. I hope everything's OK.
Lxxx
PS I'm sorry if I was in a bad mood after the cinema last week. I know you were just working and that you did your best to get there on time and you were right it was *only a film*. I'm just silly sometimes.

He covered his face. Of course it had not been 'only a film'. It was her hopes and dreams that he was going to ask her to marry him and she had sat alone with them in a cinema on a Friday evening while he emailed and delayed at work. He had been late out of lack of love for her. Why put it any other way? It amounted to the statement 'You are not good enough for me'.

Things are far simpler than we like to say, he thought. But we always show it.

Then he wrote back, having decided it would be best to do it immediately. His fingers hit the keys hard:

From: Luke, Langford <cool_hand68@hotmail.com
Sent: Monday, April 18th, 2002 13:25:01
To: Lucy, Whittome <lucy.whittome@hddl.com
Subject: Re: Hello!
Dear Lucy,
Yes – things have been frantic at work. I'll give you a call tomorrow.
Glad you're feeling better.

He paused, then wrote: Luce, maybe we could try and meet up. I think we need to talk and regretted it, imagining the shock she would get, reading this at work. He knew her – she boasted to her friends about him. They filled in astrological love-match surveys over their lunch. He thought of the novel under his sink:

> 'Well, that's lucky, isn't it?' Gus said. 'Because I've got a plane ticket here. You see, I thought you might like to come with me.'

That was the ending she dreamt of.

His finger pressed delete until the shock disappeared. Instead, he said he would call when things were 'calmer' and put Much love, Lx. Maybe she would get the point from the number of kisses, because they always put three.

Was this a way to break up with your girlfriend? By scaling down enthusiasm, by *editing out kisses*? He hated himself.

The truth was, though, he was as broken up from Lucy as he could be. He genuinely found it hard to remember what she looked like. He couldn't reconstruct his sense of her at all – not her smell or the feel of her skin or the sound of her voice. She was part of a muted existence in which nothing had really stood out.

For a moment, his callousness appalled him, the way he had just packaged up his heart and moved on. But it was, at the very least, reassuring to know that he would never, ever behave like this again. Not now that he had met Arianne.

In fact, could it not be said, after all, that good had come out of it? he asked himself cautiously. Terrible things happened, yes – and in this case they had happened to Lucy – but you just had to put the past behind you and see that this was the way of the world. Lucy must learn to accept this just like everyone else. He knew this was what he would do in her position and he suspected that it would make him stronger and wiser and so on. All of a sudden he found himself smiling with hope for all three of them – for himself and Arianne, and for Lucy, wherever she was.

That afternoon, Arianne photo-messaged him a picture of her bare legs on the tangled sheets of his bed. Purple nail varnish on her toes. At the edge of the picture, he could see a bar of chocolate, a packet of cigarettes, a magazine. This was her existence. He was missing it. He felt a pang of longing so acute it was like being kicked in the stomach by a horse.

He checked his watch and wondered if he could get more time off, if he could say he was still in pain – somewhere. It would be hard to seem convincing, given he had not planned in advance for this by wincing or limping or massaging his neck. As he sat there thinking, a text arrived: 'My fingers just aren't as good. Hope you got the picture . . . ?'

She was life and the office was mere illusion.

It was only three o'clock. He picked up his jacket and his coat and left, thinking he might not be missed for a few hours since there were no presentations. He promised himself he would come back: he would work the whole evening.

Of course, he didn't go back. His secretary, or 'assistant', because it was a non-hierarchical firm, called at six and asked if she should maybe switch off his computer. Thinking it best to give away no sense that he knew he had behaved strangely, he just said, 'Thanks, Jenny. That'll be great. See you tomorrow, then.' He could hear Arianne running them a bath. The steam crept under the bathroom door like smoke as he jogged towards it.

Walking around with Arianne (she held his arm and limped – they had an unspoken agreement it was only stairs she couldn't manage) was an uncomfortable experience. He had thought he would feel proud and virile, but he was shocked by the ugly behaviour she inspired. She got old-fashioned wolf-whistles from wolves. She got blaring car horns – and his head spun frantically in search of their origin as if he were looking for a sniper. Men in pairs actually named parts of her anatomy to each other as they walked past: they groaned, '*Legs*', or '*Tits*', and pointed in animal appreciation.

Luke was astonished it didn't upset her. She contrived to ignore it and drew him over to ooh and aah at improbable diamonds, like a child at a fireworks display, or to gaze at comparatively cheap shoes and handbags, which he bought for her in relief.

In a bookshop one afternoon, she flicked through a collection of photographs of all her favourite actresses – Hepburn, Monroe, Grace Kelly. Her face was quiet with admiration, tenderly at peace in her dreams. He watched her lovingly. *This* was being in love, he said to himself. Not that he had doubted it for one second. After all, what else could it be?

He was moved by everything she did. From excitement to sadness to peace: all in the course of one afternoon, one *meal*. She had broadened the spectrum of his emotions and afterwards she kept him hurrying constantly from one end to the other, as if she wanted to keep the blood in his cheeks.

Just then he wanted to kiss her and he wanted to stand back and look. Delicious agony! He turned the pages of a book of aerial photographs of the earth – mountains, seas, deserts – and felt no shred of desire to glance down. What did these miracles matter beside Arianne in a slouchy blue T-shirt, which flaunted the chilli-red strap of her bra?

Suddenly a movement caught his eye. Behind a set of shelves a man in a long grey coat was scrutinizing her through a gap in the books, his hand moving frantically inside his trousers. Luke stared in horror. Suddenly, more than anything, he wanted her not to see this abomination. It was essential that she did not know this was happening. He stood in front of the bookshelf and said, 'Let me buy it for you, Arianne?'

She gazed up as if he had woken her. 'What?'

'The book.'

'The book?'

'Yes – come on, sleepy. Let's get it. I want to buy it for you.'

He tried to take it out of her hands and move towards the cash desk, but she held him still. She laughed as she surveyed the forest of shopping-bags around her feet and threw her arms round him saying no one had ever been so kind to her before. They bought her nothing but underwear, she said: knickers, bras, suspender belts – things for them, not really for her. But he was different. Why was he different? She was not good enough for him, she said. She seemed close to tears.

And all he wanted was for her not to see the man in the grey coat. He was wild with it. He spun her round – and she hopped on her good leg as if they were dancing – towards the cash desk. He returned a false, tense smile to her laughing face and wondered why he was quite so afraid. Did he think he was preserving her *innocence*? She had, after all, proved to be aware of what men kept in their trousers. Or was there some risk to himself? Was it the intrusion he hated, the sense of another man scrawling graffiti where he was writing all he knew about love?

'Come on, let's get this book and get out of here,' he said, his heart racing, his cheeks hot with panic. She closed her eyes for a second, then put out her hand and followed him.

When they got home, she studied the book for hours, showing him the pictures and calling out as he cooked supper about how beautiful the clothes were. She told him stories about her mother. They were all anecdotes about admirers and the presents they had given her; they sounded implausible, like the product of her mother's misty nostalgia and vanity. But Arianne told them with the childhood faith that had first carried them into her consciousness. Her eyes widened and moved quickly around the room as she spoke. There had been pearl necklaces, diamond bracelets, roses, sonnets – one with the phrase 'AMOR VINCIT OMNIO' diagonally in *both* directions! Once there had been a magnum of champagne and two dozen lilies left modestly on the doorstep, only to be taken away by the dustman. That was funny!

Oh, it had all been a buttoning and unbuttoning of white kid ball gloves, the way Arianne told it. She sighed and laughed. 'And sometimes they played hands of poker or roulette to see who would be allowed to ask her to dance. You can't imagine that now, can you? Not these days. The clubs we go to. The way men are.'

'She sounds amazing,' Luke said, stroking her hair.

'Oh, she was so beautiful.'

'Like you, then.'

She looked insulted. '*God*, no. *Much* more beautiful than I am. I'm just nothing. She was the most beautiful woman my father ever saw, let alone met. He still says so.'

Luke almost said, 'But your father was unfaithful to her from the start,' because this was something Arianne had told him with tears in her eyes, something she said she could 'never forget'. She had gripped his arm when she told him as if she wanted him never to forget it either – and he half wondered if she expected him to apologize in some way.

Her father had been serially and humiliatingly unfaithful to her mother. Arianne had watched him seduce other men's wives at their Christmas parties, she had walked in on him once, with a half-naked

82

red-headed girl, in her own bedroom. And, from the age of five, she had knowingly observed her mother's attempts to laugh off the other women, to ignore the brazen telephone calls in the night. Mrs Tate was widely thought to be a model of restraint, but Arianne had twice come home from ballet to find her mother unconscious. She telephoned for the ambulance with the empty pill bottle in her hand.

Of course, her father had been sorry for all the mess. Max Tate had been so desperately sorry that he had had little kiddy-sized evening dresses made to appeal to his daughter's developing tastes. Rolling his fond eyes, he allowed her to try out his girlfriend's makeup, then whisked her off for dinner and champagne, calling her 'my darling', indulging her sweet, seven-year-old's fantasy that they were husband and wife.

Luke wondered how she had suddenly forgotten all this horror. It seemed that the beautiful stories could be separated from the ugly ones in her imagination. It would have felt sacrilegious to force them together but, even so, he found that he wanted to – desperately. He was afraid of the distant, half-ecstatic look in her eyes, of the sheer fantasy in which she could plainly exist. He had an urge to shake her out of it with rough facts, because this was another means by which she got away, leaving him alone with his fear that she might get bored of him. But he felt so tenderly for her that all he could do was stroke her hair and her neck and let her talk.

That evening she did not appear to want to have sex with him. She put her head on his shoulder and tucked her legs up under her sweater. They drank a bottle of Chianti and made a dent in the lasagne Rosalind had taught him to make and which he always forgot was designed to serve six. Then Arianne said she was tired. She usually slept naked but that night she put on one of his shirts when she went to bed. When she fell asleep, she was holding the fluffy rabbit and he felt almost brutal, dangerous and hairy, getting in and lying beside her. Ought he to sleep on the sofa? She was so tired and she had recently complained that he snored. Again, his heart ached with a protectiveness he did not know how to express; he tried to, awkwardly, stroking her face and knocking a glass off the bedside table with his elbow. Thankfully she was too deeply asleep to be disturbed.

After all that, it came as quite a surprise that she woke him at six the next morning by unbuttoning her shirt, climbing on top of him and whispering ferociously in his ear. She bit his neck so hard that she made a ring of purple bruises. She unhinged the headboard from the wall.

Chapter 6

Luke was finding it more and more difficult to persuade himself to go to work. He called in and tested Sebastian's non-hierarchical compassion. He used an impressionistic excuse he had once heard Adrian Sand call on: he said he had 'issues at home' and he might just use the laptop if that was all right.

'Of course it's all right,' Sebastian said. 'It's not like you're one of our dossers and skivers, Luke. I hope it all gets sorted quickly, mate.'

Meaning to be honest, Luke switched on the laptop, bracing his hangover against the sunrise graphics, the euphoric trill – then he went back to bed, to warm pastures of Arianne.

Love seemed to Luke to be a decadent kind of resignation. He saw no reason to go out into the world any more. Having abandoned every other important aspect of his life – work, friends, family – he found he had never been happier. And yet, at times, he would catch sight of his placidly grinning face in a mirror and be struck by a rising panic: surely there was *something* he ought to be doing. Arianne would get bored of his grin, wouldn't she? Would she? What did she expect from him?

He glanced at her through the kitchen doorway where she stood nonchalantly in a devastating little pink bra and a pair of his boxer shorts, trying to open a bottle of Coke. She struggled for a moment and then she hurled the bottle violently into the bin – as if to punish it.

Of course she would get bored of his stupid grin! It was a sickening inevitability. Surely there was something the man was meant to *do* so the woman didn't get *bored*.

84

He wished there was some act of heroism he could perform. Flickering in his mind was the iconography of all the Hollywood films he had ever seen: the men who threw themselves in front and took the bullet, the men who leapt out of helicopters to rescue the weak from the icy sea.

But all he could do was carry her up and down the stairs and, after a while, Arianne seemed unimpressed. He really couldn't blame her. She lay back in his arms, requiring this gesture at the very least, her eyes skipping over the wallpaper as they moved.

One evening he watched her putting on her makeup, sipping from a glass of wine he held for her, telling him something spiteful and funny about one of the girls in her drama class. He was not really hearing what she said. In a riot of pride and fear of losing her, he was thinking Arianne was the girl he would always have dreamt of – if only he had been blessed with the imagination. But she was an idea too amazing for the scope of his expectations. He watched her dab rouge on her cheeks and draw neat black lines beneath her eyes. He found himself terrifyingly, deliciously unable to predict her next move.

His relationship with Lucy had made him unhappy precisely because it had made him powerful. He had hated his capacity to devastate her hopes with a casual word. Strangely, her vulnerability came to seem ruthless because it caused him to feel so much guilt. She built intricate symbolism round the things she asked of him, investing some stupid party or lunch arrangement with all of her hopes: they were like glass cathedrals.

He and Lucy had gruelling diary sessions together.

'Oh, OK. No, that's fine. Well, are you free for lunch on the twenty-seventh, then? It's Mummy's birthday, Luke. They're doing a lunch in the country. I mean, Hannah and Sam are going, *and* Jane and Benjy . . .' (*Men who were going to marry you went to your mother's birthday lunch. Men who really loved you did not put their work before an important family occasion.* He watched her thinking it out. And he thought she was right. He resented her – at times he hated her – for being right. Was the casualness in his voice designed to impose a sense of proportion, or to knock her out with just how far she was from *winning*?)

'Oh, Luce, I *can't*. I've got to work. There's the – er – the big presentation that Monday.' And then he would have to watch the glass cathedral shatter behind her eyes, to see the disappointment twitching across her mouth.

'Oh, yes, of course. I must have forgotten,' she said. She wrote,

85

'L – PRESENTATION!!!' in rather manic capitals across the whole of Monday – as if it would be her sole preoccupation that day.

His ego might have been flattered by the control he had over her. Friends said as much with envy. But he hated it. Power only appeals to those who feel healthier, safer, for denying others their humanity. Having grown up with two parents who had done all they could to make their good marriage and the decency of their friends seem like an inalienable right, Luke had a lot of faith in the natural justice of the world. Not in Africa, perhaps, no: obviously he saw that in hot, war-torn places things were different, but here, in England, people were essentially lucky and good and he trusted them. He was conscious only of a fear of loneliness, rather than the more distorting fear of betrayal.

Consequently love had always sounded to him like a semi-religious experience, a displacement of the ego, an absorption into another. In other words, love was the exact opposite of the power he had over Lucy. All he wanted was to get closer – always closer – to Arianne. He could not bear to lose her for even a second to any of her modes of escape.

By the end of the month, Luke felt his arrival at work noted in a way it never had been before. He saw the way ambitious younger colleagues looked up, then quickly down again as he rushed in late, saying, 'Sorry, guys,' aware that he smelt of cigarettes and that he had toothpaste at the corner of his mouth.

He began to eat lunch at his desk to show dedication. Twelve thirty came and, very conspicuously, he *didn't move*. The others all got up, of course, but he merely clickety-clicked his mouse and called out, 'Have fun, you lot,' to the frivolous young. He felt like an idiot behaving this way. Eating at your desk was miserable and he spilt soy sauce right into his keyboard where it congealed into a tar-like substance, which, it occurred to him, also looked disturbingly like dried blood.

During one of these desk-lunches, his assistant, Jenny, came over and told him, with a mixture of concern and spite, that his absences had been mentioned in a board meeting. Perversely, faced with fact rather than paranoid fantasy, he found it hard to care. He offered her a California roll.

'Oooh, yummy, thanks. So, what's going on?' she said. He grinned at her and she shook her head. 'Oh dear. I hope it's legal.' She put the roll into her mouth. 'They're good, these. You go to that posh place on the corner, don't you? How the other half live.'

She looked plump and forgiving in her straining pink shirt, the black trousers taut round her crossed legs. He appreciated her gentle mockery – mostly because he was beginning to feel afraid that he was losing control of his job and her winking and smiling somehow domesticated this fear. He wanted to think of a reason to ask her to stay, to eat her lunch at the desk with him, be an ally against the younger faces, who were all plainly wondering if Arianne was going to leave him. (No, that wasn't it. They knew nothing about Arianne, for God's sake. He had to get a grip.)

But it turned out that Jenny had her own work to get on with. She slid off the desk with a tight scrape of the lining of her trousers against her tights. 'Righty-ho. Shall I print off that file Damian Green sent or shall I just email?'

Her sudden professionalism hurt his feelings. 'Oh. Um – just zap it out. I've got a copy. Yes, do that. Thanks.' He wanted her to ask him again if everything was OK, because just then he would have liked to tell her all about Arianne. He would have liked to go out for coffee with smiling, plump Jenny and tell her about his intense fear of losing his girlfriend. He would have liked to hear her smiling, plump interpretation of it all. Was it normal, the panic he felt when Arianne looked away, out of a window or deep into her glass? Was it standard, during supper, to feel you were plummeting down a lift-shaft?

A few nights before, in one of her desperate moods, Arianne had said, 'I *have* to get my fucking *life* together, Luke. I need some stability. I have to set up some things I can believe in. You know? Why is it so fucking hard?'

She hurled a hairbrush against the wall and it bounced back on to the floor and skidded towards them on its bristles. They watched it slow down and stop.

'Hey, you've got me, Arianne. I'm stable, aren't I? I *love* you.' He tried to undo the shirt she was putting on and she slapped away his hand.

'I'm being serious, Luke. I mean *real* stability – *money, career.*' She sighed deeply and slugged back her wine.

Luke thought how much he would have liked to see Jenny's face listening, nodding, the shiny pink lips pressed together in sympathy. Could he look pitiful and regain her attention? He watched her walking away across the open-plan office, the whistling prairie. Was it normal, this desire to ask everyone what they thought of the most private details of his life? Perhaps he should call his mother, he thought.

He looked at his phone to see if Arianne had sent a text message. She had not.

Why? *Why* had she not sent a text message? Just three weeks ago she had sent him one or two an hour.

He tried to control his breathing and opened an email from Lindsey Wicks at Calmaderm.

Without discussing it, Arianne and Luke began to see friends together, rather than spending all their time alone. Luke thought the stimulation would do her good. In fact, he found it did him good, too. One night, at a dinner party at Ludo's flat, he was happily surprised to see Jessica, who had recently been working all hours on some kind of a film and was known to refuse all invitations if she had a job.

At the start of the evening, looking disappointed, Ludo had told Luke that Jessica couldn't make it because of work. But at around ten thirty she called and said she had finished early and were there any leftovers? Ludo told her to come quickly because the tiramisu looked positively X-rated. It turned out she was already on the doorstep with a bottle of wine.

It was typical of her. She was ravenously hungry and she happily ate the tepid remains of the couscous and two helpings of tiramisu and Luke spent the rest of the evening catching up with her. She was co-producing a documentary and the things she told him about the filming genuinely fascinated him. Luke loved taking photographs and had once dreamt of doing a course, but it had not been something he felt he could mention to anyone. He had taken a lot of photographs during his gap-year, and he still did whenever he went on holiday, but it was a peculiar fact that he had never taken any in England. Not a single shot. Somehow, in his own country, he was always conscious of the judgement of his father or his sister – and he felt sure that even his mother would think photographs were just a big nothing in comparison to oil painting. And, anyway, he knew perfectly well that he wasn't creative. He was an account manager.

He and Jessica had a natural, easy friendship and, for a few moments, he was consciously glad to be free of the obligation to please Arianne. He felt himself relax and simply enjoy another person's company. Talking to Jessica was like crossing the equator to a temperate climate.

'God, you two have been in your own little world, haven't you?' she said. 'You're missed, you know. I'm not being all preachy, but friends are important.'

'Yes, I know,' Luke said. He felt close to tears. What a wonderful, peaceful, *simple* thing friendship was. He couldn't believe how much he had undervalued it these past weeks.

'You are OK, aren't you, babe?' Jessica asked him. 'You look all sad and tired. Do I need to worry?'

'Oh, God, I'm fine. I'm just – I'm just *feeling* so much, these days. You know what I mean?'

'I think so,' she told him. This was so unlike him that she wondered if Arianne had got him doing too much coke. She considered Luke to be incredibly restrained and English, really – like his mother. She couldn't account for this outburst. 'Babe, you'd always call me if you needed anything, wouldn't you?'

He studied her gentle, intelligent, *forgiving* face. 'You're so fantastic, Jess,' he said.

When they said goodbye, he and Jessica hugged each other for a long time. She whispered, 'That's a very highly strung girl you're involved with.'

'Yes, I know,' he said. 'It's a bit difficult sometimes. But love's supposed to be sort of demanding, isn't it? And I mean just look at her.'

She didn't look at Arianne but smiled at him and although he smiled back, she couldn't help but be struck by the gloomy incomprehension in his eyes. He seemed mystified by this girl. 'Oh, Luke, do be careful. You must remember to look after yourself. You're no good to her if you don't.'

'No, you're absolutely right. And I am,' he assured her.

Arianne was silent on the way home. She had accused him of ignoring her at dinner. She had hissed at him in the hallway. The way her tiny ponytail bounced as she trotted down Ludo's stairs ahead of him was the most frightening thing Luke had ever seen. And now that they sat in the back seat of a mini-cab, he watched the streetlights running over her closed eyes and her beautiful, passive face in increasing panic. When they got back she went straight to the bathroom and locked the door.

This was the first time she had shown a desire for privacy. Luke sat in the kitchen, listening resentfully to the water pouring over her body. He was astonished by how jealous it made him feel. He actually considered turning on the cold tap to see if the water would blast out hot on her, making her jump out, breaking up the lovers' tryst. Then he thought he must be going mad and he laughed and massaged his temples and poured himself a large gin and tonic. Was he jealous of *water*?

But he felt uneasy until he heard the shower stop and the door open. She came into the kitchen, naked, a white towel wrapped round her hair. The heat came off her skin and she smelt of shampoo and body cream. She paused by the fruit bowl and rolled a grape between her fingers.

'Arianne?' he said.

She rolled the grape down her arm and flicked it from her elbow into the palm of her hand again. Her actions were all this precise. What on earth were her thoughts like? She was supple, glowing from the shower.

'Look, I'm really sorry,' he said – though he was not at all sure what he had done wrong. Surely she didn't think he was interested in Jessica.

'I don't know your friends, Luke.'

'You know Ludo and . . . well, you know Jess.'

'It's not being a gentleman to leave a woman alone in that way. It's not *manly*.'

He couldn't understand what she meant. She had been sitting between his friends James and Joe, who were both great fun and Joe had plainly thought she was stunning, which always pleased her. But he had not been 'manly' in some way. He took her word for it and was appalled. 'I'm so sorry,' he said. 'I won't let it happen again.'

She put the grape into her mouth. 'OK.'

'I really am, Arianne. I never want to upset you.'

'It's OK. Stop apologizing. I'm a bitch. Forget it all.'

'But I've hurt you.'

'No, you haven't. I'm just – I'm just crazy.' She covered her face with both hands. 'Ugh – just don't listen to anything I say! I'm horrible and you're lovely. I'm an evil bitch and you're a good, honest man. And now we're going to go to bed and I'll do anything you want, OK? Anything. I don't even care if it hurts. In fact, I want it to hurt.'

He stood up, a little uncertainly, and held her in his arms. He kissed her for a moment, and the kiss contained the full, singing force of a last-minute reprieve, a note delivered to the executioner. Then she swivelled round and leant over the kitchen table, turned her head back and smiled broadly at him as her hands gripped the aluminium legs.

★   ★   ★

90

It would have been hard to say at that stage which was the expression and which the reality of his love – sex or emotion. His mind and body were inextricable. Emotion characterized sex and sex reiterated emotion. There was no sense of release from either. Afterwards he lay beside her, thinking and feeling, feeling and thinking in the tangled sheets.

It seemed natural to him to assume responsibility for all Arianne's practical concerns. He felt it was the least – while fearing it was the most – that he could do. He guaranteed a loan for her from her bank, which had been sceptical about the financial reliability of hopeful young actresses. 'You're my guardian angel,' she said, 'aren't you, baby?' and Luke knew he had never felt more pride.

He made sure the local deli delivered all her favourite food: plain yoghurt and bran sticks, double chocolate fudge ice-cream and vodka; apples – green, not red *ever*, he had made this fatal error once – and butter and honey and crumpets. It was all wildly inconsistent.

'I think it balances me,' she explained. 'Maybe not. Anyway, who cares?'

He adored watching her eat – anything, really, but particularly crumpets. She spontaneously toasted them in the middle of the night after a bubble bath. She sat on the window-seat in her knickers. Her mouth shone with butter and she let him lick the drips of warm, buttery honey off her bare legs, giggling at him. 'Oh, Luke – it *tickles*!'

'Sorry, darling. Should I stop?'

'No, no. You can carry on – "*darling*",' she teased, with the rest of the crumpet stuffed into her mouth.

He paid for cabs to take her to her drama class and to bring her back home again. They were booked in advance. She did not walk anywhere if she could help it. The swelling had gone down on her foot, but she still limped heavily. She refused to see a doctor, saying she was sure it was healing perfectly normally. Did he think there was something *wrong* with her, she wanted to know, that she was somehow too *incompetent* to get better without some *man* in a white coat? It was sexism!

'Look, you don't have to carry me if you don't want to – if that's what this is *really about*,' she said. 'But you'll just have to allow extra time when we go out or whatever, because you know I can't do anything quickly, Luke. Not with the pain.'

He felt terrible. She always wondered what people's words were 'really about'. She had no faith in the literal. She expected lies and subtext.

'Hey, don't be silly, darling. I'm just worried about you, that's all. I love carrying you up the stairs. It's romantic.'

She smiled at him – a sad, unconvinced smile.

He castigated himself. What had he been thinking? Again he had let her down with his mundane nagging about doctors. He deserved the flash of fear, the shock of anxiety her words 'allow extra time' had sent through him.

What '*extra time*'? he thought. Already he was spending it all on her. He had no time to work, less time than ever to see his friends. She demanded everything of him. And when she looked away sadly, beyond what he was already doing, he followed her gaze to a wasteland of his own inadequacy. He must not give her reason to doubt he could cope, not for one second.

In this way he spent all his energy.

Then, one evening a few weeks later, he came home to find Dan sitting on his suede sofa. 'All right? Howzit going?' Dan said. 'You must be Luke, I'm guessing.' He raised his hand like a warrior, coming in peace.

Implausibly, Dan and Arianne were drinking tea together. She had put biscuits on a plate – as if he were a visiting relative. His huge fingers pincered a chocolate Florentine. 'Dan's just dropped by,' Arianne explained. 'I saw him on the way out of drama class. He was passing – on his way to see someone. Weren't you, babe?'

Dan nodded and took a nibble of the biscuit.

'Right. I see,' Luke said, staring at her.

'So, have you had a good day, *dear*?' she asked him, in her nasal, American accent. She couldn't help satirizing their domesticity in front of other people. Must she do it in front of Dan, though? he thought.

Actually, he could not have begun to tell her what kind of a day he'd had. His desk now held his own bodyweight in unread paperwork. Paper was in his dreams – it pursued him down alleyways; thousands of pieces of paper snowstorming his imagination. He was on the run from it as soon as he woke, and his invaluable sportsman's calm was now monopolized by the need to conceal this from his colleagues. But faced with the unintelligible horror of finding Dan in his flat, he found the paper had all blown away. 'I had a pretty good day, thanks,' he said. 'How was yours?'

'Oh, Jon says I need to rethink my Shakespeare piece. My Miranda. My best fucking piece. I'm really disappointed in him as a teacher this term.' She smiled at him, half expectantly. Was he meant to reply?

'Right,' he said. 'I'm sorry about that.'

She picked up her teacup and drained it. Then she looked into her pack of cigarettes and found it was empty. She stuck out her bottom lip, crushing the packet. 'All gone. No fair,' she said, then smiled cleanly at both of them. One, then the other. 'So, Dan wants us to go out for supper.'

Luke put down his keys and looked at her, unable to think what to say.

Dan cleared his throat. 'Actually, I kind of meant I want you to come out for dinner *alone*, Arianne. No offence, man,' he said.

Dan looked at him, and then Arianne looked at him. Luke found her expression unreadable.

'Oh,' she said. 'Oh, right.'

Luke felt intense shock – he felt sweat break out, hairs stand on end and he returned her gaze like a lost, sweating zoo animal, behind glass.

'Yeah I thought we could go to Lanton's, babe,' Dan was saying. 'You know, with the cushions and all the incense and shit. You love that fucking place.'

She clapped her hands like a little girl. 'Oh, yes, I do. I *love* Lanton's! They do the *yummiest* crème brûlée, Luke. Not too sweet, not too creamy. It comes all golden with sugar and you press your spoon on the top and it goes . . . *crack*! Just perfect.' She sighed, still turned towards Luke. Again her face gave away no emotion. In fact, had he ever seen such a blank face before? Surely this was a diagram of a face.

'Look, you're cool about this, aren't you, man?' Dan said. 'I mean, I haven't seen Arianne for, like, a month now. It's been pretty hard. You know what I'm saying?'

He stood up and walked round the room, his leather trousers creaking with the strain of accommodating his thighs.

'And I know she's been missing me too. Of course she has. You don't mind me saying that,' Dan assured him. 'It's, like, you just don't have a relationship with real feelings and it just *ends*,' he punched his right fist into the palm of his left hand with a horrible thwack, 'in *one day*.'

Arianne sat down and crossed her legs. She had found more cigarettes in her pocket and she lit one. They watched her blow out the smoke.

'You know what I'm saying, man,' Dan repeated. 'Right?'

'Yeah, I know what you're saying,' Luke said. His voice sounded weak.

'It's basically, like, I think maybe everything happened in a hurry here. OK? I mean, you have this accident, right? You feel,' he made quotation marks in the air with his fingers, like bunny ears on either side of his head, '"*bonded*" deeply . . . But then, like, suddenly she's here *living* with you? Ask yourself if it really makes sense. I just want a little time to talk to her, OK?'

Arianne broke a biscuit in half, then left it untouched. It was impossible not to be aware of her blinking, breathing, observing. And it was impossible to misinterpret Dan. Luke gazed at Arianne who gazed back at him. Again: the diagram, the printout of unintelligible numbers in place of the human expression.

'Why?' he said stupidly. 'What do you want to say to her?'

'I think we understand each other,' Dan said.

Some sign of emotion? *Any* reaction to this? Luke stared, imploring her from behind his paralysed face. She stubbed out her cigarette neatly and squeaked her finger on a dirty spot on her shoe.

'So Arianne and me are going out for dinner, then,' Dan said.

It occurred to Luke that he was repeatedly asserting this so as to provoke either himself or Arianne to contradict him. Barely perceptibly, he pushed back his shoulders.

'OK? Because I just want to take her out to a nice restaurant for a nice dinner so we can *talk*, which we haven't been free to do with this whole *situation*.' He drew out his hand across the room, implicating the furniture, the walls. He looked morally sickened.

And Luke had nothing to say to him. He had never felt more ashamed and frightened. He knew he would not be able to defend himself physically against this huge, steroid-boosted man – and any comment he might make would be seen as provocation. He would be knocked out in front of Arianne – like Andy Jones. He would be humiliated in front of her. At a loss, he simply observed.

'It's a *nice* restaurant. We'll have a *nice* dinner, a little wine – and Arianne and I will do some talking . . .' Dan said, still trying his luck. Luke appreciated that the technique had probably been learnt from experience: it was so hard to know what she really thought. He had obviously judged her attachment to other admirers by seeing if she cried when he knocked them out.

Both men waited. And then suddenly, by one of her miracles of physical communication, some slight relaxation of her posture, Arianne let it be known that she had no intention of standing up, of walking out of the door, of going to Lanton's with Dan. Luke saw this and, trembling, put down the briefcase he was still ridiculously holding. He walked to the front door and opened it, praying he had not misread the sign.

He heard something muttered, then creaking and then footsteps. Out of the corner of his eye, he saw the huge mass of black leather coat arrive beside him. It paused – for several lifetimes – and then, with a strong, salty smell of cowhide, it passed him by.

When Luke clicked the door shut and turned round, Arianne was taking off her skirt. He was too tired to try to understand what had happened. He accepted the odd, staged quality of her kisses feeling he did not deserve them.

'I can't believe the nerve of that guy,' she said, but she appeared distracted, rather than outraged. 'You're so wonderful, Luke,' she told him, but it did not sound convincing.

Was this her first flawed performance? Surely she knew he had been a coward, he thought.

There was an unnerving calm and then she threw her knickers on to the coffee-table and pushed him down on to his knees. He put his face between her legs and felt lost. After a while he moved away and was about to pull her down on to the rug beside him when he saw that tears were coming down her face. 'Arianne? What's wrong?'

'I'm sorry,' she said. 'I'm not good enough for you. You shouldn't let me do this to you.' She pushed his hands off her legs and ran away into the bathroom, slamming and locking the door.

At a club later that week, he came back from the dance-floor to find her with a tequila shot in her hand, licking salt off his friend Joe's neck. Joe had not seen him approaching the table and Arianne made no signal to him, although she had seen Luke clearly. Joe held out the lime between his teeth and she knocked back the tequila and bit into it, watching his eyes catch sight of Luke as her teeth sank into the fruit. He pulled back, leaving it in her mouth, and she spat it across the table.

'Hey, *Luke*!' Joe said, standing up. 'Come and – come and have a shot.'

'No, thanks.'

'OK, then,' Joe said. 'Fair enough. I think I might just go and see where Sam is, then. All right.' He squeezed Luke's arm lightly as he passed.

Luke watched him go. 'What were you doing?' he said.

Arianne held up the empty glass and waved it at him, 'Tequeeeela shots.' She laughed drunkenly, through her nose. Her voice was slurring, her face was flushed. She looked incredibly beautiful – as if she had just had sex. '*You know*, Luke – salt, shot of tequila, bite of lime?'

'Licking it off his *neck*, though?'

'What, Joe?'

'Taking the lime out of his *mouth*? Yes, *Joe*.'

'Joe?' She shrugged. 'He wanted me to and he bought the drinks, so I thought why not?'

'Because he *bought the drinks*?'

'Oh, what are you fucking saying, Luke?'

'Nothing.'

'Yes, you are.'

'No, Arianne. I'm not.'

'Bullshit.'

'What's bullshit?'

'You have no right to make that insinuation. You think you're so *superior*, don't you?'

Hadn't he once said this to Lucy? Lucy, with her infinitely greater, cleaner love for him, when he was only able to muster a soiled kind of fondness for her? He pushed away the thought and its implications with horror, '*No*, Arianne.'

'Yes. You think I'm a little slut. *Slut whore slut*. You think I'm just a bitch who should be shot and tossed on to a rubbish heap.'

He had heard her talk this way before. Long monologues of horrifying insults to herself. She could become quite hysterical. 'Please, darling. Don't do this,' he said softly.

Jessica, who was sitting at the other end of the table, said something about really needing to dance and stood up. Luke gazed away after her as she left. Just then it seemed that her presence had constituted the last vestige of civilization. He could see Ludo on the stage, spraying people with a bottle of champagne. His friends were all in another world and their joy was nightmarish. He wanted to cover his head.

Love had made his mind and body inextricable, and now jealousy and hate had forced them apart just as effectively. If his body had genuinely reflected his mind, the paramedics would have come through the crowd with defibrillators, shouting, 'Stand clear!', shooting thousands of volts through his heart to start it up again. A small group would have stood by, marvelling at his survival.

96

But instead he smiled and sat down beside Arianne, out of grim necessity, out of the overwhelming fear of making things even worse. 'Hey, come on,' he said, 'I want you to have a good time. Let's not argue. OK? *OK, darling?*' He kissed her cheek.

He had recently begun to appreciate how free, in relative terms, he had always been to show his emotions in the past – as a child, a teenager. He remembered his father telling him to pull himself together when a schoolfriend chose to ask the other member of their gang of three to go on holiday with him and his family. This betrayal had occurred on his sister's birthday and Luke was meant to be changing for a big family supper. For some reason he had been alone with his father, who had said, 'It's rotten luck, but there'll be other holidays and you've simply got to pull yourself together for Mummy and Sophie, Luke.'

'You don't under*stand*, Dad,' he shouted, throwing his hockey-stick across the kitchen in helpless grief.

'I *do* understand, Luke,' his father said. 'It's very tough thinking you're missing out and feeling as if someone else has all the luck when you deserve it as much as they do. You just have to cope sometimes. So, come on, buck up.' Luke had run away up the stairs, choking and sobbing at this insult to his emotions, this soul-destroying, eat-your-greens advice.

'You just have to cope sometimes.' It chilled the heart.

He put his arm round Arianne and squeezed her shoulder. He remembered the day his aunt Suzannah had come by to tell his mother that their father had died. They had talked privately for a while and when Suzannah left, wearing big dark glasses, his mother had gone out into the garden with her gloves and her sunhat. She said she was just going to weed the border because it was in a wretched, terrible state. She smiled at them as they sat at the lunch table reading the Sunday papers, and shut the door behind her.

They had all assumed she was fine until they got hungry at around eight and realized there was no smell of cooking. It turned out she was still outside, on her hands and knees, weeding. They all observed her sadly through the window and wondered what to do. Luke remembered that his father had gone out for her with a glass of whisky in his hand, and from the kitchen window he and Sophie watched them hugging each other in the half-light. When she came in, she said, 'I am *so* sorry. I completely lost track of the time. You're all starving, aren't you?'

But his father wouldn't let her cook. He took them out for supper that night and held her hand all the way through. They went to the Holland Park Brasserie – her favourite fish restaurant.

In the club toilets, a little later, Luke found himself crying at the thought of the tenderness that was sometimes there between his parents. They seemed to go for long periods in which his father didn't really notice his mother's presence, but then suddenly they would silence him and his sister with a little display of enduring love. He found himself thinking about Lucy and wondering how she was, what it had been like to get that final email from him, with its logical explanation:

It's simplest just to do it this way, Lucy, because you know there'll only be a dreadful scene if we meet up. You know you wanted to get married and I just wasn't heading that way and neither of us could understand it, really, because you're so lovely, Luce. But I think I've worked it all out now. And the reason I'm so sure is because I've found what everyone's looking for: when it just 'feels right'. I know you'll think I'm a wanker, but I think this is for the best, in the long term, for both of us.

That had been weeks and weeks ago. She had never replied. Lucy was a good person. She had genuinely loved him; and that morning he had eaten her mother's jam on hot croissants, the taste of Arianne mingling outrageously well with the home-grown strawberries and the creamy butter and with his huge, orgasm-fuelled appetite.

He went back to the table and the tequila shots and they sat together and drank cocktails and talked to the others. There was no argument. It was such a good show that even Joe felt able to come back and sit with them. But later, when Luke carried her up the stairs to the flat, her weight even more dead than usual, after all the tequila, a terrible thought flashed through his mind. It occurred to him that, if he really wanted to, he could just drop Arianne over the edge of the banisters, on to the marble-tiled floor.

The weather had been getting warmer and now came the hottest June in fifty years. London did one of its quick changes. Supernaturally white limbs were exposed to the open air and gradually turned pink, music wafted out of shop doorways, adults ate children's ice lollies in the street, and people wore every colour of the rainbow. Every evening, tree-lined avenues were filled with the smell of barbecues – a mixture of beer and burnt sausages and charcoal. With the smell came the sound of adult laughter and of children joyously dodging their control and setting up camps at the far end of the garden.

One Sunday evening, Luke and Arianne carried a bottle of rosé towards his friend Matt's house. Arianne had begun to regard Luke with open scorn – and, as a short-term solution, he had decided to avoid direct eye-contact with her.

Matt's girlfriend Leila opened the door and said, 'Hey! Come on in,' in a voice turned honey sweet by the sunshine. She was wearing a blue cotton dress, which tied in a bow at the back of her neck. Behind her, on surround sound, was the French DJ everyone seemed to have discovered a week before. They followed her in, towards the bright french windows on to the garden, beyond which groups of people were holding glasses and talking.

Arianne had not been in the mood to have sex with Luke for just under two weeks now. His frustration was such that even watching her fingers open a packet of cigarettes was painfully erotic to him. In the garden, he eyed vicious little appetizers of raw ham and melon. Matt held out a plate of them. 'Hi, man. Hey, gorgeous. *So*, how are the happy couple doing?'

Luke wondered if there was an implied doubt of him in everything people said.

The party went on – and on, mercilessly. Candles burnt down and bowls piled up with filthy cigarette butts. Ice-cream pooled on the plates in the hot night air, trapping innocent flies and moths. Luke made insignificant conversation with friends he saw only once or twice a year, and in each case he remembered why this was. Arianne had been tugged away long ago by a girl called Laura to whom she had just been introduced. Laura was the tall, emaciated, hysterical type of girl who developed passionate friendships with strangers, only to throw them away with her empty cigarette pack at the end of the night. She had seemed almost to fall in love with Arianne. Luke had known her a long time and frequently avoided her at parties.

He left them to it. He had been hoping to see Jessica, but she texted him to say she was working late on set and couldn't make it. He absorbed the disappointment and took a bottle of wine to the end of the garden. It really wasn't his crowd – they were all drama queens, literary types who obviously thought he was a thick rugby player with nothing original to say. Well, maybe he was. He rolled and smoked a joint, then fell asleep on the cool grass.

He woke up at around three a.m. to the sound of a girl collapsing the deck-chair she was dancing on. Arianne was not in the garden any more. Suddenly concerned, Luke got up and began to search for her. There were no lights on in the house, and even by running his hands in vast circles along the walls, he couldn't find a single switch. He stubbed his toe on a zinc Buddha by the sofa, then tripped over a salad bowl on the kitchen floor. There appeared to be a light at the end of the corridor and he made his way towards it. When he pushed open the door he found a boy he did not recognize being sick into the loo.

Gradually, his eyes became accustomed to the darkness and he made his way up the stairs where there were still a few candles burning in little pink shells dispersed along the landing. At last he found Arianne in the bathroom. She was sitting in an empty bath with Laura and Laura's boyfriend JJ. Arianne was kissing Laura and JJ had his hand on her breast in a drunken, perfunctory way.

Luke stood in the doorway.

'*Luuuke*. Hello, *you*. Come and join us,' Laura said. 'I have borrowed your delicious girlfriend.'

JJ said something indecipherable that was, apparently, still deeply amusing to himself.

'I'm sorry, I can't, Laura. We're leaving,' Luke said.

'Leaving? *Noweeyaren't*,' Arianne told him. She sounded incredibly drunk.

'Yes,' he said.

'Whaddoyou mean, *yes*? *No*.'

'Yes. The taxi's here, Arianne.'

'What *taxi*?'

'I ordered one.'

'*Oh*, didjou now? Well, you can jus' geddinit, then.'

Laura put up her hand to halt the conversation. '*Or*,' she said, '*or* he could come and geddin the bath.' She levered herself half-way out for her glass, which was sitting among the bottles of shampoo, then flopped down again, spilling some of the wine into her lap, saying, 'Oopsy-daisy, who's a silly cunt?'

'Oh, that's easy, darling – *you*,' said JJ.

Laura ignored him and stared at Luke, her head tipped on one side. 'You know, I do like your boyfriend, Arianne. Known'm fer *years* but he's never shownenny interest. *Fucking* insulting, really. Tell the truth, I thoughtee might be one of those rugby queers. You know – the ones who protest jusaliddle too much?'

This idea struck Arianne as hilariously funny.

Laura went on, 'But now he's got you. And we can't argue with tits like that, can we?'

Arianne glanced down at her cleavage and giggled.

Laura said, 'Almost makes me wish I was a real dyke, not just at parties. But I can't help preferring him. He is pretty, isn't he? *Very pretty boy*. I want'm to geddin the bath, acsherly. Use your charms on him, darling. Oh, *go on*, Lukey-Luke, stop being such a lovely, broad-shouldered spoilsport.'

They were coked up and blind drunk. He hated their simple way of talking. It was supposed to be sophisticated to sound like spoilt children when you talked about sex.

'Canchoo *make* him, Arianne? Jusfer Laura?' she said, pouting. 'We could have loss and loss of fun.'

'He won't, babe. Only thing he's geddingin's his fucking taxi. Watch him.' Luke turned and walked out. He heard Arianne laughing: 'See. Offee goes. That's all, folks.'

But, of course, Luke didn't get into a taxi because he hadn't really ordered one. He walked back through the dark streets to his flat. It took almost two hours.

The days of longing for a mode of self-sacrifice had passed. All that complacent philosophizing! He could not believe he had ever felt at leisure to do it. Now he just wanted her not to humiliate him, not to leave in the middle of the night. In fact, he had started waking up in the middle of the night just to check she was still there at that vulnerable time. He listened to her sighs and wondered who she was dreaming about. Other men? Dan? Or were they sighs of despair? Was his comprehensive inadequacy causing her to feel *despair*?

It was five a.m. when he heard her come back from Matt and Leila's. He listened to her filling a glass of water in the kitchen, dropping her clothes on the bedroom floor and getting into bed. He stood in front of the bathroom mirror, brushing his teeth intricately and crying.

Was this normal – this crying, this toothbrushing?

As it happened, Arianne did not leave him in the middle of the night. She left him on a sunny afternoon. She said, 'Look, you know and I know. You *know* you do.'

'No, I don't know.'

'You do. You know *really* – if you really think about what's good for you.'

He had never heard her so reasonable before, so rational. Normally her emotions were a deep blue sea she choked in until he hauled her out. Lately she had slipped out of his hands – and now, for some reason, she had appeared on dry land, and was waving casually across. Leaving him was apparently bringing out the best in her.

She smoked her cigarette efficiently and her eyes darted about the flat for things that belonged to her. She saw a pair of earrings on a bookshelf and walked over to them. Her heels were loud on the wooden floor – she had declared her foot completely better and could wear them now. She slipped the earrings into her pocket.

Luke said, 'But I love you, Arianne. I mean – I genuinely *love* you.'

This was too much for her. She spun round and gesticulated wildly, spreading out both her arms like someone recommending good, fresh air. 'It's not *healthy*, Luke.'

Hadn't he seen her make this exact gesture in the lit window at Dan's flat? 'Why isn't it healthy? Why not?'

'I don't know. But it isn't. Things are mysteries. You need someone more – more *you* than I am. You *know* what I mean.'

'No, I don't.'

'Look, I'm really sorry. I don't want you to think I'm not sorry. That's the main thing.'

It was not the main thing.

'But where will you go?' he said.

'Oh, I'll be fine.'

The fear of what this certainty connoted was almost intolerable, but he could not bear to ask the question again. She went into the bedroom and came out with the cardboard box, Dan's old sports bag and an armful of jumpers and other objects. 'Where do you keep plastic bags?' she said. 'Of course it's outrageous that I don't know.'

'Under the sink.' He watched her go into the kitchen. Why would she be 'fine'? Who would she be 'fine' with?

'Hey, Luke, what's this? Whose is this stuff?' she called through. 'You've got, like, makeup and stuff under your sink. What the fuck is *Oh, Serena!* about?'

He had never been able to send back Lucy's things. The timing of this discovery slotted neatly into the horror. It was hard not to perceive a creative intelligence behind the course of heartbreak. Arianne was smiling knowingly when she came out. She said, 'I'm guessing those things belong to the owner of the makeup remover in the bathroom cupboard.'

So she had acknowledged its significance. She had just never mentioned it, having absolute confidence that this other, shadowy girl would be an irrelevant detail in comparison to her presence. With her eye on the big picture she had decided not to start an awkward conversation full of irritating, messy details.

'The mysterious *lady of the pink toothbrush*,' she said, smiling. And, with brutal logic, she tipped her head on one side and said, 'Well, *there you go*, Luke. Life goes on, hey. Doesn't it just? It's all a trail of plastic bags, really, isn't it?'

Arianne set down her things on the coffee-table. Inside the bag, the strange and painful mixture of objects held some terrible revelation about what had happened to them, but just now Luke couldn't say what. He took in a few details – the top right-hand corner of the *Hollywood Icons* book he had got her, the edge of the plate they had found in a market, the flex of her hairdryer, the bosom of the Russian doll they had discovered in an antiques shop and which she had simply had to have.

'OK. So, I should go. I've got a big audition tomorrow.'

His mouth went dry at this foretaste of her independent life. 'Audition? How come?'

'Oh, it's just – it's just through someone I met. It's a West End play. Something called *Hotel*. New writing – someone amazing, apparently.'

'*Hotel*,' he repeated numbly. 'Won't you stay and we can try to work this out?'

'Look, this was always a temporary thing, Luke. Life's a journey, right? Who wants to settle down and all that?'

'*Me. I* want to settle down. I want you to stay.'

She picked up her things, balancing the box on her hip and holding the two bags in her right hand. The buzzer went. She had tears in her eyes. 'Shit, my cab's here,' she said. 'Luke, I just want you to know that I'm sorry life's so fucking appalling and painful like this. But it's not my fault. Please try to remember that.'

And then she left. He listened to her running down the stairs.

Chapter 7

That Arianne had gone was all Luke needed to know about the world or his place in it. Food was grotesque – vast lumps of substance to be swallowed for some forgotten purpose. And the prosaic satisfaction derived from drinking a glass of water – this was an affront to the complexity of his feelings. He did not want to take in or receive anything except her. He was conscious of a universal pain; he wondered if it was possible that his cells ached. There was no rest: sleep tossed him off its surface right up at the big black sky. He sat on the sofa with the TV on and let the bright signal pelt against the lacquer of his grief.

He listened to messages from work playing out on his answerphone, with a vague interest in the development of the narrative.

'Hi, Luke, it's Jenny,' his assistant said. 'Just calling because we haven't heard from you and Calmaderm anti-dandruff's just been scheduled for next Monday. I thought you'd want to know.'

Then, the next day: 'Luke, Sebastian. Could you check in with me ASAP? It's nine fifteen now. Thanks.'

And the day after: 'Um, Luke . . . it's Jenny again.' Her voice was hushed. 'Look, are you OK?'

He managed a call to Sebastian and explained he had gastric flu and that he was sick to his stomach. If he had felt capable of amazement, he would have directed it at the fact that he had never called in sick like this before. It was so easy. He saw why the neurotic 'creatives' behaved as they did. To think he had always felt he was the one in possession of the facts when it had been them all along! He had been so superior. He had always found Adrian Sand's volatility absurd, for example, and been unable to see why he got so upset if someone criticized an idea of his in a meeting. It was work, for God's sake: a matter for the mind. Why take it to heart?

Why take it to heart? Because what else was there of any importance? It was only the heart that mattered! Luke put his head in his hands.

All in all, he preferred TV to life outside the flat. At night, people sold their houses: they redecorated with teams of experts so they could sell up and move somewhere else. In the day, they tried new ways to lose weight, they gave face creams marks out of ten, they called in about child-abuse or alcoholism or low self-esteem. Luke developed primitive loyalties to particular daytime presenters. He felt quietly blessed when they smiled at him. On the fourth morning after Arianne had left, his favourite one gazed at him lovingly in her soft lavender V-neck, twinkling caramel highlights curling softly at either side of her face. Luke smiled back weakly at the screen. She said: 'Our phone-in *today* is about *low-carbohydrate diets*,' and a memory reflex twitched in him, like a facial tic. Hadn't the phone-in been about *domestic violence*? It was then that he realized he had been sitting on the sofa since the programme aired twenty-four hours before.

He did not care now to debate whether this was normal or not. There was only one instinct in his body, one physical longing: mother. He could think only of his mother. His mother would understand; she would *know*. As he dialled the number a new chasm of self-pity opened within him and he cried out inarticulately from it.

'Oh, Luke! *Darling?*' Rosalind said. 'Try to calm down, darling. Just try to breathe slowly. Will you do that?' She waited a few moments. 'There, that's a bit better, isn't it? What's happened, Luke?'

He began to cry again and she said, 'Listen, you don't have to explain what's happened now if you don't want to.'

'It's all just – just – ruined,' he said.

'Oh, darling, you sound tired out. Would you like to come and stay at home for a few days, get yourself back on your feet? Would that be nice?'

Luke could sense the permanent texture of home behind her – so unlike this hateful, wobbling stage-set in front of him now: the ostentatious plasma screen, the purple suede sofa with its horribly eloquent stains. He could smell his mother's floral scent down the phone. He stuttered and sniffed his way through the word 'yes'.

'Shall I come and collect you, Luke? Would that be best?'

'Mmm. Might be. Might be a good idea, Mum.'

When he had put the phone down he switched off the TV and started to sob. He sobbed for forty minutes straight, as if this was work to be done, until he felt as if he had taken his broken heart for a long and arduous run.

The buzzer went – on one of the outermost orbiting stars. He walked over to the entryphone, letting tears roll off his chin and splash on his dirty shirt, dropping his bare feet carelessly – thud, thud, thud – on the floor. This would be the sound of his existence from now on, he told himself: *thud*. He leant on the door and listened to his mother coming up the stairs.

'Oh, goodness, Luke,' she said. She was genuinely shocked by his appearance. Her son looked gaunt, exhausted. The word 'dope' flashed through her mind. She held his front door open with her foot while he threw himself on to her.

He buried his face in her hair, her scent, her soft cotton blouse.

'Luke, darling,' she said again, half-questioningly.

And he loved her, he loved her, he *loved* her. His heart was beating against her heart as he clung to her in the hallway. She was perfect as she always was – the gentle colours she wore reflecting the passing seasons and the quiet music of her existence. He liked to think of her glancing up at the sky and wondering if it was going to rain a little for her roses.

Why would it have occurred to him that there was anything wrong in her life? How could he have known that, just two days before, she had been telephoned *in her own home* by the police? Detective Inspector Pendry had been sorry to have to inform her that Mr Langford had been attacked by two youths with a baseball bat. She had not yet told either of her children. Somehow, she couldn't bear to and kept putting it off. It wasn't so much that she was afraid of worrying them, more, as she explained it to herself, that she wanted 'to get the whole thing straight' in her mind first. She shied away from the peculiar implications of this. Twice she had tried to get hold of her daughter, but she hated making recordings of her own voice and gladly allowed herself to be defeated by voicemail.

The moment she replaced the receiver on DI Pendry, she grabbed her handbag and car keys. She ran up for Alistair's pyjamas and dressing-gown; she ran down for a bag of fresh fruit. Then she drove over to the hospital.

This had happened to her husband! Not to a person on the six o'clock news – to *Alistair*. She spent the drive working herself up with the essential question: what kind of a world is it in which bad things happen to good people at night? When she arrived at the hospital she was so full of urgent tenderness and indignation that she was too impatient to listen to the nurse who led her along the corridor. She felt later that she had been ill-mannered and was ashamed of herself.

But she would never forget walking through the door of Alistair's hospital room, and how her indignation fell away like a disappointed smile. Something in his expression, in the total absence of self-pity, the lack of any demand for her sympathy cut off her instincts at their root. The tears dried in her eyes. She felt stark, bereft of a vocabulary, as she sat beside his bed. She held his hand to prevent the scene falling apart – and he gave it to her for the same reason – but all she felt was a growing fear. She looked at his face – but only when he looked away. He said he couldn't bear to talk about what had happened just yet but that he was quite all right, as she could see. She observed the injured leg. Yes, this she could see.

On the portable TV by his bed they watched a late-night programme about gardening in which he would normally have had no interest whatsoever. She sat there, knowing something had gone from their lives, knowing that this strange vigil was an ending to some aspect of innocence she had never thought to single out as corruptible.

Two days had passed now and she was still letting her thoughts brush over this knowledge as fingers might brush over a lump, a telling abnormality in the skin.

Rosalind found an overnight bag in her son's cupboard and filled it with T-shirts and jeans and clean socks and boxer shorts. Unconsciously she picked clothes he had worn at nineteen, when he had last belonged to her and lived inside the body of her home.

Luke watched her for a while, until he had built up the courage to go and get his toothbrush and razor from the bathroom. This was the most dangerous room by far – it was a minefield of Arianneness: stray glossy blonde hairs, discarded makeup, an empty bottle of her shampoo in the bin. There were two smears of foundation on the basin – he noticed one in the shape of half a heart. He looked at the bottle of shampoo. The bottle said 'hair' to him and the word 'hair' said 'head' to him and the word 'head' said 'face'. And the mental picture he had of Arianne's face emitted a laser of pure white pain right into the centre of his body. He had to get out of the bathroom or die.

'Come on, then, darling. Let's go home,' his mother called out. He followed her down the stairs, feeling he had come to the end of an unsuccessful experiment: adulthood.

'So, how's Dad?' Luke asked, as he ate the cold pea and mint soup she had put in front of him. He looked out at the garden, at the antique roses, the honeysuckle, the orange blossom. He sighed, feeling like an invalid leaning back on a cool fresh pillow. Rosalind put down her spoon and pushed back her hair. 'I was actually going to call you and Sophie later today. Dad's not very well, Luke,' she said. 'He's actually staying in hospital for a few days because he's been hurt. It's nothing too serious, so don't panic.'

'What? *How?* Was it an accident? A car crash? Oh, my God.'

'No, no – it wasn't a car crash. He was attacked, Luke.'

'*Mugged?* Dad was mugged?'

She was glad merely to agree with this simple explanation.

'Yes,' she said. 'Mugged. On his way back from Julian and Elise's. I wasn't there.'

'Dad was mugged in *Knightsbridge?*'

'Yes.'

'I can't believe this. This is terrible.'

'He's in hospital,' she said. 'They're taking very good care of him. His kneecap's been smashed and there's bruising all down his leg. But they said he can come home tomorrow so there's no need to panic.'

'My God, Mum.'

She stood up to fetch the jug of elderflower cordial. Luke felt there was something peculiar in her manner and wondered if she was protecting him, concealing how bad his father's injuries really were.

She felt him staring at her and she jerked the kitchen window open a little more. She said, 'The main thing is, he's going to be perfectly all right, Luke. Nothing's too serious. There was an extremely nice doctor. There really isn't any need to panic.' She put a few more ice cubes in the jug. 'Would you like some more elderflower? I find it very cooling. Incredible how this has all sprung up on us, isn't it?'

Luke was about to agree with her grimly that, yes, this was a world of sudden car crashes and muggings and heartbreak – when he realized she was talking about the weather. The shock of the literal sent his mind reeling in confusion. To him, the external world was merely an assortment of triggers for ideas more or less connected to the loss of Arianne. What else could account for the existential agonies he felt when he looked at his double bed, or for the sense of savaged ideals when he ran his fingers across his purple suede sofa? Most poignant of all, perhaps, were his meditations on the apples in the fruit bowl. They were her apples – and this was what apples made him feel, and so it would be with any apple for the rest of his life. Even the hot weather was a depiction of feverish grief.

His mother said, 'Yes, apparently it's going to be over a hundred this weekend. Really scorching.'

He tried to go through the things she had told him since he sat down at the table. First, that his father had been hurt and was in hospital. Second, that his father had been mugged. Third, that elder-flower cordial was very cooling and it was going to be really scorching this weekend. What the hell was going on? He cleared his throat. 'Aren't you going to visit him, Mum?'

'Oh, yes. No, absolutely. I'll go in a bit,' she said. 'You can go until seven thirty, so there's no rush.'

No *rush*? Something was definitely wrong. This was not his mother. She sprang into action for the sick, she made soup, she put her cool hand on the perspiring forehead and insisted on plenty of fluids. She *rushed* – whatever the official visiting hours – as if she had been blessed with a brief opportunity to prove the strength of her love.

But just as Rosalind did not dare to ask Alistair what accounted for his strange resignation, Luke did not dare to ask her. On a funda-mental level this was the way their family survived. It was as if they all feared there would be a knock on the door one day, a grand repos-session of the furniture and all the good memories, and the best they could do was keep quiet and hope not to attract attention prema-turely. Only Luke's sister, Sophie, ignored or fought this instinct – and the other three found they couldn't look into her eyes when she slammed down her fork and screamed about *communication* over the dinner-table. Luke could never understand why she had to choose mealtimes anyway, and, moreover, why she even had a knack for choosing the meals their mother did best. Beef casserole followed by pear and almond tart with crème fraîche, for example, had been callously spoilt on more than three occasions.

Rosalind smiled at her son. '*Oh*, it's lovely having you, darling. Even if it's a sad reason it's lovely for me to have you.' Her eyes narrowed a little, like someone struggling with an eye test, as she looked out at the garden. It had begun to dawn on her that she was going to have two men in the house to look after. Two men who would want lunch and supper. For a moment, this thought irritated her and she wanted to drive to the showroom on her own and go through the accounts. She did not want this double arrival of masculine emotion, which would be a demanding, ungovernable presence, like someone else's spoilt child.

But years of maternal self-discipline, of putting her children's needs long before her own, brought Rosalind's focus sharply back to her son. Luke had always moved her to near-painful protectiveness. She stared intently at his face. 'Do you want to tell me about what happened, darling?' She stroked the hair off his forehead. 'Only if you want to . . .'

He looked down at his salad plate and toppled a pile of walnuts and rocket with his fork. 'Mum, I really love her,' he said. 'I really do.'

She was intensely relieved that this was all it was. No disease, no dope addiction, she told herself. Just a wretched girl.

'But Lucy loves *you*, Luke,' she told him. 'I've never seen a girl so obviously in love with someone before. Lucy adores you, darling. You know she does. I don't mean to underestimate this for a minute, but don't you think you might patch it up?'

Luke felt deep shame. She had no idea what had been going on. How could he bring his filthy life before his mother? Shameful images consistent with such a life pulsed in his mind: Arianne in the bath with JJ and Laura, the little bag of Lucy's things under the sink with the oven-cleaner and the dishcloths, Arianne in her see-through négligée, trickling maple syrup up her thigh. The things he had done to her – in the car, in the hallway, before they had even got through the front door. He had smacked her bottom for her, just as she begged him to, calling her a 'naughty little girl'; he had suffered hours of torment handcuffed to the bedhead while she tried out underwear combinations and, occasionally, according to her whim, ran her tongue over all of his erogenous zones but one. And he had enacted a horrifying scene in the communal hallway of his apartment building – though it had honestly scared him that she wanted this – in which he was a rapist and she was a young girl coming home from school. *Dirty* things in *public* places. His mother would never forgive him.

'This was another girl, Mum,' he said.

'Oh. Not Lucy?'

'No.'

'But you were . . .'

'No, I know. But this was a different girl.' He lifted a spoonful of soup but his mouth soured with self-loathing and he lowered it again.

'Do try to eat,' Rosalind said. She put some more cheese on his plate beside the untouched salad. 'It only makes things worse if you feel ill.'

Luke had always enjoyed thinking that his mother didn't know how ugly life was. What he liked to think was that for her life was all about Christmas and their birthdays and the garden and Sunday lunch, and that a timeless aspect of her was perpetually engaged in cutting up carrot sticks for him and his sister. But now he found himself faced with a dilemma. For the first time in his life he would have liked her adult advice – or, at least, her adult sympathy – because she must know something about love, mustn't she, even if she was that much older? But he saw that to ask this of her would involve the loss of an ideal, that he would have to bring her out of her Eden. Just then, with principles crushed like muddy cigarette ends wherever he looked, this seemed too great a price.

So, rather than tell her about Arianne, he spread butter on the walnut bread and ate plenty of green salad, like she said. He ate a bowl of strawberries and cream for pudding, like she said. With each mouthful, he felt he was taking in the peace of his mother, the sweet simplicity of his mother. He was not surprised he felt sleepy afterwards.

'What about a snooze, Luke? I'll wake you up at about four so you'll sleep tonight.'

'OK, Mum.' He stood up.

'Good. I think it's just what you need. Oh, no, darling – leave all that. I'll stick it in the dishwasher. You go on up and snooze for a while.'

Her word 'snooze', the vase of flowers she had put by his bed, the full stomach, the faint smell of her scent in every room of the house, the encapsulated story of his childhood . . . He lay in the foetal position in the little single bed and then he fell asleep.

It was his first uninterrupted hour of sleep since Arianne had left. He dreamt about his father being mugged. He dreamt the muggers had broken both his father's arms and legs and stripped him naked on the street. At first Luke felt devastated, vengeful. His face contracted with anger as he slept. But when the doctor told him that his father would need to be in hospital for a *very long time*, he felt oddly relieved. He felt lighter. It turned out that it was all for the best because, actually, he and his mother would live very happily in the house without his father. In fact, life would be altogether better without him. This was the conclusion of the dream.

When he woke up it was to the sound of his mother knocking on his door. Luke felt disgusted by his own imagination, by the violence he seemed to have wished on his own father. Rosalind sat on the end of his bed and looked down at her hands. She had changed her shirt for a dark blue linen one. She had done something to make her hair more bouncy.

'I'm going off to see Dad for a bit,' she said. 'I thought I might as well just go now. Then that's done, isn't it? Are you going to be OK, my darling?' she said.

'I'll be fine.'

'Will you have a nice bath? And I've left some tea-things out – those caramel biscuits you like.'

They had been a passion when he was about twelve. 'Thank you. You're amazing, Mum.'

'No. Not at all.' She tucked her hair behind her ears. 'Far from it. Well, I'd better go.'

'Dad is going to be all right, isn't he, Mum?'

'Oh, yes. Yes, of course. They said he can come home tomorrow,' she told him again.

'I just – I thought you might be trying not to worry me. You aren't just not saying how bad it is, are you?'

'No, no . . . It's just the kneecap and the bruising on the shin. Which is bad enough, of course. Poor old Dad.'

'Has he seen the police? I mean, obviously the police are involved.'

'Yes. Actually, they caught them – the two boys. Julian saw them run off and called the police in the nick of time.'

'He actually *saw* them? So this was right near the house?'

'I know. Awful to think of it, isn't it? Just down the road – beside Julian's car.'

'What did they want? Money? Money, of course.'

'I don't know, Luke. They didn't take anything,' she said.

'What? *Nothing?* You're not going to tell me *Julian* scared them off?' He imagined his spindly, myopic godfather getting every last bit of mileage out of this.

Rosalind smiled and shrugged at him, as if to imply that she understood his scepticism but that this was what had happened. In fact, she knew perfectly well that Julian had not scared them off. He had told Rosalind the two men were already running away when he came out

112

of the house. They had just *not taken anything*. Julian had said he thought it was rather odd, and didn't she?

'Look, I don't know much about it, darling. Dad hasn't wanted to talk about it yet,' she told Luke.

'Really? Has he not?'

Now nothing sounded right to him. His father was relentlessly logical – that legal mind of his would have sorted the facts from the impressions before he had even begun to feel the pain in his leg. ('That's not a coherent argument, Luke. It's all fuddled with *emotion*,' he heard his father tell him – as he had on so many occasions when Luke attempted to make conversation with him.) Instinctively, Luke thought that part of his father would simply enjoy an opportunity to show the nurses and the police what a great lawyer he was. This was how essentially weird Luke found Alistair. As a child, if ever he had cried, his father had been ready with a rational solution. This he would deliver in due course, when hysteria had subsided appropriately, with the full authority of his forensic detachment.

Luke felt Rosalind waiting for him to say something. He took in her anxious face. 'Well, when you think about it, Dad's actually really lucky,' he said. 'They must have been the worst thieves in London.'

'Yes, they must.'

Rosalind laughed, in obvious relief. Then she stood up and quickly started moving his clothes from the overnight bag into his empty chest of drawers. He watched her refolding the T-shirts and rolling up a pair of socks that had come undone. It was intensely reassuring to watch.

He had no idea then that she needed to do this just as much as he needed to watch it being done.

When she had finished, she said, 'Well, I suppose I should go. I won't stay all that long, but the traffic will be a nightmare. I imagine I'll be back at about six thirty. I'll be quicker if I possibly can.'

She leant down and kissed him, just as she used to when he was little and he pretended to be ill so as to get off school, so as to be kissed by his mother in just that way.

The velvet-textured silence of a car had always been a thinking space for Rosalind. She felt solitude wrapped around her, luxurious as a cashmere shawl. In a twenty-year period in which she had done more than her fair share of kissing goodbye at the airport, of loading shopping-bags into the boot of the car, of dropping Alistair off at King's Cross or Sophie at piano or Luke at rugby, she had learnt to value these moments of peace. First came the modern, high-tech thunk as the door closed, and then, suddenly, immunity.

After the shock of what had happened to Alistair, she wanted nothing more than to sit alone and think for a while, but the builders had been in repairing the conservatory roof and twice when she had been sitting on the steps with her coffee one of them had called out jarringly, 'Cheer up, love. Might never happen.'

Whether it was her sister or her friends or the builders, somehow there was always someone around wondering what she was thinking about, asking if she was all right, if she had a headache. She did not have a bloody headache!

Was Luke watching her from his window now? She started the car and moved off. Someone was always ringing the doorbell, selling something, delivering something. The world was not private enough. An image of the desert came into her mind: red sand blown gently into ripples. She had never seen a desert.

She indicated left and got on to the main road. And, again, she found she was thinking about their friend Julian on the night of the attack. He had insisted on staying with her in the hospital waiting room while Alistair was taken off to have his head X-rayed. Julian had handed her a ribbed plastic cup of scalding coffee. 'Ooops – I think I might have pocketed your change,' he said.

'What?'

'For the coffee. Your change.' After a lot of searching, he pulled twenty pence, bright and shining, out of his pocket and handed it to her. She looked at him as if he had handed her a watermelon.

Julian contracted his eyebrows. 'D'you know what I keep thinking? I keep thinking that it just is a bit strange, isn't it, Roz,' he said, 'that they *didn't try to take anything*? Not money, not his watch or his wallet or whatever. *Nothing.*' He was thinking of his daughter's mugging. They had taken her money, cards, earrings, her coat, her shoes.

Rosalind brought the cup to her lips. She did not drink.

'The police were very odd about it,' he told her. 'I mean crazy, really. They asked me if there was any reason anyone might be getting revenge on him.'

'*Revenge?*'

'I know. *Barmy.* They have to rule things out, I suppose.'

Well, it must be ruled out quickly, she thought. There was no place for this concept in their lives. The word gave off the same neon glare as the miniature envelope of white powder she had once found in

114

Sophie's old winter coat, as the times when Suzannah had turned up drunk on the doorstep and had to be rushed out of sight of the children. Worst of all, it gave off the same glare, the same deafening static, as the shocking magazine she had found in Luke's room when he was about fourteen.

In fact, Luke's 'livewire' friend, Ben, had bought the magazine for him as a birthday joke. Luke hadn't known what to do with it, how to dispose of the evidence, feeling afraid he would be judged not only by God but also by the dustmen, whom he had often seen looking meditatively into the bin lorry while the rubbish churned. So he hid it. In fact, Rosalind's had been the only eyes to look through it, taking in the spread legs, the clitoral close-ups, the crotchless knickers and peep-hole bras. She put it back carefully in his right ski boot and hurried back to the phone to say, sorry, Luke's boots were a size ten, so they'd be no good for her friend Charlotte's son Rory.

'Oh, God, Roz, I'm sure it's a standard question, really,' Julian had said, causing her to feel even more worried. 'It's just that it's the middle of the night. Everything feels *extraordinary* in the middle of the night, doesn't it? We all need to sleep.'

She nodded at him, with the flat-lipped smile of resignation people use to restore order to the face. 'Exactly,' she said. Then she took a sip of the coffee and felt consoled by the way it burnt her throat – like pouring boiling water on filthy ants in the kitchen.

'You do look tired, Roz.'

'Do I? Not surprising, I suppose.'

'Yes. What a stupid thing to say,' Julian said. 'I'm sorry. Why do people say that?' He was a self-absorbed man, who often picked himself up on tiny points of grammar or found a loose thread in his sweater with an overly dramatic expression of shame. It irritated her. There was something repulsively effeminate about it and she felt grateful for Alistair's occasional brusqueness with her, what she saw as his masculine impatience to get on with important work. She was glad she had never succumbed to the charm of all those love-letters Julian had written her a million years ago. He was certainly a loyal friend now, but it was a mystery to her that Elise put up with his endless puns and his frivolity and his nervous glances in the mirror.

She gazed at him and felt a wrench of guilt. When had she started finding people she loved so irritating?

Now she parked the car, feeling deeply confused. Why did she suspect her own husband of – what? *What*, exactly? – so easily? An

115

educated man, a successful man, an eminent barrister, she told herself. She thought of him quietly reading the biographies or histories he got for Christmas with a cup of coffee beside him. In a dislocated memory he glanced up and smiled as she passed through the room with a plant pot for the conservatory, and she smiled back, appreciating their life together. Children home for Easter, him reading, a lily waiting to be potted. This was trust.

But part of her had always known that Alistair's excellent legal mind told her the truth and nothing but the truth, but not the whole truth. What was more, she knew she had made way for his dishonesty in the first place. There were places in that mind of his that she watched him go to – as if he was visiting a long-term mistress whom she had come quietly to accept.

The nurse led her down the corridor to Alistair's room. His head swung round as she came in. He looked up at her – as if he had forgotten to lock the bathroom door, she thought. A book lay unread on the sheets beside him. 'Hello, darling,' he said. He leant forward so she could kiss him.

She chose the very top of his forehead. 'How's the leg doing?' she said.

They both looked at the plaster.

'Not bad at all. Really not bad. The painkillers are fantastic. Everyone's been marvellous.'

'We must write and thank the nurses,' she said.

'Yes, darling. You always have the right ideas.'

She was not really listening to him. He was staring at her sentimentally and it frightened her. Everything was beginning to frighten her. Her son had literally thrown himself on to her in the hallway at his flat – a drowning man.

What had happened in the air? It was like a curse, she thought – like a curse from ancient times: 'a blight on fathers and sons'. She said, 'The nurse said the police were in again.'

'Yes, that's true. Yes, they were,' he said. He was using the level voice designed for the less-educated members of the jury. For the first time she was aware that it was entirely inappropriate.

'*Why*, Alistair?'

'Why? Well, it's complicated.'

Alistair knew he had about thirty seconds of his former life left. He clung to them, blinking, feeling his heart beating, studying his poised wife.

Chapter 8

Just inside the entrance to the newer wing of the Old Bailey there is a line of policemen behind a long window of bulletproof glass. Beside them is an airport-style X-ray machine and a metal-detector security arch. After coming through the rotating doors, jury members, judges, reporters, barristers and solicitors, court clerks and QCs, canteen workers and expert witnesses must all pass through this second gateway under the weary scrutiny of the policemen's eyes.

No one is exempt from suspicion. Years of IRA trials mean the child with the pink rucksack, the spectacled lady with the embroidered shoulder-bag may very well be carrying the bomb. Each person is checked for guns, or explosives or knives or drugs. In the eyes of the police by the X-ray machine, there is a joyless knowledge, which comes of years of looking into strangers' bags.

At times it is a delicate procedure and, as the barristers come through, the policemen's faces carefully imply neither judgement nor suspicion. For their part, the barristers appear preoccupied with more ethereal concerns, submitting only their physical selves to this security check, with its faintly absurd implications; the younger ones are vague and intellectual, the older ones place their bags on the conveyor-belt with an air of sympathetic efficiency. These modes of detachment are all that preserve them from the amazing things people do every day. To a barrister, amazement is a professional hazard, a risk to the healthy legal mind, and it must be suppressed, along with fear and hate and despair. The Old Bailey is a building dedicated at every level to the punishment of instinct and the suppression of instinct, in the name of law and order.

Alistair and the junior barrister who was assisting him, Sandra Bachelor, and her pupil, Ryan Townsend, had been going through these twin entrances every day for two weeks now. The case of Regina v. Giorgiou was the kind of trial barristers hope to get – long and lucrative, genuinely interesting – and there was the not insignificant allure of seeing one's name in the papers. It was a kidnap trial, one that involved the only son of a wealthy Greek shipping family often photographed in *Hello!* magazine. Alexis Giorgiou was a handsome young man in his early thirties with a devastating gambling habit to feed.

Throughout the traumatic period of ransom demands, the police sat with Mr and Mrs Giorgiou, both of whom were predictably distraught about their son. Had it not been for the kidnappers' unguarded insistence that, in spite of his protests, Mr Giorgiou certainly could lay his hands on two million pounds in cash, because he need only 'flog that fucking Reardon sketch', there would have been no reason for them to suspect their own son's criminal involvement. But, as Mr Giorgiou said, his face visibly draining of blood while he loosened his cravat and groped like a blind man for his wife's hand, no one knew about this hidden treasure. The sketch was kept in a bank vault in Switzerland and the documents concerning it were in one of the files in a locked compartment in his dressing room, to which only his son and his wife had been given a key. To discover the existence of the sketch would have required a thorough and premeditated search by one or the other of them.

The police subsequently raided the kidnappers' address, which they had long ago traced, and discovered both the kidnappers and Alexis Giorgiou himself sharing a bottle of claret and playing five-card stud.

Alistair couldn't help being affected by Ryan Townsend's naïve excitement about the case. The boy sent text messages to his mother if there was a chance she might spot him on the London news. It was a different sort of excitement from that with which he had started his career. Ryan seemed modestly thrilled to be included: he watched the court proceedings as if they were a spectacular show to which he had won a ticket. Alistair had always been defensive and vain really; he had always brandished his ticket and focused his attention on the effect his career was having on his personality, his demeanour, his quest for self-improvement. Essentially, Ryan looked outwards while Alistair looked inwards and, like all introverts, Alistair perceived a moral sweetness in the extrovert's cheery smile.

Sandra Bachelor turned out to be extremely able. She was good and useful to work with and Alistair enjoyed debating points of law with her. But the real pleasure, as always for him, was the immense satisfaction of turning the lead weight of fifteen ring-binder files into the pure gold of an argument. When he was working, and he was almost always working, he thought in these terms: of lead and gold, right and wrong, guilty or not guilty. The expulsion of vagueness left him at peace.

Alistair loved his life as a barrister. The collegiate feel of the Inner Temple; the camaraderie of the barrister's robing room; the defiant fried eggs and cigarettes in the bar mess before court; the friendly teasing – '*Langford?* Good God – you still allowed in?'

It was a congenial atmosphere. He liked the lunches out with clever solicitors and grateful clients. He liked having drinks at El Vino, where women were still not allowed to order at the bar and men had to wear a tie. He enjoyed a good steak and a glass of claret at a restaurant on Fleet Street, often alone, with his papers spread out on the table in front of him. And it pleased him to use Latin phrases in his everyday work – who else could claim that privilege? *Prima facie, sui generis, mutates mutandes*: the words themselves carried the scent of old books and churches. They were old and trusted; they authenticated the user. To speak them in an argument was to hit the meeting-point between intellectual and sensual pleasure.

When dusk fell, Alistair could look out of the window of his room in chambers at the courtyard, which was much like an Oxford quad and still gas-lit at night. From there he could watch the eternal London rain as it fell indifferently both on the barristers' cars and on the barristers themselves, who were hurrying, always hurrying, with their red bags slung over their shoulders. It was good to watch, a familiar dance, and the steps had the dignity of centuries of English law.

To Alistair, what was old was safe – archaic phrases, traditions, buildings, laws . . . Like artefacts in a museum, what was old was protected by a thick cord over which the mob was not allowed to lean in too close.

But modernity crept in everywhere. Your mobile phone went off in your pocket and threw you off your speech. 'My pacemaker, my lord,' he had once wittily explained when this happened, much to the amusement of the courtroom. But he hadn't got into his stride again and felt he had lost the jury. He never forgave the flashy little machine. Even so, he had learnt how to use his email, when chambers set up work accounts for them all. But he had done it joylessly, with the aggressive thoroughness he had developed early in life to challenge his fear of change. Alistair was never easy on himself: he had always suspected he was prone to disproportionate fears.

Around his room were bookshelves crammed with mass upon mass of law reports, legal textbooks and piles of briefs tied with ribbon; dark pink was a defence, white was a prosecution. His desk was Victorian mahogany with an inlay of walnut and pieces of ivory. There was a carved lion's head at each corner: big, solid carvings – roaring lions.

Of course, it was not a working life without frustrations. He had not been made a Queen's Counsel or 'silk' until the relatively late age of fifty-two. Barristers waiting hopefully for silk are known as 'senior juniors', which has a ring of disappointment to it. It had always made Alistair picture trouser legs an inch too short.

Given his excellent record, he felt sure the delay had been caused by a letter he had written to *The Times* when he was buoyed up after an argument – or, rather, an extended and euphoric agreement – between himself and two colleagues at El Vino. The letter complained, in precisely the terms that had caused his colleagues to order a fourth bottle of burgundy in his honour, about the prevalence of prosecution-minded judges at the Old Bailey. What were we all to make, the letter asked, of judges repeatedly interrupting defence counsel, judges virtually cross-examining defence witnesses themselves, of judges whose theatrical summing-up to the jury cast *lurid* doubt over the defence case?

The issue had come to the front of his mind because he had just appeared in a murder trial before the most notable example of this species of judge. Alistair knew he had been stupid not to see that his words would be taken personally. He would always remember the thud of dismay when his clerk winked at him the next Monday morning and said, 'Susan showed us all your letter, sir. That'll put the wind up old Hanging Judge Simpson, won't it?'

Simpson was a fiercely insecure man who always smelt faintly of whisky. He was also a great friend of the Home Secretary, who was himself an ex-barrister, and of the newly appointed director of public prosecutions. It turned out that the three of them had been insepa-rable at Cambridge. The good cases Alistair's clerk had grown used to receiving for him simply dried up. This went on for five years and it took Alistair another three to regain his previous sure footing.

He regretted writing the letter because it had changed precisely nothing – and he had only sent it because he had been particularly pleased with the way it was phrased. He had liked the thought of colleagues reading it over their toast and marmalade on Sunday morning. And he had thought it would healthily banish any residual shame he felt about his speech at last year's Bar conference. He still suffered this shame because he had forgotten a whole section of what he had meant to say, even though he knew the points he had made were widely thought to be excellent.

Alistair's letter inspired a few articles about the issue and he had to endure the increasingly irksome mention of his name again and again in connection with it, along with the back thumps of colleagues whom he knew to feel he had acted rashly. 'Good for you,' they said, 'bloody well written letter.'

This was the darker side of the camaraderie: the potent sympathy for a colleague's failures.

Aside from the loss of earnings involved in missing out on good long trials, Alistair was forced to see many friends take silk before him. Each of them asked him to have a drink with them to celebrate. Sometimes there were dinners. He raised his glass and felt himself passed over.

But it finally happened – after a nine-year delay. At last came the ceremony at the House of Lords, where he was sworn in by the Lord Chancellor. Rosalind came along and looked very beautiful in a pale blue suit. He was aware that the picture his daughter Sophie took that afternoon had caught in one moment the satisfaction of nearly all his ambitions. How many people could say they had as much?

He went to the House of Lords loo and had to suppress nervous laughter as he stood at the urinal. Did anyone ever lose the sense of having sneaked in uninvited? He straightened his shirt and reminded himself that he had earned his invitation to this place fair and square. It was a satisfying thought, although, by implication, it threw out a net of uncertainty over the rest of his life. He went out again brightly and knocked back his glass of champagne.

And now the defining photograph of that day sat on his desk, beside one of Rosalind on a boat in Crete and one of Luke and Sophie in their ski-clothes aged around fourteen and sixteen. Alistair found he looked at these photographs to remind himself of himself – just as Luke did when he stared into his fridge. The comparison would not have rung true to Alistair, though: he thought himself irrevocably unlike his athletic and mildly dyslexic son. He was also of the opinion that this kind of thinking was, philosophically speaking, meaningless, and so he was surprised by how often he did it. He did not like the implication that he was somehow separate from his own mind, that in some sense it ran on without him. This sounded chaotic, risky – and, of course, philosophically meaningless. Who exactly was making this implication, after all? The question made him feel tired. It sent him over to the shelves for a volume of *Blackstone's*, thick and leatherbound and heavy in the hand.

In the House of Lords photograph, Rosalind was holding down her pale blue hat in the breeze and Alistair had noticed recently that there was a single bird in the fragment of sky above her head.

The satisfaction of nearly all my ambitions, he thought . . .

What was left? He had been a QC now for eleven years. He had been offered the chance to become a judge but had felt he would miss the life of a barrister and that judicial solitude would not suit him.

He was a popular man at the Bar, well respected, and even though he liked to eat alone sometimes, he was just as likely to ask colleagues along or to hear a genial knock at his door on the days he worked in chambers. It was agreeable to be among so many like-minds. It was reminiscent of his Oxford days, only he knew how to talk now: he had all the right accessories.

Seeing his clothes, his house in Holland Park, his impeccable wife, his children, no one would have suspected that he had grown up in a shabby boarding-house and that he did not know who his father was. Alistair had a silk bag for his wig and gown, just like everyone else.

Ian, his clerk, had made quite a show of the kidnap case. 'This'll have you in the papers,' he said, when he handed over the brief and the first box of ring binders. And Alistair had soon thought it was possible Ian was right, though one never knew what would seize press attention. At any rate, it was an interesting case. The Crown Prosecution Service had sent it to him at the express request of the junior barrister in the case, a woman named Sandra Bachelor, who had particularly wanted Alistair to lead her. He had never met her before. It was always a pleasure to meet new barristers, particularly when they had paid you this professional compliment.

She was in her mid-thirties with frizzy brown hair and acne scars on her cheeks. Sandra's intelligence made her stutter, as if she was hurriedly bailing out her observations for fear of drowning in them. Sometimes she blinked too hard in the frenzy and dislodged a contact lens – she carried spares for this eventuality. Her pupil, Ryan, was twenty-four and had just finished his law conversion course, having done his first degree in history at Edinburgh University. He did not speak very fluently and Alistair suspected he would not be offered a tenancy at Sandra's chambers. It was so competitive, these days. Perhaps there would be a backstage career for him in the Crown Prosecution Service.

He was an extremely handsome boy with light brown hair and a pale, smooth complexion. He used the word 'fascinating' a great deal, which made Alistair and Sandra smile and avoid each other's eyes for fear of laughing when he did. It was good to be around his excitement. And it was good to be around his beauty, even if it did heighten Alistair's sense of sexual invisibility when he saw how women stared at Ryan. It was so frank – the desire. He had been looked at like that once.

They had prepared the case, with numerous conferences, over a period of many weeks. When it came to court, they soon found themselves entrenched, and it was obvious that this case, in all its complexity, would take precedence over all other commitments.

Court thirteen at the Old Bailey became entirely familiar. It is one of the modern courts, with strip-lighting and the barren smell of a new car, which never leaves it. Every day, between ten thirty a.m. and one p.m. and, after a break for 'the short adjournment' – known to ordinary people as lunch – followed by the afternoon session, they sat in this room. The defendant looked broad-shouldered and almost obscenely fit when compared to his diminutive barrister, Randall Schaeffer.

Randall had been a contemporary of Alistair at Oxford, two years above. He had always been thin but now he was hunched as well. And he seemed to have developed a squint. It shocked Alistair to observe the sudden ageing of his friends. Not just furrowed brows or grey hair but painful limps, actual loss of height. You saw people you hadn't bumped into for a year and they appeared to have shrunk inside their clothes. This would happen to him, of course. Soon enough.

He had begun to avoid looking into mirrors a few years before. Between twenty and thirty he had barely changed: youth had grown on trees. Between thirty and forty he had noticed only a slight decline – usually on holidays, when he levered himself out of a swimming-pool, uniquely aware of himself as a picture, as film footage, the water running down his brown back, the strong, male legs flipped up on to the side of the pool. But between forty and sixty-three the changes had been quick and violent. His hair grew thin and its texture had altered, becoming coarser and less orderly. It was as if it had evolved, like grass and bracken, to prolonged rough exposure. His back- and shoulder-ache suggested he had been on a long journey, carrying heavy bags. He woke in the night to urinate two or three times and invariably a little fragment of a sad and embarrassing conversation would lodge in his mind as he stood before the loo. His old friend Henry had leant towards him – on the *tube* of all places! – and whispered with quiet agony, 'My equipment's just *stopped working*, Al. I'm no use to Katherine at all. *No use at all.*' Henry slapped his newspaper against his leg.

Alistair read Pascal, Montaigne to lift himself out of these bodily concerns. But being fifty-eight made him feel *bodily*, made him feel lecherous in a way he never had before. He looked at young women – and, very secretly, at young men – and desire was a kind of envy, a longing for the suppleness of youth.

They passed through the metal detector and turned right for the lifts up to the Bar mess and the barristers' robing room. As they walked through the doors, there was a smell of eggs and bacon, which drifted down the stairs from the kitchen.

They went into the mess for coffee and to have a brief discussion of the case. The canteen tables were already unevenly strewn with newspapers and plates and along them sat barristers, already in their wigs and gowns, drinking coffee and smoking and hurriedly writing speeches.

'Morning, Langford,' said Richard Evans. He was at the head of the short queue, just paying for a few pieces of fruit and a yoghurt. He was one of those who had kept himself in good shape; he always had a rather suspicious-looking tan.

Alistair smiled and nodded. 'Evans.' Many of the older barristers still addressed one another by their surnames, as they had at boarding-school. Of course, Alistair had never been to boarding-school, but this detail was long hidden.

Evans said, 'Not seen you about for a while. You've got a goodie, haven't you? How's it coming on? Something of an Athenian playboy, I'm told.'

'Defendant? Yes, he is. I'm against, actually – he's Schaeffer's chap.

124

Not going too badly, thanks. Cross-examining the girlfriend this afternoon, if all goes to plan.'

'Really? Blonde and gorgeous, no doubt. Playboy bunny!' Evans chortled lustily and Sandra Bachelor sent some oranges bouncing out on to the floor.

She chased after them and put them back into their basket, saying, 'Oops. Clumsy clogs. Sorry,' and blushing deep red.

He beamed and approached with his hand held out. He was immaculate with women. 'I don't think we've met,' he said, 'Richard Evans.'

'How d'you do? I'm Sandra Bachelor.' Her whole arm jolted as he shook her hand. 'And this is my pupil, Ryan Townsend,' she told him.

'I'm her pupil,' Ryan repeated, still feeling the need to justify his presence in these rarefied surroundings. He recognized Richard Evans because he had seen him speak at the Law Society dinner. It had been a fascinating speech about legal reform. These older male barristers seemed to Ryan to have a priestly, incense-scented gravitas. He stumbled towards it urgently, terrified that he might just drift, playing 'Dragonman 4' all day as he had done before he decided to do the law course.

'Well,' Evans said, 'I'd better get mobilized. I'm up for drug-smuggling in court nine. *Would* you believe it? I had *five kilos* of raw cocaine in a car boot full of children's teddies.'

'*Did* you now?' said Alistair.

'And I've got *absolutely no idea* how it all got there.'

'*Extraordinary.*'

They went on in their superior sing-song (this rather inhuman game was another mode of detachment, another strategy for survival) while Richard Evans straightened his gown and Alistair paid for his breakfast.

'Yeeees. No idea at all . . .' Richard Evans sighed, shaking his head. He pulled the thick pile of papers into his chest and turned towards the stairs. 'He's going to go whistling down, I'm afraid. Not a lot I can do for him.'

They exchanged a wry smile.

Alistair said, 'Are you going to be at Philip's retirement dinner next Thursday?'

'Yes. You?'

'I shall see you there.'

'Good, good.' Richard nodded to Ryan and half bowed formally to Sandra Bachelor. He took pride in being particularly courtly to plain women.

When they had eaten breakfast and finished discussing the strategy Alistair would employ in his questioning of the arresting police officer, Inspector Radley, they heard their case being called over the Tannoy: 'Would all parties in *Giorgiou* please come to court thirteen immediately? All parties in *Giorgiou*.'

By the time of the short adjournment it seemed it was going to be an uneventful day. Sandra popped out to get some things from the chemist, Ryan read a novel about a hotshot American attorney and Alistair ate his shepherd's pie in silence while flicking through the newspapers. He noticed there was a new biography of Gladstone, which had got very good reviews, and thought he might like to buy it.

After this, the early part of the afternoon was devoted to a series of expert witnesses. Professor Aitken and Dr Ellis offered their respective analyses of voice recordings and various medical details, such as the curious absence of chafe-marks on Giorgiou's wrists, which had allegedly been bound for seven days.

After a great many technical details, it was obvious the jury was flagging and the judge thought it wise to allow a little recovery time. He suggested a short break. The court would sit again at three forty-five.

And so, after their respective sandwiches and bars of chocolate and telephone calls and quick trips to the loo, the human components of the courtroom shuffled back into place for the last session of the afternoon. The solicitors, who had ventured out of the Old Bailey at lunch for a large curry, sat behind the barristers in a sleepy gang. Along the benches at the side of the room were the twelve members of the jury in their various shapes and sizes. At the head of the room was the raised dais from which the judge presided. One level beneath it were the court clerk, an obese woman with a florid, sceptical face, and the inspired-looking figure of the court stenographer, permanently bent over his keys.

After everyone had settled down, then risen for Judge Morton and settled again, an atmosphere of anticipation grew and spread around the room.

In terms of entertainment, it had been a bleak day. Inspector Radley, the arresting police officer, had proved to be a man with no exceptional features, either physical or behavioural. He had mousy-coloured hair, a bland, even face and a level, bureaucratic voice. As he gave his account of the conditions in which he and his fellow police officers had discovered Alexis Giorgiou, several members of the jury struggled to stay awake or found themselves wondering what the life of such a colourless person might be like. Did he have a lonely boiled egg for breakfast? Did he have a cat? Did he go for walks on his own in the park?

Neither of the expert witnesses was cause for celebration either. They had the generic brutally scrubbed look of scientists, and their evidence was soon reminiscent of interminable physics lessons at school.

Even without this day-long drought, though, the arrival of Karen Jennings would have been an event. Inappropriate as it was, the jury members were in awe of Alexis Giorgiou, who looked, as the foreman himself had conceded, 'like a genuine celebrity'. Everyone wondered what the girlfriend of this proud, muscular, TV-looking Greek would be like.

Not one of them had got it right. She was not tall and elegant; she was not posh; she was not spoilt and sulky. She was a miniature mousy blonde with a cartoonishly erotic figure and a permanent smirk on her lips.

As the usher brought her in, Karen Jennings peered about her, seeming unable to contain her amusement. She had the appearance of a giggling schoolgirl brought before the headmaster and her small, plump, playfully mocking presence worked a friendly kind of magic on the room. She made tired people smile, men and women alike. Sandra Bachelor, who was one of these, decided immediately that Karen was the sort of girl who would ask for a lick of your ice-cream and that no one on earth would refuse it. There was something innocent about her sexiness because, even though her curves were almost a parody of the female form, she appeared to take an uncomplicated pleasure in her body, enjoying her youth and her health as much as her power to seduce. In essence, she appeared to be having a good time – an adventure, a laugh, and at no great expense to anyone.

Karen was, in fact, less than five foot three, but she carried herself with a defiant sensuality. This attitude gave her more stature than she actually had, and although it did not make her intimidating, it did make her impossible to ignore. Sandra Bachelor noticed, with a faint envy (because her tall, thin body never had and never would have this effect), that some of the male members of the jury were rapt. In particular, she watched the tattooed, stubbly man in the back row whisper to the spectacled man beside him. They were unlikely friends, but at the sight of this potent dose of femininity, they both grinned the same grin.

Karen was wearing a partially transparent white cotton blouse and a breathtakingly tight dark blue skirt. The heels on her shoes were so high and narrow that it was a kind of miracle she could walk at all. Her clothes seemed to have been designed to inhibit her but, as if this was all part of a wicked double bluff, they served only to emphasize the fluid action of her waist and her hips.

As soon as she had taken her oath, which she punctuated with curious little glances about the room, Randall Schaeffer cleared his throat and began: 'Are you Miss Karen Jennings of Flat 234, River Court, Balham?'

Karen drew a long breath, then giggled with relief. 'Well, this one's easy at least,' she said.

A few of the jury members smiled in identification with her; they sympathized with her all-too-human nervousness and her all-too-ordinary London accent. This was a girl who ate fish and chips with her brothers and sisters, whose dad watched the football with a can in his fist. She was not like the rich Giorgious, or the sneering barristers. Karen had immediately generated an atmosphere of us-and-them: overworked, dry, stuck-up lawyers versus young, plump, smiling girls. She pressed her hand to her chest to calm her nerves and even the female members of the jury were visibly charmed.

Sandra Bachelor did not believe in Karen's nerves for a second. She looked forward to hearing Alistair's cross-examination and hoped Randall would not draw out the defence questions for too long.

Thankfully, Randall obliged and it was soon Alistair's turn. He rose to his feet and, as was his habit, flipped pages for a few seconds, to establish an air of imperturbable purpose. Then, in a firm voice, which suggested he had not in fact noticed the exaggerated breasts, or the wild arc of the hips or the frank outline of the knickers in the dark blue skirt, he said, 'Miss Jennings, am I right in thinking that you and the defendant have been conducting a relationship for some eighteen months now?'

Karen nodded and shrugged.

'Please just answer yes or no, Miss Jennings,' said the judge.

'Sorry. Yes, then. We have been,' she lowered her voice and frowned portentously, '"*conducting a relationship*" for eighteen months odd. Just to be certain, the way I can remember is because it was since I went darker blonde so, yes, that's about right.' She wrinkled up her nose at her own silliness.

'I see,' Alistair said. 'And am I right in thinking that you were in the habit of meeting Mr Giorgiou at Buzzy's Restaurant and Casino in Piccadilly every Friday evening?'

Karen seemed oddly flattered and puzzled by the emergence of this personal detail. 'Yes,' she said, 'you are.'

'And am I right in thinking that *after* dinner, you invariably went on to the casino downstairs at which Mr Giorgiou would gamble?'

'Well, you don't really need *me*, do you?'

There were a few titters from the jury. Sandra noticed how Karen's eyes discreetly checked the arrangement of her breasts in the tight blouse; she also noticed that Alistair was having trouble with his wig. He kept adjusting it at the back of his neck in a rather irritating and visually distracting way. It was slightly mystifying, but he gave the impression of being embarrassed. It was a boyish embarrassment – a genuine, if inexplicable agony. He had the look of a teenage boy enduring the last throes of a TV sex scene on the sofa beside his parents.

'Please just answer the question, Miss Jennings,' said the judge again.

'Sorry,' she said. '*Yes.*'

Alistair went on, 'Miss Jennings, would you say that Mr Giorgiou was a reliable man?'

'Are you *kidding*?'

'I'll rephrase that,' he said. 'Would you say that Mr Giorgiou was a *punctual* man?'

'Well, depends if there's gambling or sex, doesn't it? Like all men. If there's blackjack or poker or a bit of something he wants, he's there like clockwork.'

'I see. And would I be correct in stating that on Friday the fifth of January you went, as usual, to Buzzy's Restaurant and Casino, expecting to have dinner with him?'

'Yes,' she said. 'You would be correct.'

'You expected to have dinner together and then to go through to the casino, to gamble, as usual?'

'Yes,' she said. Then she smiled because this evasion seemed absurd to her. She stage-whispered, 'To gamble, *then to have sex.*'

'Yes, I see. But on that evening Mr Giorgiou didn't arrive, did he?'

'No, he didn't.'

'And you waited for him for several hours? Is that right? Until the restaurant closed?'

129

'Yes.'

'Why did you wait so long?'

Karen laughed incredulously. 'Do I *look* like the sort of girl who's used to being *stood up*? I kept on thinking he'd turn up any minute with a bunch of flowers,' she said.

Sandra Bachelor glanced at the jury, who seemed to be watching a tennis match. She was beginning to feel concerned that, in the atmosphere of hilarity, they would not appreciate the significance of Alistair's questions. To continue as he was, in a stern voice, might only add to the comic effect of Karen's performance, but she appreciated he had little choice. The depth of his embarrassment now amazed her and she stared at the small figure on the witness stand and wondered what it would be like to have this rather shaming effect on a man.

'Ah. Yes, I see,' Alistair said sternly. 'So you were extremely *surprised* that he didn't turn up. Would that be a fair description?'

'A polite description. Yes.'

'You were surprised because, as you say, he's punctual if there's gambling involved and because, *naturally*,' he bowed his head, because he could ham-act for the jury, too, 'you aren't the type of girl who is accustomed to being *stood up*?'

'You got it,' she said, raising an eyebrow.

'But eventually you went home.'

'Well, yes. There are limits, aren't there?'

Again the jury tittered collectively. It struck Alistair that they were about as intimidating to a potential perjurer as cooing barn owls. In all his years as a barrister, he had rarely seen anyone so unfazed as Karen by the solemnity of the courtroom. He had seen plenty of angry defiance, from etiolated car thieves or swarthy pimps, but all of these had suggested at the very least an acknowledgement, an aggrieved reverence, for the authority of the court. Karen, on the other hand, was simply unable to keep a straight face. She was a genuinely anarchic figure – and he couldn't help finding this acutely exciting. He felt his face going red and wondered if it would be noticed. The thought was appalling.

He went on, still more severely, 'And the following Thursday, that's Thursday the twelfth of February, *again* you went back to Buzzy's Restaurant and *again* you waited for Mr Giorgiou for several hours?'

'Yes. And I don't mind telling you, I was *not* a happy bunny,' she said, pouting slightly.

Alistair felt his face flush redder still and was suddenly afraid that he would actually make a fool of himself in front of a judge and jury if he could not keep better control of his demeanour. This had never happened before. He rested his hand casually on the table in front of him. 'No, I can imagine you weren't,' he said, playing along. 'But, none the less, again you waited, and . . .' he made a tumbling motion with his hand and pushed out his lips to imply their easy understanding '. . . and again, all the while, you imagined that Mr Giorgiou might suddenly turn up because it was unlike him to miss an evening's gambling or to stand up a girl like you.'

'Exactly,' she said, visibly impatient.

'I see. And did you receive any kind of explanation from him about why he had not turned up?'

'Explanation? Well – no.'

'*No?*' Now he felt himself regaining control – the first foothold.

She looked at him as if he was an idiot. 'How could I? He was *locked up?*'

'Ah, yes, *of course,*' Alistair said, all but slapping his forehead. 'I wonder then how you *explained* this to yourself – I mean, the fact that he didn't call. How did you account for this, Miss Jennings?'

For a moment, she looked almost startled. Then her eyes seemed to catch sight of something in the far corner of the room and she said, 'Thought he was playing hard to get.'

'Oh, I *see*. But he had never behaved in that way before, had he? You described him as – what was it? – "like clockwork" if there was . . . *gambling* involved.'

'Look, I do it to him all the time. You play hard to get and then they appreciate it when you give them what they want,' she said. 'Does a man no harm at all. He could've been giving me a taste of it. Why not? That's what I thought.'

'Indeed,' Alistair said. 'You sound, Miss Jennings, like something of an expert on the male ego.'

She giggled and wrinkled up her nose at him. 'Ooh, is that what *barristers* call it, then?'

His only option was to press on, deaf to the laughter (to which even the judge seemed prone) and simply to ignore her asides. Again he consulted the ring binder, in a bid to return the jury's focus to the facts. 'Surely, though, Miss Jennings,' he said, 'in your – well, in your *expert* opinion, there must be more effective ways of "playing hard to get" than sitting in a restaurant until closing time *twice in a row*. Aren't there?'

She raised an eyebrow. 'Yes, but he wasn't to know, was he?'

'Ah, no – of course. Of course he couldn't have done. Forgive me – I'm simply trying to put it all together. Perhaps you would further assist me, then, by describing what was going through your mind, Miss Jennings.'

'What? In the restaurant?'

'Yes – I mean what with waiters coming and going. It's a well-known restaurant, after all. People must have been served mouth-watering food to the left and right of you. You must have been terribly hungry . . . and yet it would appear that you didn't order anything.'

She snorted and tossed back her hair. 'I'm not paying a hundred quid for my dinner, am I? What do you take me for?'

'No. Quite. But you said you expected Mr Giorgiou to turn up at any moment with a bunch of flowers. Would he have begrudged you a starter?'

'Look, Lexi's the kind of man who orders for you,' she said. 'That's the kind of man I like.'

The insolence was astonishing, he thought. He imagined her in red stockings, laughing at him, in a see-through black négligée, not letting him come near. He looked forward to seeing his wife.

'Ah. Yes, I see. But, as I say, I'm curious about what you were *thinking* at the time, Miss Jennings. I mean to say, did it perhaps occur to you that your boyfriend might have had an *accident*?'

'I don't know. Maybe. It probably crossed my mind.'

'I can imagine. He might, after all, have had a car crash or broken a leg – who was to know? Certainly not you. And, let's face it, you were waiting, with no occupation, for *over three hours*. Even the steadiest mind would run riot under such conditions.'

He glanced up at her, but she made no response. She was plainly not going to speak unless she was asked a question. It astonished Sandra to see that Karen looked intrigued, rather than nervous – as if she viewed her cross-examination as a flirtatious game and was interested to know who might win. Sandra wished she could stop Alistair's constant fiddling with his wig: he was plainly unaware that he was doing it and it gave a dreadful impression of nerves, which surely couldn't be genuine, given his experience, she thought. Perhaps he was feeling unwell, she told herself. The redness of his face might simply have been caused by a fever. That was probably it, she thought, but still she felt somewhat let down by this eminent QC whom she had so longed to work beside.

132

He went on, 'Did it perhaps also cross your mind that your boyfriend might be *ill*?'

Karen shrugged and sighed. 'Did I think he might be ill? Oh, I guess so. I can't really remember, to be honest, but it probably did, yes.'

'Of course. You must have been very worried. So there you sat, thinking all these unpleasant things,' he circled his hand to add a falsely reassuring breadth to his point, 'and yet, Miss Jennings, it did not occur to you simply to call his mobile phone and find out where he was.'

He registered the changed expression on her face. It brought him the usual quietly violent satisfaction. He then consulted a record (which in fact he had mislaid on the large desk and was now representing with a sheet of blank paper visible to none but himself) and continued, 'It seems you made no telephone call either to him, or to any of his friends, or indeed to any member of his family, on *either* evening or at *any point* between the fifth and the seventeenth of February, when your boyfriend was discovered by the police.'

He made eye-contact and removed his glasses.

'Miss Jennings, can it be true that you made *no attempt* to visit or to contact Mr Giorgiou, your *boyfriend*, in *any* way, for almost two weeks, during which time he stood you up, without explanation, *twice*? Is that correct?'

She stared at him. A flicker of pleasure passed over her lips and she smoothed down her clothes as if it might literally have disturbed them.

Alistair said, 'You see, all of the telephone numbers that attempted to contact his mobile phone during that time have been accounted for.' He turned to the judge. 'I refer, my lord, to exhibit eight, the telephone records. Usher, please hand a copy to the witness.'

He waited for her to cast her eyes over the first few pages and then he continued, 'As I say, Miss Jennings, none of his close friends recall having heard from you by any means. Nor do any of his family. And it's plain that you did not call him *directly*, and yet records from the last eighteen months show us that, even under *ordinary* circumstances, you were in the habit of calling your boyfriend, *on his mobile phone*, up to two or three times a week.'

She laughed. 'Oh, you keep saying "*your boyfriend*" like that. Like my mum. So I called him sometimes. Sometimes I didn't. So what? You don't really seem to get it. I don't have rules. It's not like we're serious or whatever. With me and Lexi it's a *casual* thing, yeah? You know.' She pouted indifferently and leant very slightly forward as if she was sharing a deep secret with him alone. 'It's *sexual*,' she said.

133

To the rest of the courtroom, Alistair then appeared to make a note on the pad in front of him. It was, in reality, merely a wiggly line. 'Yes,' he said. Then he repeated to himself: 'Yes.'

And when he raised his face, she said, 'Yes,' in return, and smiled conclusively.

(This little exchange of yeses was vibrantly parodied by the jury members in the canteen the next day.)

Alistair straightened his waistcoat. Then he straightened his wig, and his gown, and then he rearranged his feet on the carpet. He frowned for a moment and cleared his throat. 'Am I right in saying that the next time you heard from Alexis Giorgiou was when *he* called *you* from the police station on the seventeenth?'

'You are.'

'But he was allowed only *two* telephone calls, Miss Jennings. Were you not extremely surprised that he chose to ring you – given you aren't in a "*serious*" relationship, given *you* didn't try to call *him* once, in two weeks, during which, after all, you had an unlimited number of telephone calls at *your* disposal?'

Karen gave him a level stare and he felt a deep thrill at the direct eye-contact. She was certainly not beautiful – she was vulgar-looking, really, but then her effect on him was not exactly sexual. At any rate, it was not sexual in any recognizable sense. There was sweat on his forehead, his cheeks were burning, his clothes felt fundamentally *wrong*.

Again, she gave her shrug. 'Well, *who knows*? Maybe he missed me more than I missed him. Is that possible, Mr Langford?'

In spite of her mockery, there was no escape from the net he had created. It had been a successful cross-examination. But now that he had reached its crescendo and was able to put it to her directly that she had known all about the kidnap and was merely attempting to provide Giorgiou with a cover, he found that the usual predatory fulfilment was missing. She denied all prior knowledge of the kidnap outright, of course, but the jury was plainly alerted and he put no further questions. As he sat down, he felt a peculiar, almost a devastating sense of anticlimax.

He had caught the defence witness in a lie but, what with his red cheeks and his crazy waistcoat-straightening and the intolerable itchiness of his wig (which he now removed so as to scratch his head all over in luxurious surrender), he was the one who felt shown up.

He could not blame Karen. She had done her insolent best to devalue his questions, certainly, but he felt sure that she had no more idea of her anarchic power over his body than spring itself. This was a peculiarly sentimental thought and he hurried it away with his papers and highlighter pens.

Sandra Bachelor, Ryan and Alistair took the lift back up to the Bar mess and the robing rooms without looking at one another. There was an obvious awkwardness in the air and Sandra said something banal about it being a late sitting, with which Ryan enthusiastically agreed, as he did with everything she said. It was becoming increasingly plain to Alistair that Sandra had noticed how flustered he had been and that she did not know what to say. Her comment on his cross-examination was conspicuously absent. Thankfully, Ryan was robustly oblivious. And, better still, it was the weekend and there would be no need to call Karen again as a witness.

In the silks' robing room, where his locker was, Alistair was accosted by an old friend, and by the time he came out, carrying his coat and his various bags, the hallway was teeming. As always on a Friday night, the Bar-mess area contained an end-of-term excitement that spilled down the stairs and into the hall. Sandra stood by the stairs, hurriedly reloading files into a bag whose handle had torn. Ryan was waiting beside her. 'Oh, *wretched* thing,' he heard her say. 'I really *must* get a new one.' Then she turned and smiled at Alistair – who was now obliged to exchange a few non-professional words with them. He went over to join them.

Sandra was saying, 'Are you going anywhere nice this weekend, Ryan?'

Alistair had noted all her attempts to make the boy relax.

'Well, it's my sister's twenty-first tonight. We're all going clubbing,' Ryan told her.

'I've always thought,' said Alistair, 'that particular activity sounds like the most awful blood sport.' He grinned at Sandra.

Ryan looked embarrassed. 'Oh, yeah. God, I suppose it does, doesn't it?'

'Will there be lots of you?' Sandra persisted – and immediately Alistair regretted his stupid joke.

'Tonight? About fourteen. Hopefully lots of my sister's pretty friends.' Ryan grinned, his habit of self-effacement giving way for the first time to a youthful ego. His face was beautiful, the eyes were a rich brown and there was a natural flush of health in his cheeks. Alistair studied it longingly, hungrily.

135

Sandra giggled. '*Goodness me*. Sounds like they'd better watch out.'

'Yeah, maybe. How about you? Are you doing anything fun, Sandra?'

She folded her gown and laid it on top of the files, looking pleased to have been asked. 'Yes, I am, as it happens. I'm going out for dinner with a very nice young man.'

'Are you? Maybe *he*'d better watch out,' Ryan ventured, smiling nervously.

'Yes. Actually, Ryan, I think he probably had.'

Was no one going to ask him what *he* was doing, Alistair thought. *Old people's* things, it was assumed. Something slightly embarrassing, something *poignant*. He noted the new camaraderie between the young and fertile as they put on their coats, smiling like conspirators.

Alistair had never been fooled by the sense, which had threatened to plague his twenties and thirties, that there was a great carnival called 'happiness' going on, just one street away, and that he was the only one not invited. He had always known that this was a message from the false heart to the long-suffering will. It was designed to tempt you away from your purpose. The only solution was to use your will to spite your heart into submission; to shut that damned heart up once and for all. And he had done exactly this, working on in his study when there really was no need, no hurry, listening to the family sounds of Christmas through the floorboards or the tap-tap of croquet on the lawn in the summer. He could relish his imprisonment in his own ambitions, ritualizing it like an act of obedient prayer. There was much to be thankful for, after all: he might have had a very different sort of life.

And when happiness came, it was nothing like a carnival, of course. It had simply always been there, waiting quietly to be recognized and he would catch it in the corner of his eye. There it had been while he looked through the windscreen at the approaching view of sunny French vineyards and golden hills, his arm resting outside the open window, Rosalind beside him and the two children singing in the back. These had been moments of fulfilled egotism, essentially, when the world had seemed to show them themselves – their youth, their hope, their fertility. It had been enough to make you believe God was a great artist.

Alistair set down his bags and put on his coat because it was a nuisance to carry. It was too heavy over his suit. He felt encumbered, stifled. He wondered if he had ever appreciated how valuable, how *perishable* the sensation of approaching those hills really was.

136

God the great artist, Alistair thought, with His devastating sense of proportion.

He said goodbye to the other two and to a few loitering colleagues as he made his way into the lifts and back through the rotating doors. When he walked out, it was dusk, a melancholy London early evening, with a faint metallic taste in the air like dust from the silver grey sky. There were lights on in the pubs along Old Bailey and Fleet Street – the Magpie and Stump, the Old Bell, the Tipperary, Ye Olde Cock Tavern. They implied festivity, leisure, the bachelor's freedom to hang around after work.

Suddenly he felt reluctant to go home. The thought of having supper with Rosalind made him lonely and sad. Then he remembered that Anne and David Nicholson and the Grants were coming for dinner. Peter Grant had a new wife in her mid-thirties. It was all rather uncomfortable – Erica was devastated and there were torn loyalties. The women were appalled, threatened. Alistair wondered how Peter had the energy – or the inclination – to begin a marriage and a family all over again in his fifties. It required such faith, such optimism.

He turned into Hare Place, an alleyway that led from Fleet Street, near the Royal Courts of Justice, into Mitre Court and onwards into the Inner Temple. Then he heard a voice say, 'Hello, there,' and he looked up to see the unmistakable figure of Karen Jennings coming towards him. He couldn't think what she was doing there.

In fact, Karen had left her bags at Randall Schaeffer's chambers that morning and had returned for them after court. He nodded as he passed her. 'Good evening.'

She giggled behind him. '*Very friendly*,' she called. 'Nice chatting to you.'

He stopped and turned around. 'Forgive me. I – it's not allowed. We can't speak outside the courtroom, I'm afraid.'

She wrinkled her nose mischievously – as if he had suggested she ought not to have a second helping of pudding. '*Oh*. Why not?'

'It's not ethical if you're involved in a case. Those are the rules. I'm sorry – it's nothing personal.' He wondered why on earth she would want to talk to him anyway. He must leave immediately.

She walked a few steps towards him, widening her laughing eyes, 'But no one can *see*, can they?' she said.

He felt painfully self-conscious. Of course he must seem absurd to her. He was also aware that at any moment a colleague might come round the corner and discover him talking to a witness. Again he told himself he must go back to chambers *immediately*.

And yet he stood still.

She chewed her gum for a few seconds, 'D'you want to come for a drink?'

'A *drink*? I can't. It really isn't allowed.'

At the end of the alleyway, behind her, he could see the cars moving slowly, unreal. In the flat light they were like a film of London traffic projected onto a screen. It was the indistinct time of the evening, when the quality of the light and the subtle muffling of city noise could have belonged just as easily to the early morning. He stood there for a moment, lost. Karen kicked her tiny high-heeled shoe against the cobblestones with a sudden, sharp movement and he felt himself wake up. This was a busy passageway and anyone might walk down it at any minute. He said briskly, 'Well, I should be going. Good evening.'

'Oh, come on. Are you sure? What about if we went somewhere no one could *see* us? Then would it be all right?'

'No, it's really not possible. It's not ethical. One can't be seen to be conversing—'

She smiled and interrupted him, 'Yes, I know. You said. But if we weren't *seen*—'

He glanced behind him, having imagined he heard footsteps. Why did he not leave immediately? He really must leave immediately.

Karen chewed her gum and opened her handbag. He watched her, with stunned curiosity, as she brought out a pot of lip balm, put her little finger into it and smoothed it over her lips. He could smell . . . what was it? Artificial strawberries. It reminded him of his daughter Sophie and her friends, an indistinct tumble of girls coming out of the steamy bathroom with towels on their heads, trying not to giggle in their face packs. Fourteen years old and synthetic-fruit scented. He missed his daughter with a kind of physical hunger. It was a father's hunger for that blonde-haired, green-eyed benediction she used to give him when she threw her girl's arms round his neck.

'I just thought it would be nice to have a drink with you,' Karen said. 'That's all.'

'With me? I mean – *why*?'

She laughed and shook her hair off her shoulders.

He started violently as a group walked past the mouth of the alleyway, one of the men saying, 'Relax James, I'm agreeing with you

138

– I'm not surprised the jury didn't find him credible, either, to be honest . . .' And somehow the strain of bearing this imminent danger added to the song of her lilting, girlish laughter.

She said, 'Why wouldn't I want a drink with you? What's *wrong* with you? You're interesting. You're the first lawyer I've ever met – except *Randall Schaeffer*.' She crossed her eyes in mockery of his poor sight and Alistair felt a pang of sympathy for his old colleague. The young were so vicious. 'Can't you see that might be *interesting*?' she said.

Did she want to discuss a possible career in the *law*, for God's sake? It was all very unsettling. He felt embarrassed and – old. Increasingly he found himself worrying that he was the victim of a joke. And, aside from these faintly paranoid concerns, at any given second anyone might discover them talking!

She laughed at him again. 'Don't you ever do something just because it's *interesting*?'

'No,' he said. 'And I'm afraid I'm too old for that formula to sound as exciting to me as it does to you.'

At this, Karen's manner altered. She tilted her head on one side. 'Oh, OK, whatever. Is it any wonder I need a drink, though? You gave me hell in there today. You were *really scary*, you know? Oh, I see, you think it's *funny*, do you?' she said.

'I'm sorry – I was just wondering if I'd ever seen anyone look less scared.'

'Oh, that's all front – that's all bullshit. We're all bullshitters, aren't we – in our own ways?' She spat her gum into the gutter and grinned.

'Yes,' he said.

Any moment, anyone, he told himself, '*Langford, talking to a witness.*'

'Just one drink between old bullshitters, then. How about that?' She winked at him and he smiled involuntarily. 'Look, I don't want to discuss the sodding case anyway. I'm bored stiff of it.'

'There truly isn't anywhere we could go.'

'God, you haven't got much imagination, have you? For a *brilliant barrister*.'

'Barristers aren't required to have imagination. We wouldn't want to lose hold of the facts.'

She tapped her shoe again on the cobblestones – from side to side, as if she was about to dance. 'Oh, yes, but there's other bits in your brain – other than the barrister bits. You haven't got to be anywhere, have you?'

'No,' he said, 'but that doesn't mean—' Who had told her he was 'brilliant', he wondered.

'*Well*, then. We could go somewhere you won't know anyone.'

Alistair tried to imagine this place. His mind was immediately crowded to suffocation with a hundred friendly salutes and falling smiles of confusion from nearby tables, with friends putting on their wives' coats, catching sight of him: 'Isn't that Alistair? Alistair Langford?'

'Where? Good God! *Yes*, but who's he *with*, darling? Don't *wave*, for God's sake.'

Karen drew in her breath sharply. '*I* know. A *hotel*. Why would anyone who lives in London be in a hotel?'

He laughed – at what he felt sure was the spontaneous presentation of a tried and tested formula. He suspected there were other jewels in this box – 'You went back and bought it for me? That expensive dress?' – and so on. Then, unexpectedly, he felt a brandy-like flood of warmth through his body and realized this was what it felt like to contemplate the idea of a drink with a girl in her twenties with sooty mascara and comic-book curves.

She said, 'We could go to the Ridgeley, couldn't we? By the river. That place with the big things outside – oh, you know.'

'This is totally impossible,' he said, thinking there really was not the faintest chance of anyone he knew being at the Ridgeley. It was a new hotel done up by some fashionable interior designer, catered by her celebrity-chef husband. He had read about it in the business section of *The Times*. It had flaming torches outside it. He would be the oldest person in there by thirty years.

She smiled hard at him. 'Oh, *go on*. One drink on your way home.'

His mind felt weightless. It was professional insanity to have a drink with a witness. It was enough to get you disbarred.

But for some reason – and perhaps it was simply out of indignation at the conspicuous lack of interest Ryan and Sandra had shown in his life – this dangerous idea appealed to him. Somehow his thoughts insisted the only alternative in the world was going straight home to dinner with Rosalind. And suddenly this felt like dying. (There was a terrible silence in the house sometimes – the ticking clock, the thick curtains, the paintings still and heavy on the walls and Rosalind's pale absence from the room. Sometimes it occurred to him that this silence was not so very different from the silence at the boarding-house when he was a child, when the beds were done and his mother had gone to the shops. He would listen to her shut the front door as if it was the lid of his coffin. Then he would sit at the kitchen table digging the varnish out of the cracks with his thumbnail, hot tears in his eyes for the horrifying randomness of where God chose for you to be born.)

Just then he should have been laying his briefcase on the passenger seat of his car and heading back to his gently lit house in Holland Park. He would kiss Rosalind, tell her there were lovely smells coming from the kitchen, go up to change (cords, a checked shirt, a cashmere V-neck, loafers) and come down to help her by decanting the wine and laying the table, perhaps. But his mind presented him with two choices: recklessness or death. He felt like laughing, like crying. Why was he feigning a belief in this intoxicating rubbish?

'Just one little drink in secret?' She wrinkled her nose and smiled.

He met her eyes and felt another thrill pass through him. It was not exactly a sexual thrill – although she was almost comically attractive, an illustrated pin-up – it was the same thrill he had felt the time he stole a shilling from the floor underneath the till in Geoff Gilbert's shop when he was eight. It was the same thrill he had felt, perhaps a year or so later, when he stole a custard tart from the plate in Ivy Gilbert's kitchen. Aunty Ivy and Uncle Geoff, who were poor like them – whom he *stole* from. He had lost the shilling as he ran up the road towards the cliffs, but it hadn't mattered. The custard tart had got so coated in fluff from his pocket it was inedible and he had chucked it to a stray dog. But it hadn't been the shilling that was important; it hadn't been the custard tart. What was the important element? What had made him run as hard as he could up the cliff path feeling an electric storm in his chest?

He really must go home to Rosalind, he told himself. There would be a delicious dinner and good friends and the lullaby of their quiet habits at night: her light off first, her hand sleepily pressing his arm as she turned away from him. 'Don't read too long, darling,' she always said. Her face cream smelt of lilies – as it always had. On his bedside table was the same photograph he had on his desk, of the day he was sworn in as a QC, the picture that constituted the satisfaction of *nearly all his ambitions.* He was ashamed that he rarely looked at it without wishing it had been Luke, not Sophie, stuck out of the picture behind the camera. He missed his darling little daughter and the lost, picnic days of her perfect admiration, the days when he had known the answer to everything. It was so hard to believe she was thirty now.

Feeling as if he was setting fire to himself, but also to this terrible sense of dread, of loss, of tedium, of death, he said, 'All right, one drink. Why not? But I'll have to meet you there. You get a taxi and I'll come on afterwards.'

He followed her a few steps towards the road, watching the outrageous curve of her hips outlined by the streetlight ahead. He waited at the mouth of the alleyway, feeling a breathless relief to be out of such imminent danger. And he felt a kind of passion, too, though this was still somehow an abstraction from the idea of desire − a variation on the theme of desire, rather than the feeling itself, he thought. It struck him that Karen was the kind of girl his son would find attractive and this appealed to him shamelessly. Physically, she was an amalgamation of all the girls Luke had brought back. But Luke's girlfriends − in particular the current one, Lucy − were all dull, obsessive, preoccupied with becoming wives. They were all terrified of Alistair, sycophantic to Rosalind. It irritated Alistair to the point of incomprehension. There was no need for Luke to marry a girl like that because, unlike him, Luke had been lucky enough to start out with every advantage in the world. That boy had everything − *everything*!

Karen put out her arm to a passing cab and it stopped beside her. She said something through the window to the driver and walked back towards him, smiling. 'If I go, you will definitely come? You won't just leave me waiting there like an idiot?'

She looked hopeful as a child in the streetlight in front of him, and his heart moved protectively. It was the first time she had shown her age by accident, rather than flaunting it calculatingly, like a low-cut dress. Of course, it was more dangerous this way. He told her he would meet her in the bar at the Ridgeley. She could order him a whisky and water.

To pass a little time he stood inside a delicatessen, pretending to examine a packet of breadsticks. What did she see him as? he wondered. A wealthy older man, the source of some unspecified luxury, some dubious paternal reassurance. Well, it was an age-old formula, wasn't it? The man behind the counter asked if he could help and Alistair said, no, he was fine. Just looking, he said.

He picked up a different packet of breadsticks and thought: What exactly is so awful about a drink, a little flirtation, the possibility of more held tantalizingly ahead and . . . approached, like golden hills and sunny vineyards? Of course he would turn back delicately at the last moment. He could do what the older man did − buy her some good champagne, order her some oysters, or whatever accorded with the picture in her mind. Attempt to fulfil the role – as he always did.

And in what sense was this role so inferior to the others he played? Just then it seemed only to be a rather wearisome question of aesthetics. What right did he have to think in these rarefied terms, anyway? The truth was, he did a passable tired-but-loving-husband but he undermined it by losing the thread of what he was saying, by pausing to wonder if his wife heard his voice any more. He did an uninspired wise-but-vague-loving-father and was secretly frightened of his own children, wary of exposure to their problems, of exposure *by* their problems. He really did not know how to help, what to say to them – and they must know it, he thought. Not that Luke challenged anyone much. Quite unexpectedly, he had put that terrible bolt through his eyebrow, but when he finally found a job that interested him, he simply took it out again. Old Luke was resilient, predictable. His darling, brilliant little daughter on the other hand – she starved herself, she cut her own arms. What did it all mean? He couldn't bear to imagine.

Sophie had begun to kiss his forehead when she greeted him – as one kisses children, or the old and confused.

Where was the beauty in any of this? These were thin performances and he saw through them *himself*. Somehow, in the years since both the children had left, since the satisfaction of *nearly all his ambitions*, he had got lost outside his own life. He did not know how to signal to Rosalind. Not that she would have noticed: she was so busy, these days, with those dreadful friends and their furniture catalogue.

He waited until three taxis had passed. Then he put down the breadsticks, walked on to the road and hailed one. He slammed the door after him.

There was plenty to distract the eye along the river. The Oxo tower stood out against the sky, lights were coming on in the restaurant boats and across the bridges and in many of the penthouse river-view flats, and each one of these lights was reflected in the glittering Thames. Very gradually, London was putting on its jewellery in preparation for Friday night.

Alistair began to feel calmer, less reckless. He told himself that there had been plenty of occasions on which he had noticed other women before. *Of course* there had been other occasions in almost forty years of marriage. But as he tried to remember these occasions, this sly old habit of his, he could come up with only one example. He had once had dinner with an Italian solicitor at a pub in King's Lynn when he was staying there defending a murder charge. Otherwise he had not been alone with – or alone and attracted to – a single other woman. Surely this avoidance of desire had taken thought and planning. It was almost frightening that he had never been conscious of it.

His briefcase slid across the seat as the taxi rounded a corner and some papers came out of the side pocket. He gathered them up and stuffed them into his pockets. Sylvia, her name was – the solicitor. Sylvia Dolci. She had been working on another case; she had been there only for the night. They had eaten good fish pie together and drunk Chablis and she told him about her little daughter, her useless ex-husband. She was very funny, dry as the wine. He had liked the smell of her thin cigarettes. And all the way through, particularly when they had finished their coffee and the moment came for one or the other of them to ask for the bill, he had felt an overwhelming sense of missed opportunity. He remembered it as a physical sensation: it had been like rushing back for your towel down a corridor of hotel rooms and seeing someone else's room through a half-open door, an unlicensed glimpse for no more than a few seconds – the maid flipping up a sheet, brilliant in the sunshine, the better sea view, the brighter sunlight across the wall. The sensation was longing: for another life, which might so easily have been his. It had been Sylvia who asked for the bill, sighing conclusively.

They had said goodbye outside her room: 'So, *Alistair*,' she said, with the charmingly random emphasis that made her words seem translated and all the more exotic, '*thank* you. It was a lovely evening.'

'Yes, it was.'

'*Yes*,' she said. She put her key into the lock and he noticed her eyes close tightly for a second. Then she turned back and kissed him on the cheek. '*Well*. Sleep well, then.'

'You too, Sylvia,' he told her.

And so he had passed on, twirling his key on his finger in an imitation of indifference, listening to the sad music of her door clicking shut. His heavy heart had dragged him deep into sleep.

That had been contemplating infidelity. What exactly was he contemplating now?

Chapter 9

Alistair paid the cab driver and walked up the steps of the Ridgeley, past the absurd torches and the cream-jacketed doorman and through the rotating doors. The floor was white marble and the interior walls were made of frosted glass. Ahead there was a reception desk of glass twisted to look like gnarled branches with glass leaves that bounced the light off their rainbow surfaces. Two thin girls in white shift dresses, their hair scraped back, attended to a huge book of reservations. A young Japanese man approached the desk and both girls raised smiling faces.

To Alistair's left was the entrance to the bar. Sylvia Dolci, he thought, as he went through. They pronounced their Ts a little further forward in their mouths, Italians. He had watched her, anticipating the sight of her tongue against her teeth as she did it. She had shown him a picture of her dark-haired little girl. 'She's very, very pretty,' he had told her, hoping Sylvia would catch his implication.

Karen was sitting discreetly in the corner behind the bar. She waved at him as he came in. Her face was a floodlight of youth, a blaring stereo of youth, which he wanted to tell one of his children to turn down immediately. What the hell was he doing?

'Here we are,' he said calmly, putting down his briefcase. He would have one drink.

'Whisky and water,' she said, holding out a glass to him. 'That's you done. Me? I still can't decide. They do hundreds of things here. Look.' She held out the clear plastic menu at him.

It was full of pretentiously conceived drinks that involved improbable verbs: 'muddled' blueberries, 'smashed' limes. Her face was a mixture of confusion, intimidation and excitement. It made him smile. 'Have a Bellini,' he said. 'You can't possibly go wrong with peach juice and champagne.'

She seemed pleased with this formulation. He had drunk Bellinis with Rosalind on their honeymoon in Rome. But, then, it was not inconceivable that everyone else he knew had drunk Bellinis on their honeymoon in Rome. The waiter stood beside them. 'A Bellini, please,' he said. 'And could we have an ashtray?'

He lit a match for the cigarette she had been holding uncertainly in the palm of her left hand.

'Oh, thank you. I've been *desperate* all day. There's nowhere to smoke any more, is there? Always one of those signs up, spoiling the party.' She scraped her hair off her face.

This was how she would look leaning back on her elbows in the bath, lifting her wet hair out of the water, he thought. 'Looks nice,' he said, 'your hair back like that.'

Why on earth did he feel able to speak to this girl so intimately? He checked himself – like a man who has fallen over and wonders if he has torn his coat, scuffed his shoes – and found himself intact. Karen held the cigarette in her teeth and tied back her hair with a band she had on her wrist. He was mystified but increasingly flattered by her desire to please him.

'Don't you smoke?' she said.

'Not any more.'

'Oh, shit, it's gone in my eyes. It only works in black-and-white films, doesn't it – holding it in your mouth like that?'

'Here.' He held out a napkin for her.

'I wish you smoked. It makes you feel guilty smoking on your own.'

She had left a light smudge of mascara under her left eye, which at once made her seem like a child dressing up in her mother's clothes. He wondered if he could draw her attention to it somehow, because it added to a fear that the immaculate young at the other tables were staring at him, appalled or amused.

'What the hell?' she said, exhaling. 'I can cope with a little guilt.'

The waiter arrived with the Bellini and a little bowl of what looked to Alistair like broken crackers in self-consciously irregular shapes. He picked one up, wondering what this meant. It sprang from an aesthetic he felt he was too removed from, too old, to appreciate. It tasted like nothing at all.

'So, d'you like being a brilliant barrister, then?' Karen said. 'You enjoy it all – wearing your wig and cape and all that?'

'Oh, I went into it for the wig and cape,' he said, smiling.

'*Wigs*,' she said, rolling her eyes. 'This is so delicious. What's it called again?'

'A Bellini. I'm surprised Mr Giorgiou didn't introduce you to those.'

'Mr Giorgiou doesn't take me out much,' she said. 'He spends all his money on gambling anyways. And all the other girls. And you said we shouldn't talk about him.' She lengthened her mouth and put on a mock-pompous voice. 'It's unethical, I'm afraid.'

It was hard not to like her. She had finished half her drink already – in three gulps – and Alistair watched her push it away. 'Look, I'm rather old and predictable,' he said. 'Why don't you tell me about yourself?'

'About me?'

'Yes.'

She thought for a moment, and then she laughed and picked up the drink again. 'I can't think what to say . . . God, I'm nothing special. What can I tell you?' Her mind ran through a series of the actions that apparently constituted her existence – eating toast in the tiny kitchen at home, putting on her makeup in the bathroom mirror, the way she banged drunkenly into the side of the toilet cubicle in a club when she pulled up her knickers and tights. None of it was good enough to tell him. For a moment, she felt despair – the despair that came when she watched her brother stoned unconscious in front of the telly. She felt her feet sweating in the cheap shoes and wondered if there would be dye on her feet.

Imagine if they made you show your feet, she thought, picturing a surreal humiliation in the hotel lobby, in which wealthy and clean were divided from poor and hopelessly stained. Her heart thudded in anger. I'd kick them in the face, she told herself. Fuck the lot of them.

'Well, I can tell you what I want to be, if you like,' she said brightly. 'I want to go into fashion – you know, design dresses and stuff. Beautiful dresses and coats and skirts. Maybe I'd do jewellery too. Underwear. Who knows? I'd love that. It's not just bullshit – I've applied for the course and everything.'

'I didn't doubt it. You seem very determined.'

She eyed him suspiciously for a second. 'Yes, well, I am. I've had to be, with my family. Not that I do that whole blame-it-all-on-your-parents bullshit American thing, but it does get you down. My parents are just slobs, really. Fat whales on the couch – that type. They drink. My little brother nicks cars. It's your dream set-up.'

'I'm sorry.'

'Gives you something to run from, doesn't it? God, don't get me started,' she said, her eyes full of humour, which she abruptly held back. She looked at him, at his suit and tie. She took in the expensive watch, the cufflinks, the good cashmere coat on the seat beside him. He had a handsome face even if he was old. There was friendliness in it, genuine curiosity, which was not how men usually were. Usually they looked at your legs, your tits, over your shoulder until you'd finished talking. They waited to get their sex. And he was nervous, too, which was sweet. He kept glancing at the people at the table near them wondering if they were watching him. She took out another cigarette and he lit a match for her and leant across the table with it. She liked him. Why not tell him about herself? Even though he was posh, he was not like Lexi and his friends, always thinking people hadn't realized who they were and had given them the smaller table or forgotten to comp them the champagne. Alistair looked like he cared more about people than things.

'So my parents are disgusting,' she said. 'You wouldn't believe it. It's like – as an example – this Christmas my dad wandered off in the middle of our dinner. Mum had done turkey, sprouts, the works. We couldn't believe it because it's usually a row and something out of the freezer, but not this time. This was like your Christmas miracle.

'But, of course, Dad has to ruin it. Why – who knows? He's just one of those people that spoils things. Like my brother, I guess. Anyway, the exact second it's ready he goes out for a "breath of air" and it all starts to go cold. My sister, Yvonne, she's older than me with three kids and one on the way – I know,' she said, shaking her head at Alistair. 'Birth control? They're always at it, her and Mick. Anyway, Yvonne goes, "Oh, just let him fuck off, Mum, it'll be nicer without him." So we gave his to the dog. Yvonne puts this paper hat on him and sat him on Dad's chair. It was pretty funny. A dog at the head of the table! And it *was* nicer without Dad – until he didn't come home for a *whole week* after that.'

'What on earth had happened?'

'*Drunk.*' She swung her head from side to side in time to her words: 'Drunk, drunk, drunk. Bastard got so drunk, when they found him in the doorway of Tesco in the high street he couldn't remember who he was.'

'My God.'

148

'*Couldn't remember his own name.* He had forgotten his whole life. Can you imagine that?'

Actually, he could. This evening, he *could* imagine lying nameless in the doorway of Tesco. 'You need another Bellini,' he said.

She looked at her empty glass. 'Oh dear. My father's daughter, hey?'

'Not at all. Please don't if you don't want one. Don't let me—'

'Oh, no – I'm not being like that. I do want one,' she said. 'But I'm not getting all tipsy on my own, though – you have to as well.'

He picked up his glass and drained it, returning her smile with his eyes. It was impossible to feel sorry for her, in spite of the depressing family life, which he could imagine only too well. He remembered his mother drinking, laughing in the kitchen with a male guest – the horror of seeing a parent disgraced like that. Why did he not feel sorry for Karen? Perhaps she was simply too young. It was good to be near her. This was doing nobody any harm.

'Look, shall I order a bottle of champagne?' he said.

'Oh, a bottle of champagne would be *lovely*.' She clapped her hands. '*Thank* you. That would be *lovely*.'

He ordered a bottle of Dom Pérignon and some more cigarettes for her – because he had noticed she only had a few in her packet and this felt like the right thing to do. As he ordered, he watched her from the corner of his eye and noticed the way she tempered her excitement, schooling it under her nervous hands, holding it down in her lap. It touched him. He felt moved to nostalgia by the mock-up of knowing sophistication on her face. Must his own face have been like that at one time?

While they drank the champagne she told him stories about her life, her school, her friends. She spoke well, with a compelling sense of irony that had her rolling her eyes at the ugliness of her family. How superior this was to the tortured secrecy of his own youth, he thought, to the wincing and the clenched fist and the short sharp lessons he had taught himself in the privacy of the loo. He had punished himself viciously for those early catastrophic errors at lunch with Rosalind's family, at dinner with her father at his club. He had left doors open in those days, exposed himself by accident to their scrutiny—

'But hang on – your parents were *married*, surely?' his new sister-in-law had asked, silencing the lunch-table. Even the carpet had seemed to hold its breath. And on some other occasion his father-in-law had laughed, sherry in hand, still certain he must have misheard—

'What? *Never* been abroad in your whole life?'

It still made Alistair shudder to remember these incidents. It had never occurred to him to make a joke of his background, as Karen did. But, then, he mustn't forget that times had changed, England had changed. People were 'themselves' now in a way that had not been encouraged when he was young. It had been an unspoken agreement between himself and Rosalind that he should at least appear to be the right sort of young man. How could she have married him otherwise? As it was, her parents had been deeply disappointed by his obvious lack of private wealth.

'Five of us,' Karen was saying, 'with this fake "Save the Rainforests" tin, dancing to this old Madonna tape. You can't believe people fell for it, really. People actually gave us money.'

He refilled their glasses and enjoyed the work the champagne was doing on his empty stomach. His face felt flushed – but with exhilaration rather than embarrassment now. The colour had come into her cheeks, too. He thought she was incredibly pretty as she smiled at him, saying, 'God, different *worlds*, hey?'

Could *sympathy* breed desire? He wanted to kiss her panicky mouth, to hold down all the fluttering energy with the weight of his own body. 'No. Not so different,' he said.

'Oh, come on. You must think I'm awful. Vulgar little tart.'

'No. I think you're going to get exactly what you want out of life and that you must be very careful what that is.'

'Oh, what does that mean? That's one of those Chinese riddles.'

He laughed. 'Nothing Chinese about it.'

'You know what I mean. Something that sounds all meaningful but you can't work it out.'

'Well, I meant it,' he said. 'And it was supposed to be a sort of compliment.'

She observed him for a moment. 'I've never met a man who said so little about themselves. I mean, I don't know anything about you. Most guys have found a way to tell you what they earn and what they drive within five minutes. Not you, though.'

'Maybe I'm too old to show off.'

'You're a man, aren't you?'

'You don't think we improve with age?'

'Well, I'll tell you in a bit, shall I? I've only seen you drink.'

He looked away and tried to rationalize the longing. His mouth was watering and he swallowed. His throat felt swollen. Again he saw her in red stockings, laughing cruelly at his old body.

She giggled. 'Come on – play fair! *You* know I've got a no-good thieving brother and a sister at it like a rabbit and two disgusting, drunk parents. *I* know you've got a grey coat and a briefcase and – what are they? Green? *Green* eyes. Is that some kind of barrister's trick?'

'No tricks, no riddles,' he said. 'I think they're green, aren't they? I'm told they're green. My daughter has them.'

She leant across the table and put her hand on his cheek. He felt her breath on his mouth and his heart jolted.

'Green,' she said. 'Same age as me, probably – your daughter. What's her name?'

'Sophie.'

'Sophie,' she said delicately, trying on the more refined existence like a diamond bracelet.

She sat back. 'So, what about *you*, then?'

'Me?'

She tilted sideways and glanced under the table. 'You'll have to do. I can't see anyone else.'

'Goodness, I'm no good at this. Where should I start?'

He looked so shy, so anxious, she thought. 'Oh, wherever. Just say something.'

Oddly, it did not occur to him to pick a detail from the past forty years of his life. 'Well, I grew up in Dover,' he said. 'I grew up in grotty seaside Dover in a dingy little boarding-house with my mother. She wasn't married and I don't know who my father was. That was pretty scandalous in those days.'

A waitress passed with a tray of drinks. He felt his heart racing with a kind of hilarious excitement.

'My mother always told me they were planning to marry when he got killed in the war, but I suppose it stopped adding up as a story when I reached the age of, oh, about eight. I remember I threw all my toy soldiers into the sea. I can't imagine anyone else believed it at all. Nothing was ever said, though. She was popular in the area – grew up there and so on – and to talk about it would have meant judging her, I suppose. People hid it for her so they could carry on enjoying her company, really. We never discussed it either. I haven't seen her for, God, forty years now – is it forty years? – possibly so as to avoid the conversation.'

He felt like laughing. Not only had he never told a single person the naked facts of his past, he had never arranged them in this way.

Could forty years really have been spent in avoidance of a conversation? Here he was, suddenly able to tell it all to a girl he had never met before.

Karen was open-mouthed. 'Shit. How come you're so . . .' She circled her hand.

'Educated?'

'No. So *posh*-sounding.'

He laughed hard. Yes, that was the interesting bit. How come he sounded as if he had grown up like his wife, like his own children? 'Oh, it's fake,' he said.

'What do you *mean*? What d'you mean it's fake?'

'I mean it's put on. I learnt it at university. I copied my friend Philip's accent.'

She began to laugh now, uncontrollably, gleefully, and he felt himself tumbling after her, down a grassy hill, landing breathless at the bottom in the sunshine. 'I think that's *brilliant*,' she said, 'fucking *brilliant*.' She raised her drink. 'Two old bullshitters?'

They clinked glasses, but as he drank, she whispered, 'You know what I think?'

He had no idea what she thought – or what he thought himself. And what did any of it matter? 'No idea,' he said.

'Let's get a room.'

His heart almost stopped. He watched her finish her drink and press her lips together with sudden pragmatism. 'It's pricey here, though,' she said.

'Is it?' he said, not hearing himself speak. He felt rather dizzy after the whisky, which must have been a double, and more than half a bottle of champagne. He had only had a bit of shepherd's pie for lunch.

'Yeah, it's pricey. But what's money for?' Karen said.

He stared at her in a kind of blank panic and she stared back. She seemed to want an answer. 'I don't know,' he said quickly. 'I'm not sure.'

It was true: he didn't know what money was for. He had known when the children were at home, when there were school fees to be paid, family holidays to go on. And he had bought Rosalind a pearl necklace with an emerald and diamond clasp for her fifty-ninth birthday. That was something. Something beautiful in a velvet box: 'the good things in life'. Wasn't that a phrase of his mother's? He remembered how he had loathed the pleasure she took in her 'precious' ornaments. He had run away from her 'good things in life', dreading them physically as if they were radioactive waste.

'You can *afford* it, can't you?' Karen said casually, her gaze as steady as a jeweller's on his face.

'Yes.'

'Well, I think money's for doing exactly what you like,' she said.

'Yes, I expect you're right.'

'Well, what do you *like*, Alistair?' She was beginning to feel confident, sexy. Your shoes didn't matter, for Christ's sake, if you were young and pretty. This older man, this brilliant barrister, was all nervous in front of her because she was young and pretty. It was so funny she had to bite her lip. 'I bet I can guess some things,' she told him.

His mind ran involuntarily through a rather unexpected list of pleasures: the taste of whisky, the smell of lilies, eight dusty chimes from the clock in the drawing room signalling the end of the day, the creak of his leather armchair and the weight of a book in his hand. Was that really all there was? He could not tell her this. He could not tell himself this. What about the red stockings? Suddenly he couldn't summon them up. 'Isn't it sad?' he said sarcastically. 'I seem to have forgotten.'

'Maybe you're depressed. It's common in men your age.'

He laughed sadly and finished his champagne. He wanted to ask her how she knew so much about men his age, but he feared she would say, 'My dad's about the same age as you,' and that this would make him feel even more disgusting for contemplating the idea of removing her clothes.

His own thoughts stung him: removing her clothes? Why? Why would he do that? He had not seen another woman naked in over forty years. A spell would be broken . . .

It was getting darker now and the lights on the ground floor of the hotel fell in bright golden squares on the pavement. The traffic moved past slowly, the rain trickled down the window-panes, the flames on the torches outside swayed in the wind. London seemed to be engaged in a languid dance.

'Well, do you like *me*?' she said.

'Oh, Karen, I'm old enough to be—'

'So *what*?'

'So what?'

'Yes. So what?'

'And I'm *married*.'

153

'Well, I've got a boyfriend. As you know.' She giggled – keeping her disappointed vanity secret from him, confining it to the stiffened corners of her smile. '*Don't* you like me?' she said, making her voice playful, wanting to press a sharp object, a lighted cigarette, into the palm of her hand. She longed to be older sometimes, past the stage of constant hopeful auditioning, when you must have learnt to know your place.

He looked at her face. Just then he almost hated her. He hated the arrogance of youth. He hated the faith she had in her physical superiority. Where do they get the idea that the important things get done in your twenties? he thought. All the bright pictures in magazines, in films, telling them a beautiful lie. You had to wait and wait and wait for success, for acceptance. It had nearly killed him, the waiting. She had better realize that quickly. Briefly, he felt the desire to humiliate her and to teach her a lesson about disappointment.

The wind picked up outside and the rain pattered on the glass. A double-decker bus paused close enough for him to see windows misted with human breath, faces blurred to abstraction behind them. It was only seven o'clock. Hardly a dangerous hour. Was it possible that, after all, everything he cared about mattered less than he thought, that he invested his actions with far too great a significance, that he was a self-important fool? And, after all, no one could actually *see*.

'Oh, look, Alistair, I won't ask you again. If you don't want to . . .'

He shook his head hard to compensate for the fact that he was finding it almost impossible to speak. His mind was evenly split into three emotions: lust, cruelty, fear. 'Want to,' he told her. He spoke from the point at which all three emotions met and combusted. *Want to*. The charred little fragment of a sentence shrivelled and flew up out of his burning mind.

Want to what? Betray my wife? Humiliate myself? But why would he humiliate himself? Unlike Henry's, his 'equipment' had not stopped working. And this had nothing to do with Rosalind. This present moment was as irrelevant to her existence as that untidy past of his, which she never condescended to mention. Half an hour or so of untidiness – a little out of synch – and he could simply consign it to the river of forgetfulness, which flowed just beneath their bedroom window. The details Rosalind had forgotten on his behalf . . . He could forget this on her behalf.

'Don't you want me?'

It was agony. 'Yes,' he said. 'Look, stay here for a few minutes and then ask them for the room number at Reception. I still think it's best we don't go up together.' He was aware this did not make much sense.

'OK.'

He grinned at her, telling himself to try to relax. It was only seven o'clock. When had he started to dread Rosalind? The girl's cheeks were red with excitement and alcohol, her face almost painfully excited. It was funfair excitement.

'See you up there, then,' she said.

He paid the bill, then he left her in the armchair with the empty glasses and the smudge of mascara under her eye and he walked away towards Reception, as if they had done this a hundred times before. Again, he was reminded of how easily his hand had slipped Uncle Geoff's money into his own pocket – like a practised thief. A practised adulterer, he said to himself.

He felt unsteady in the bright lights of the lobby. He walked as confidently as he could towards the icy teenagers at Reception. 'I'd like a room,' he told one. The phrase sounded wrong.

'Certainly. Single, twin or double?'

'Double.'

'Will you be wanting breakfast in your room?'

'No. That won't be necessary.'

'We'll need a credit card, sir.'

He handed over his identity and was given a card-key in return. No, he had no bags. No, there was no need for the porter to help him up. No, he would not be requiring a wake-up call.

'It's on the third floor, then, sir. Turn left as you come out of the lift. Enjoy your stay.'

And that was that. He paused uncertainly and the girl smiled harder at him, as if she suspected he had run out of battery and required this mega-boost. He recoiled from her, startled.

Enjoy his stay. Yes, he would. All he needed to do was stop thinking about the wrong. Think about the *enjoy*, think about the arms, wrists, thighs. Her boozy breath on his face. She was not really his 'type', though. He liked shining dark hair and long, elegant limbs. She was altogether too functional, what with the breasts that would one day spurt milk, the hips that would heave around sons. And the shrill, exhibitionist laugh, the eyes that would damn well squeeze out their

155

money's worth of joy. There was chipped pink varnish on her finger-nails. Her shoes were cheap.

Why not go home? he asked himself, pressing for the lift.

He had told her things that ought to have brought the sky down, collapsed the film set – and yet here was the Muzak still playing serenely by the oversized cactus. It was impossible that nothing meant anything anyway. He caught sight of himself on a mirrored pillar and thought: Drunk and nameless in the doorway of Tesco.

In the lift there was a flat-screen TV with a nature film on it. Flamingos raced over a rainbow of salt flats. The standard, treacly American black female voice sang through the speakers, 'Oh, yeah, cos what you did to me baby . . . stole my heart, stole my soul, made my dreams come *true* . . .' and spotlights flashed in sequence on the ceiling. Again, he wondered, what did it all mean? What notions of sophistication or luxury did all this convey to his children's genera-tion? He was simply too old to receive the message, to unpick it from the atmosphere of intense irony.

The card-key beeped and he went in. The room was vast and bright. A glowing fridge set back into the wall three feet high was full of champagne, Dutch lager, diet Coke, Swiss chocolate, sushi, and packets of what turned out to be facial mud. The bed was low and wide enough for three people, half covered in a white fur throw. There was a bathroom with a sunken bath and a chandelier hanging low over it. The windows were elaborately draped in white sackcloth with ice blue wooden shutters behind. He sat on the bed and waited for the knock at the door, feeling as if he needed Karen to act as an interpreter.

When it came, she ran in past him bursting into laughter, just as Sophie and Luke used to do on holiday in the race for the best bed. One, much like the other, had always acquired a mystical status and he had drawn up rotas for them to highlight the importance of sharing, of fairness in this life. He sat down again.

'Oh, my God, it's *incredible*. I wish I had a camera,' Karen said. She aimed the remote at the TV and a picture of a girl dancing on a beach appeared. 'MTV!' she said. 'How cool is this?' Her eyes did not really see him as she searched his face. 'And this fridge!'

She ran into the bathroom, then out again and over to the window, and then she looked back at him, her hands over her mouth. Something in his smile must have made her remember herself, because she picked up the remote and turned the volume low, sending diminishing trian-gles flashing across a close-up of the singer's midriff. She took off her shoes carefully and sat down in front of the bed, by his feet. He watched her as she put her hand inside his trouser leg, just above his sock. Her fingers were cold.

'*Karen*,' he said.

'What?'

What were the right words? He scoured the sterile corners of the room. 'I don't . . . I don't know what's happening here.'

She giggled. 'Well, I do. Don't worry – it doesn't hurt.'

His laugh was ugly with fear: it was a mean, shrunken sound. 'I'm just . . . concerned,' he said – and the understatement was enough to collapse his heart like a punctured balloon.

'Are you saying you don't fancy me, then, Alistair?'

He stared – he had never been spoken to like this by a woman. She was literally offering herself to him. It was appalling, amazing. 'Why the hell do you want *me*?' he said.

'I just like older men. I've always liked an older man. When I was sixteen I went out with a guy in his fifties. He bought me a car.'

'Did he?'

She pushed her hand round the back of his calf and he felt his breath catch. His eyes closed. He had forgotten how hot the body could get. Hot, sticky. '*Karen*,' he said.

'It was a crap car and my brother ended up selling it for parts. Nice for my brother, though – having something to smash up like that. Not my stereo, for once. Or my hairdryer.'

'Karen,' he said again, speaking from some desperate part of himself, his voice almost whiny, 'I really don't think you should let yourself be used like this.'

'*Used?*' She removed her hand. She felt a rising sense of panic. She noticed her shoes on the carpet, spaced out as if they were running away. She remembered the stains on her feet and said quickly, 'Can we have some more champagne?'

He let out a burst of relief: '*Yes*. Yes, why not? Good idea,' he said, getting up. He walked over to the fridge and took out a bottle, opening it as slowly as he could with his back to her. 'This should be delicious,' he said. 'This is quite a bottle for a mini-bar, I must say. What a *place*,' he said, speaking mechanically, sociably. He remembered he had dreamt of hell once – a huge valley between two cliffs, one of which he had wandered on to inadvertently. There was no wind, no sound. He stared down into a blanket of pure white mist. At the deepest point, barely visible, were faint-coloured lights. They moved

157

slowly, incredibly beautiful, and he knew: This is hell. He thought of the sequential flicker of lights in the lift on the way up.

It was a great relief to be engaged in the simple action of opening a bottle. He picked up two glasses, thinking he would tell her amusing stories about cases because he did this well. People laughed. This was something he did. But when he turned back, he saw she had taken off her clothes.

Why this was happening, what he was doing in a scene from another man's life, ceased to matter beside the fact of her naked body. She was a little too skinny about the ribs with her clothes off, the breasts were far too heavy for her frame, but her skin was smooth and new in the electric light. She laughed at his surprised face and the noise went through his body like gunfire. He walked towards her.

'Exactly,' she told him softly. 'You just need to relax.'

He put down the empty glasses and lay beside her on the bed, his entire self silenced by her youth and her nakedness. The muted TV ran on in the background, wild with unintelligible images, flickering their shadows up the wall as he kissed her. Her sly fingers undid his tie and shirt. She rubbed her cheek on his chest and kissed her way down his stomach, running her tongue in a line above his boxer shorts.

What could possibly be in this for her? He was old. His stomach was not hard like his son's, his arms were thin, there was grey in the hair on his chest. This must be some enactment suggested to her by a deprived and abused childhood. Perhaps her father had . . .

He heard himself say her name in a gasp.

'What?' she said, raising her face and smiling, 'What, Alistair?'

Suddenly his life seemed to have been one of almost constant justification, argument, verbal evasion, but he knew that now he had absolutely nothing to say. And so he let her continue whatever unhealthy game she was playing so happily with his body. He smelt her different hair, her different skin with an animal curiosity, and when he turned her over and pushed himself inside her, barely conscious of the little face on the pillow, he felt an exquisite sadness for the things he had never done in his life – almost as if this was the moment of his death. Why had he not loved Rosalind better? What was it that she had done wrong? He simply couldn't forgive it. The bedside lamp dazzled his eyes and he wanted to switch it off, but the girl clasped her legs round him, urging him on with her hips, and the idea rapidly lost its shape.

At last he closed his eyes in bright sunlight, remembering sunlight, remembering closing his eyes.

Chapter 10

When Alistair's daughter came back from travelling in India during her gap-year, she brought her father and mother two simply horrifying little figurines. 'Meet Ganesha and Kali,' she said. 'He's god of all existing beings, she's transformation through death.' Sophie did the knowing smile she had acquired on her travels, her teeth very white against her brown face. Alistair sat with the tissue paper in his lap, his knees pressed together awkwardly, looking at the elephant head, the grotesque fat belly, and the other with its waving greedy arms. He tilted it towards Rosalind and smiled as best he could. This is *not* my culture, he thought, staring at them, repelled.

When Sophie left he wanted to hide the ghastly things in the hall cupboard, but Rosalind insisted they keep them out so as not to hurt her feelings.

'But they're *hideous*,' he said. 'What do they *mean*? We don't believe in them. They're *hideous*.'

'Yes, darling, I know,' Rosalind had told him, putting them on the mantelpiece, by a crisp, card wedding invitation, which suddenly looked as if it had come from another planet. She had seemed unduly irritated by him.

He thought these thoughts – about his daughter and his wife and the two Hindu gods – in rapid succession, while sitting on the edge of the hotel bed. He was putting on his pants and his socks and his crumpled shirt while Karen was doing something in the bathroom. At first he hurried to dress, in an irrational panic of modesty and shame: his body, his ageing body. Then he stopped this and sighed deeply and put his hand over his heart.

He listened to the brazen trickle of Karen's urine and did up his tie, rather tightly. Then he heard the loo flush and out she came, grinning, wearing the hotel bathrobe – and his barrister's wig. The robe, adult-sized, was poignantly enormous. Her legs were posed seductively, one in front of the other. She had her hand on her hip and the robe fell open over her left breast and all the soft skin he had kissed and licked just a few moments before.

Yes, that had been him – my mouth, my hands, he thought. His eyes moved up her neck to the giggling, winking face and the disfiguring horsehair wig. What sort of joke was this? It was such a sinister muddle of vocabulary. He felt lust and sheer horror and a desire to hide either her or himself immediately, to throw a cloth over the squawking canary in the cage.

Alistair's had been a life spent on the run from the grotesque and he had never developed a sense of humour with which to confront it.

Her smile fell. 'Oh, you're dressed,' she said.

'I – yes.'

'Oh.' She tossed the wig on to his bag and fluffed up her hair.

'Listen, Karen,' he began, in the voice of order, as he straightened his shirt, 'it's all – it's all paid for, this room. You may as well stay the night if you'd like to.'

'Are you going, then?'

He bent down to tie his shoes – and also to be nearer the floor. 'Yes, I've got to go,' he said.

She walked over to the bed and lay across it, spreading her hair out behind her. She was the picture of the tragic starlet. 'So are we going to do this again or was this a one-time-only thing?' There was a pause and then she met his eyes. 'Oh, don't *worry*. I knew it would be just this once really. Not your style, right?' She checked his face one last time. 'Nope, thought not,' she said.

He walked across the room for his coat and he heard the TV volume go up again on another music video. Of course she had known it would be one time only, he told himself. She was wise beyond her years and would hardly have entertained fantasies about being kept as a mistress. Oh, who did he think he was, for God's sake? She would not even have *wanted* to be his mistress. She was merely being polite.

He said, 'Karen, could I order you some supper up here? They could bring something to the room for you, if you like.'

'Oh, my God, you mean like *room service*? Yes, please. How cool. Is it really OK?'

'Of course . . . it's the least . . .' he said, struggling. There must, of course, be a kind of etiquette – but he had never had cause to learn it.

She said, 'I should order it now, shouldn't I? Then you can pay on your way out.'

Such earthy delights, such robust pragmatism, he thought. Was it all too much for his prissy little butterfly heart? 'Yes, I suppose that would be sensible,' he agreed.

The very least he could do was try to remember – if only in the name of good taste, for God's sake – that there was no place for disappointed romanticism in a hotel room. He cleared his throat. 'I must just . . .' He pointed at the bathroom and escaped behind the door.

He did not look into the mirror. He touched nothing. Suddenly he was afraid to leave his fingerprints anywhere, afraid the hotel would leave signs, marks, would subtly adhere to the surface of his skin. After a moment or two of absolute stillness, he walked towards the toilet and flushed it. Then he heard Karen calling, 'What's . . . Kewsa . . . koyza . . . something-dilla?'

He ran the tap for a second over the empty basin, watching the water run down the drain, aware of infinitely refracted versions of himself in the mirrors on each side of him. His hand moved and ten thousand hands moved. His shameful legs were ten thousand shameful legs walking towards the door. He was his own strange god.

When he came out she was cross-legged under the bedside lamp, smiling up at him. 'I think it's Mexican food,' he said. 'Quesadilla.'

'Oh, is it? I'll have that, then. And a Bacardi and Coke, please.'

He called Room Service and ordered. When he replaced the receiver, she put her hand on his arm and he jumped. '*Hey,*' she said. 'What on earth's the matter?'

He turned round and took the fingers – and, with infinite gentleness, he let them go. 'Jumpy,' he told her. 'I'm sorry.'

She looked down at her hand, knowing it contained their momentary intimacy – a souvenir as small as a ticket stub. 'Why are you sorry? No harm done.' She rubbed his arm with the other hand, 'You know, maybe you should have ordered two dinners. I'm starving.'

He said goodbye, he said, 'Thank you very much,' to her in the bathroom, where she was arranging the complimentary shampoo and soap bottles along the side of the bath, singing along to the TV. The hot water crashed in. She kissed him on the mouth with her hands on either side of his face and wrinkled her nose up at him, saying, 'Go easy on the guilt.'

'The guilt?'

'Look, I know I'm young and I know fuck-all, really, but everyone deserves a bit of pleasure, you know? Life's not long, is it?'

'No.'

'The way I think about it is, it doesn't matter if nobody sees. Didn't happen. Haven't you ever started wondering if something you just remembered really happened or if you dreamt it?'

He nodded vaguely, afraid to commit himself to agreement.

'Well, then,' she said, 'that's what things are like if nobody sees. If there's just you to say what they are, then they could be a dream, or you could *call* them a dream and nobody's going to know better.'

She was smiling at him and stroking his face and he did not know how to reply. He watched the water pounding into the white bath, whipping up a thick foam of bubbles.

'Anyway,' she went on, 'I had a lovely time. I think your wife's really lucky.'

He kissed her goodbye and left.

It was just after a quarter to nine when he got home. It was dark now and the air was damp and smelt of recently fallen rain, of wet paving-stones and brick. Drips came off the railings and the leaves along the avenue where he lived. The dripping was part of the darkness: it seemed to be the sound of the darkness. For a moment it was almost unbearably beautiful and again he put his hand on his excited heart.

He got out of the cab outside his house and glanced up at the drawing-room window. The curtains were drawn. Friends must be behind them already, having drinks, wondering where he was. A halo of light escaped round the edges of the window. It would have been sensible to call Rosalind from the taxi, but he had not felt able to.

He walked up the steps and patted his pockets for his keys, but they were not there. He remembered he had left them in his study at chambers. Had he gone back there, as he had intended to after court, he would have seen them on the desk and slipped them into his pocket. Not once in almost forty years of marriage had he forgotten his keys. He rang the bell. Rosalind came to the door and opened it to a flood of home: the dappled hall light, the warmth from the kitchen, her face . . .

'Oh. Alistair? I assumed you were Peter and Isabel,' the face of his wife said. And around it poured the hall wallpaper, the vase of lilies under the mirror, her perfume, the umbrellas in the rack.

He smiled at her from underneath this tidal wave of sensory information. 'Alas, it's only your husband,' he said.

'*Alas?*' She laughed. 'What d'you mean, darling? I'm actually rather relieved to see you're all right. Where on earth have you *been*?'

'I left my keys behind,' he said, pointing at the door by way of an explanation. She looked at the door and then at him.

'Yes, I see that. Are you all right, Alistair? What kept you so long?'

'Working,' he said. '*Working. Working.* May I come in?'

Rosalind leant over to kiss his cheek. 'Darling, I'm sorry. Come and have a drink. Goodness – another drink,' she said, smelling the alcohol on his breath. And then, as she went towards the drawing-room door, '"*Alas*"? What a funny word.'

He couldn't help agreeing with her. Guilt appeared to have poor taste in language. With distorted emphasis, he heard the dark rain dripping off the trees as he followed her inside.

It was very, very bright in the drawing room.

'*There* you are!' Anne Nicholson said, setting down her glass. 'We were all beginning to suspect you didn't want to see us.'

'Poor man's just been working late,' David Nicholson said. 'Honestly, Anne.'

Alistair received the hugs. As Anne pulled away from him, she said, 'Goodness, was that your stomach?'

'Yes, how very embarrassing. I'm so sorry. I – I'm evidently rather hungry.'

Peter and Isabel arrived shortly after Alistair. It was strange for them all to see Peter without Erica, to whom he had been married for twenty-eight years, and as Rosalind took coats in the hallway and was politely amazed by a rustling bunch of flowers, they each prepared themselves for a good show of civility.

Peter looked tired but very much in love with his new young pregnant wife. He brought her in protectively, with his arm round her. She was a rather fat, not particularly pretty girl, but Peter couldn't take his eyes off her. Alistair, whose face was still hot from sex, who still had the flavour of another woman on his tongue, was appalled by this flagrant lust. The world was plainly drowning in it. As they went into the dining room, Peter took hold of his arm. 'Isn't she fan*tas*tic?' he said.

Alistair nodded, wanting his friend's incriminating hand off him quickly.

Rosalind had made an opera of a meal. To start with there was fried pink bream in a fish and vegetable broth. Just before serving it, she sprinkled finely sliced raw vegetables over the fish – orange peppers, mushrooms, fresh coriander and spring onions. Alistair watched her quick fingers as he waited to carry the tray through. The broth was clear and spicy and slightly sweet, and with it they drank a good Riesling. The main course was a fillet of beef in filo pastry. Hidden in the crisp, golden pastry, over the beef, was a stuffing of wild mushrooms, garlic, chilli and parsley. The meat was pink and velvety and complemented perfectly by the earthy spiciness of the stuffing. For pudding there were caramelized apples and pears with hot butterscotch sauce and cold, tart Greek yoghurt. This she served in their wedding-present champagne glasses. And then there was cheese, Explorateur, St Marcellin, Époisses, St Félicien, with biscuits, crisp sweet grapes, and fig chutney. Alistair ate ravenously, indulging his body in spite of his mind, which reprimanded him with deeply distasteful biblical images of dry bread and water.

Around him, the gentle talk went on: was Tuscany overrun these days? Parts of Spain were just as lovely but then there was the far less interesting food. France, of course, would be utterly fantastic, if only it weren't for the French.

'Where are you two going on holiday this summer, Al?' said David.

Alistair forked spinach on to his salad plate. 'We thought we might stay with Chris and Lara in Malta,' he said. Then he looked at his friend and thought: You have absolutely no idea who you're talking to. If you knew, you'd leave. He said, 'How about you? Andalusia again?'

'*Absolutely*. If it ain't broke – that's what I always say. Can't bloody wait. A chair and the sun,' David sighed, capturing the idea between his raised hands, like a photographer, implying this was all he had ever wanted out of life.

By the time Alistair was helping Rosalind bring through the cheese, he was telling himself that he must regain control of his thoughts. He would contain the aberration in the hotel room within himself and he would most certainly resist the childish desire to confess.

He looked around the table, then he let his eyes fall on his wife's smiling face. Rosalind had always been beautiful. What a lucky man he was to have spent his life with one so beautiful. When was the last time they had made love – or even kissed each other? He felt intense love for her and a desire to be physically close. He wanted to make love to his wife and to have her familiar body wipe away the other woman's fingerprints. He longed to apologize to Rosalind physically.

I have been unfaithful to my wife, he thought. I am an unfaithful husband. There were tears in his eyes.

Then he listened to the conversation, to Isabel talking with what seemed to him to be a feigned respect about schools with the older women.

'Well, Luke *hated* Eton,' Rosalind was saying. 'It really only suits some characters. He's so sensitive, that was the thing. We had to move him. Alistair was disappointed, of course, but obviously he never let Luke see that.'

So, family life was beginning all over again for Peter. Alistair found it so exhausting to contemplate he had to stifle a yawn. Erica was a lovely woman and he thought his friend had been an idiot to throw her away. There was Peter, grinning murderously.

'We thought maybe weekly boarding, actually,' Isabel said. 'I mean, Westminster's very good academically.' Her fingers reached over to Peter's.

Oh, why bother sending it to school? Alistair thought. What did any of it matter? Another identikit education, another job in the City, another mortgage, another marriage at twenty-eight in a rented manor house, another first child at thirty-two. He looked at the self-satisfied young mother face and told her silently, 'It's an illusion, that sense of identity your swollen belly gives you. We unmake ourselves in a matter of seconds.'

She looked up at him with a slightly anxious expression. She had plainly noticed him staring. He forced a smile. 'Not long now,' he said.

'Two months. We're so excited,' she replied, the uncertain hand scrabbling across the table for her husband's again, 'aren't we, darling?'

Dinner was over. Very calmly, Alistair decided that it was quite late now and he really ought to be going. This peculiar thought made him laugh out loud and he managed narrowly to suggest it was in response to a story David was telling. He felt safe until he saw that the pregnant girl was looking at him again. She turned away, embarrassed.

A little while after they had moved back to the drawing room, Rosalind said, 'You did put the coffee on, didn't you?'

'Coffee?'

'Oh, Al. I did ask you.'

'Darling, I'm so sorry, I forgot. Forgive me, Rosalind.'

'Of course I'll *forgive* you.' She laughed. 'Darling, what's the matter this evening? Are you all right?'

Why did she keep asking him that? Yes! Yes, he was all right! 'Forgive me' was just a figure of speech, for God's sake.

'I'm fine,' he said, 'just tired out. That was an incredible meal.'

'It wasn't bad, was it? Even if I do say so myself,' she said, smiling shyly.

He squeezed her arm. 'You're very talented, darling.'

'Thank you.' She appeared touched – flattered, even moved by his approval. It struck him that these moments of bland encouragement were all that she lived on.

'I'll do the coffee now, shall I?'

'Lovely, darling.'

The guests wanted two black coffees, one decaffeinated coffee with cream, a mint tea and a camomile tea . . .

He crept out of the room, smiling amiably. Although, of course, nobody knew what he had done that evening, he felt utterly humiliated. When he remembered his weird laughter at the dinner table, he was afraid that he might start talking to himself. He was, essentially, talking to himself then. And the tone of the conversation seemed at best ironic and at worst horrified.

He did not want to talk any more, because he had said quite enough already. Least said, soonest mended, his mother always used to say.

Why was he thinking about his mother so much all of a sudden? It was just plain odd that he had talked about his past with Karen. And now, just for having mentioned it, he felt his concealed history sticky on his fingers and arms and hair. He sniffed his fingers and smelt sex.

His childhood had no place in his real life. It was just a crackly black-and-white film sodden with shame and sentiment. A far greater proportion of his life had been spent in these surroundings, in Holland Park, in corduroy trousers and a cashmere V-neck, than in Dover. If the number of years counted for anything, he was unquestionably Alistair Langford, QC – the man in the photograph at the House of Lords, rightfully there because of his own achievements. He must simply put out of his mind this terrible evening and the pervasive sense of his own fraudulence. It had all been a rather devastating species of Freudian slip – and now he would continue with what he had meant to say. 'A Freudian slip is what happens if you say one thing when you mean your mother,' a friend had once joked.

166

He flicked the switch on the kettle and heard it start up. This was the way life functioned, he told himself. You put lots of things out of your mind – starvation, torture, wars, famine. Terrible things, which, if attended to, would make ordinary routine impossible. This was the purpose of good manners – he glanced through to the dining room – this was the purpose of nineteenth-century tables with silver knives and forks lined up, each one to be attended to carefully. Etiquette slowed the painfully racing heart: it distracted you from the things that did not bear thinking about.

He heard Karen's soft voice – 'You've got a beautiful cock, haven't you?' – and flinched. The different age-group with its risky liberation. But it was not his problem. It was his son's problem, his darling daughter's problem. And yet those words he had used in the hotel bar when she suggested they get a room: 'Want to,' he had stuttered. '*Want to.*' The shard of desire in his eye.

He took out the cups and saucers and spoons and put them neatly on the tray. As the kettle boiled, it made him shudder to think how terribly cold it must have been, in late December, for one unconscious in the doorway of Tesco, one so drunk he had forgotten his own name.

The phone call about his mother's death came two weeks later. Rosalind received it and wrote down the details on the phone pad. She stared at them for a long time after she had put down the receiver. She decided to wait until Alistair got home before telling him – it was inappropriate to do so during the working day. She had great respect for what he did, and in all their years of marriage, she had interrupted him only once at court, when she had gone into labour with Luke.

At around eight, she heard him shut the front door and drop his keys into the bowl on the hall table. She walked out into the hallway. 'Darling, there's been some news,' she said.

'Really?'

'Yes.'

He was loosening his tie. 'What have our children done now?'

'No, it's not them. It's about your mother.'

'My . . . ?'

'Alistair, she died last week.'

'Really?' he said again. He put down his briefcase very softly. He had told Rosalind his mother had died just before they got engaged.

'I don't really know what to say about it,' she said. 'As you know, it's a shock to me, too.'

'Yes. Yes, I see that.'

'So, I'm just going to tell you the facts, Alistair.'

'OK.'

She had received a call, she said, from an Ivy Gilbert. His mother had died of a heart-attack. It would not have been a drawn-out thing, Rosalind told him. Apparently the doctor had been quite certain about that. It was sad, though, that she had lain undiscovered at the bottom of the stairs for a few days. It had been Ivy who alerted the authorities, concerned that she hadn't heard anything from her friend for a while. Ivy had said she felt that Alistair ought to be told, as he was his mother's son, no matter how long it was that they hadn't seen each other. Because of the circumstances in which she had been discovered − so long after her death − she had already been cremated.

As Rosalind spoke, they went into the drawing room and stood a little way apart from each other in front of the fireplace. When she had finished, she looked right at him. His eyes ran over the room, skipping from the chandelier to the carpet, along the shelves of books to the orchid in the pot by the door. She was reminded of the way his eyes had done this when they first met − and how she had thought at the time that it was as if they were seeking refuge, a place to rest.

'Well,' he said, 'I'm quite shocked.' He looked hunched − stiff.

'Yes. Let me get you a drink.'

'Thank you,' he said. And, as he had been on so many occasions, he was intensely reassured by her presence − and by her good manners. She must be angry and confused, he thought, but she would never lose her temper, not Rosalind.

She poured him a glass of whisky, put a little water into it and brought it to him on the sofa. He took the glass and she looked at him until he averted his eyes. She said, 'Alistair, I have lived countless years thinking your mother died before we were married.'

'Yes,' he said.

'You've lied to me. We've lied to the children.'

'Yes. Well − not you. You haven't lied to anyone, darling.'

'Look, I'm not going to make you talk about it now − I'm not even sure I can face it myself − but . . .'

'But I owe you an explanation.'

'I think you do,' she said. 'My God, Alistair, you do. I know you didn't get on with her, but this is really . . . I can't even think of the right word.'

'No,' he said. 'I'm not surprised.'

She sighed very deeply and then she held his hand. But it was he who squeezed her fingers.

'I expect you're in shock, aren't you?' she said, as if she was offering him an excuse for not explaining himself just yet.

'I think I am, darling,' he said.

'Oh, God, Alistair, I've just remembered that I'm meant to be going to our table supplier in Sussex with Jocelyn tomorrow. This is hopeless. We won't get back till very late – you'll be on your own all evening. I'm going to call her and cancel.'

'No, no. Don't, darling. You must go. It's . . . important,' he said. Then he slapped his forehead. 'We're meant to be going to Julian's for dinner.'

'Tomorrow night?'

'Yes. I – I forgot to say.'

'Oh, Alistair. Well, we'll cancel that, too.' She had just enough room in her mind to think how unlike him it was to accept a midweek invitation to dinner and how unlike him it was to forget to tell her about it. She squeezed his hand, attributing his uncharacteristic vagueness to the news, even though she knew it had preceded it. She had noticed an odd, hunted expression on his face and a new habit of jumping as she walked into the room.

'No, let's not cancel *anything*,' he said. 'You go to Sussex. I'll go to Julian's. It's probably the best thing for me. I'll explain I didn't warn you – all my fault.'

'You really think so?'

'I do. I think it's best we carry on as normal. It'll be best for me that way.'

'Well, if you're sure.'

'I am.' His voice sounded sure, too. The flawless performance was his only protection from an evening alone with his loving wife.

When Rosalind thought over the events a few weeks after this, she couldn't help dwelling on the subject of fate. This was a concept Alistair had always laughed at – he thought it a preoccupation of neurotic women, like her sister Suzannah, and at first she felt embarrassed. It was her instinct to check whether her thoughts would bear her husband's scrutiny. But suddenly she pushed open the french windows and went out into the garden, thinking angrily that it was not exactly as if Alistair's brilliant mind had been right about everything, was it?

But before this came the night of Julian and Elise's dinner, the night of the attack, of the whirring car alarm and the two figures running away in the dark.

Afterwards, at the hospital, when the doctor had examined his leg, Alistair found he was still clutching the little card Rosalind had written for Julian and Elise, to apologize for her absence. The words were smudged with his sweat: '. . . so disappointed I can't be there . . .' he read, '. . . have been lovely . . . miss out on Elise's delicious . . .' He was in a great deal of pain and he read his wife's gentle words while the doctor asked him if he could move his toes and rotate his ankle.

After his X-rays, he was told that Rosalind was on her way and he was put into the private room he would stay in for the next week. Detective Inspector Pendry sat on a chair by Alistair's bed. He spoke highly of Julian's swift telephone call. 'That's a good friend you've got there,' the efficient policeman told him.

Two constables in a nearby squad car had caught the attackers on the high street minutes after the attack. Just half an hour later they were signing their names at Knightsbridge police station.

'I must just ask you a few questions,' Detective Inspector Pendry said, taking out a notepad. 'First, do the names Anil Bandari and Michael Jensen mean anything to you?' he said.

Alistair had never heard of Anil Bandari. The other name, though – the other name he did know. He felt his mouth go dry with fear. Michael Jensen was a defence witness in the Giorgiou case, a friend of the defendant.

'I'm sorry,' he said. 'I've never heard of either of them.'

When Detective Inspector Pendry had gone, Alistair thought it all through with terrifying clarity, resolving the outlandish details into a story that really did fit into his life.

There could be no doubt as to the motivation for the attack: it was an act of revenge, the lashing out of a male ego. It was about a girl.

He could not believe Karen's indiscretion had been malicious. She would have seen it as something to giggle about. He felt absolutely sure of this and amazed that he did. But he trusted Karen – he trusted that her betrayal had not been a desire to expose him to anger and violence, but merely to make a joke at his expense. She would only have wanted to laugh about it with someone, to entertain a friend with a funny story about her adventure with an old barrister. He imagined her talking excitedly with a drink and a cigarette in her hand. He remembered how sad she had been that she didn't have a camera to record the way the hotel room looked. She was young enough to find private experience lacking and to believe it must be validated by the envy or approval of another, no matter what the risk.

Obviously it had got back to Giorgiou. And that proud, vain young Greek could never have let it pass – although Karen had said he was openly unfaithful himself. He could picture the reaction: 'What? *Karen?* With the prosecution barrister?' the spoilt mouth would have asked. 'With the barrister who is trying to *put me away?*'

Karen should have known her friend better. Why had she not known her friend better? He closed his eyes in desperation. But she was very young, he thought, and we all have our quota of mistakes to make and learn from. This episode had undoubtedly been her short, sharp tutorial on discretion.

It was possible that even Giorgiou could not have foreseen the ultimate outcome of his revenge. That the men had been caught was the factor no one could have predicted. If only they had got away, it might have been passed off as a mugging and Giorgiou would still have inflicted his punishment on Alistair's leg. But Julian, the good neighbour with his mobile phone, had ensured the bad guys were caught, and now there was the signature, 'M. Jensen', scrawled in the police book, signalling something curious, something to be looked into, to anyone who cared to notice.

Alistair lay in his hospital bed, waiting for someone to notice, his hours punctuated by visits from the doctor, the physiotherapist and the nurses – and his increasingly suspicious wife.

Astonishingly, he managed to cling on through Rosalind's initial questions, buying himself more time. But the questions quickly took on the essential theme: why had the police come back *three* times to visit him? Wasn't it strange that muggers had not even *attempted* to take anything?

One moment had been almost comic – if it's possible to laugh as you dig your own grave. Rosalind had arrived in a determined mood, as if she was going to insist on some kind of explanation. Alistair told his heart to enjoy the last moments of its former life. Within seconds he would have to tell her about Karen. But one heartbeat – literally one heartbeat! – before he began to speak, a nurse came in, saying it was time for his bed-bath.

Miraculously, Rosalind was defeated by this interruption, and after the wash was done, she talked only about Luke, who had come to stay that day and was terribly upset about a girlfriend.

On her few visits after that, before he was discharged, Alistair feigned sleep and listened to her sitting silently beside him for as long as he could. And when he woke, plainly too weak and confused to be interrogated, she seemed too preoccupied with their son to ask him questions anyway. She didn't stay long – she must hurry home, she said, she was desperately worried about poor Luke. When he looked back on it, he wondered if this wasn't her way of clinging on, too. They had always been accomplices in that sense.

But on the morning after she brought him home, to the newly laundered bed and the cut flowers on the dressing-table, there was no longer any way to avoid what had happened. The sun shone outside the bedroom window, a tray of toast and coffee sat beside him on the duvet and already the filthy papers were waiting in the shops.

Again, Alistair was sure it had not been Karen who had sold the story. It occurred to him that his faith in her might spring from the false intimacy, the false expectation of loyalty he had always thought would be created by casual sex, but this did not ring true. He remembered the tenderness with which she had said goodbye to him in the hotel bathroom, while she sang along to the TV. No, it had not been her, he thought – she was too good-natured. She laughed too naturally. It might have been many people: the indiscreet friend, one of the attackers or even one of the police. But not Karen. And, anyway, the long delay between their night together and Giorgiou hearing of it and the papers being alerted had a brutal clumsiness to it, which suggested a stranger's involvement. Had Karen felt guilt towards Giorgiou, or spite for Alistair, or even plain greed for a newspaper pay-off, she would have told her story immediately, a couple of months ago.

So, Rosalind had checked he had everything he needed and went out as usual for *The Times* at around nine. All that morning he lay ignorantly in their bedroom drifting in and out of sleep, distantly aware of ghostly doorbells and phones, of Rosalind's feet hurrying to answer them. He began to wonder who all her visitors were and why they did not come up to see him. Why did *she* not come up to see him? He put the breakfast tray on the floor and picked up a book.

At last, at around one thirty, he was actually hungry and thirsty and called out to her: 'Darling? Darling, I've finished my water, I'm afraid. I'm so sorry about this.' He was embarrassed to be so dependent on her.

He heard her feet coming slowly up the stairs and leant back on his pillows. Then he took in the white, pinched face in the doorway, the improbable coffee splash she had left unsponged on her shirt. 'Darling?'

'*No*,' she said.

She put the paper on the bed and left the room.

The *Sun* headline read: '**FAT CAT QC BEDS SEX-KITTEN WITNESS**', and there was Karen, photographed by a battered front door, looking amazed, looking about fourteen.

His eyes skimmed the opening paragraph, picking out the phrases printed in bold, '**London's trendy Ridgeley Hotel**', '**quaffing expensive champagne**' and then, further down, '**"She looked young enough to be his daughter," said barmaid Angela Jessop, 23**.' They had even interviewed the staff.

He put the paper down and laid his hands neatly at his sides. '*Rosalind?*' he shouted. '*Rosalind?*'

But a few minutes later it was his son who came into the room.

Chapter 11

It was the kind of summer's day that has Londoners staring up at the sky and speculating about the hole in the ozone layer. TV and radio voices carried through open windows, reciting weather statistics, saying 'heatwave' and 'global warming' and 'possible water shortages'. It was already stiflingly hot at ten to nine. There was primitive fear on the tube trains — of thirst, suffocation, fire — as they thundered through their network of underground tunnels.

As he dressed, Luke thought how glad he was not to be on the Piccadilly line on his way to work. He could imagine the smell of it. This was his second week off. He had told the office there had been a death in the family — which, of course, there had — but he knew they would all have seen the papers and assumed his father was the reason Luke had asked for compassionate leave. He imagined he was much talked about next to the big photocopier outside Sebastian's office. He really didn't care.

He went down the stairs for breakfast. On the way he heard his father moving around and felt glad that he and his mother would be alone for a bit. He knew his father hung around in the spare room long after he woke up. As he reached the bottom of the stairs, he heard the sound of the toaster popping up.

'Morning, darling. Did you sleep?' Rosalind said.

'Nope. Did you?'

'A little. A few hours. Oh, the pair of us.' She shook her head and put out toast and marmalade and coffee. 'I'm afraid I dropped the eggs, Luke. All six of them broke, would you believe it?'

'Oh, Mum.' Luke rubbed her arm.

'But there's cereal, too. And my yoghurt – not that anyone else likes it. Look, is that going to be enough for you?'

'Mum, you must stop worrying and look after yourself. You do need to, after . . . everything.'

'Yes,' she said, 'I know.' She looked desolate for a moment and Luke was sorry he had even referred to it. She seemed to hold herself together so long as no one mentioned that anything was wrong. He understood this because they were essentially similar. When things had fallen apart with Arianne he noticed that he himself had developed what Sophie referred to as their mother's 'first-lady' smile. It was a relentless kind of smile, used to ward off bad spirits. Rosalind did it at him over her coffee cup and he wondered how she would cope while he and his father were away for the day in Dover.

The plan was to go and look at the house with the surveyor and put it on the market. They were also going to pack up the rest of the clothes and funny ornaments and old bits of furniture. Luke felt no connection with the idea that he had had a grandmother – or had always had a grandmother – whom he had never met. It was as if no one had owned that little house and those possessions: they had fallen out of the sky with an incalculable significance, like a doll found in a bush where a plane once crashed.

As for the other issue, what his father had done with that slutty-looking girl, it was incomprehensible and too psychologically threatening to contemplate. Luke simply couldn't stand any more disillusionment just now. Instead he worked himself up into a deep resentment of his sister, who had not been round once since the story came out in the papers. Resentment was a welcome relief from humiliation and it was not without its sensual qualities.

'Have you spoken to Sophie?' he asked.

'I called her this morning.'

'Right. So when's she coming over?'

'She's not.'

Luke's face reddened. 'What?'

'She isn't planning to come over just yet, darling.'

'She's not coming over.'

'No, Luke.'

'Why? Why not?'

'She just won't, darling. She says she can't face seeing him.'

Luke felt intensely angry with Sophie. Couldn't she tell their mother needed them at the moment? Was he the only one with any sense of

175

family responsibility? *He* didn't exactly want to spend time with his father himself, but he was doing it, wasn't he? Because that was real life, that was being an adult, both of which were things Sophie didn't understand – for all her brilliant exam results.

Sitting at the breakfast table with his fist clenched, Luke entirely forgot that he had been brought home by his mother for his own sake and all but carried up the stairs like a child asleep after a long bout of tears.

'What about seeing you, though?' he said. 'That's my whole point, Mum. That's what this is all about.'

'She just can't face it all yet. Luke, it was terribly embarrassing for her at work.'

'Uh-huh.'

The *Telegraph* had covered the story, like all the other papers. Sophie had watched colleagues file copy about her own father. It wasn't that Luke didn't sympathize: it was just that they were always making allowances for Sophie's greater sensitivity. She always got away with looking after herself – because she was so very *sensitive*.

'She's very sensitive, darling,' Rosalind said. 'You know that.'

Yes, he knew that. Any minute she might cut up her arms with a razor blade so you saw the scars when she reached out for her cup, or she might turn up on the doorstep weighing five and a half stone, shaking and crying. He knew all about it. He wanted to bring the subject back to himself. As usual, he felt he was doing the dutiful, boring stuff while everyone worried about his sister's feelings.

He really didn't want to drive his father to Dover. He had already done the journey once a couple of days ago and that had been awkward enough. Apart from the fact that the idea felt unreal, distasteful – even sinister, like everything connected with his father at the moment – the truth was, he did not want to give up another whole day that he might have spent lying on his bed, thinking about Arianne. He was also terrified that Alistair might attempt to explain himself – although there was no precedent for any kind of personal discussion in their relationship. But Luke had noticed a kind of mellowing in Alistair since they first visited Dover. There was something approaching senti-mentality in his eyes and, instinctively, Luke thought it might go with making confessions.

When Luke thought about what this conversation might sound like, he was aware that he had never before rehearsed dialogue in his mind in which he heard the other person speak and then struggled to breathe, let alone to do an impression of his own voice. 'Mum, do you really think I should go to Dover with Dad? I mean, is it strictly necessary?' he said.

Rosalind furrowed her brow, 'Luke, you've got to. You've just got to. He can't drive all that way with his leg.'

'I know that. I just don't understand why he can't just send people in or whatever. Why does he have to go himself?'

'Because it was his mother, Luke. They're her things – and that was his childhood home. Anyway, the house has to go on the market and it belongs to Dad now. You have to deal with that kind of thing in person. You just have to. You and Sophie always have this idea about *sending* people. Where does it come from? What *people*?'

Rosalind looked at her son and wondered frantically for a moment if she had done everything wrong – not only marriage, but Luke and Sophie too. Were they spoilt and irresponsible? Was that why Sophie couldn't find a husband, why Luke went to pieces like this and showed off about his salary all the time?

'Removal people, Mum, that's all. Look, it just feels so weird, is all I'm saying – doing him a favour.'

'I know, I know,' she said, softening with compassion again as she watched her son's hurt face. 'My poor darling. But, Luke, it's you or me driving him. That's what it comes down to.'

'God, hasn't he got any friends?'

'Not at the moment, no.'

'No, I suppose not.' He put his hand over hers and felt a rush of love and protectiveness and pride that he was such a good son. She looked gratefully at him and then she heard Alistair limping and tapping his stick down the stairs, and flashed her eyes. 'He's coming.'

Rosalind behaved as if her husband was literally dangerous, yet he couldn't have seemed more cowed as he came lumbering in. He attempted to grin casually – a sort of prolonged wince – and then he drummed his fingers on the sideboard in a bright little flourish: it betrayed his heartbeat. 'Morning, darling,' he said, unable to meet her eyes.

Rosalind took her full coffee cup over to the sink, tipped out the contents and washed it. 'Good morning.'

They listened to the fridge humming.

'Goodness, ten fifteen already,' Alistair said. 'Well, shall we head off soonish, Luke?'

'What? Right now?'

'Twenty minutes or so. That's my thinking.'

'Aren't you going to have any breakfast, Dad?'

Alistair glanced at Rosalind's back. 'No, I don't think so. Better just get on. That's my thinking.' He stood still.

'OK,' Luke said. 'Well, I'll just eat this toast, then, if that's OK, and then we'll go.'

'Good, good. That sounds good. Right.'

He walked rather formally into the hall, and after a moment, Rosalind shouted, 'I've put some trunks out, Alistair.' She paused, then began again more quietly, 'Luke and Sophie's old school trunks? They're on the landing. I thought they might be useful for packing things up in.'

Alistair hurried back into the room. 'That was – that was very thoughtful of you, darling.'

'It was nothing,' she said, turning away again.

By eleven, they were on the road, heading for Dover. Luke had not driven his father anywhere before these trips to Dover and he found himself conscientiously checking the mirror and moving his hands on the wheel like a new driver, seeking Alistair's approval.

But Alistair didn't notice any of it – he couldn't have cared less about his son's driving: he was filling his lungs with delicious air. As they set off, he felt himself rise, kicking, up to the bright surface. He inhaled deeply. He felt so relieved that he smiled – and immediately hoped his son had not seen. Luke had caught him laughing at a silly item on the news the day before and for a few seconds had seemed to regard his father with open horror before informing him that supper was ready. Alistair could see that it was in very poor taste to smile.

But the fact remained: today was a beautiful day – and the smile came back. Since the hurdle of the first visit to Dover had been cleared and a few days had passed with no mention of his name in the papers, he felt increasingly detached from the circumstances of his life. He felt OK, so long as Rosalind wasn't there, so long as he couldn't see his wife's face. He was aware that this was emotionally crass, but there it was. Perhaps he was having some kind of a breakdown and the memory of these false calms would later serve to emphasize the storm.

Alistair suspected he ought to have a nervous breakdown, that, morally speaking, it was the only adequate reaction. But in his heart, he knew he was perfectly sane. Helplessly, he grinned at the perfect blue sky and said, 'What a beautiful day.'

Luke squinted through the windscreen. 'Mmm. Might turn viciously hot, though.'

They drove the rest of the way listening to the radio. There was Chopin playing and Alistair found it restful to be driven by his son and to stare out of the window like a dreamy child. In this way he ate and drank, too – accepting his lunch from Rosalind with boyish gratitude and a little smile that also communicated his emotional negligence, his inability to confront what he had done to their adult relationship.

As Luke and Alistair got near to Dover they found themselves driving behind foreign number-plates and left-hand-drive cars. Billboards advertised McDonald's hamburgers and milkshakes in French and English. Bottles of Lisco lemon-and-lime crush could be purchased for just €1 or 75p a litre. Because it was August, plenty of holidaymakers were heading off in their cars for the ferry terminal; many contained a whole family and a great crush of suitcases and sunhats and beach-balls. There were bored children asleep in the back with vast bags of crisps in their arms, and story-tapes in fatuous adult voices – a universal sing-song – could be heard playing through the open windows as the cars slowed for the roundabout. All around were the signs not only of travel but also of import and export. There were lorries behind and in front of them, with exuberant slogans in Dutch and French and Spanish across their vast tarpaulins.

The sea and the cliffs came into focus as they reached the roundabout, and beyond the sunny haze, somewhere on the horizon, was Europe.

'You forget you're on a little island, don't you?' Luke said. 'You really feel it here, though. This is like the edge of England. The last outpost.'

'Yes, I know what you mean. Yes,' Alistair said – always surprised if his son made an observation of any subtlety.

Luke noticed that some kind of demonstration was going on near the ferry terminal. It was just possible to make out a crowd and several placards. The two vast lorries ahead roared off towards the docks and Luke turned the car in the direction of the town centre.

They drove up York Street, towards the town hall. In spite of the threatening start, it had become a pleasantly warm afternoon. The scene in the town centre looked sunny and ordinary: young mothers pushed prams; adolescent boys walked around in scowling gangs; two old ladies clutched each other's arms at the zebra crossing; an

179

enormous man in a vest put his hand up and simulated a jog across the road in front of their car, his belly jerking over his belt.

It struck both of them that people were noticeably fatter here, more garishly coloured than they were in London. Neon orange, lime green, scalding pink T-shirts strained across vast bra-less breasts and rolls of flab. Alistair watched female hands covered with cheap rings, male hands covered with tattoos, flash in the side window as the car moved along the road. They held beer cans and choc ices and cigarettes. Every face appeared to be chewing or swallowing something contained in bright packaging.

Cheap food depressed Alistair. He stared out at what struck him as conspicuous poverty. This sugary, colourful plenitude actually signified deprivation – of the capacity to discern what was good or bad for the body in the strobe flash of media images. Wealth, on the other hand, would always be a seamless absence, an opting-out of the mass market: pure as mineral water, discreet as a navy blue cashmere coat.

Thirty years ago, the crowd's noise and colour had come from pub sing-alongs and 'New! Luxury!' goods aspirations, but time and TV had effected this gaudy change. His head shook slightly as he remembered the spiritual awe with which his mother had longed for an American ice-box. Back then, it had all made him so angry and desperate. He had felt stifled by the material limits of their desires.

But they looked so joyous – and they always had. Dover had always contained this abundant human energy. How much happier these fat young mothers looked than the starved joggers in Holland Park. They were smiling and laughing in the busy street just as they had smiled and laughed when he was last here. He saw how patronizing he was being, but his relationship with the place he grew up in had always contained this uncomfortable quality. How could it not when he had been condemned to estrangement by his unexpected brain?

Had he been handed to the wrong mother? He remembered the elaborate fantasies he had constructed along these lines: the wealthy professor who came to the door, arms outstretched, calling him 'son'.

But his mother had been his mother, all right – he had her nose and her hands and her feet. These were not to be argued with.

Eventually he had come both to love and hate being the superior outsider. It had been lonely having only his ambitions for company, never being able to share enthusiasm for a book – except with one or two teachers at school, which always exposed him to bullying. And as he got older his awkwardness increased. It became harder and harder to join in with his old friends, with his mother and Geoff and Ivy drinking shandy in the garden. Without understanding why, the lonelier he felt, the more he had made terrible scenes about needing to study without interruption. He had slammed his books on the table and said no one understood how hard it was to win a scholarship to Oxford – but he was bloody well going to, though. His mother told him not to use that foul language in this house – and he shouted and stormed at her about how little she understood or cared about his brilliance, his plans.

At last everyone took him at his word and tiptoed past his door in silence. He nearly died of peace.

Alistair shook his head and smiled. What a lot of his life had passed sitting alone at a desk, listening to distant sounds of celebration!

He looked out at the sunlit pavement, at the shopping-bags and hairdos and thought: Perhaps it matters very little what your aspirations are so long as they are occasionally fulfilled. An American icebox, the latest pair of trainers, a five-bedroom house in Holland Park. Perhaps there was only the most arbitrary of differences. Perhaps success was all a question of accrued sensation rather than meaning, after all.

If this was true, then what a very long way he had come to realize it. Or what a short way, he thought, as they turned on to Maison Dieu Road.

'Well, here we are, Dad,' Luke said.

'Goodness, yes. You got us here quickly. The surveyor isn't coming until a quarter to two. Shall we get some lunch first?'

'Fine by me. Where should we go? You're the expert.'

'Yes, I suppose so – although my information may be a little out of date. We could go to the White Horse – just up here and on the left. There's a little car park, I think. There used to be a little car park, anyway.'

They pulled up outside the pub, which was by a ruined church, on the corner of three roads. One led up to the castle and the cliffs; another stretched down to the sea and the third towards the town centre. Alistair sighed. 'My God, I haven't been here for . . .' but he tightened his lips rather than supplying a number, which would have been meaningless to his son anyway. It would have been meaningless to *him*, really. He levered his bad leg out of the car and stared along the road, his head still shaking gently.

Luke had begun to observe that his father would be an old man one day. He had never seen Alistair injured before and the limp and the walking-stick were like a foretaste of old age. It was frightening and oddly exciting at once to contemplate this.

'So, do you remember it all, Dad?' he said, genuinely curious. 'After all these years?'

His father had a distant smile on his face. 'Oh, perfectly.' Alistair took his walking-stick out of the car and shut the door. 'Come on, they used to do good grub in here.'

The White Horse had been bought in the late nineties by a childless Australian couple who had needed a pet project. The husband worked behind the bar with his wife. They were tanned and muscular, at odds with their pink-and-white English clientele. The husband pointed out of the window at the pub garden. 'Have you guys come for lunch? We're doing a barbecue out there if you're into shrimps or steak or chicken.'

This was plainly not the White Horse Alistair remembered. Luke noticed his father's shock and couldn't help adding to it mischievously. He said, 'It says on your board you do kangaroo steak.'

The wife came over to the bar, 'Ah, yes, normally we do, but we just had a party of eight and they ate the lot. Big, greedy boys!'

'Kangaroo steak?' Alistair said.

'Yes, it's a little like pork.' The wife beamed healthily and handed him a menu. 'But we're all out, love,' she added gently. 'There's the barbecue – or we have great sandwiches, if you prefer.'

'Well, I know what I'm having. I'll have the grilled chicken panino with pesto, please,' Luke said.

'Yes. And I'll have . . . I'll have the egg and cress – er – *bloomer*. What exactly is a bloomer? Type of bread, is it?'

'A bloomer? That's a typical English roll. Soft – delicious,' she said. 'You'll love it. You're all right with a bloomer.'

He remembered Karen asking him what a quesadilla was. Why would he be 'all right' with a bloomer? The barmaid plainly saw him as old and decrepit, and seemed to think she was indulging him with her patronizing manner.

'A roll. Right. I'll have one of those, please – just with simple egg and cress. And a pint of Old Simpson. You do have that, do you?'

'Yes, we do. That's a good, traditional English cider.'

'Make it two,' Luke said.

The woman smiled, first at Luke and then at Alistair, as she pulled the pints. 'Are you two father and son?'

'Yes,' Alistair told her warily.

'You don't mind me saying – but what a strong resemblance. Not just face shape and noses and whatnot. Just look at that body language!' She laughed.

Luke and Alistair checked themselves and then each other and found they were standing in an identical pose, Luke leaning on a bar stool, Alistair on his stick, each with one arm folded high across the chest and the hand tucked under the armpit, the head bowed. Both found a reason to move.

'Aaah,' she went on. 'Dad and son out for a nice pub lunch together, hey?' She put the second frothing pint down on the counter. 'Here you go, fellas.' Her hand shot out neatly for the money.

They carried the drinks over to a table in a cool, dark corner.

'Kangaroo steak,' Alistair said. They laughed and Luke lit a cigarette.

'Changed a bit, then, Dad?'

'Yes. But no more than I have, I suppose.' He sighed.

In forty years Dover was very different. And yet, like the photograph of his white-haired mother, it was still undoubtedly the same. The town centre and the bleached seafront hotels and the cliffs and the grey Channel itself were the essential bone structure.

What about the people, though? He wondered what Ivy Gilbert would look like now. He had not spoken to her since she had telephoned and told Rosalind about his mother's death. He had taken the coward's way out and written instead of calling her back and hearing a ghost's voice. But of course he must see her at some point – and if too much time had passed for him to see her out of affection then he must see her out of simple courtesy.

Ivy would be a very old woman now. His heart moved as he thought this and he knew that, really, the affection had remained unchanged through all the years. He had carried it around and it had survived miraculously, like a dog-eared love-note in a soldier's pocket. Would dear old Geoff still be alive? he wondered. He did not like to think of Ivy alone. Not all alone – as his mother had been.

'I wonder what that demonstration was about,' Luke said, 'by the seafront.'

'Demonstration? I didn't notice.'

'Yes. There were about thirty people holding these signs up just by the ferry terminal. You couldn't see what they said, though.'

'There are often things bubbling up there. Animal rights a lot, I think. Protest about live export.'

'I might go and see while you talk to the surveyor. Would that be OK? I'd like a walk.'

'Yes, of course. This is all so boring for you,' Alistair said. He felt embarrassed, unexpectedly beholden to his son. He watched Luke drinking his cider, his eyes focused on nothing in particular. It was not to be envied, really, that lost look of youth. 'Luke, thank you for driving me today,' he said. 'It's a shame we didn't get much done last time. I think I was just a bit – well, thrown, really. I'm sorry you've had to drive all this way a second time.'

It was such an odd reversal of roles but, again, this was not an unpleasant sensation to Luke. He felt mature and highly reasonable as he said, 'That's OK, Dad. It's not as if you never drove me anywhere I needed to go. Think of all those rugby matches.'

'Yes,' Alistair said, but he was guiltily certain it had almost always been Rosalind who had done that. He had found the thinly veiled competitiveness of the other parents intolerably petty and depressing. And sport was meaningless to him because it was not academic achievement: it got you nowhere, taught you nothing. You just went up and down a field. Claiming work pressure, he had avoided almost all the back-of-car picnics, Rosalind's sausage rolls and Scotch eggs, and the cheering in the rain. Consequently he had missed almost all Luke's sporting victories, too. Instead, he heard them lovingly misreported by Rosalind over family suppers. Luke would blush and correct her: 'It really wasn't the only try, Mum. Stephen Falconer got two.'

'Well, Mr Sanderson said *you* saved the game, darling. He *did*, Luke.'

Alistair watched his son now, stubbing out his cigarette, and thought he basically didn't know him at all. Could this extraordinary display of grief, the weight loss, the sobbing in his room at night, really be over a girl? 'Rugby or no rugby, I'm grateful, Luke,' he said, knowing this was not at all what he meant. Then he caught sight of their food coming over and was glad to put an end to this unfamiliar type of conversation.

After lunch, Luke dropped Alistair at the old boarding-house. The surveyor, a thin man in a slightly shiny grey suit, was waiting on the doorstep with a clipboard tucked under his arm. From the car, Luke watched his father greet him and lead the surveyor inside.

Luke thought it was a horrible-looking little house, with greying net curtains and dark green paint peeling off all the window-frames in large curls. The garden in front was all weeds and people had thrown rubbish into it. A black bin-bag flapped in the hedge. At least half the

184

mosaic paving stones were missing on the path up to the door. It was a total mess and probably riddled with damp, and Luke wondered if his father would get anything for it anyway.

Luke knew a bit about property – after all, he had bought two flats for himself in London. Yes, his father had stumped up for the first one, but Luke had gone on to make a good profit by selling it at just the right time. For this reason he thought of the second flat as the fruit of his own labour. It gave him a great deal of satisfaction.

He sighed and hoped his father was thinking clearly about selling this dilapidated little house. He wasn't sure why he hadn't brought the subject up at lunch, as it was one area in which he might actually have seemed worthy of his father's attention.

But he could never assert himself in front of Alistair. He became what Alistair had decided he was: the stupid, sporty one who didn't even understand wine the way his sister did.

He looked at his watch and wondered – as he did every time he looked at his watch – what Arianne would be doing now, and who she was doing it with. He could taste the food she was eating, the cigarette she was smoking, when he thought about her. He had heard nothing from her. But she had not been in touch with Ludo or any of their other friends either. She had disappeared. She had run away on her incredible legs.

The thought of her legs sent lust through his body like a wind through long grass and he put his head into his hands and lost himself to memories. She was lying naked underneath him on the hall carpet, her legs circling his hips, her calves banging against the back of his thighs as if he was the winning horse. It had all been such a delicious panic.

But there had been times when the urgency was even greater: when she arched herself over him, her hand pressed against his chest to keep him still and he felt her tense every muscle one by one in a ritual of agonizing precision. It was like being children, playing a game of blinking, or eating doughnuts without licking the sugar off your lips – who would give in first to the body's desires? Slowly, slowly, she would build the longing in their nerve endings – and then, shaking and crying out, she would kick and slap it away.

It had all been so wonderful – his designer lamps got knocked over, wine bottles rolled, pouring wild streams across the floor, and they shouted out all kinds of passionate nonsense without caring what it meant or who heard it through the wall. At last she would fall exhausted on to the pillow beside him, saying, "Hanks, baby," in her baby voice.

Why the baby voice? he wondered. It had always been slightly sinister, belonging to the realm of things he didn't understand about her, like her rages and her sudden fits of crying.

One thing he knew with absolute certainty was that he would never again experience as much physical pleasure as he had with Arianne. She had a capacity for total sensual abandonment that he had not seen in any other girl he had slept with. He had never heard a girl cry like she could, either. She cried as voluptuously as she made love. He had felt as inadequate before her sadness as he did before her sensuality and had not known how to help when she bawled and rocked, hugging her knees.

He had let her down time and again. At the end she had seemed to hate him most of all when she cried and he laid his stupid, inadequate hand on her back. She jolted it off, saying, 'Oh, just *fuck off*, Luke.' Once, in one of their last arguments, she had actually punched him in the face.

Girls could really hit. Luke knew this because his sister had hit him once, too. Not just kids' play-fighting, but a genuine attack just a couple of years ago. Sophie had caught his cheek and his nose with a sweeping backhand after a row about who had lost the remote control and who, by extension, was the more spoilt and irresponsible. The impact made a comic-book *thwaaack!* and his nose started to bleed. He stared at his sister's shocked face, saying, 'What the . . . what the . . .' until she ran out of the room in tears.

Luke thought: What if, fundamentally, women consider men an enemy and basically want to humiliate and destroy them?

But – he loved girls! Were they getting back at men for making them do the vacuuming and the cooking for all those years? He felt on the verge of deep understanding and rubbed his head and his eyes. Then he thought fondly of Lucy, who said things like 'Oh, you are such a lovely *man*, aren't you, darling?' when she undid his shirt and stroked the hair on his chest. He thought of his mother and the way she had hugged him that morning in the kitchen, relying on him.

No, it was just these crazy women who hated men. He wondered if his sister was good in bed like Arianne and decided immediately that she would be. This was a profoundly disturbing thought and he got out of the car quickly, slammed the door and locked it.

★   ★   ★

He walked down towards the crowd of people on the seafront. The demonstration had grown. Sixty or seventy people stood along the marina, holding placards and shouting. Their physical anger seemed unreal to Luke. He had spent so many sleepless nights surfing the Internet that real life was like a complex website and he felt his index finger twitch for 'click here' when he opened a door or reached for something. The Internet, the TV and the weird moonlit reticence of his parents were many times removed from these loud voices and raised fists.

'Out! Out!' they shouted.

> 'Out! *Out!* Scream and *shout!*
> *Do*ver *re*sidents, use your *clout!*'

Luke read the placards as he got close enough to see.
'Illegal Invasion!'
'Swamp France Instead!'
'Dover is not Asylum Alley.'
It was one of the demonstrations his aunt Suzannah had mentioned seeing on the news – a mixture of local residents and nationalist groups campaigning against the influx of asylum-seekers. He had read about the latest in a series of government 'crackdowns', which had involved giving police man-sensor machines to help catch smugglers as they drove off the ferries. The machines were passed against the sides of goods lorries; they could detect the sound of a human heartbeat.

Luke stared out at the crowd, all pink-faced and squinting angrily in the sunshine. On the wall in front of a TV camera and a reporter was a girl in a tight T-shirt with a swastika on it. She had large round breasts, which distorted the obscene symbol; her legs were fat and white and muscular. She glanced in Luke's direction and the idea of eye-contact with her frightened him so much that he hurried on with his head down. Two men wearing 'Save Dover' baseball caps came briskly across his path, their bodies already attuned to the vigour of the demonstration. A police helicopter circled and buzzed threateningly overhead. Mounted officers in riot gear, like space-age knights, flashed sunlight off their plastic shields as their horses jogged and stamped.

Luke walked on past the crowd and stopped by one of the seafront boarding-houses where three teenage girls stood smoking and observing from a safe distance. 'Matt's down there,' one said, nodding her mirrored sunglasses at the crowd.

'Yeah?'

'Yeah. He done his big sign this morning.'

'Yeah? Matt did? What's it say?'

'He nicked one of Mum's sheets – she went *men*tal.'

'What's it say, Michelle? What did he put?' the youngest-looking one asked.

'It said, "Scum down the drain not in Dover." '

'What's *that* got to do with anything?'

The other two laughed and rolled their eyes at each other.

'*Asylum scum?* Ring any bells, Saz?'

'Fuck – I'm still mash-up from last night.' She shook her head as if she was clearing it of a blockage.

'You *al*ways say that. D'you know you always say that?'

'No.'

'Well, you do. We ought to get down there, really. Don't you think, Jem?' A little way off, two police officers had stopped a young man and asked him to empty his pockets. One searched through his wallet, while the other watched him take things out of his jeans and hold them up in a pantomime of scandalized innocence.

'Don't, Michelle,' Saz said, eyeing this spectacle. 'It's dangerous.'

'*Ooooh*,' laughed the other girl. 'I wonder who sounds just like their mum. Like their do-goody leftie mum.'

'Come on, I don't,' Saz said, knowing full well that, unlike her weirdly passionate mother, all she felt was fear of physical harm.

'Yeah. Your mum's a loony leftie, Dad says. She'd let all the dross in to take all the jobs and housing in Dover. She'd probably give them her *bed*, too. Bit of money for a fucking *ice-cream*.'

Michelle and Jem laughed.

'No, she wouldn't,' Saz said. 'That's just crap. We *hate* them.'

Jem spat her chewing-gum into the road suddenly and said, 'They should burn. They should petrol-bomb the lot of them, the scroungers.' She looked right into Saz's face as if it had been discovered that she was to blame and this was the moment of confrontation. 'Taking all our fucking jobs and money,' she said, 'bringing in AIDS.'

Luke walked quickly away from them along the seafront. He had never heard anything like this before. English people hating like this. Girls hating like this. Young girls – no more than fourteen years old. Behind him the crowd shouted, 'Out! Out! Out!' and he walked as fast as he could until he could no longer make out the words.

He wound his way back towards the town centre where it felt

188

safer. He could not believe this was where his father had grown up. He walked past the slot-machine arcade and the pawnbroker with its shamefaced-looking watches and rings and televisions and the 'Everything under £1' shop where you could get dusters and plastic laundry baskets and hairspray and felt slippers. There was the sweaty smell of onions and burgers frying and in a nearby street an ice-cream van played its melancholy, tinkling music.

When Luke thought of his own childhood and schooling and the house he had grown up in, he knew he carried them with him wherever he went. His mother's taste was evident in his choice of ties; his father's professional authority was behind his capacity to send bad food back in a restaurant; his school sporting victories had given him the physical confidence with which he swung open a door or caught a bunch of keys that were thrown to him across a room. Where had his father allowed his past to contribute to *his* personality? Looking around, it was impossible to say.

It had never occurred either to Luke or to Sophie before that their father did not refer to his childhood and had only mentioned vaguely that he went to a school in Sussex that they would never have heard of. Luke imagined Sophie had also pictured a minor boarding-school – a little like their schools, but smaller. But his father's life had been nothing like theirs. Their father had been poor. He had grown up alone with his poor mother in the kind of house that poor people lived in, with damp stains and rust and worn-out furniture.

What did it mean to hide that much about yourself? Wasn't it pretending to be someone else? For a moment, Luke felt as if he had been burgled. He had frightened himself and he pictured his father and thought: *Who are you?*

But Luke had recently had reason to become passionately conscious of how easy it was not to be yourself, to become a fake or an approximation. He felt that he had not been himself at all since Arianne left. In fact, he distinctly remembered feeling that he had not been himself until the day she arrived. This meant he had been himself (except in the presence of his father, in front of whom he was always someone shy and awkward and hateful) for a total of about twelve weeks.

Twelve weeks, out of all his twenty-eight years. This was plainly ridiculous. Wasn't it? He did not like the idea – and this would apply to his mother, too – that other people were as chaotic and unfixed as he had proved to be.

Automatically he had made his way back to the seafront again and the broad, flat sight of the Channel was consoling after his intricate thoughts. He stood still and lit a cigarette.

'Hello, excuse me? Do you have free cigarette, please?' said a foreign voice. Luke spun round to see a tall, black-haired man with a deeply furrowed brow. He was wearing a woman's anorak over a threadbare blue jumper. A dirty handkerchief was tied round an injury to his wrist. On the wall, a little way off from him, was a starved-looking girl. Something mutually affirmative about the angle of their bodies suggested they were together.

'Yeah, sure,' Luke said, fumbling in his jeans pocket. 'D'you both want one?' He glanced at the girl. Her skinny legs dangled like one at peace in her daydreams, but the heel that banged the wall in triplicate from time to time gave her a tense, military air, as if a marching tune was playing in her head. The man called out, 'Mila, *cigaretu?*'

She was gazing out to sea and at first she seemed to be squinting at the distance or because of the strong sunshine, but when she turned her pinched face in their direction her expression remained the same.

'Thank you,' she said, as she arrived beside them. Luke handed her the cigarette and she waited for him to light it, saying, 'Thank you', again in exactly the careful way Luke said, '*Grazie*', all the time in Italy, because it was all he really knew how to say.

'Can you speak English?' Luke asked her.

'Very bad,' she said, and lowered her eyes.

'I speak,' the man said. He put out his hand. 'Goran. Great to meet you.'

'Luke,' said Luke, a little unnerved by the man's unexpected American accent.

'This is Mila.'

The girl shook his hand awkwardly.

'So, where are you from?' Luke said.

'You know Kosovo?' said Goran.

Immediately Luke felt that he did not watch enough news, that he skipped the long articles in the papers, and that he lacked original opinions for dinner parties.

'Um – yes. Yes – the war,' he said, unthinkingly, remembering something about the Albanians and the Serbs and a news clip of a girl with a gun on her back, saying she would defend Serbia until she died in the snow. 'Yes, of course. Of course I do.'

'We are from there. We are Serbs. And you are English?'

'Yes.'

Goran nodded approvingly.

'Pretty boring, really,' Luke said, smiling.

'What is boring?'

'Just English – I meant.'

'I'm sorry I have misunderstand you.'

'No – just I mean so much more interesting to come from Kosovo, that's all I meant, not just from boring England.'

Goran laughed. 'Boring England? I hope it is the most boring place in the world. This is why we came. We have enough of interesting Kosovo.'

'Look, I'm sorry – I'm not putting things . . .' It was not as if the articles were that long – or as if he had anything so much better to do. He read the Style section, the sports pages. Why? Because he was superficial. That was why Arianne had got bored with him.

Goran waved his hand genially, dismissing Luke's embarrassment. 'So, you live here in Dover?'

'Me? No. God, no – I'm from London. Holland Park. I'm just here for the day. A day trip.'

'Ah, yes? From London?'

'Yes. Have you been there?'

Goran smiled. 'No. We have been inside England just twenty-four hours.'

'Yes I see. Not much time to look around, then.'

Luke listened as Goran and Mila began to talk in whatever their language was. The exchange became heated, with Goran appearing to disagree with something Mila had suggested. It was odd how you could work it out. Goran ended the conversation firmly with '*Ne*, Mila.'

She stared at him with her ravenous eyes and Luke thought she would have been quite pretty if her face had not been so thin. But she looked feverish – endangered. Luke wondered how old she was and decided she might be anything between twenty-four and thirty-four.

'OK. Thank you for these cigarettes,' Goran said. 'We must go now.'

Luke wanted to ask where they were going. He wanted to ask Goran how old he was because he might have been about the same age as Luke, but he seemed much older.

This act of comparing himself with other people of his own age had started to preoccupy Luke. The talk-shows he had watched obsessively for the past two weeks had fascinated him in this respect. Every

191

so often little descriptions flashed up at the bottom of the screen, under the shouting faces: 'Shewanda from Detroit, 21. Mom of three'. They all looked so much older than they were and it had occurred to him for the first time that this was what happened to you if you had a difficult life, if you were poor. He had studied his stupid baby face in the sitting-room mirror and wondered if he would look older for losing Arianne. 'OK, then. Was nice to meet you. Goodbye,' Goran said, raising his hand.

Luke wanted to stop him. He wanted to say, 'Excuse me, but what have you come to England for? Will you tell me about your lives, because I never read the long articles in the newspapers and I don't know anything about the world.' But instead he stood there with a paralysed smile on his face as they walked away in the sunshine, smoking his cigarettes.

Chapter 12

'You'll appreciate the property is in poor condition, Mr Langford,' said Mr Wilson, the surveyor. 'There is rising damp, there is rot – both dry and wet – and there is significant structural damage to the roof. I'm also sorry to inform you that the plumbing is in poor repair and . . .'

There was something obscene about this summation. To Alistair, it was almost as if his mother's body was being criticized, not her house. Her worn hands, her aching hips and back, the ankle that had always given her trouble since she twisted it trying to carry in the coal when it had snowed.

'. . . and I'm afraid the boiler is nothing short of a museum piece,' he went on.

'Yes, I appreciate all of that,' Alistair said. 'Why don't we just decide on a realistic price and do this as simply as possible?'

'OK. Well, I'll give you a detailed breakdown, of course, but I think we might get £40,000 for it, Mr Langford. At a push.'

Suddenly Alistair wanted him out – him and his clipboard, his breakdown, his pushing. He wanted to be alone in the house with his nostalgia, free of this earthbound presence in its shiny suit.

'As I say, I will send you through a breakdown in the next few days, Mr Langford.'

'Yes,' Alistair said, hurrying him towards the door. 'Thank you. Thank you very much.' He could not help reacting to the surveyor's alarmed expression: 'I'm sorry – I'm in a bit of a rush,' he explained.

'I see. Well, goodbye, then, Mr Langford.'

'Goodbye.'

When the door was shut, Alistair let the familiar dim light of the hallway sink into him. It felt like drinking. He ran his fingers along the uneven wall, he inhaled the musty smell of the old carpet and then he pressed his weight on the second stair up to hear the creak. He found there were tears running down his face and he rolled his eyes in gentle mockery of himself and sighed.

He had not been alone in the house for a moment when he and Luke had first visited it and he realized that his son's presence had spared him these depths of . . . whatever it was that he was feeling.

He looked down at his shoes on the patterned carpet. His mother had died just where he was standing. He moved his feet quickly as if he were walking on her grave. Then he sat down on the stairs and looked out at the hallway for the first time like an intimate of the place, one whose eyes were ready to forgive and love any deterioration they saw, as one loves the lines on an old friend's face.

His mother had written to him once, after the birth of Sophie was announced in *The Times*. She had been shown the clipping by Geoff, she said. Alistair remembered how Geoff had always skimmed through the births and deaths in every one of the newspapers he ordered into his shop – 'Just in case,' he would explain smilingly to a young, fidgeting Alistair. 'Because life's going on, Al, beginning and ending all over the place,' he would say.

Alistair had been allowed to sit on the counter beside the till, his eyes rioting over the penny sweets in their glorious rainbow of jars on the shelves. Jelly babies, flying saucers, sherbet balls, liquorice sticks, chocolate buttons and strawberry chews. Geoff flicked the pages of a newspaper in the background, indulging his peculiar, boring adult whim. Then he would ruffle Alistair's hair, reach up behind him and put his magician's hand into one of the jars. Geoff could produce pear drops, peppermint creams – anything.

'Yes. Just in case.' He would sigh contentedly, brushing off his sugary fingers on his apron, carrying the papers to the rack by the door. 'It's a job keeping up with it all – with life and death and all that.' As it turned out, it was all just in case of:

LANGFORD
On 6 June,
to Rosalind (née Blunt) and Alistair, a daughter,
Sophie Rose Catherine.

194

His mother's letter had been brief:

Dear Alistair,
I saw on a clipping your Uncle Geoff showed me that your wife give birth to a little daughter and I thought why not write and congratulate you and wish you and the little one all the best. I hope you and your wife are truely happy and she is now comfy and all rested up at home. Funny how it makes me remember having you. It's been a long time since we saw each other but I do think of you.
God bless —
Mum.

He never replied. He had thought about it and just not been able to imagine how his life would accommodate his mother, how her ungainly griefs and sentimentality, her vulgar anxieties and resentments (which would play out so obviously in her clumsy syntax) could ever fit into his smooth new reality. It was too late anyway. He drove Rosalind home from hospital. She was wearing the elegant navy blue suit she had purchased for the occasion. Sophie was wrapped in a white cashmere blanket on her lap, and Rosalind's own mother was stern and formidable in the passenger seat, her pearl earrings catching the sun like armour each time she turned to check that all was well.

When they got home, Alistair went upstairs and threw away the letter, tearing the incriminating evidence of his past self into hundreds of pieces and flushing it down the toilet.

What an act that had been — so impulsively performed. Had he really known what he was doing?

He had told Rosalind a version of his childhood, of course; a picturesque version containing intimations of noble struggle against adversity. His mother cleaned and sewed, he told her — 'For *other people*? For a living, you mean?' Rosalind gripped his hand.

'Yes. She had to.'

But blessed with innate culture and breeding, in spite of the poverty and widowhood into which Fate had cast her, his mother had also made money translating French poetry and novels, literary ones, not silly romances, long into the night. How fondly he remembered her teaching him French and reciting Shakespeare's sonnets while she mended the rich women's blouses and skirts. And after she had kissed him goodnight she would go to her desk and translate.

It was all so poignant! He drew tears from his blue-eyed girlfriend with this Cinderella story. He even fed her the line about his father being killed in the war. Somehow this felt like the worst lie of all – perhaps because it was the first he had ever been told: his archetypal lie; the charged source of all lies.

Some of what he had said to Rosalind was true – that he went to a grammar school, not a public school, that he had been bullied for being more interested in Greek than football. But none of the real sordidness was there. He had edited out the boarding-house with its smell of fried eggs and sleep, and there was no mention of the male guests who stayed up drinking and talking with his mother. Talking and drinking, drinking and talking, long into the night, until he couldn't stay awake to listen and worry any longer.

He saw no need to mention these details at all.

But, of course, as soon as he had given her this story of himself and the miracle had occurred – the delicate, refined girl, falling in love with *him*! – he could not risk exposure. It was as if her love was maintained by a potion: alter the recipe even slightly and she might wake up and open her beautiful eyes!

His mother would only have had to speak. She would only have had to sip her sherry and burp, or to use a singular verb with a plural subject, and the whole story would ring false. And people who did elegant translations of Racine did not say 'Scuse my French' if they swore – which they did *all the time*.

The absolute impossibility of introducing her was further heightened by his own struggle to be accepted by Rosalind's family. They had held 'high hopes' for Rozzy's marriage, her father had explained, when Alistair and he had had their highly significant first drink together. 'I'm sure you understand what I'm saying,' he said, swirling the brandy in his glass. 'It's just that – as I said – we had very high hopes.'

'Yes,' Alistair said.

'Now, I know you're considered to be terribly bright and all that . . .' Rosalind's father had failed his Oxford entrance exams. He had subsequently developed a philosophy in which 'common sense' and 'decent manners' outranked all other virtues. He derived a great deal of relief from the slights life had dealt him by mocking the 'impracticality' of his brilliant wife – or that of anyone else who might have succeeded where he had failed. '. . . but one has to be *practical*,' he said. 'There are certain things Rosalind has been brought up to expect. Clothes, restaurants, holidays. It's all very well to be an intellectual, but—'

'Yes, I understand. Of course. One has to be practical.'

'And, not to put too fine a point on it, but who are your people? We don't know anything about them.'

So, while he sat there in Mr Blunt's study, holding a cigar, which had to him the sublime flavour of acceptance and conventionality, Alistair began the murder of his mother. There was no choice – it was done in self-defence. He gave her lymph cancer and she died shortly before they announced the engagement.

Six months later, people kissed the bride and said it was a great shame Rosalind and her mother-in-law had never met. They pressed the groom's hand and said how sorry they were that Mrs Langford could not be there on that day of all days . . . and Alistair, whose eyes missed nothing, felt sure he saw relief on his new mother-in-law's face as she took a neat forkful of kedgeree.

He had just four guests at his own wedding, all acceptable friends from Oxford, one of whom was Rosalind's cousin Philip, who had introduced them.

What he couldn't understand now was why, after the early days of love when, like all couples, they had both been prone to infantile sensitivity, he couldn't simply have admitted his dishonesty and ended it. Surely he could have talked openly to his wife, she could have forgiven him and they could have set about repairing the damage together. Couldn't they?

But when he thought of the distance, which, for one reason or another, had always been there between himself and Rosalind, he knew it would not have been possible. In the difficult first year of marriage, they had felt this distance painfully whenever it tested the elasticity of their dreams. Suddenly they would be forced to see each other simply as a man and a woman lying in a large bed together, rather than 'powerful husband' and 'devoted wife' in a novel or a glossy advertisement.

They had quickly learnt to fill the distance with life – with searching for Sophie's hamster or Luke's hockey boot, with rushing into the back pews at the carol service, with ski-trips and dentists, with tearing the clingfilm off the salmon and pouring the Chablis just as cars pulled up for lunch. They had been very, very busy for years.

As he told himself this, Alistair knew there was more to it. He knew that at times there was a knowing, conspiratorial look in Rosalind's eyes – when someone asked him where he had grown up or where he had gone to school and he replied evasively. On occasion she had too conveniently spilt her drink, needed help in the kitchen, or remembered a dull anecdote, just when he seemed to have no escape.

What was he to make of those times? He had made nothing of them. He had blocked them out as one blocks out the dirt on a glass when one is terribly thirsty and – well, the water tastes perfectly good.

The truth was, he had not been able to bear the idea of even Rosalind – his *own wife* – knowing the truth about him and his background. It was not because she would have told anyone – she would have been discreet for her own sake as well as his, fearing her mother's disapproval, her sister's glee. He had not been able to tell her because his performance required a globally captive audience, and the idea that her imagination could be roaming outside its boundaries would have thrown him off altogether. He really needed to think she believed him.

He had begun lying about himself before he met Rosalind, of course – at Oxford. He acquired a reputation for being a man of mystery because, with a tragic air he had adopted in a moment of inspiration, he said he 'loathed discussing Mummy and childhood'. This declamation had been made, of course, in Philip's public-school accent.

For the first year he felt guilty, but this changed. In the Michaelmas term of his second year, after much delaying on both sides, his mother came to visit him. Afterwards he thought he would never get over the experience and from then on he was able to justify each lie by working himself up on the rarefied surroundings of Oxford, running his fingers over his books and telling himself he had too much to lose. This was pure self-preservation – red in tooth and claw, he thought. In addition to this, he told himself that by excluding her from his life he was protecting her from ridicule. His friends would have taken one look at her and tried generously to assume that she was his old nanny or some other indulged retainer. It had seemed unbearable.

As he put her on the train at the end of her visit, he felt as though he was locking the cage on a wild animal – only he was not sure if she was the wild animal or his new life was.

She had arrived on the four o'clock, feeling 'sick as a parrot', wearing a vulgar green headscarf. He noticed immediately that her shoes were very battered. He rushed her away as quickly as he could, saying they could see his room after tea. Philip would be at church by then and John had an economics tutorial late on Thursday afternoons.

The strange thing was, his need to hide his mother from his friends was coupled with a desire to impress her with them. Ideally, he would have liked her to look through a hole in the wall as he and his chums were witty and incisive together in his room after dinner. He wanted to say: 'See, *this* is who I am, Mum. *This* is why I was never any good at home – I needed all this to bring me out.'

As they climbed the steps to the Victoria tea-rooms, he acknowledged that he was feeling something like anger and that maybe – secretly – he even wanted to intimidate his mother a little. This was the place where Philip always met his parents when they visited. There was nothing like it in Dover. He watched her flinch as they walked in through the chintz and mirrors and raw silk. Yes, he wanted her to know this was how far he had come from her damp kitchen. He saw her eyes widen at the chandelier, the bone china – and, yes, he wanted to sock her in the face with his Lapsang Souchong sophistication. He was sure she didn't know you drank fine China tea without milk.

But in spite of all this – and at the same time – he wished they had gone somewhere simple together, where she might have been able to smile and speak naturally. Where she might have been his wide-hipped raucous mother with her grin and her intolerance of fools and those big hugs she gave him when he had fixed a tap or put up a shelf after hours of unmanly struggle. She could make him feel so proud – if only it had ever been for something he was genuinely good at! He handed her a menu and suddenly wanted to undo a little of the damage he had done by using the Victoria tea-rooms against her. 'They have good scones,' he said, 'just normal ones. And nice jam.'

'Do they? This is very posh, Al.'

'It's not really, Mum.'

'It must be ever so dear.'

'Look, I'm paying so don't worry about that. I told you, I won that essay competition. Five quid. You did get my letter, didn't you?'

'Yes. That was a turn-up, wasn't it? Well done, Alistair.'

She had not written to congratulate him and his face reddened with anger at the belated praise now that finally he had it there, withered in his hand.

'I won against two hundred other people,' he said, disgusted by the brazenness of his desire for her approval. 'Logical positivism. It's an interesting subject, actually,'

'It sounds ever so complicated. Too clever for me by half. Oh, Al, do you think my clothes are good enough for in here?'

He sighed. 'No one *cares*, Mum.' But this had not occurred to him and he glanced around uneasily at the tweed skirts and pearls on the other women. Did she stand out? He knew nothing about the right clothes for women. He had known the headscarf was wrong but, thankfully, she had put that in her bag now. Maybe it would be best to get things moving.

'What will you have, then, Mum?' he said.

'Oh, you order me something, love. Only not bread and dripping.'

'They won't do that here anyway.'

'Well, I think I'll go to the Ladies.' She put on a mock posh accent for a moment and winked at him. 'Ay shan't be long – Ay must just powder may nose.'

He winced in case anyone should have heard. He had no appreciation then of how valiant she was being. He had his youth, after all, he had the full potential of his brain to protect him from glib categorization. But, unarmed, she walked the full length of the polished wooden floor, stared at by each of the tables, because it was perfectly obvious – from her brassy hennaed hair to her ungloved hands that she was not exactly *a lady*. She was shaking in spite of her private indignation.

As she reached the end of the room, Alistair watched her do a big, flashy, showgirl smile as she addressed one of the waitresses and all he could think was: Please, God, let her say 'cloakroom', not '*toilet*'.

Tea was a disaster: they barely spoke about anything other than the food – all of which had struck her as mysterious or too rich and exotic. The cucumber from her sandwich fell into her lap and, not knowing where was the right place to put it, she tucked it into her cardigan pocket and said rather frantically that she could always have it if she got peckish on the train. Alistair became so agitated himself that he spooned a great slop of cream right past his scone and on to his shoe and had to mop it up with his handkerchief. They were like a pair of zoo animals, he thought. His mother rounded it off by apologizing to the waiter for having used the napkins. 'Seems a crime,' she said, as he cleared their plates, 'when they're all beautifully starched and pressed like that.' The young man smiled patronizingly.

When he had gone, Alistair spoke through gritted teeth: 'Why did you say that about the napkins, Mum? That's what they're there for. You've as much right to use them as anyone.'

'Yes, love. I know that,' she said absentmindedly.

It was then that he noticed she had her handbag on her lap and that she was holding something inside it with her right hand. It was her return train ticket. It was with a mixture of genuine sympathy and almost voluptuous martyrdom that he sighed, 'Tired out, are you? I expect you are.'

And, as he offered her the escape, he felt the full weight of his loneliness crash down. She smiled with obvious relief. 'Oh – well, yes, love. You're not wrong. I'm ever so tired. I was up at five to get the rooms done.'

'Well, perhaps you'd like to get the earlier train,' he said – and immediately she was looking in her bag for the timetable,

'You know, I think that might be best. Yes – best get the earlier train.'

'You don't want to look round my college? See my room?'

'Next time, love. I'll come again soon. Maybe Ivy and me could make a day of it. A proper jaunt.' She squeezed his arm, but they both knew that this was a fantasy. Of course she never came back.

What an idiot he had been. They could have gone to a little café and had mugs of tea and sausage rolls or crumpets and he would have heard all about home. He would have loved to hear about home because, hate it as he did, he missed it too. He missed Auntie Ivy and Uncle Geoff and the seafront and the sugary buns at the Igglesdon Square bakery. He missed those rare occasions on which he had helped his mother to understand a bill or some legal document and she said, 'Clever little sod, aren't you?' and the high note of happiness was literally painful in his ears. He shattered with joy.

And he had heard that Ivy and Geoff's 'real nephew' Martin was staying with them for a few months while he did an apprenticeship with a local craftsman. Alistair was still senselessly in awe of Martin's celebrated carpentry skills and the news had filled him with envy and anxiety. This great hulking favourite would obliterate his memory altogether. It was no wonder his mother had not rushed to visit him.

Throughout Alistair's childhood, Martin had stayed with his uncle and aunt in the school summer holidays. Martin was the older, more muscular boy, who spoke of having half a pint of beer with his dad from time to time and swore he regularly kissed girls. When he was fourteen, Alistair remembered Martin bringing his mother a present. It was a sealion he had carved in oak. She had never been more thrilled and Alistair, who had been saving the big news all week, for the first day of the summer holidays, said nothing about his history-exam result, which was the best his school had ever seen.

Why was it that even when he was an Oxford scholar he was still crushed when he was shown a 'marvellous' table or a 'smashing' book-case that his old pal Martin had made?

He saw his mother on to the earlier train and walked back to his college. Although he knew his memory might be exaggerating to emphasize the point, when he remembered it now, he was sure he had sat in the college dining room at a table of strangers that evening. Philip and John and the others were at a dining society for Old Etonians.

When Luke was born, Alistair half wondered if he would hear from his mother again, but there was silence. She had given up. And he continued the business of forgetting her and the boarding-house and Dover.

The sound of the doorbell reached into his mind as an alarm clock reaches into a deep sleep, at first existing only as a sound, then acquiring significance. Alistair woke to the present moment, stood up and opened the door to find his son standing there.

'Dad?' Luke said. His son looked scared and Alistair remembered he had been crying and that his face probably showed signs of it. He turned away quickly, wiping his eyes, and Luke followed him towards the kitchen.

'So, all done with the surveyor,' Alistair said. The paperwork was spread out on the kitchen table and they both glanced at it.

'Well, that's good,' said Luke.

'Yes, that's out of the way, at least.'

'So, just the packing up to be done now.'

'Yes. I'll give most of it to charity. There are one or two things she'd have wanted the Gilberts to have, though. Mementoes – photos and things. Nothing valuable.'

'You'll keep a few things yourself, won't you?'

'I – I haven't really decided.'

'No. Right. Well, we'd better get on with it, hadn't we? I'll get the boxes out of the car, shall I?'

Luke smiled good-naturedly at him and Alistair felt a rush of pity for his son, who must be struggling to comprehend so much. 'Luke?'

'Yes?'

'Listen, there's truly no need for you to do this with me, you know. It's not as if there's anything to lift and carry. It's just sorting through old things. I've been thinking,' he said, although it had only just occurred to him, 'if you like, you could leave me here for the night and come back for me tomorrow afternoon. I'll have it all done by then and you can get it into the car for me and drive us back and so on.'

Luke's heart raced with joy.

Alistair held back his smile: his son's feelings were as transparent as his grandmother's had been.

'Are you sure? I mean, will you be OK?'

'Of course I'll be OK. This is a depressing business for you.'

'No, no – it's been . . . fine.'

'Well, even so, I'm sure you'd rather be out with your friends.'

'OK. Yes,' Luke said, thinking there was nothing he would like less – other than staying here with his father – than to go out with his friends. His friends, a few of whom had called him from a bar to tempt him out, had appeared to be high on some appalling stimulant, which rendered them emotionally tone deaf. They would not even hear the subtle range of his longing for Arianne and sitting beside them, listening to the percussive jangle of their one-night-stands talk, their promotions talk, their parties and flat-hunting and new-car talk, would be torture. At least his mother's sadness had musicality.

'Will you explain to Mummy?' Alistair said.

'Yes, I will.'

'Of course I'll call later tonight but, well, she doesn't need me phoning all the time. Best if you just say I'll be staying here and then I'll ring later and just say goodnight.'

'I'll explain.'

'Thank you.'

Alistair felt an intense nervousness – half excitement, half dread – about the idea of being alone with his mother's things, at liberty to look through them with a clear conscience, as one can with the possessions of the dead.

Luke drove away quickly. As he got to the end of the road, he saw two figures sitting on the wall by the hedge. It was the Serbian couple to whom he had given cigarettes just half an hour before. Again, he was overwhelmed with curiosity about them. He slowed the car and ran the window down. 'Hello again. Is everything OK?'

'Yes, we are OK. We must wait here because of the—' Goran shook his fist in the air and twisted his face into a grimace.

'Because of the demonstration? The people down there?'

'Yes. They throw a bottle at Mila.'

'*What?*'

The girl had a hand over her left eye, and when she lowered it, Luke could see it was slightly inflamed.

'Yes. In her face.'

'My God. I'm so sorry.'

'It is not your fault,' Goran said.

'Look, can I take you anywhere? I'm going to London. Would that help you at all?'

'Yes,' Mila said, looking up at Goran imploringly.

'We will find work in London,' Goran explained.

'Well, perfect. Why don't I take you there? I can drop you at your friends' house or wherever you're staying. Listen, it'll save you the train fare – and it's no trouble.'

'Trouble?'

'It's easy, I mean. Not a problem.'

The man and the girl looked at each other and gradually Goran's face took on the hopeful expression she radiated at him. 'You are certain?' he said.

'Yes, of course. Where have you been staying? Shall we collect your luggage?'

'This is what we have. This is all.'

Luke took in the half-filled black bin-bags at their feet. Then he got out of the car with the keys in his hand. 'Well, let's get it in. The central locking's broken, I'm afraid.'

'We can put it in the trunk,' Goran said excitedly.

'The trunk? Yes.' Luke smiled as he undid the lock.

'What is funny?' Goran said.

'Oh, nothing. Just you saying "trunk". In England we say "boot". Trunk's American, I think. But it really doesn't matter at all.'

'Yes, it matters.'

'Oh, no, really – no one cares about things like that.'

Goran looked at Luke straight on for a second. 'In this way you will lose your language.'

'Oh, I'd never really thought about it,' said Luke. He opened the back door.

Mila slipped in silently, her hand still held against her eye. 'Thank you,' she said.

'It's nothing. Really nothing,' Luke told her.

Goran was obviously worried about Mila and said he would sit with her in the back. As they drove out of Dover they passed two

204

TV news vans. The chanting was louder now and constant: '*Out! Out!*'
In the rear-view mirror, Luke could see Mila peering out of the
window at the crowd with their daubed bed-sheets and cardboard
placards, their savage misspellings:

'ASILUM BACK TO FRANCE!'

'BOWGUS SCROUNGERS! OUT!'

Luke noticed that Goran paid no attention, he kept his eyes straight
ahead and put his arm firmly round Mila.

Chapter 13

They had been on the motorway for about forty minutes before anyone spoke. The enclosed space had heightened their strangeness to each other. In the rear-view mirror, Luke watched Goran staring out of the window at the flashing fields, trees and cars; Mila was asleep on his shoulder. Eventually Luke said, 'You must both be very tired.'

Goran met his eyes in the mirror and smiled. 'Yes, it was long, bad journey.'

'And then you had all that shouting – the bottle and everything – when you got here. How terrible.' Luke glanced at his hands on the steering-wheel. 'D'you want another cigarette?'

'Thank you, Luke – I would love, but no. I will wake her. She must sleep. Mila is ill.'

Hastily Luke put the cigarettes back into his shirt pocket, 'Oh, no! Poor thing! What's wrong?'

'She gets a bad fever. For three days now. You see she is very thin.'

'Goran, you must take her to a doctor. You really should, you know.' There was no reply. Luke said, 'Listen, you know you won't have to pay or anything. Just so you know that's not an issue. It's not like in some countries where it costs a fortune if you haven't got holiday insurance or whatever. I mean – not that you're on holiday. You know what I mean.'

Goran looked down for a second, and then, speaking gently, he said, 'Luke, do you understand we are illegal? We have no passports. You know this?'

Luke bit his lip. 'I – I wasn't sure.'

Goran nodded. 'Now you are sure. Do you want us to get out of this car?'

'No! God, no. Not at all. *No!* It's not as if anyone can tell by looking at you. I mean – *is* it?'

'No,' Goran said, laughing. 'Thank you, Luke.'

An enormous truck towered beside them for a moment. Through the narrow slats an improbable number of wet animal snouts sucked at the air. Were they cows? Small horses? Then it overtook, sending out tufts of straw, which caught and spun in the turbulence behind the exhaust.

'Goran?' said Luke.

'Yes?'

'When we get to London, have you actually got a friend to stay with?'

'No.' Goran watched a motorbike pass and strained to see what model it was.

'I just assumed . . . Where will you sleep?'

'I don't know. *But* we will be in *London.*'

Luke found himself smiling with pride at Goran's excitement. But this feeling was quickly followed by vague shame. 'Yes, but you can't sleep on the street,' he said.

'Ah – it is better than many places where we sleep. It is more safe than in my bed at home in Priština.'

Luke observed the tense, melancholy face.

Then Goran waved the back of his hand at the sky. 'And also it is warm now in England.'

'Well, it's really not that warm at night, Goran. And Mila's ill.'

'I think she will be OK,' he said, stroking her hair. 'The worst time is finished for us now. Now we can begin.'

Luke stared ahead at the road. He had never slept outside before – other than on school camping trips – except once, for a couple of hours, when he had forgotten his keys and was too stoned to handle waking his parents and communicating with them. He had bunched his jacket up under his head and passed out. His mother had spotted him slumped on the doorstep when she came down for the Sunday papers. She had made him a big cooked breakfast, he remembered, and he had allowed her to become almost tearful at the thought that he had slept outside solely because he could not bear to disturb his mother's sleep. She said he smelt 'funny' – it was Ludo's skunk – and he told her he had been in a horrible smoky pub and had just wanted to come home all evening. She kept kissing his head and ruffling his hair. His father and Sophie must have been out somewhere. It had been lovely, actually. He loved his mother very much.

Luke overtook a car pulling a trailer with a small powerboat on it. A man with spiked blue hair was driving, drinking from a can of beer.

The radio was doing the top ten: 'And in at number *eight*, with a *cracking* new entry from *Hea*ther de *Wayne*, it's 'U . . . R . . . my . . . world . . .' There was an audio-waterfall of sickly notes.

Luke switched it off. 'Look, you can't sleep on the street,' he said. 'You just *can't*.' For a moment, he imagined letting them use his flat for a couple of nights, but it was impossible. The flat was a time-capsule, an inviolable shrine to himself and Arianne. It was this, rather than the thought that he had no idea if he could trust them, that stopped him suggesting it. No. His stomach lurched with nausea at the thought of other people – any other people – being there. Even he could not go back into that flat without her. It had to be them together or he would sell the place. It felt right to think in this apoc-alyptic way – it contained all the force he had lacked while they had been together.

Suddenly he felt a surge of excitement. 'Look, I've got an idea,' he said. 'There's this annexe, like a little flat, at the bottom of my parents' garden. We've never really used it. It's not beautiful or anything. I mean, it's full of old garden furniture and stuff, but at least it's got a roof and a shower and a loo – and I know they work because we use the loo when we have our garden party. Anyway, I'm just thinking you could stay there for a night or two. You know, if—'

'Luke, I . . .'

'If it would help. But, listen, we couldn't tell my parents.'

Luke knew it would be impossible to ask Rosalind and Alistair to agree to have total strangers sleeping under their roof. Perhaps they might have agreed ten years ago, if he had said this exhausted couple were friends of a friend, but now they would be frightened, shocked, disoriented by the question. Luke was aware that his own perspective was unusual. Arianne had made him reckless in happiness and she was making him reckless in unhappiness, too. But it was all very well for him to be reckless: his parents were a different matter. Apart from the strain of recent events, they had long been acquiring a new vulnera-bility.

With a kind of sad curiosity Luke had noticed his parents were less and less resilient to the unexpected impact of humanity: the phone call during lunch, the spontaneous visitor on a Sunday afternoon, could knock them breathless, leave them searching each other's faces in a kind of panic or mutual pleading. How could he bring this about deliberately – especially now? Unlike Sophie, whom this 'neurosis' deeply exasperated, he understood. Instinctively, in his guts, he knew it was just another sign of ageing. He knew by feeling what might have been explained more cerebrally. What he had noticed was his parents' need to keep the stars, the seasons, each other in place by little efforts of will, little acts of obduracy, now that convention was losing its precedence to death.

Luke shook his head firmly. 'It's just that my father and mother – well, they're going through a lot at the . . . Basically it's just simpler, that's all. We would just have to keep it quiet – not put the lights on and stuff when it gets dark. *Would* that help at all?'

Goran squeezed his eyes shut. 'It helps! Yes, it helps very much. Luke – *thank* you.'

Luke felt his heart swell with satisfaction. He flicked the indicator switch and slowed down as he moved into the left-hand lane. 'Come on,' he said. 'Let's get you something to eat at this service station. I need a coffee and you're probably hungry, aren't you?'

Goran lowered his head, but when he looked up, it was with a smile of open gratitude and a sigh of relief. 'Yes,' he said. 'We do not eat for two days.'

'My God. Well, here we are. I'm going to buy you a welcome-to-England lunch. We can do better than that awful demonstration. I can't believe people do things like that.'

'They are just scared,' Goran said. 'All people are the same.'

The service station opened out in front of them in a vast arc of futuristic optimism. It promised, on first sight, that it had an answer to every possible human need. Enormous up-lit billboards announced brand names in ecstatic lists, as if they were famous actors in starring roles. There was a chemist, a petrol station, a bookshop; there were two fast-food counters, a video-games parlour, a sunglasses shop, a newsagent, a coffee bar, a miniature pub and an Easy-Dine Cafeteria, which was a chain in which Ludo's family had a large stake. (The two of them had had a lot of laughs on what Ludo referred to as 'Easy Money'.)

Luke drove around, hunting for a space. The car park was crowded with a mixture of cars, the odd motorbike or caravan and huge tour coaches, which were mobile advertisements for themselves:

'www.splendorofeurope.com';'www.twilight-tours.co.uk';'www.Best-years.com', they read.

There appeared to be hundreds of old people helping each other across the tarmac, between the cars, around the wing-mirrors. By two of the coaches, Luke spotted bizarrely similar tense-faced women wearing bright lipstick and slacks. They were each waving a stick with a coloured rosette on it, one green and one yellow. White-haired men and women in beige and pale lilac and dove grey made their way towards the brighter colours.

As Luke pulled into a parking space, a small child's voice shouted, 'Daddy! Daddy!' right beside him and made him jump. At first he couldn't see the child. A man was locking the next-door car; then he leant down and lifted a little boy of three or four on to his shoulders. The child had on shorts and a white T-shirt with green stains on it. The man was about the same age as Luke. Among Luke's affluent, educated, procrastinating friends in London, it was possible for him to forget that people were fathers at his age. The little boy said, 'Ride, Dad? Go on a fire engine?'

The father noticed he was being observed and he grinned, adult to adult. 'Always an expensive stop at one of these places,' he said.

Luke got out of the car and casually slammed the door. 'Total rip-off,' he said, then blew air up at his forehead and rolled his eyes as if he was a father too: a father who faced tough money worries just like this man, not someone whose parents still took him on holiday and said he could bring a friend. Not someone who had spent five thousand pounds on a suede sofa.

A heavy pulse of shame beat through him as he watched them walk away. The loss of Arianne was making him relate to the world with a new humility. He realized he did not feel immune, he did not feel *special*, any more. Almost immediately, this was unbearably poignant.

Goran and Mila got out of the car. Mila stretched and Luke noticed how thin her arms were – curiously thin. She was as thin as Sophie sometimes made herself with all the crazy dieting. Mila's fragility was a wonder: it made her sacred somehow. She was miraculous after her journey, like a tiny artefact in an archaeologist's knapsack.

'Right. Let's go to the cafeteria,' he said firmly. 'We can get some hot food and sit down.'

As they set off, Goran stumbled and reached for the side of the car. His face had become very pale and the stubbly beard was pitiful against it. The dark hair grew in sparse quantities over his prominent cheekbones and reminded Luke of the patches of weeds you some-times saw in the middle of French or Italian motorways. It had once struck him that it was as if those plants sprouted there, in the parched tarmac and the double rush of traffic, solely to remind you that nature is strong. Mila put her shoulder under Goran's arm.

'*Nema problema*, Mila. *Ja sam* OK,' Goran said. 'I am so sorry, Luke.'

'Don't be silly. Please. You're both exhausted. Come on, let's get you in there,' he said. As he spoke, he thought how much he liked the good-natured insistence in his voice, the gentle authority. 'Listen, you must eat as much as you like,' he said, and spread his arms wide. 'You must eat the *whole restaurant*, if you like.' He put his hand on Goran's shoulder and Mila smiled at him with deep gratitude. This unexpected opportunity for largesse had made Luke feel purposeful and elated. What an amazing thing it was to be able to help two good young people! How very much more pleasant it was than wondering who had their hands on Arianne, whose lower lip she was biting in her excitement.

He had not eaten in a self-service restaurant since he was at univer-sity and even then it had been on only a few occasions when, on one of their road trips, he and his friends were ravenous with 'the munchies' after smoking comical quantities of dope. Since then the food had improved immeasurably. He remembered gorging helplessly on solid fried eggs and baked beans dried out under the lamps, on brutally stunted frozen waffles, waxy choc-ices, flat Coke and bitter instant coffee with little packets of dried milk. But England did not seem to produce food like that any more. Jessica said it had given up its defiant stand against Continental sensuality.

Now there appeared to be a little something on offer from selected corners of the world: Irish stew, *coq au vin*, couscous, steak and kidney pie, chicken tikka, mushroom risotto, Swedish meatballs. The dishes were listed on a printed *faux*-blackboard in a novelty 'handwriting' font.

Another blackboard announced ice-creams, jam sponge and custard, New York cheesecake and tiramisu among other 'Sweet Treats!'. There were rows of plastic cases from which portions already served on to plates could be removed through transparent hatches. On the 'chilled drinks island' beside the till, there were little bottles of Chardonnay or lager, Coke, orange juice, apple juice, mineral water, guarana wake-up soda, diet lemon-lime crush.

Goran and Mila queued with their trays and Luke went straight to the coffee counter and ordered himself a cappuccino and a white-chocolate-chip muffin. When he looked round to check that the others were OK, he saw that Goran was swallowing frequently, his mouth watering hard at the sight of the hot food. Again, Luke felt his heart race with – there was no other word for it – this was a kind of *love*. It was love of his fellow man. He was overwhelmingly afraid that Goran and Mila would not take enough food, that they would be shy about the expense and come away hungry.

They *must* eat, he thought. Did they realize how absurdly rich he was in comparison to them? He tapped his fingers on the aluminium counter until his coffee arrived, wondering how he could persuade them to take enough. A soup-bowl-sized cappuccino was set in front of him. 'Chocolate, cinnamon, vanilla or nutmeg?' the boy asked him, pointing at a rack of shakers.

'It's fine like that,' Luke said. He picked up the tray and rushed over to the '*Something for dessert? (Go on, treat yourself!)*' section. He chose a plate of cheeses, some French bread and a couple of slices of fruit cake, which seemed to have an international quality to it, unlike the sponge pudding, which, he thought, might well offend the Serbian palate. He had never liked sponge pudding himself. As an afterthought, he picked up two apples, a packet of dry-roasted peanuts and a king-size Go-Go bar.

Goran moved away from the hot-food queue while Mila was served. He stood facing out into the room. Luke got into his eye-line and beamed, clownishly, lifting his tray, but when Goran gazed back at him it was with a remoteness that was like a blast of cold wind. It was as if he had forgotten what Luke looked like; as if the shape of yet another pink-faced, spoilt English boy standing near the till had failed to register in his consciousness.

Tentatively Luke tried the smile again and, holding the tray with his left arm, he raised his hand a little and waved. Goran shook his head as if he had been dreaming, then grinned with recognition. But Luke knew he had fallen out of significance for a moment. He felt slightly deflated as he pointed at the till. Goran and Mila brought over their trays and placed them beside his on the conveyor-belt.

'It's . . . um – it's all together,' Luke told the cashier in a half-whisper, making a little circling gesture with his down-pointed finger. Goran was obviously uncomfortable and Luke wished he would just go and sit down with Mila. He hadn't meant to embarrass anyone. It must be the right thing to do, mustn't it, to buy lunch for people in need?

The cashier made a great show of counting up all the food. 'Right. Where are we? So, that's two main items, no, *three* main items . . . oh, no, *two* – I *was* right, because that's a snack item, isn't it? I never know with the sandwiches. *Right.* Then *three* dessert items . . .' She stood on tiptoe and leant over the till to count it all up. It came to thirty pounds. Goran shifted uneasily. He put his hand on Luke's arm and said, 'Luke, you are sure you—'

'Please, Goran,' he said quickly. 'Forget it. It's *nothing*. God, I spend this much on—' He had been going to say that he spent that much on a jumbo-plate of sushi for lunch sometimes – and usually left half. But how could he admit that? He said, 'Seriously, just forget it. Could you take the trays over and I'll follow when I've – when I've done this?'

'Yes. Thank you, Luke. You must know we will . . . In some way we will pay you back.'

'Of *course* you will, Goran. You think I won't make you? You can take me out for dinner in London,' he said. 'I'm *crazy* about caviar and champagne.'

Goran laughed. 'Thank you, Luke. You are a kind man.'

Luke noticed with horror that Goran had tears in his eyes. He felt crushed by the force of this gratitude: he knew it came out of a scale of pain that he did not have the imagination to understand. 'Well, wait until you taste your food. You and Mila may never forgive me. That might be couscous but it was still made by an English cook.'

Goran laughed again. 'Ah, no. We are safe.' He nodded in the direction of the women serving the food. 'One cook says she is from Jamaica and the other is from Taiwan.'

'Oh. Well, *thank God for that*,' Luke said. He smiled, but he felt lonely and uncertain. He was suddenly afraid that he did not know how to behave and that he wasn't sure what was rude and what was polite any more.

When they got into the car, Mila lay down in the back and Goran sat in the front with Luke so that he could smoke a cigarette with him. Mila stretched out and fell asleep straight away.

They headed out on to the motorway again. The sky was deep blue. It was the blue Luke thought of as 'church blue' because it was always in paintings of Jesus or angels or the Virgin Mary. He had never forgotten the oils and frescos he had seen at sixteen on a school trip to Florence – yet he had never been into a gallery since. It was odd. He particularly remembered the Fra Angelicos in the little monks' cells and how the men in the pictures had often fallen asleep while the women were still quietly praying. It was a little joke still audible through the centuries – and it had touched him. Why had he never looked at paintings again?

It was as if all that sport, all those stupid parties with Ludo, had stolen an important aspect of life. Why had he let this happen? Just then, he wanted to go back and see those frescos again and, forgetting about Goran and Mila and even Arianne for a second, he wondered if that was exactly what he needed to do. Yes, to see frescos, he thought, to see a bit of church blue and smile again at that tender old joke. He wondered where his camera was.

'We are lucky to get here alive. You know?' Goran said. He blew the smoke in a sharp jet out of the side of his mouth. 'We could be killed many times.'

Luke let go of his thoughts about frescos as if they had been so many balloons. He stared straight ahead.

'Our journey was very bad. We go Serbia, to Croatia, to Slovenia. We take always these buses. You know? Terrible buses with so many people it is hard to breathe.' He made little legs out of his forefingers and walked them across the dashboard. 'Then we walk Slovenia all way to Austria – through Alps mountains.'

Luke heard the inappropaite sound of skis. He bit his lip, pushed back his hair.

'It was bad time in these mountains. We sleep outside three nights – in the forests. Black trees and black sky and wind Mila say is sound always like somebody crying. It was very cold. Bad cold in your body, in blood. You know?'

'Yes,' Luke said quickly.

'Then we come to Austria and we have a name of truck company. The driver you can pay them and they will take you in England. They drive Austria to France and then on this boat to Dover. It was pizza truck. You know? Twenty people. No light,' he said. He pinched the bridge of his nose. 'I was very scared. Mila she just hold me like this always.' He clenched both fists to show the force of Mila's grip.

Luke's hands imitated it on the wheel. '*Twenty* people?' he said.

'Yes. All kind of people – dark, light, eyes like this and like this.' He stretched his eyelids to show the different races. 'Where are they

214

from? From nowhere. Nobody has passport. Nobody has identity.' Goran checked Luke's face to see how much it was safe to say. 'We throw our passports away in mountains. We burn them.'

'But why? Why did you do that?'

'Because you come from nowhere then where they will send you back?'

Luke nodded.

'We leave Kosovo quickly. We sell everything – TV, stereo, bed, all clothes. Albanian woman wears Mila's necklace.' He laughed, then his face became serious. 'But we must sell everything for money for our journey. You know? We just say: *Now. This is life. Go.*'

'My God.'

'No. God was not there. Not in Kosovo, not in mountains, not in this pizza truck.'

Luke allowed a Porsche to overtake him and watched it accelerate out of sight. 'How long were you in the truck?' he said.

'I am not sure. There is no light so we cannot see if a day has passed. I think maybe it is two days, maybe three. We had no food. We try to eat these pizzas, but it is not cooked and it makes you sick. We drink the ice in the freezers. It is very hot with twenty people. This is why Mila is ill. In Kosovo she is a beautiful strong girl. I also am much stronger. I lift weights. Ninety kilograms. You do this?' Goran smiled and squeezed Luke's biceps.

'Sometimes,' Luke replied, not sure what he was saying. 'I mean, I haven't for a few weeks.'

'Oh, I have women's arm!' Goran said. '*Look.* But I become strong again soon. And Mila also. I think we *cannot* die, Luke. What is left? Milošović, Nato air strike, UN in our city, Priština. And then this bad, bad journey.' He threw his cigarette butt out of the window.

'It sounds . . . Shit, I'm just so sorry,' Luke said.

'Why you are sorry? It is your fault?'

'No, I just . . . It's just a way of saying it's not fair, that's all – when I'm so lucky.'

'I am lucky, too. I have Mila.' Goran swivelled round in his seat and put out his hand to stroke her leg. She seemed unconscious. 'We are together since fourteen and eighteen,' he said. 'We will get married. She is Serbian Orthodox Church and she cares about this, you know? Me, I don't care, but for Mila I will do anything. Her family think I am a bad man for her because I do not go to church, because my parents do not have family feast in the old way. Also it is because I

215

am not very rich man like this *amazing* Vladimir, the cousin husband. You are married, Luke? You have girlfriend?'

'No.'

'*No?*' Goran tilted his head and frowned. 'Why not? English men are all as handsome as you? Like Hollywood film star?'

Luke laughed. 'Oh, most of them are far more handsome. I'm a terrible example. No, my girlfriend left me, actually,' he said, rather enjoying the bracing honesty. 'It all happened a few weeks ago.' He smiled lightly at Goran, hoping both to be understood and mis-understood at the same time.

Goran's face contracted in sympathy. 'You love her?' he said simply.

'Yes. Yes, I do.'

Goran was fascinated by the childish determination on the other man's face. He thought Luke was like a little boy smacked by a bully, struggling not to cry. It was strangely primitive – disarmingly so. He said, 'Oh, Luke, it is very bad. I am sorry.'

Luke turned, smiling at him.

'Why are you sorry, Goran? Is it your fault?'

Goran brushed invisible dirt off his jeans and looked out at the road, 'No,' he said, 'nobody's fault.'

It was still broad daylight when they arrived and Luke knew there was no question of getting spare pillows or sheets from the house until later, when his mother had gone to meet Suzannah as she had said she was going to do. The best he could do now was to take Goran and Mila down the side passage, rather than across the lawn, and let them into the annexe. He would come back later. He would have to wait until his mother went out before he could rummage in the linen cupboard. Somehow she knew what went on in the house – she always had: she *sensed* people in rooms and had a habit of coming to see if she was right, no matter what time it was. When he was about fifteen she had once sensed him and a girl called Hattie Matthews (who, rather fascinatingly, never wore knickers) in the double bed in the first-floor spare room. She said she had 'actually felt it' when the pipe burst in the cellar. And, of course, she had sensed Sophie at four in the morning, lying unconscious on the kitchen floor, having swal-lowed every last aspirin in the house.

Luke parked the car and led Goran and Mila up the side passage, then told them to wait behind the hedge while he went into the house and found out where his mother was.

Rosalind was in the sitting room, at the little desk, writing a letter. She glanced up anxiously as he came in. He explained that Alistair was staying in Dover for the night and she nodded wearily, her eyes glazed.

'Writing a letter?' Luke said.

'Yes.'

Feeling he had now adequately dealt with the formalities of arrival, Luke patted his pockets and said, *would* you believe it?, he must have left his cigarettes in the car.

'Oh, darling, you don't need those awful things,' Rosalind said, out of long and fruitless habit.

'I do, Mum. Back in a minute,' he told her – and he watched her turn safely back to her letter before he left the room. He took the little key off the hook beneath the coat rack, went out of the front door and jogged down the side passage.

Goran and Mila followed him to the annexe. It was a simple building, the size of a small bedroom with a little bathroom attached. The previous owners had apparently referred to it as 'the granny flat' and Luke had always felt sure he could tell that an old lady had died in it. In fact, there was nothing sinister about it. It was painted pale yellow inside and out. The entrance was through a rosy pink door, which was conveniently obscured from the house by a huge tree peony at the end of the passage.

Inside, it smelt damp and the light was dim and greenish, rather magical. It filtered through the ivy and wisteria that grew over the little windows. The room was full of garden furniture and family history: art projects, his sports cups, Sophie's countless framed music certificates for flute and oboe and piano and violin. There were stacks of board games with grinning, victorious children on the front; there was the boules set they always took on holiday; there were countless old tennis rackets of various sizes. His enormous teddy bear, which, aged seven, he had imaginatively named Bear, was sitting in a deck-chair, under the orange parasol they had bought on a beach in Greece.

Along the left-hand wall, there was a mirror and the old TV (which looked so dated he couldn't believe how proud he had once been to show it to his friends) and, beside it, the ancient pink drawing-room sofa, which Sophie had insisted was of sentimental value to her. Luke suspected she had lost her virginity on it, but he would never have given her the pleasure of imparting this information to him with one of her so-what grins.

217

With the small camp-bed and the sofa there were two fairly comfortable places for Goran and Mila to sleep.

'Look, I hope that's OK for now. I'll bring you some sheets and pillows later,' he said.

'We are so tired Mila and I can sleep anywhere. I can sleep three days.'

'I'm sure. But I'll come back later with blankets because it might get cold in here at night. I know my mother's going out for a bit this evening, so I'll do it then.'

Luke jogged back down the side passage towards the street. When he reached the end of the path he stopped dead and watched. His friend Jessica was on the front steps of the house, talking to his mother. 'I just thought I'd drop by and see how he was doing,' she was saying.

'That's so thoughtful of you,' Rosalind told her.

Luke knew his mother liked Jessica. This surprised him as Jessica swore all the time and very obviously disliked his sister. Jessica called Sophie 'daahling' and rolled her eyes behind her back.

'I wish I could have come sooner, Mrs Langford. I've been away assisting on a documentary,' she said. 'I've been calling but his phone's been off and it's taken me ages to figure out that he might be here. I've been working hard, to be honest – not much brain power left over.'

'You're doing a film? How exciting. That's what you've always wanted to get into, isn't it, Jessica?'

'That and sculpting – but yes. At least there's a *tiny* bit of money in this.'

'Well, that's not everything. Making money's not everything. Your parents must be thrilled to see you doing something you love.'

'Actually, my parents are both dead, Mrs Langford.'

Rosalind literally stepped backwards. 'I had – I had no idea.'

'Please don't worry. My father died when I was a child, and Mum was over six years ago now. *Please* don't think you've said something terrible.'

'Thank you,' Rosalind said, deeply impressed by this girl's ability to say exactly what she meant. She had always liked Jessica's direct manner. And she had particularly enjoyed seeing her correct Alistair's misquotation of Shakespeare one evening when Luke had first brought her back from university.

Luke stepped over the furthest corner of the low garden wall. Then he walked extra casually along the pavement so it would seem as if he had come from the car.

'Ah, there he is,' said Rosalind.

Jessica turned and they both smiled at him.

'*Hey*, Luke,' Jessica said. She put out her arms and hugged him. 'Where have you *been*? You've been missed a lot. I've missed you most, though.'

Rosalind said she was going out to meet Suzannah for a bit so they could have the house to themselves. She said she would be back in time to do supper and Jessica looked away tactfully while Rosalind checked whether Luke would prefer 'a lovely piece of salmon' or his 'favourite creamy chicken and spinach'.

After she had gone upstairs, Luke took Jessica into the kitchen. 'D'you want a coffee?' he said. 'Actually, it's a bit hot, isn't it? Iced tea? Lemonade?'

'Have you got a beer?'

'Good idea,' Luke said, clinking bottles in the fridge. He opened them and gave one to her.

'Let's go outside,' she said. 'I'm guessing there won't be a garden party this year – and your mum makes it all so gorgeous. It's such a shame to miss it.'

'No, you're right,' Luke said, following her.

'Oh! Roses, roses, *roses*!' Jessica held up her hands like an Italian in a traffic jam. 'Just smell that. You were so *spoilt* growing up here. Lucky you. Our place was a little . . . well, different.'

They sat on the stone steps down to the lawn.

'So,' Jessica said. She took a long drink.

'So?'

'So, I'm intrigued. What's your *strategy* here?'

Luke stared at her brown-leather boots and her old jeans. There was clay on her jeans and he wondered if she was doing her weird sculptures again. Ludo's father had bought one of them on the single occasion that he had visited Ludo at university. Sandro had told them all Jessica would be famous one day and Ludo and Luke had watched her giggling and making their shepherd's pie and felt a bit frightened.

She put down the frothing beer bottle beside her and took a packet of cigarettes out of her bag.

'My *strategy*?' he said.

She spoke out of the side of her mouth while she lit the cigarette: 'Yup.'

'What do you mean, exactly?'

219

'Well, with your job, for example. Are you actually *trying* to get sacked or is this, like, a test of their selfless belief in your talent?'

Luke waved his hand, brushing away her remarks as if they were flies. 'Yeah, yeah,' he said. He wished she would go away because he was getting used to exile, to his expat status at home where, with no one but himself to maintain them, the old peer-group standards were ceasing to apply. But he was torn because, conversely, he was intensely relieved to see his intelligent friend because he could trust her sense of proportion, even if he found it brutal at times. She was generally thought to 'take no shit' and he often wondered why this was. How did a person get that way? He had a vague impression of hardship in her childhood – money, possibly violence or alcoholism – and, of course, there was the loss of both her parents by the age of twenty-two. He couldn't begin to imagine what it felt like to have no parents – no *mother*.

'Gimme one of those?' he said.

'You can have a cigarette if you *promise* me you won't lose your job.'

'What if I don't want my job any more?'

She tossed the cigarette at him anyway. 'Oh, God. Not you too. I heard about bloody Sophie *daahling*.'

'What about Sophie?'

'Shit, don't you know? Your parents *must* know.'

'Know what?'

'Sophie handed in her notice at the *Telegraph*.'

'What? Why? To do what?'

'Don't know what she's doing. My mate Caroline just said she left. That's all.'

'Caroline?'

'You know Caroline. My friend at uni? She used to come and do her philosophy essays on our kitchen table. This is terrible – you probably can't remember her because she isn't five foot nine and a size ten. Her name's Caroline Selwyn. Very bright. A really interesting person.'

'Oh, sure. Of course. No, I do remember. She had bad skin.'

'God, Luke. Yeah – that's her. Anyway, Caro said it was like the big shock of the month, apparently. I mean, obviously things weren't easy with the whole thing about your dad, but life goes on, doesn't it? And *shit*, Luke, that was a hell of a job to throw in.'

'Yes, it was,' said Luke, feeling frightened for Sophie – and for himself. Were they just a no-good pair? Were they a bad batch of genes?

'I'm just throwing out ideas here, but maybe you should, like, *call* her? You're her brother. It might be friendly. Do you lot communicate at all?'

'I will call her,' he said. 'No, I will.'

'But I didn't come here to talk about *Sophia*. She gets quite enough air-time in my opinion. This is all about *you*. What's up?'

'You know what's up.'

'*Arianne?*' She frowned.

Luke nodded and tapped the ash off his cigarette. He glanced at the annexe windows: it was still and dark behind the leaves and glass.

'So what are you feeling? Will you tell me? It might help,' Jessica said. 'Look, it might help *me*, OK, because you've got me dead worried.'

She stroked his hair in the peaceful, maternal way she had and Luke said, 'It's simple, really. I love her and I have to have her back. I just have to. That's all there is to it. It's that or I've missed my chance, Jess. Because what she and I had – well, that was *it*, what everyone's waiting for. She was *it* and I let her go. Not let her, exactly, but sort of lost her. It's complicated.'

Jessica sighed. 'Oh, Luke.'

'What?'

'Why was she *it*? Yes, she was beautiful, *yes*, she had the whole damaged and manipulative Monroe thing going on and, sure, everyone turned to look when she came in. But, really, was that what you actually wanted to *live* with? It was all a fucking performance, Luke. She was your consummate actress. What was real?'

Luke took a drag on his cigarette. He remembered how, at the end, he had wondered if Arianne was faking the seductive little sighs she gave while she slept. In bad moments, after she had stopped wanting to sleep with him, he had been sure she did things to taunt him, to punish him for his global inadequacy. While he attempted to work from home, for example (which he had done more often when he became afraid she might call his supposed friend Joe and ask him over to keep her company), she had begun to give disproportionate attention to the smoothing of moisturizer on to her bare legs – up and down, up and down on the sofa beside him. She had padded about in a rainbow of G-strings, making an X-rated reflection in his computer monitor and, absentmindedly, she had often paused in the kitchen doorway to bite into pieces of fruit, letting juice run from her wrist to her elbow, then chasing it back up again with her tongue.

Or had she just been *eating fruit*, for God's sake? Was it not possible for an individual to be so close to perfect that their fruit-eating, their sighs, were precisely what 'eat' or 'sigh' had always meant in your imagination? Jessica was sceptical about perfection because she had not been exposed to it. He wanted to tell her this, but he was afraid she might call him an idiot and tell him to go back to work.

She was so sharp and clever about people and he knew she would have theories about Arianne, but he did not want to hear them. Jessica saw human nature neon-lit under a microscope and although he could always see she was right when she explained herself, he was glad his mind naturally blurred life a little and made it softer to look at.

Jessica went on, 'What a girl. No, I'm not surprised she's doing so well really.'

'*Is* she?' he said. 'I haven't heard anything about her.'

'Oh, well, I haven't *seen* her either and nor has Ludo, I don't think, but she's been in the press a bit recently. You really have cut yourself off, haven't you? Not even reading the Style section. Good Lord.'

Luke's mouth went dry with fear. Here it was: Arianne's independent life. It was about to crash into him head on. 'In the *press*? Why?' he said.

'She's in that play *Hotel* in the West End. It's being directed by that Hollywood actor, Jack Cane – oh, you know, from that film where the thinly disguised Arab types plot to blow up the White House? He's in loads of stuff.'

'She got the part.'

'Yeah, she's replacing the lead actress indefinitely – maybe the whole run. Apparently the real girl was "exhausted". We all know what *that* means,' Jessica said, tapping her nose.

'Wow. That's – that's fantastic.'

'Yeah. All worked out nicely for her. No, she must be pretty talented, actually, if they thought she could learn the whole part in a few weeks like that. Not that she didn't get a little help, of course.'

'Oh?'

'From – oh, you know, Jamie wotsit.'

'Who? From who?' Luke said. 'Why did he help her? Do I know him?'

Jessica stubbed out her cigarette and a drank some beer. 'Oh, it's nothing. He's just some crappy TV actor with floppy black hair.'

'And she's — what? She's friends with him?' Luke said. He felt the garden slope violently away from him. He was almost too weak to breathe.

'I . . . I really don't know,' Jessica said, appalled at her tactlessness. She just found it impossible to believe that Luke genuinely loved that agonized narcissist, no matter how good her legs were, so she had not taken enough care to be discreet.

'You do know,' he said.

'Look, I'm sorry — I really don't. I only know he helped her get the part because his dad's the major backer of the production.'

Luke put his head into his hands and then he put his head in his hands on his knees, and then he drew his knees and his head and his hands up into his chest. It was as if being smaller might shrink the pain.

'Oh, babe,' Jessica said, 'they *might* just be friends, honey. I really don't know.'

'They're not,' Luke said. 'She's sleeping with him.'

'Luke, you don't know that.'

'Yes, I do.'

Jessica sighed and looked away. They sat in silence for a moment and the wind stirred the bushes and blew a few rose petals out across the lawn. Eventually she said, 'So have you just ditched your amazing flat?'

'I'm just staying here for a bit, OK? Basically I'm not going back there without her, Jess.'

'*What?*'

'I mean it. I'm not doing anything without her. Life, I mean. None of it.'

'Luke, this is *crazy*,' she said. '*Luke?* How do I make you listen to the voice of your friend who loves you?'

'I always listen to you.'

'OK, then. What if she *is* going out with this Jamie whatever-his-name-is?'

'Turnbull,' he said, remembering Arianne mentioning she had met him. How insignificantly the name had trickled into his life! He recalled her saying, 'Yeah, I met some new people this evening — a few models, an actor. Mostly twats — except this swanky actor called Jamie Turnbull. Want a bubble bath? I'll go and run it.'

Unable to drink, Luke put down his beer bottle. 'I know who he is. He's the one from that hospital thing,' he said.

'Yes, *that's* him. He's like the "lovable rogue" who's secretly a genius but has-a-drinking-problem-and-is-wasting-his-incredible-potential-to-be-a-brain-surgeon-like-his-highly-respected-brain-surgeon-father. *God*, those shows are crap – psychiatrists must *wince* if they see them. Anyway,' she said softly, seeing she had lost him – he was staring out across the garden, '*anyway*, what if she *is* going out with him, sweetheart?'

'No,' he said.

'Because you probably should just try and be ready for that. I suppose that would be sensible.'

'No, it's OK. She can't be, Jess. She isn't. She *couldn't* after what we had. Not so soon. The reason I know is because it wouldn't be humanly possible.'

'"Frailty thy name is woman,"' Jessica said. She hated the glibness with which she was avoiding her friend's unhappiness, but she had not been prepared for it. It occurred to her that, oddly, she sounded rather like Luke's emotionally paralysed father, who was a mine of apposite quotations if ever warmth was required. It was unlike her, but she felt thrown. Of course, she had seen other friends heartbroken before, but to see Luke in this state somehow constituted an end of innocence. If her broad-shouldered, privileged, sports-playing, hand-some friend Luke wasn't immune to this depth of pain, no one was safe. Here was the rose garden of his childhood – and here was Luke, pale and slouched before it.

He looked at her as if she had been trying deliberately to confuse and scare him.

She said, 'Oh, sweetheart, I'm sorry. All I'm saying is, you know what Arianne's like. I mean, I don't know her that well, but wasn't she seeing some guy when you met her? Didn't she leave him in exactly the—'

'*No*,' Luke said. 'It's not the *same*. Oh, my God.'

She saw tears in his eyes and went on, rather desperately, 'But, Luke, think about it calmly. Please try. She wasn't the easiest of girls, was she? Let's face it, she was a total nightmare. Don't you remember that evening at Ludo's – the dinner party? She went completely mental because you stopped checking on her for five minutes so you and I could have a little gossip and catch up. Do you remember? She didn't like you having *friends*, Luke. She didn't like you having a *job*. These are commonly thought to be bad signs in a girlfriend.'

'It was just she didn't know many people that night. She thought I was ignoring her.'

'*Oh, right*. OK – because she's so *shy*. Yes, I can see why that would have been a problem.'

'She *is* shy. Underneath it, I mean. You don't know her. It's all very complicated. There's basically been a *huge* confusion.'

'What confusion, Luke? OK – no, I don't *know her*. But I do know love isn't meant to be *complicated*, there aren't meant to be huge *confusions*. To me, you either love someone or you don't. And, Luke, if you do love someone, you *respect* them.'

'But I *do* respect her.'

'Fuck! I'm talking about *her*, Luke, not *you*. Wake up! She practically kissed your friends in front of you. Remember Joe and that whole tequila-shot incident? Everyone fucking gossiped about it, babe. They were all, like, "Luke should have more self-respect." Is that what you want?'

'Well, I know why she didn't respect me. And I just need a chance to show her who I really am and then she will.'

'Who you really are? Who were you then?'

'I don't know. I was just – I was *scared* all the time. All I could think about was her leaving me. I was not myself. I wasn't a real man.'

'Yes, you were. What's a real man? That was you. Luke, you were what she made you into – you were both what you made each other into. And you *still would be now*. That's the Arianne-Luke, just as much as this is an aspect of the Jessica-Luke.'

He shook his head slowly. 'God, you really think that's how people are? *Chaotic* like that? *Changing, changing, changing?*'

He sounded slightly manic, but Jessica did not notice this. She enjoyed theorizing and could forget her context in the rush of mathematical excitement. '*Definitely*,' she said. 'We're like colours. You put one shade of blue next to another shade of blue and it can look green, but put it next to green and it's blue as the sky, put it next to red and it looks purple. No one's fixed. And, Luke, Arianne made you invisible. You disappeared on us.'

'Not at the beginning. It wasn't like that at the beginning.'

She sighed. 'No, it can't have been. I know. But maybe it wasn't ever meant to be a long-term thing. Maybe it was always just a little bit of the journey.'

This was almost exactly what Arianne had said to him. He remembered her standing there with her weird assortment of possessions, sinister in their disparateness as ingredients for a spell. She had said, 'This was always a temporary thing, Luke. Life's a journey, right? Who wants to *settle down* and all that?'

Luke turned to Jessica. 'A journey?' he said desperately. '*Where?*'

225

'Well, I mean I don't know, exactly. Why would I know? But this is what people say is the interesting—'

'*Don't tell me that.* And I don't see why you're so sure you're on a *journey*, anyway. You only call it a journey if you know you're going *somewhere*, right? If you were just going round and round you'd call it—' He broke off in wordless frustration.

'Just going round and round,' she said.

'So how can you tell that isn't what we're doing?'

'I . . . You can't.'

'Well, then.'

'Well, what? I don't see how this relates to you and Arianne.'

'No,' Luke said, 'neither do I. I think I've forgotten.'

But even though the idea could lose its logical formation, he could not really forget. Although he could not explain it, he knew that his belief in God and heaven and in human progression altogether was inextricably connected to the salvage of all that wasted love. That it should simply be lost and forgotten implied facts about the world too terrible to contemplate.

'Sweetheart, if you want my honest opinion – and I'm well aware you've given me no reason to believe you do – I think you should move on. *Mend* yourself and *move on.*'

'Oh, you make it sound so . . . How would you know? I'm sorry, Jess, but *how would you fucking know?*'

They sat quietly while he cried, and then Jessica said, 'Luke, haven't you ever wondered why I don't have a boyfriend?'

It took a moment for her words to reach him. 'I suppose,' he said. 'You're pretty secretive about things. Private, I mean.'

She laughed. 'No, secretive was the right word. But you're so unsuspicious, Luke, aren't you? You just accept things – the way they look on the surface.'

'Oh, I'm *thick*, you mean?' he said, remembering how frequently his sister had made this poisonous observation. 'You mean I'm *thick* and *conventional*.'

'No!' she said, although if you stripped away the fond indulgence that was what was left. 'No,' she said more quietly, ashamed of herself. 'Anyway, I'm trying to tell you I'm gay.'

Luke flinched as if he had been punched in the stomach, and she couldn't help giggling at the artless honesty of his reaction. 'So, what do you think?' she said. And then, unable to stop herself before it came out, 'Are we still friends?'

'Of *course* we're still friends,' he said. He put his hand on her arm and then, as if in response to a new understanding of her, he shook it and thumped her on the back.

She smiled lovingly at him. 'Good. I'm sorry I didn't say before.'

'I – well, you *should* have. How long have you known? I mean – oh, God. Does Ludo know?'

'Yes. I told him a couple of weeks ago. Actually, I introduced him to my new girlfriend the other night.'

'Your—'

'Cally,' she said. 'I'd like you to meet her. She's doing a doctorate in philosophy at Cambridge.'

'Wow.'

Jessica blushed with pleasure and excitement. 'I know. She's *gorgeous*, too. I have no idea what she's doing with me, which is a completely great sensation.'

Luke felt a stab of jealousy. 'That's really fantastic, Jess.'

She put an arm round him and kissed his cheek. 'Thanks, babe,' she said, again reminding herself not to sound so grateful in future. Cally was always telling her off for this – and she was right. You had to start on the right footing – no defensiveness – particularly, as Cally said, if you'd been crazy enough to pretend for as long as Jessica had.

'So, you see, I do know what it feels like, Luke. I know what love feels like. I understand how overwhelming it can be and how you can't tell left from right from wrong.'

He looked at her seriously and it occurred to him that he had probably been this obtuse in his own happiness. Perhaps everyone was. Hadn't he almost wanted to tell his ex-girlfriend Lucy not to be sad about them splitting up because so much *happiness* had come out of it? He had wanted to draw her attention to the *sum total* of happiness because, for a moment back there, he had felt sure good old Lucy would understand and be pleased, if only she thought about it.

Happiness was an ugly condition to be in, really, he thought. A picture came back: himself, overexcited by a new red bike on his eighth birthday, running round the house shouting his joy like a Red Indian, accidentally stamping on Sophie's hamster. 'No,' he said bitterly. 'Now you'd have to feel it all turning into *hate*.'

Jessica looked at him and nodded. Then she put her arms out and he let go of himself into them and cried into her long hair.

When she had gone, he went into his father's study and typed Arianne's name into the search engine: 20,024 hits in 0.45 seconds.

'Jamie dating again! But who is the mystery girl?' he read. He clicked on the link:

www.starsandcelebs.co.uk
Jamie Turnbull, who split just recently from sexy co-star Elaine Dance has been spotted in the arms of a new babe. At the 1st birthday bash for trendy restaurant 'kink', Jamie's date for the evening was the mystery-girl who recently replaced Cindy Tayler in *Ho—*

He clicked back and tried another site, for something – *anything* – better. Surely the world could do better than this.

www.hotgosmagazine.co.uk
Bad luck girls! It looks like our Jamie has found love. With her sultry looks and sexy French accent, Arianne is going to be tough comp—

He turned the computer off at the mains.

It was an hour or so before he returned to himself. Gradually, he noticed his face in the polished surface of his father's desk. Then he wiped his eyes and looked out of the window at the annexe. He must take them their sheets and pillows because his mother would be back soon. It was getting dark.

He went to the linen cupboard and took the sheets for the bed in the first-floor spare room, then he went downstairs and gathered some of the cushions from the cupboard in the conservatory. He took the picnic blankets from the chest of drawers in the hall. On the way through the kitchen, he went into the storecupboard and took a packet of biscuits and a bottle of lemonade because they – or, rather, Goran – had eaten everything but the apples and the Go-Go bar at the Easy Dine Cafeteria.

Luke was rather astonished by his efficiency. He was learning things about himself. He put the biscuits and lemonade under his arm, balanced the huge pile of bedding on his outstretched wrists, steadying it with his chin, and walked down the garden steps, past the empty beer bottles that he and Jessica had left there in a time of relative innocence.

At first there was no answer to his knock. He said, 'Hello? It's OK, it's me, Luke.'

Then Goran came to the door. He was swollen-faced with sleep. Luke gave him the bedding and explained he would have to go straight away as his mother would be back at any moment. He promised to come and wake them in the morning and tell them when it was safe to go out.

Goran took the bedding and put it on the table by the door.

Luke said, 'Oh, what am I doing? I nearly forgot to give you these. It's not much – just a snack. I hope that's OK. I can get you something more if—'

Goran accepted the biscuits and lemonade. 'No, Luke, this is very much already. Please. Mila and I, we have talked.' He glanced back into the interior darkness to which Luke's eyes were not yet accustomed. Mila came out of it. Her hair was tangled and there were crease marks from the sofa cushions across her cheek. She tucked herself under the outstretched arm. 'Luke, we don't know what to tell you to say thank you,' Goran said.

'Thank you,' Mila echoed. She glanced up uncertainly at Goran, who gripped her shoulder in encouragement. 'Thank you sincerely,' she said.

'Yes. Like Mila says, we thank you sincerely. We rest for tonight and tomorrow we find job. I have address to go where is work.'

Luke studied them briefly. They had brought out their best English word for him; Goran clasped Mila more tightly and rubbed her arm as if to emphasize his gratitude, as if she was a musical instrument on which to strum it out. She rested her head on his chest, absorbing these good-natured blows. They were a forcefield of emotion and hope.

'One day there is *something* that we will do for you, Luke,' Goran said. 'You will tell us. We will never forget this help.'

Luke tried to smile. He tried to make sense of the tears that had rushed into Goran's eyes again, just as they had by the till in the service station, but he could not. Goran, too, seemed amazed by them and wiped them away roughly with the back of his hand.

'I hope you both sleep well,' Luke said. This practicality was all he could manage. 'I must get back . . . inside.' He raised his hand.

As he walked off, he heard Mila call softly, 'I hope also you will sleep well.'

She had a lovely gentle voice. He pretended not to hear it.

Luke knew that he would not sleep well. Why would he sleep at all? Arianne was with another man: 20,024 hits had brought this fact home. Her independent life had roared her off in a jet-plane, a space-ship, into a rarefied atmosphere he was not equipped to breathe. She was mixing with famous people now.

His stomach, the battleground for all Luke's anxieties, clenched painfully. He told himself to remember that in a room behind him were people struggling to survive, sleeping in forests, hiding in lorries, not eating for two days. He remembered Goran's voice: 'We will never forget this help.'

It was touching that all of their acts were mutual — even the most abstract, even memory. They had no money, no possessions, no home, no country, but wasn't it true that they would sleep deeply because they were together, while he would be tossed out alone on a cold star?

Luke stopped by one of the rosebushes and, feeling like a very old man, he leant down to smell one of the blooms. He had not felt lonely like this until he met Arianne. She had brought with her all of the sharp emotions his life had been lacking — or free of. He thought about their first kiss, after the car crash, when she stood in his bedroom doorway, sleepy and confused by the painkillers. 'Does your head hurt?' he asked her.

And then had come the first of her unforgettable scenes: 'No . . . It was just . . . I dreamt I saw God.'

What was it she had seen? A 'burning, devouring light' — that was it. He had soon learnt that she loved those words: 'You know what? After pudding, I feel like *devouring* you,' she would say, with her hand down his trousers in a restaurant booth crowded with friends. 'Fuck, I'm absolutely *burning* for you,' she would whisper, in the middle of the film. 'Any ideas, Luke?'

It was strange that it was in these terms that God had appeared to her. It was all very confusing and a little bit sinful. He shook his head. When he had sex with Arianne, his fear of life diminished in propor-tion with the distance between their bodies. For him, there had been no more terrified speculation about whether he would be a failure or not, about whether his father acknowledged his potential or even his existence: he had simply arrived at her mouth, at her soft stomach, at her hips and her breasts. Why had it not been this way for her? Sex with him had increasingly seemed only to amplify her fear and afterwards she took to lying silently beside him, like the survivor of a shipwreck, naked and vulnerable to the elements.

He peered through the trellis at the next-door house. The family were all in the kitchen, eating. There was wine on the table, the smell of garlic and pastry mixed with that of the fresh-cut grass on the lawn. Upstairs, in a dark room, an unwatched TV pulsed light up a bare wall; Luke wondered if this was the loneliest thing he had ever seen.

Was *this* what Arianne felt when she cried like that? Was this the fear with which she had come hurtling into his complacent arms? He hadn't even begun to understand it. It was no wonder she had not trusted him to protect her. Perhaps he had actually needed to lose her before he could understand.

Didn't this revelation, which, after all, he was accepting with a considerable degree of nobility, didn't this signify human progress?

Suddenly he felt capable of miracles. Of course he would get Arianne back.

'Oh, Luke!' Rosalind said. 'Are you in the garden, darling? I've been calling. How lovely. Isn't it a beautiful evening?'

'Mum?' Luke said.

Carefully, Rosalind picked a few dead leaves off the honeysuckle. 'Yes, darling?'

'Do you think you're ever going to be able to forgive him?'

231

Chapter 14

Rosalind sat down at the kitchen table in front of a tuna salad with a light vinaigrette dressing. She poured herself a glass of sparkling mineral water and laid her napkin across her lap. A brown roll lay on a plate beside her and to its right a pile of letters, which had been building for two weeks. She couldn't think what had stopped her opening them. There had been desperate empty tracts of time spent staring at her shoes, her teacup, her hand – but somehow she had never picked up the envelopes.

It was an unexpected luxury that Alistair had decided to stay away for the night. She had slept more peacefully free of the thought that her husband was in the spare room: even separated from its full significance, when her mind had expertly filled itself with practicalities, this thought was a loose thread on her hem or an appalling wine stain on the cream sofa.

But last night Alistair had straightforwardly been away. Nothing could have been more ordinary. It was lovely to feel well rested for the first time in two weeks, and now that her son had gone back to collect him from Dover, there was no denying it was lovely to be alone in the house. No men wanting sympathy or wanting to be forgiven. Luke had attempted to discuss her feelings about Alistair and she had successfully put him off by saying she needed time to think. She did. She leant back in her chair, consciously enjoying the sounds you only hear when you are alone: the clock ticking in the hall, the hushed spin of the washing-machine, the birds in the garden. A lawnmower was running a little way off.

She took a mouthful of crisp lettuce and started on the letters. She began with the bills, saving the handwritten envelopes for last. Her mind habitually began with practicalities: the personal letters would be a reward, like chocolate for Luke and Sophie if they had their jabs without making a fuss, or unpacked and brought down the laundry right away after a holiday. After years of this kind of thinking, she still mothered herself.

The bills were all overdue, a fact which would normally have caused her deep anxiety. But today she felt nothing. There was one from the dry-cleaner, who had recently done the drawing-room curtains, there was the car insurance, which Alistair would look at, and there was her subscription to *Town and Country Interiors* magazine. There were various offers and big prize draws, which scattered out of the envelopes in novelty shapes and insistent colours. It was irritating to have to pick them up. One said: 'Spot the hidden monkey and win £100,000!' The world seemed very mysterious.

At last she got to a stiff, pale mauve envelope, which contained a card. It was from her friend Cynthia, who was 'just sending love at this difficult time'. There was another card saying much the same thing from their dear old au pair Claudia, who had married and settled in England. She appreciated her friends' tact: 'Thinking of you and all you are going through'; 'Just wanted to send a quick note to let you know I'm here for you.' They conveyed sympathy without hurting her by appearing to know all the sordid details.

It was unlike Rosalind to be so conscious of the mechanics of friendship. In the past couple of weeks, though, she had found herself overwhelmed by the intricacy, the complexity of human relationships. The number of conflicting things you could feel about a person as you filled a cup with coffee and passed it to them! This was something that had occurred to her.

Lastly, there was a plain white envelope addressed in familiar handwriting. She could not quite place it for a moment. She recognized the looping 'L' of Langford, the dramatic, oversized 'W' of 'W8'. She opened it and took a sip of her mineral water. She read,

Dear Mum,
   I'm writing to you from Heathrow airport.

Rosalind put down her glass. It was Sophie's handwriting – although it was Alistair's she had remembered because it was almost indistinguishable from Sophie's. She continued:

I've decided to give up my job and go to Ghana for a year. You remember I did that course which qualified me to teach English as a foreign language? You probably do remember — I'm sure it cost you and Dad a lot of money. Well, I thought I might as well use it, I suppose. I know I did the course ten years ago but I really haven't moved anywhere since I was twenty anyway.

Mum, I know you'll think I'm doing this because I want to run away from Dad's mess. Well, you'll just have to believe that's not true — or, at least, that it's not the whole story. The main thing is that you and Dad — and Luke in his own way — have done nothing but worry about me for years, since I first got ill with the anorexia, and I'm sick of it. It's like I've diagnosed myself and, whatever was wrong with me before, at least I know what's wrong with me now: I'm sick of being an emergency.

I'll write as soon as I get there and let you know I'm OK. And I will be OK. Please don't see this as another disaster for you to cope with. This is the most hopeful I've felt in years — ever, really.

It's funny. You know I would have written this letter to Dad if all that terrible stuff hadn't come out. I'm sure you know what I mean — just that he's the one I would naturally have confided in. Well, I wanted you to know that I'm glad I'm writing it to you — I'm glad you're the one I'm telling.

I'm thinking of you, Mum, all the time, coping with so much betrayal. I'll send an address when I'm settled. I know Luke will think I'm evil for going away, but I have to do this. I'm not sure why I feel this so strongly, but I know you'll understand.

Love,
Sophie

Rosalind's daughter left her breathless. She always had. The emotion, the power of that thin, blonde girl, exploding right in your face. 'Coping with so much betrayal' — there it was, in black and white. Sophie exploded, she attacked, she *insisted*. These were not Rosalind's ways. Sophie had her father's loud voice and she actually screamed during arguments: terrible emergency screams, like someone trapped in a burning building. The loudest thing Sophie had ever screamed was 'LET ME SPEAK!' when she had refused to go back to boarding-school and Rosalind and Alistair found her sitting on her trunk in the hall in protest. She and Alistair had instinctively covered their ears and the glass lampshade on the hall table had hummed for a few moments afterwards.

When Sophie was fourteen, she wrote words on her arms with razor blades: 'bitch', 'meat', 'whore'. It was as if she was a piece of paper for writing angry letters to the world on. Like letters to the editor of *The Times*, which Alistair got so heated about. Rosalind remembered a christening they had been invited to, a row about whether Sophie would wear a silk shirt with long, concealing sleeves, which Rosalind had ironed for her. Sophie took it and dropped it out of the window like rubbish. It was so disorienting later to walk out into the garden and lift the shirt off the dripping wet blackberry bush where it had caught.

Sophie brought together unlikely things to sinister effect, forcing you to hear a crackle of strangeness just beneath the surface of the ordinary world. It made Rosalind want to sort through the cupboard in the pantry as she was always meaning to do. It also made her want to go to church and sit very quietly listing the things she was grateful for, as she had done at school. She remembered holding her rosary, oddly conscious that there was a lot about her parents and the rest of the world that she didn't understand, and that she would never feel so safe again as she did then, in her starched school uniform, with the bell going for lunch.

She and Sophie had never been very close. It was a great sadness to Rosalind, an absence powerful enough almost to invalidate the satisfaction of those sunny weekend mornings when she walked about the house checking the plants and looking at the framed photographs of her family.

Basically, it had not been what she expected – having a daughter. Even as a little girl, Sophie had wanted mostly to play chess with Alistair or to read a book in her room, and so it had always been Luke who made fairy-cakes or pom-pom animals with Rosalind. A further disappointment was that Sophie hated clothes, and by the age of five had thought dressing up was 'for babies'. Rosalind had kept ribbons and pieces of fabric for the Dressing-up Box since she got married, saving them carefully while Sophie grew, but none of it was ever used. It wasn't suitable for Luke, who had shown a slightly unhealthy interest in trying on her jewellery, which she knew perfectly well she had been tempted to allow.

She had longed for a pretty little daughter with whom she could re-enter the fantasy world of her own childhood. But Sophie was not interested. And it was just plain humiliating to be grimaced at by a six-year-old when you suggested dressing up as a lovely Fairy Queen for the square garden fancy-dress party.

The party – or one of them, since it was an annual event – stood out in the story of herself and Sophie. It was put on to raise funds for the upkeep of the pretty communal garden in the centre of Burton Square and it was held in the summer, when the garden was heavy with magnolia. All the neighbours contributed party food and helped with balloons and tables and streamers. All the children had pretty hand-made costumes. Hiring was seen as terribly vulgar. It was an event fraught with feminine rivalry. Some of the women began work on the costumes months in advance.

Sophie, after much argument about whether she would go at all, had insisted on going as a judge. She was a sallow, thin little figure in her father's wig and gown. She went about thumping her toy hammer by the other children's plates, making the crisps jump. One little boy burst into tears and Rosalind noticed Sophie being spoken to on several occasions by James Wardell from number thirty-eight.

She had rarely felt more disappointed in her daughter than she did that afternoon. She stood behind her big smile, holding a bucket, collecting the children's five-pence pieces by the coconut shy. She could not help seeing the other mothers stare at her weird little daughter as they arrived and released their Cinderellas and Little Red Riding Hoods into the sunshine in a shimmer of frills and ringlets. At least Luke looked perfect as a sailor-boy, she told herself.

But as wonderful as Luke was – and he was wonderful – she had always wanted a wonderful daughter. And instead she had Sophie. In her darkest moments – when Sophie had overdosed on sleeping pills and been taken into hospital aged fifteen – this was what Rosalind allowed herself to think. It was simply appalling for a mother to think something like that! It had made her feel so guilty that she stayed at the hospital all night, sitting on a chair by the bed, even though the doctors said Sophie was in no danger and would not wake up until morning.

It was then that she gave up on her dream daughter. She grieved for this beautiful figment in instalments – during the arguments or the visits to the anorexia clinic, where she and Alistair sat with their teacups surrounded by all the weirdly thin girls, angular as bicycles beneath their clothes.

Her own mother had come to visit the hospital the day after that first overdose and looked despairingly at Rosalind, her expression not without a tinge of judgement. Rosalind had wanted to remind her that Suzannah had been a total mess for years, but she would never have spoken to her mother in that way.

Did her mother *ever* look at her without a tinge of judgement? Rosalind had spent her life attempting to meet the woman's standards and it had never done any good; in fact, there seemed to be far more appeal, far more romance in Suzannah's imperfections. Suzannah had got away with everything. She had once stolen one of their mother's brooches and sold the diamond out of it. Shortly after the theft was discovered, Suzannah had overshadowed the incident, with what Rosalind considered to be chilling expertise, by bringing home the heir to the Ellerson sugar fortune for Sunday lunch. Her sister had bought herself a whole new wardrobe with the money from the diamond. She made no secret of her purchases. But that autumn Hugo Ellerson was regularly to be seen in their hall, helping Suzannah on with her new fox-collared coat or waiting while she tightened her new pearl earrings in the mirror. Drunk on grand visions of the future, in which her father went shooting with Ralph Ellerson and her mother sat chatting in the drawing room at Nordean, Rosalind's parents stood by with indulgent smiles. It had shocked her most deeply of all to discover that her father made an insurance claim for the brooch, saying it had been lost.

What a lot of secrecy family life involved. What a lot of mean, filthy secrets, she thought, pushing away her plate so hard that she splashed the water out of her glass. And then she remembered something Sophie had said when the anorexia was really bad and she had sat before an untouched plate, like the spectre at the feast, at every family meal. It had been raining hard, genuinely battering on the windows. They had just sat down to supper and Alistair had said he couldn't make it to something Rosalind had hoped he would come to. As far as she could recall, it had been the Holland Park Mothers Against Vandalism meeting, which it had been her turn to arrange. She had known perfectly well that Alistair would be bored stiff by the event and that he loathed all the women involved and thought they were 'silly twitterers'. But she had wanted him to be there as many of the other husbands were going and it would look odd if he wasn't.

'Oh, I'm sorry, darling, I've got a big case on next week. I'll simply have to stay on at chambers on Tuesday evening,' he said.

'Really? Oh, well.'

'Yes, it's a big case,' he said.

'I'm sure. Never mind.'

'What a bore.'

'Gosh, no – really. *Really*. Not important.'

'This is wonderful partridge, by the way, darling. A real triumph.'

Sophie snorted. 'Wonderful *partridge*?'

They all looked at her leaning back against the wall, behind her untouched plate. She was doing 'the face', a mixture of disgust and despair. It signified a point of no return.

'Do you *know* how much you patronize her, Dad? Why can't you just go to her fucking mothers' meeting? She goes to your boring legal dinners all the fucking time. How often does she ask you to do anything for her? Name one thing in the last ten years and I'll give you all my money. No, tell you what, I'll give you all my *cigarettes*.'

Rosalind put some more peas on to Sophie's plate and said, 'Darling, Daddy works incredibly hard for us *all the time* so we can have everything we need. And you aren't meant to be smoking, Sophie. We agreed.'

'*You* agreed. I like smoking. And, no, Dad works incredibly hard because he *loves* it – because it's what he *enjoys* doing. Because it's a way of *avoiding time at home or doing anything he doesn't want to do*. Isn't that true, Dad?'

Sophie stood up and looked straight into her father's face. (Wonderful, Rosalind thought. She won't eat anything now.) Alistair looked back, his mouth twisted into a crooked smile or frown, which was strangely embarrassing to stare at, like a facial spasm on a stroke victim.

'*Isn't* it, Dad?' Sophie shouted. 'Why couldn't you just go to one little meeting for her – make her feel *respected* for once?' She turned to her mother. 'But, Mum, what I *really, really* don't understand is, why do *you* take this shit?'

Rosalind found herself saying pleadingly, 'Sophie, everything's fine. Please sit down. Please. Everything's all right.'

Sophie laughed. 'You and Dad want to know why I can't eat? Big fucking mystery! This is a fucking *hunger strike* against *lies*.'

'Hey,' Luke said, leaning back in his chair in an attitude of paternal authority, 'calm down, Soph, for goodness' sake.'

Sophie threw her water in his face and left the room.

Now Rosalind looked at the tuna salad she had pushed away from her across the table. A hunger strike against lies. She could actually understand that. Had she always understood more than she had allowed Sophie to know? How terrible! Why on earth would that be?

Or was this bizarre self-accusation unfair? After all, Sophie had

238

always given her reason to doubt her insights from the moment she began to trust them. Because, as angry as Sophie could be, the day after an incident like the one over her speech at the Holland Park Mothers, she and Alistair would often behave as if nothing had happened. They would sit in the drawing room discussing newspaper articles in raptures of mutual appreciation.

Just as Suzannah had always been forgiven, always remained their father's favourite, whatever wine she opened or whatever time she came in, Sophie was forgiven by Alistair. Their reunions were obscurely embarrassing to Luke and Rosalind, who stood up in silence and cleared the plates while father and daughter played word-association games in French or Latin and giggled at their private jokes. Luke and Rosalind did not look at each other while this sort of thing went on in the background.

Rosalind's daughter was a wild and frightening mystery to her. One thing she felt passionately, though, was that, unlike her, Sophie did not hide things from herself. It was a painful way to live – there was no doubt about it. You could not see Sophie, with her emaciated arms and legs and the scars on her forearms, and say it was not a painful way to live.

Suddenly Rosalind was proud of her daughter in a way she could not have expressed – in a way that deeply confused her, given all the anxiety Sophie had caused. Her cheeks had flushed and she looked at the letter again:

I'm writing to you from Heathrow airport.

Her heart raced with excitement. Then she read the end:

I'm not sure why I feel this so strongly, but I know you'll understand.

Why would she understand? Rosalind felt completely unworthy of this trust and her fist clenched in exasperation.

She was the least adventurous person who had ever lived. Where had she ever been, other than on family ski-trips with her parents or family holidays with Alistair? She had only ever planned one journey without a family, without a man. It had been known as the Big Italian Adventure. She remembered this and cringed internally. It was poignant, but it was also embarrassing.

She and Lara Siskin had planned the trip for months when they were both twenty and doing their secretarial courses in Chelsea. Alistair had been doing his law-conversion exams at the time and they saw each other rarely. She did not know that he could not afford to take her out to dinner and that his only option was to hope to be invited to the same drinks parties as she was. She imagined he took out other girls – clever Girton or St Hilda's girls, unlike her in every way. It was lovely to see him by chance at a party, though. She had told herself she must get on and forget the extravagant promise of that May Ball, over a year ago now. And, anyway, she couldn't help thinking it probably was more interesting to be dreaming about travel rather than weddings, as her friends always were.

But in spite of these independent tendencies, love was still the incentive behind all action. She and Lara had bought a map of Italy and a guidebook, which they took out every day over lunch, saying things like, 'Well, *I* think some dashing Italian will ask you to marry him on the Spanish Steps, which is where Keats died in 1821.'

Then the other one would grab the book and flick through the pages, 'Well, *I* think you'll fall in love with a vineyard owner's eldest son in Montepul – Montepulciano.'

Lara would giggle wickedly. 'You'd better not say yes if it's you on the Spanish Steps, Roz, no matter how dark and handsome he is, or someone's heart will be broken.'

'Oh, what are you talking about?'

Lara made a face: pompous, self-conscious, lovestruck. It was Alistair to a T.

'Lara. Stop it.'

'Well, he's mad about you. Everyone says so. Philip says he nearly *faints* if someone mentions your name.'

'I don't know him that well,' Rosalind said, biting her lip to suppress the smile of pride – even if she didn't think it was true, it was nice to be thought of by her friends as an object of someone's desire. But she could not quell her natural honesty and modesty for long. 'Really, Lara, it's not as if he's endlessly taking me out to dinner or anything.'

'Who knows what goes on in men's minds?' Lara said, sighing like a woman who has reconciled herself to much disappointment. In fact, she had never had a boyfriend. 'Anyway, Roz,' she said, 'there's lots of time for getting married, isn't there? You aren't on the shelf till you're twenty-five.'

They took Italian lessons on Tuesday and Thursday evenings with an enormously fat woman named Elena Forli whose house smelt mouth-wateringly of fresh pastry and icing sugar and vanilla. Signora Forli had faintly alarming baby blue- and pink-hued pictures of Jesus all over her walls and He smiled down at Lara and Rosalind like a patient nanny as they struggled with the past perfect and licked their lips.

During their dull shorthand lessons, they hid their Italian grammar books just beneath the desk, smiling conspiratorially at each other. '⟋⟍ ⌒ ⌐' was '*Andiamo in Italia*', which was 'We are going to Italy.'

Lara made pasta out of flour and eggs and they ate it reverently, even though it was revoltingly overcooked. Was this slimy stuff what the Italians were famous for, they wondered. It was all part of the mystery of adult life, of a piece with the thrilling uneasiness that came of imitating grown-up talk at their parents' dinner parties. There was a distinct sensation of fraudulence, and eye-contact with each other at the wrong moment might have blown their adult personae apart in an avalanche of stifled giggles. They solemnly avoided this eventuality. Each secretly vowed to pretend to like tagliatelle, almost as if this constituted a rite of passage in itself.

Two days before they were due to leave for Rome, Lara's appendix ruptured. Mrs Siskin called Rosalind's mother to explain. There was simply no question of Lara going away for at least three weeks – and she was due to start at her finishing school in September. Both mothers agreed it was a great pity, although Rosalind's mother had no idea how frustrated Mrs Siskin was to lose this opportunity to cement what she saw as a highly suitable friendship for Lara.

Rosalind had never cried like that before. Perhaps she never cried like that again. In the end her sister came in and sat on her bed. Rosalind could smell Suzannah's face cream.

'Rozzy, you're making the most frightful racket – it's heartbreaking,' she said.

Rosalind lifted her head from the pillow. 'I'm sorry.'

'Poor old you. God, why don't you just go anyway?'

'What? Don't be barmy. I can't.'

Suzannah went over to the mantelpiece and took down the tickets. 'What a waste of all that planning. All that ruddy gossiping.'

'Please don't, Suzannah. I know. *Don't*.'

'Don't what? I'm not just rubbing it in. I'm saying, '*Go*'. Go on your bloody own. It's what I'd do.'

Rosalind lifted her face from the pillow and looked at her beautiful

241

sister holding the tickets as if she had just been presented with them as a prize for vibrant personality. 'But I'm not you, though,' Rosalind said.

Suzannah took this in. Her expression became serious – as if she had appreciated how irresponsible she was being. She exhaled soberly. 'No, I suppose not.' She walked back to the mantelpiece and propped the tickets against the clock. Then she stretched and yawned and said, oh, well, she must get a bit of beauty sleep and she was sure Rozzy would feel better in the morning. If she carried on bawling like that, she said, her eyes would be swollen for days.

As the door closed, cutting out the light from the hall, Rosalind felt another ending to what had already seemed to contain all the grim finality the world could muster. It literally went dark.

Six months later Alistair, who had passed his law exams and begun a pupillage at a reputable Inner Temple chambers, asked her out for dinner and not long afterwards if she would marry him. She was over-joyed and said yes straight away. Thrilled to have thought of the perfect way to put an end to the difficult atmosphere between herself and her friend, she asked Lara to be her bridesmaid.

Suzannah would have gone to Italy alone, it was true. Rosalind pictured her sister holding up the tickets, the lamplight from the hall bringing out the red in her dark hair. Their parents would have been furious – and then, when Suzannah got back, full of stories about grand somebody and grander somebody else, it would have been 'Our eldest daughter is quite the explorer, you know,' to everyone who came for drinks.

Rosalind felt keenly that she had been a bad example to Sophie. Alistair had always patronized her – it was true – and she had let it happen. Why? Because it was what she was used to. She had always been patronized – by her mother, her father, her sister, everyone.

Why had she never stolen the diamond from her mother's brooch or travelled around Italy alone? If she had been an adventurer, if she had used that boat ticket, if she had caught the overnight train from Paris to Rome, she might never have married Alistair. She might have married the vineyard owner's son in Montepulciano.

She smiled at this extraordinary thought. It was not that she had never imagined another life. There had been the affair with Rupert Sanderson, after all. She referred to it as an affair, though in fact it had consisted of a few moments of lingering eye-contact in the Sandersons' kitchen when everyone had rushed out to see a rainbow

242

and Rupert stood in front of her in his tennis whites, tapping his racket vigorously against his shoe. There followed several months of erotic dreams on Rosalind's side. She woke up scandalized by her imagination. The things she did! Kneeling on the floor and pulling down Rupert Sanderson's tennis shorts, licking his . . . his . . .

But the longevity of her 'affair' with Rupert was an exception. She had only ever imagined other lives – the poignant, domestic aspects of marriage – in abstracted fragments, which confined them safely to the realm of fantasy. She had wondered what it would be like to be in a car beside Julian, to come down the stairs with Henry Phipps – to have her coat put on by *Omar Bhattachari*! These dramatized moments required a suspension of disbelief, just like a play or a film. But Alistair was the reality she came back to when the lights went up. Their marriage was a *sine qua non*, which was an expression Alistair used. Everything was an expression Alistair used! Her whole self was an expression Alistair used. After thirty-nine years of marriage, she didn't even understand what divorce meant.

'I'd divorce him,' Suzannah had said, as they stood there with the terrible newspapers. 'It's what I'd do, Rozzy.'

And she had found herself answering her sister, 'But I'm not you, Suzannah. You've never understood marriage. You may have had four different surnames, but you've never really been *married*.'

Suzannah had studied her face in the drawing-room mirror, her knee resting on the club fender. The slightly aggressive tension in her shoulders relaxed. 'No, I suppose you're right, Roz,' she said, nodding with genuine humility.

She knew she was being eccentric, but Rosalind decided to have a cool bath instead of eating her lunch. She put the whole plate in the fridge, splayed knife and fork included.

As she sat on the bed, listening to the water running in the bathroom next door, she put her hand under the mattress. This was where she had kept the articles with the photographs of Alistair and the girl. She took them out from time to time and looked at the faces, not knowing why she felt the need to hide them, since they could hardly have been made more public already. And Alistair had not set foot in their bedroom since they had agreed it was best he move into the spare room.

The girl was not a child the way the papers made out, but she was very young. She was younger than their daughter. This fact was terrible enough – annihilating of Rosalind and her attractiveness, and faintly sinister in its own right. She looked at the photograph of her husband. To imply his amorality, the *Daily Mail* had chosen a grinning one taken on some courtroom steps after a victory a few years ago. *The Times* had opted for him in downtrodden mode, 'Miserable Sinner'. They had snapped it on the doorstep when he came out unsuspectingly to answer their ring. He appeared much smaller and older in that photograph. There was such fear in the clenched face. Part of her could not help feeling desperately sorry for him.

She, more than anyone else, could imagine his humiliation. Not only because she was the wronged wife and shared it, but also because she had long felt his disappointments as keenly as her own.

She had acquired the habit gradually. In the early days of knowing him, before they were engaged, she had noticed an agonized, tight look on his face occasionally, when his friends were chatting in a perfectly ordinary sociable way. At first she wondered if he disapproved of their frivolity – he did seem happiest when discussing something heavy and serious, like whether the Tories would win the next election, or if John Lister's new book was a fair portrayal of Churchill. Perhaps he thought restaurants and ski-trips and musicals were a waste of time. The idea thrilled her; the idea of a mind *that* superior. Perhaps his parents were strict or puritanical, she thought. This was also exciting in its severity. But he gave her no clues at all.

Then, shortly after the Big Italian Adventure fell through, when there seemed to be nothing left to hope for in life, something Philip said to her began a process of understanding. She and her cousin had bumped into each other at a crowded drinks party in a tiny flat on Ebury Street. He said, 'You're rather keen on my friend Alistair, aren't you?'

Rosalind averted her gaze, but then she brought it determinedly back again. 'Well, he wrote to me a bit after that ball you took me to, that's all. Actually, I haven't seen him for ages, and when I do it's only by chance, at a party like this,' she said.

Philip was amused by her uncharacteristic petulance. 'Well, I shouldn't be at all surprised if you hear more from him now, Rozzy.'

She looked at him hopelessly.

He laughed – he was always irrepressibly charmed by romance – and leant towards her. 'Listen, he's just been offered a pupillage at *Alan Campbell*'s chambers. You know Mr Campbell, don't you? Great friend of your wonderful mama's – probably madly in love with her like everybody else. Anyway, this is between us, but apparently there's no question of their not taking him on. Mr Campbell told my father he's the best candidate they've seen in years. Great future ahead of him and so on. Alistair's going to be a huge success.'

'Oh,' she said, nodding, not understanding how this related to her. 'Good for him.'

'He'll ask you out to dinner in no time. Bet you.'

It was just as Philip had said. At first it was merely to friends' parties, though: he asked if he might escort her, if they might *arrive* together. She was delighted.

Having the opportunity to watch Alistair with friends less close to him than Philip, she began to notice how insecure he was. She saw he was pretending to have had all the experiences they talked about so casually – shooting, fishing, skiing. It wasn't pretending exactly: he just let it be assumed that he knew exactly what they were talking about by remaining completely still and saying nothing. She could feel the brute force of his self-composure as she stood beside him. She could not imagine why he thought it was necessary, when his friends were plainly so much in awe of his intelligence – just as she was. But nothing could throw Alistair off his brilliant argument like being asked how good his tennis game was or a suggestion they all try some swanky new restaurant together the next week.

When her mother first brought up the subject of Alistair, Rosalind felt the issue at first-hand. 'Suzannah tells us you've got a young man,' her mother said, her eyes not lifting from the newspaper.

Rosalind buttered her toast, pressing out this betrayal of confidence under her knife. 'No, I haven't.'

'Oh?' The paper lowered. This simple exclamation of her mother's could mean a thousand different things. It was always an invitation to do better. 'What I mean is, he's just someone I know. That's all. A friend.'

'I see. We've met him, haven't we?'

Suzannah really was very indiscreet. Rosalind swallowed her toast and said, 'Yes, at Philip's twenty-first birthday party.'

'That friend of Philip's? From Oxford?' her mother said, plainly in full possession of the facts.

'Yes,' Rosalind said.

'With the dark hair and the rather gaunt look? Terribly earnest?'

'Yes, I suppose so.'

Rosalind thought Alistair was chiselled, not gaunt, and 'terribly earnest' did not relate at all to the vicarious thrill of sitting beside him at a party and hearing him talk on any subject in the world. Of course, the biggest joke and pleasure of all was that he would break off his brilliant argument to ask if she needed a refill! It was crazy – that intellectual young man being interested in dull, ordinary her. She had laughed and laughed internally when he told Philip, 'Tolstoy can wait a few minutes,' because he was getting Rosalind another glass of fruit punch.

'Well,' said Rosalind's mother, pausing to sip from her coffee cup and replacing it carefully on the saucer, 'I hear he's not stupid. Alan Campbell appears to think he's worth something, anyway. But, Rozzy, you mustn't go falling in love with him.'

For the first time in her life, Rosalind's curiosity overwhelmed her instinctive desire for privacy. 'Why not?'

'Why not? Because he couldn't possibly look after you, darling. One can tell things about a person's upbringing – the standards they're used to . . . There's a certain *polish*. Don't make me spell it out.'

'But he's going to be a *barrister.*'

The newspaper was already up, seemingly impregnable. 'Is he?' came the weary, sceptical reply.

'Yes. With Mr Campbell. He must have said so. It's a very good profession.'

'I'm aware of that, Rosalind, but he'd be starting from scratch. Most young men you might be interested in have already got something to begin—'

'*Mummy*, I think you've got the wrong idea about him. I think Suzannah must have given you the wrong impression. She truly doesn't know *anything* about him. He's one of Philip's best friends, you know. They're *inseparable.*'

Helena Blunt was unused to hearing Rosalind challenge her, but she respected spiritedness and she smiled behind her paper at this rather touching ploy of using her favourite nephew Philip as a sort of royal seal of approval. She could not imagine what it would be like to be as simple-minded and transparent as her younger daughter.

Rosalind had never attempted to conceal or deceive before. But when Alistair told her about his mother – a story that, after all these years, had proved to be a lie! – she had known her parents would look down on someone who did sewing for other people and lived in a tiny cottage in a village somewhere in Sussex, the name of which she could never remember, though she knew she must have been told.

The fact that Mrs Langford was a widow, that she might have been a serious writer but used all her time and talent on doing underpaid translation work would have left her father cold. Her mother might have liked the idea of it, though: she would have respected Mrs Langford's courage and cleverness. But ultimately, Rosalind knew, her parents wanted a Hugo Ellerson for both of their daughters.

There was no question of depicting Alistair as a Hugo, but she could at least manage the picture he gave of himself in accordance with what she knew about her parents' prejudices. That these prejudices were nothing more than the standard snobbery of the day was something Rosalind learnt with mounting disillusionment. Like most children, she had grown up thinking her family was rare and exceptional, engaged in a unique drama.

It did not give her pleasure to be dishonest. She had always known that certain things Alistair told her didn't ring true, or didn't contain the whole story – of course she had. Not that she had doubted for a moment that his mother had died of lymph cancer, but it had been peculiar that there was not *one* other family member to meet and not *one* friend in existence from before his Oxford days. And he was incapable of talking about his father: there was only the bald fact of his death. It was as if Alistair knew nothing about him.

But Rosalind was in love, and, improbable matchmaker though he was, dry, sarcastic Alan Campbell had spoken so highly of Alistair and his professional potential that her parents were able to contemplate the idea of a marriage. So long as his past went consistently unmentioned, he might redeem his present with his future. Under these unspoken conditions, he began to be invited round for lunch or drinks.

Rosalind saw that Alistair's quick brain had propelled him into a world whose rules she had never even defined as rules before. Just as his mind made her feel authenticated and safe from exposure to the intellectual ridicule she constantly feared, she made sure to offer him what little she had in return. She took great care slowly to lift the right spoon or fork at dinner so that he could imitate her. She said, 'Why don't I take your arm?' or 'Why don't you help me to put on my coat?', or, 'Look at me, barging ahead, so you can't even *open the door for me!*' at all the right moments. She took great trouble with her appearance and saw what good it did him to walk into a party with her on his arm.

But she also began the long habit of pretending to Alistair that she did not notice the gaps in his account of himself. Of course, it had always preoccupied her that he did not have any photographs of his 'beloved' mother or, in turn, that his mother did not appear to have left him any of her possessions. Rosalind was acutely aware that, after those first heartbreaking descriptions of his mother's work, Alistair never told a single anecdote from childhood. It was as if he had no past and she conspired with him to maintain this illusion, in public and in private, because she understood the agony of a sense of inadequacy, even if she did not understand its source in him. This subtle transformation of sympathy into deception was Rosalind's first act of love.

Now she looked down at the frightened face in the newspaper cutting. The weak, frightened, *stupid* face. Alistair had never failed her before, and she had never failed him. This was what love was: it was not failing each other. This was what they had silently agreed. And between them, with each other's help, they had never said or done anything wrong in front of anyone – even each other.

But now in her hands was a flash-lit portrait of failure: this photograph, taken by an unthinking stranger. How much better it would have been not to know about Alistair and Karen Jennings! And if only Ivy Gilbert had not had an attack of sentimentality about a son who had not contacted his mother for almost forty years, a son who had been heartless enough to tell everyone his mother was already dead! She would rather have lived in ignorance of these facts.

Yes, she answered the Sophie in her mind, *more* dishonesty. So what? Wasn't it better than this? After all, for a great many years dishonesty had looked like health and happiness, like life. And honesty? Honesty looked like her husband's shamefaced picture in the paper, like her daughter's starved body, like death.

Her lip curled. The fear on Alistair's face was grotesque: it was revoltingly intimate, like the smells you would never dream of mentioning, the sounds you pretended not to have heard. She began to cry. She felt contaminated. She pushed the cuttings safely back under the mattress because she could not stand the sight of her husband's fear any more.

Chapter 15

Alistair put down the receiver in the hall. 'Well, it's all done now,' he told Rosalind. 'I've arranged for the industrial cleaners to go in tomorrow afternoon. I left a box of things there that might interest Ivy and Geoff. I'll just send them the keys,' he said. 'It's just so much simpler that way.'

The rapid aversion of his face after he had said this made it obvious to her that he did not want to explain himself. He had said he might see Ivy Gilbert in person, and Rosalind thought he should, out of respect for someone who had cared enough to call and announce his mother's death. But he had decided against it. Rosalind sighed inaudibly and pushed the hair off her forehead.

Alistair picked up the envelope containing Mr Wilson's 'breakdown', which she had put beside him while he talked on the phone. 'Very efficient, these estate agents,' he said, holding up the letter. He was in the habit of holding things up as proof these days – cups, books, his glasses, whatever he had referred to abstractly in speech.

'Good. I'm glad,' Rosalind said. She was carrying a laundry-bag stuffed with clothes. She had it propped on her hip the way she had carried Luke and Sophie when they were little. She began to climb the stairs.

'Goodness, look at all that. Has that son of ours got you doing all his washing? Can't the cleaner do it?' Alistair said.

She turned and furrowed her brow. 'I've done our washing for years, Alistair. It's a total waste of money having Lani stay an extra hour just for two people's washing. She irons your shirts, of course. That's the hard part. I just bung it in the machine and flick the switch.'

'Oh, I see.'

Hadn't he heard her reduce the quality of her actions to mere mechanics on some other occasion only recently? This troubled him for a moment. But, as ever, he was profoundly struck by how unspoilt she was. He had made a lot of money, but somehow she had never treated it as hers, never indulged herself. She made her clothes last; she still wore the watch she had been given for her twenty-first birthday. He wished he could give her a present – but of course it would look like guilt rather than a genuine desire to see her smile about something – which, in fact, it was. He would have liked to buy her the silk jacket she had admired one afternoon a couple of months ago as they walked back from a restaurant. They had eaten lunch together – just the two of them, which was rare – and as they caught each other's eye over the menu, a silent acknowledgement had passed between them. It was a whisper, a nascent anticipation of peace to come. Stretched out ahead of them was a series of quiet lunches, discreetly luminous as a string of pearls. What could be so bad about getting old if it was going to be like that?

Retirement could seem to Alistair to be a kind of annihilation. He was liable to bouts of panic, to feeling a landslide of his identity. 'My occupation gone!' he would say to himself, only half believing that he was being melodramatic. But that afternoon Rosalind's calm gaze had penetrated the depths of his fears. Perhaps it really was for the first time that he imagined they would read the papers after breakfast, that she would prune the roses, that he would collect the Venetian glass he had always admired in pictures. One of them would say, 'Shall we take our books out on to the terrace and just sit and read for a while?'

'Yes, what a lovely idea. Shall I bring some tea? We can look at all our letters after lunch, can't we?'

Perhaps these gentle routines really would soak up the frantic significance of his dashing from court to chambers; perhaps they would blossom it all out in a garden of softer colours.

'Oh, lucky you!' Rosalind said, pointing at the menu. 'They've got Tarte Tatin, darling – your passion.'

'Aha!' he answered, thinking he really was very lucky indeed.

Yes, he thought. Her ordered mind, in which everything was clean and folded and sprinkled with lavender water, would steer him quietly towards . . . sleep. There would be no annihilation. *This* was love, not the eroticized battle of intellects which he had dreamed of in secret, which had excited him dangerously when he was up against a woman in court. Love was bringing out a jumper, an extra cushion, sweetly remembering a favourite dish. He felt wise and happy that afternoon.

The jacket was still there – he had driven past the shop with Luke. She would have looked beautiful in it: the dark pink would have brought out the elegant pallor of her complexion. Why had he not rushed in and bought it for her straight away, when she stood there smiling at it after lunch? Why hadn't he ever done that kind of thing impulsively, he wondered.

It occurred to Alistair that this last sequence of thoughts was probably typical of the adulterous husband: choosing from a range of palatable remorse options, he had decided to feel he had not bought his wife enough presents.

Rosalind had noticed he was doing the odd sentimental expression he had developed recently and she averted her eyes, faintly disgusted.

'Have you heard from Sophie?' he asked quickly.

She jogged the laundry-bag as though it had wriggled away from her. 'Um . . . yes. I was going to tell you about it,' she said.

'Oh? What's happened?'

She saw how white his face had gone and she knew he imagined Sophie had hurt herself. 'No, it's nothing like that,' she said. 'Don't worry.'

'Thank God. What, then?'

'She's just gone away, that's all.'

'Gone away?'

Rosalind came back down the stairs so that she was level with him. She put down the laundry-bag. 'Yes. She's got herself a teaching job.'

'A *teaching job*? What?'

'Yes, teaching English.'

'But she's a journalist. She's got a job at the *Telegraph*, for goodness' . . .' He spoke abruptly, without thinking, jogged by his paternal pride, which was as sure in him as the patellar reflex. As soon as a stranger exerted the slightest pressure at the relevant point, it had him boasting about his clever daughter: 'Yes, I have. One of each,' he would explain, 'thirty and twenty-eight. My daughter – she's the eldest – she works for um . . . for the *Telegraph*?' (This odd questioning emphasis had first been added to this setpiece to imply modesty, a sense of proportion that recognized there were people in the world who had never heard of the *Telegraph*. But the formula was repeated out of pride, as he soon discovered there was no other reaction available to the listener, who was invariably English, than a stressed 'Yes, of *course* – the *Telegraph*', which might refer to his odd tone – or might be an expression of awe.)

'Yes, Sophie's done tremendously well,' he would say. 'Of course, she's the real academic of the family.' He was so starry-eyed when he spoke about her.

'Well,' Rosalind said, 'I'm afraid she's given up her job.'

'But her flat. Her *job*. Her *flat*,' he said senselessly. 'She just bought that sweet place in Chiswick. What do you mean she's gone away? Where?'

'Ghana. She's gone to Ghana to teach English.' Rosalind found she was enjoying telling Alistair this. She took in the shock on his face. Was this the power Sophie had enjoyed as a teenager? She could see its appeal. She shrugged casually saying, 'Yes. She wrote and told me,' knowing this hidden intimacy between herself and her daughter would hurt him.

'She wrote you a letter?'

'Yes. I only read it yesterday. It had been sitting there for a while – I'm not sure how long, but she said she'd send an address when she was settled.'

'I don't understand,' Alistair said.

'Well, there isn't much to understand, is there?'

'But I thought she liked her job. She did so well to get it. She's worked so hard. And the flat – that was a big landmark.'

'She wasn't *happy*, Alistair. You know that.'

His shoulders sank. His eyelids lowered a little. 'I do know that. Of course I do,' he said quietly. Then he rubbed a hand over his face. 'Oh, God, is this all my fault?'

Suddenly Rosalind felt very angry. She stood up and lifted the washing on to her hip so violently that a balled-up pair of socks bounced out of the top of the bag and rolled away. 'Alistair, you're not the reason we all breathe, you know. People have all got their own lives independently of *you*,' she said.

He watched her, amazed, as she climbed the stairs. Then he bent down and picked up the socks where they had stopped by the umbrella stand.

Luke took a bag of shopping down the side passage to the bottom of the garden. In his numbed state he had wandered about the local delicatessen picking up curious food for Goran and Mila: overripe bananas and hot roast chicken, rye bread and a packet of butter, some potent-looking Italian cheese and four little chocolate truffles wrapped in foil and cellophane. He had no idea what the Serbian palate preferred. He had picked up baked beans and thought himself incredibly unimaginative. It had occurred to him that some religions didn't let people eat certain things – he knew Jews weren't allowed to eat bacon and some Indian people weren't allowed to eat beef (or was it the other way round?) but he was pretty sure no one cared about chickens. He had assumed Goran and Mila would be deeply religious in one way or another, as people who got into wars usually were.

He went down the side passage and knocked on the annexe door. There was a scuffling sound followed by dead silence.

'It's Luke again,' he said softly. There was more scuffling, uninhibited this time.

'Please come in,' Goran called.

He pushed open the door. 'I'm so sorry if I scared you. We must work out a signal, mustn't we? What about three knocks, then two short ones?' He tried this out on the picnic table.

'OK,' Goran said, and smiled, wondering if Luke thought he was in a spy novel. He didn't care if it was a game to this English boy, though – they needed him. And he was kind and it looked like he had brought them some more food. Goran stretched. He couldn't help staring at the plastic bag.

'Um – I got you this,' Luke said. 'It's nothing special but it should fill you up again.'

'Thank you,' Goran said, reaching out for it, 'you are very kind to us.'

They all sat down and Luke smoked a cigarette and watched while the other two ate. 'Were you all right on the sofa?' He picked up one of the cushions he had brought them. They were from the old playroom and they had Disney characters on them. 'Donald Duck didn't keep you awake quacking all night?'

'We sleep beautiful,' Mila said.

Luke was touched by the gesture of intimacy constituted by this complex sentence. He smiled warmly at her. 'Good. You were very tired, weren't you?'

'Yes,' she said, looking down as if she was ashamed of something – of his overt reference to her physical self, perhaps. He told himself to remember there might be religious aspects to this, too, particularly with the women.

'So, we must go to find work today,' Goran said. 'I will try to get work as driver.' He handed Luke a tatty business card, which read, 'Kwik-Kabs, W6.'

'My friend told me this place,' he explained.

'Your friend? I thought you didn't have any friends in London.'

'Not now. They send him back to Belgrade.'

'Oh, I see. Did he come over like you? God, getting sent back after all that effort.'

'No, he came ten years ago. He claim asylum. But he was involve in drugs.' Goran raised one eyebrow in a way that implied a weary suspension of moral judgement. 'It is expensive to live here,' he said.

The charmed numbers of Luke's salary danced through his mind. 'Well,' he said, 'W6 is Shepherd's Bush, I think. It's not far. This is a mini-cab firm.'

'Yes, mini-cabs,' Goran said, nodding, pocketing the valuable card again. 'I study all London roads for five months. Ask me a road. I know Ealing to Embankment to Camden Town to Victoria.'

'That's amazing. Don't you need a British driving licence, though?'

Goran shrugged and opened the packet of butter.

Luke shook his head at his own naïvety. 'No, probably not. Of course.'

'And we find Mila a job too. We know some shops and also we go to a cleaning agency we hear about.'

It occurred to Luke that his own cleaner was from an agency. He could never remember her name – and it was too late to ask now without seeming rude. Katya, was it? Where was Katya from? He had forgotten to tell her there was no need to come in while he was staying with his parents, and he imagined her unquestioningly laundering the untouched bedclothes and polishing the spotless tables as she had done once when he went on holiday. She obviously thought he was rich and crazy. Perhaps she was right.

Goran winked at him and whispered, 'And Mila also will not need a British driving licence.'

The two men laughed and Mila joined in uneasily. Luke wondered if it was only not knowing the language that made her so quiet, or if she thought women were meant to let men do the talking. He wondered if that was how it was where they were from and he was surprised by how angry this made him. He addressed her directly, raising his voice a little to compensate for the language gap and also to rouse her from this submissiveness, at least in front of him. 'Well, you'll be on your feet in no time, won't you? You'll have some money soon,' he said.

Goran answered, through a mouthful of food: 'Yes. We are better this way than many who must still work for paying their journey. We had enough to pay ours. At least we take our own money for working and we begin life now. We make some money and the first thing we must buy is EU passport and National Insurance number.'

'*Buy* them?'

'Yes. Of course. We must buy one passport and one National Insurance number.'

'Don't you both want them?'

'We buy a second later. First we buy one and also we pay two telephone bills, with the passport name and UK address on them. Then we can open English bank account for bank loan.'

'Can you do that? It's amazing you can do that.'

'Yes, we are lucky. For some – these ones who must work illegal for years before they finish to pay for their journey – the Immigration will catch them and send them back. But this will not happen for us. We will be too quick. And, also, who are we? Where we are from? Nobody knows.'

'It's quite a plan,' Luke said. 'A good plan, I mean.'

'Yes, of course. I think about only this plan for eight months, all the time while the UN they "escort" the last Serb families out from my city, Priština. You know it is only Albanians now in Priština? All Serb families must decide. Do we go to a new city – maybe to Belgrade as my uncles did? Do we go further into the north, to Vojvodina? Maybe we go west, to Montenegro. Or do we say goodbye to all of Serbia?'

'And you decided to say goodbye,' Luke said.

'You must understand, Luke, Priština is our city where we grow up and we go to school and university. All my life Albanian people are not allowed in our schools, in our university and all of this. Now we are not allowed. Now all the street names they must be changed. They put it up in Albanian language, not Serbian. For a while some streets have no name. You can imagine this?' Goran laughed and put on the voice of a dimwitted innocent: '"Hello, where do you live?" "Oh, I am sorry, I live nowhere." It is crazy, Luke. So, like I tell you, we sell everything, we leave everything. We throw away our passports. It is a good plan, yes, because it is all what we have now.'

Luke was desperate not to reveal his ignorance of what they had suffered but too grimly fascinated to keep quiet. 'I know it was terrible

255

with the fighting and everything, but won't you and Mila be home-sick? It's where you come from, after all.'

'Homesick?'

'Oh – it means when you wish you were at home, not far away like you are. It's when you think about being in your own bed and having your favourite food and all that. It's called being "homesick".'

'Yes, I understand. Maybe it is different, Luke. I think maybe I am sick from Kosovo. You know? I am sick from a broken city – from all these broken houses, these broken churches, broken shops, broken schools. I am sick from these UN soldiers who must walk around with Serbs now because Albanians they want to kill us *always*, *every day*, in our streets where we grow up.

'Now I am sick from Albanians *and* from Serbs, too, because after all what we have seen, all this killing, nothing it is really change, Luke. It is still hate – always same hate and same old, old hate stories. And still these stupid country people fathers – Albanian and Serb, too – still now they teach their sons these stories and this hate and they have a *machine-gun* on the wall. Can you believe this, Luke? The family eat the dinner and, look – here is a *machine-gun*! This is Kosovo.

'I am sick from my own country, Luke, and I am sick from my own father – *educated man* – who teaches me from a little boy also to hate in the old way and also he is so crazy he wishes there still was Communist in power.'

Goran laughed bitterly and then, as he contemplated Luke's pained face, the bitterness faded. He tapped his fingers against his own head. 'Where is your question, Luke? I talk so much it is lost. My answer: *no*, I am not *homesick*. I think maybe in England I am going to be healthy. And . . .' he tore off a large chunk of bread and a piece of chicken '. . . I cannot think sad for my own bed because I sell it.'

Goran ate ravenously, while Mila consumed a banana in tiny bites, watching Luke over the peel.

Luke was overwhelmed by Goran's speech. The scenes were familiar to him only as excerpts from action films and it was with little jerks of consciousness, like waking up with a thud from a dream, that he remembered this had been their real life. Goran was full of so much anger and hope that Luke wanted to turn away from him for rest. But Mila was not much of a relief, with her silence and her odd staring. He smiled at her again – out of nervousness. 'Is it OK, Mila? I'm sorry if you don't like it. Do have some chicken. Or – or just bananas, of course, if you prefer.'

'Yes, I like. Thank you,' she said, eating faster.

'I didn't know what you might want, really,' he said.

'I like . . .' she said, holding up the banana itself in place of the word, and smiling helplessly, her cheeks flushing with embarrassment.

Goran leant towards her. 'So, Mila, you don't *speak* him about it — you *eat* it.'

She scowled at him while he tutted and rummaged in the bag for more food. He took out the cheese, broke off a chunk and ate it like a piece of cake. Then he looked at Luke. 'So, where is this bad girl-friend?' he said.

'Arianne, you mean?'

'This is not an English name.'

'No, it's a French name.'

Goran nodded. 'French girl. Where is she? She is with another man already?'

How had Goran guessed? He was mortified that it was so easy to work out the story. 'Yes,' he said, 'with another man.'

Goran put out his hand and shook Luke's knee back and forth. 'Then she is not a good woman for you. A *bad girlfriend*. Why do you spend your time? If any woman did this to me I would say *goodbye*. If Mila ever did this to me . . .' He jerked his head towards her and she smiled innocently at one then the other of them, not having understood their conversation. Goran put his hand over hers, and Luke found that the mixture of affection and secret threat made him shudder.

'Really?' he said desperately. 'I mean, don't you think you could forgive? If someone's sorry — *really sorry* — and they want to try again . . .'

Goran shook his head. 'No,' he said. He raised Mila's hand to his lips and kissed the delicate fingers. 'What is "really sorry"? It means nothing.' Then he pointed Mila's hand at Luke, squinting along the fingers as if it were a gun. 'I kill you,' he said, 'and now I am "*really sorry*"?'

Luke was appalled. It was like being told that he was a fool and he must stop hoping. Surely there was a chance Arianne might realize how stupid she had been. She would suddenly realize and she would tell Jamie Turnbull that she had made a mistake, that she still loved Luke.

For 20,024 hits there would be 20,024 kisses. And then she could come back to him. And it would all feel natural and right.

Goran was still shaking his head and eating the cheese. Surely being sorry *counted*, Luke wanted to insist. If you were sorry and someone said, 'OK, I forgive you,' then it was as if it never happened, wasn't it? You only had to decide between you.

And forgiveness was a virtue. He had learnt this at Sunday school. After confession, Father Matthew used to say, 'Go in peace.' All Luke wanted was to say, 'Come back in peace,' to Arianne. He saw her coming through the door, he felt their hands clasped loosely in the excruciating tenderness of reunion . . .

But beneath this vision lay the knowledge that what had turned him on beyond everything else was Arianne's selfishness, that joyous lack of conscience, which had exposed him and his ordinary life to the baroque. If she had ever been sorry, even once, she would not have been herself. And he would never have known the alchemical pleasure of having his abject shame fucked into golden insignificance.

He watched Goran drink almost the whole litre bottle of water, his head tipped back, the Adam's apple rising and falling mechanically in the broad neck.

Chapter 16

Kwik-Kabs was down an alleyway, just near Shepherd's Bush Green. Two restaurants, one a Chinese takeaway and one that promised a hundred different fillings for your baked potato, backed on to it and kept the narrow path full of steaming rubbish bags and greasy packaging. Even though no more than two or three customers had ever ventured down there to book a cab in person, Bogdan Malici, the owner, had fitted flashing yellow lights above the Kwik-Kabs sign. These lights had reminded him of New York, where he had never actually been, but he had elaborate fantasies about the place, and any time there was a programme about it on TV, Bogdan would watch. Beneath the sign was a small hatch in the wall through which his sister-in-law, Zigana, was now accepting a light from one of the drivers. Above her imperturbable face, the lights flashed and rotated against the dirty brick walls. When it rained, they reflected in the puddles. To the left of Zigana's hatch was a doorway covered with a constantly rattling bead curtain.

Goran had told Mila to wait on Shepherd's Bush Green while he visited Kwik-Kabs. He left her on a bench, looking at an old newspaper she had found beside her. Two laughing little black boys were playing football and a drunk with feet bound in plastic bags sat on the grass a little way off, but Goran felt sure he would not trouble Mila. The sight of the children was reassuring.

He found the alleyway, just as Sergey had said he would, and walked down it. He smiled and raised his hand assertively at Zigana as soon as he saw her face. He spoke to her in Serbian, because Sergey had told him the boss of the firm was from Montenegro, and liked to help out other Slavs if he could. It felt almost illicit to speak Serbian to someone other than Mila. Goran said, 'Hi, I've come about a driving job. My friend Sergey Gazi told me about this place. D'you have any vacancies?'

Zigana frowned and replied in English: 'I don't speak Serbian,' she said. 'I am Hungarian, OK? You are here to see Bogdan.'

She pulled back inside the hatch and Goran heard her flip-flops carrying her down the hallway. He smiled at the driver who had lit her cigarette and wondered if he was Kurdish. He was small and very thin with a splash of white in his thick, dark hair. They smiled at each other but did not attempt to speak. They stood on the common ground of the alleyway, but it was as if what was most real in both of them still existed in different countries, far away from each other.

With an incredible rattling, the bead curtain opened and Zigana, whose slim face had not prepared Goran for the width of her hips or her thighs, which were soft and dimpled in their red leggings, signalled to him to follow her.

The hallway was dark and the floor tiles were oddly sticky and there was a strong cooking smell in the air, which he recognized. It was the smell of *rasol*: a dish of beans and dried meat cooked slowly, in the southern Serbian style. The mixture produced its own rich, flavoursome gravy, which, as his mother used to say, improved with being kept – just like a woman. His mouth watered at the thought of a plate of *rasol* and a chunk of good bread.

Another bead curtain off to the right led into a small kitchen, full of cigarette smoke and steam from the cooking. There was a TV on the sideboard, showing a tennis match, and the density of the silence for play added to the atmosphere of standstill as much as the heat and the single fly buzzing in the steam. A man in his early forties sat at the table with a dirty plate in front of him. He was drinking a Turkish coffee and smoking a leisurely after-lunch cigarette. The smoke curled up and drifted out of the filthy little window, which was open above the sink. He looked up as the bead curtain rattled aside.

'This man comes about a driving job,' Zigana said, standing in the doorway behind Goran as there was only enough room for one person to stand in the kitchen.

'You are Bogdan?' Goran said.

The man nodded and Goran spoke to him in Serbian. 'I'm so sorry to disturb your lunch,' he said. 'I'm looking for work and I was wondering if you needed any more drivers. My friend Sergey Gazi suggested I come here. He said he worked for you a bit a couple of years back.'

Bogdan surveyed Goran and said, 'Drivers come in and out. Where are you from?'

'From Priština.'

Bogdan gave a low whistle. 'My God. Welcome to the UK.'

'Thanks.'

He stubbed out his cigarette and put out his hand to Goran. They introduced themselves.

'So, Goran, you're a good driver, are you?'

'I've been driving since I was sixteen. I know all the English road laws and regulations and I've studied a map of London. I concentrated on learning the routes from here in Shepherd's Bush to the main areas in my guidebook – like where the theatres and cinemas and restaurants are, or where the City businesses are.'

'Very efficient,' Bogdan said. 'Guidebooks, maps, regulations. What did you do in Priština?'

'I was studying to be a lawyer, but when the trouble started . . . You know how it was. I stopped all that years ago. Anyway, for now, Bogdan, I want nothing more in the world than to be a mini-cab driver.'

Bogdan laughed. 'You can take me for a drive and we'll see if you're safe to let out on the road. If you crash, the police will trace the car back to me so I need to be sure you're OK. Getting a customer lost is one thing, but crashing without a driving licence is quite another.'

'I won't crash,' Goran said.

Bogdan stood up and grinned. 'Ah, it's good to speak Serbian after a wonderful lunch like that. At least that fat Hungarian bitch can cook.'

'She answers the phones, does she?'

'Yeah. She's my brother's wife, unfortunately. God knows why he chose her. Still, he fucks anything he wants behind her back.'

Goran laughed along with him, though he found Bogdan repulsive.

They went out of the back entrance and down the street to a battered maroon Ford Mondeo. Bogdan asked him to drive to Mayfair, and then to Baker Street and back. Goran did this effortlessly, not even thrown by some roadworks in Notting Hill. Bogdan could not help being impressed. Nearly all of his drivers had to have an A–Z and ask the customers for directions – not that they understood them: most of them could barely speak English.

Afterwards, when Bogdan and Goran walked back down the alleyway, Zigana peeped furtively out of her hatch, reluctant to admit to her curiosity. Her phones were going constantly now and she had a receiver hanging on either shoulder as she sucked up a milkshake through a red and white straw. The vast polystyrene cup had a picture of a smiling baked potato on it.

Bogdan ignored her and took Goran back to the kitchen. 'OK,' he said, 'It's three pounds an hour. You'll work an eleven-hour shift – seven to six. And you can start tonight.'

'A night shift?'

'Yeah, I don't need anyone in the day just now. I've got fucking Kurds coming out of my ears.'

'Three pounds an hour?'

'You got it.'

Goran had been told to expect this and it was with no hope at all, just a kind of loyalty to his instincts, that he said, 'But I thought four pounds fifty an hour was the minimum wage here.'

'Will you be paying tax, then, Goran?' Bogdan laughed.

'Maybe you know how to help me to get—'

Bogdan flapped his hand. 'Look, my brother can get you everything you need. Just start the job now and make me a bit of money and we'll get you the passport and so on later. A step at a time. I'm a businessman, Goran. I can't give you your ticket out of here as soon as you arrive.'

They shook hands.

Sergey had told him that Bogdan could get hold of excellent quality Italian and Spanish passports, and although Goran intended to ask around elsewhere, this personal recommendation meant a great deal. He didn't imagine he would find one more quickly through someone else – and even if he did, how could he be sure of the quality? Most important of all, he and Mila had only fifty pounds and they would need to rent a bed somewhere after tonight so they would have to resign themselves to being secret, illegal workers for a while, until they could purchase their new nationality and with it a few rights.

Goran felt hopeful. Bogdan seemed like as good a boss as any to work for: at least he was honest about his dishonesty, which was about as much as he ever hoped for in a person – except Mila. He went back through the bead curtain and out into the alleyway. He stopped by the hatch, and smiled at Zigana, addressing her in English. 'Hello another time. You are Zigana? I am Goran,' he said. 'I am new driver.'

Zigana grunted, unimpressed by this skinny, tired-looking man, who was much like all the other skinny, tired-looking men. Her friend Yasmine always said how great it must feel to be the only woman at Kwik-Kabs and to order men around all day, like Zigana did. But Yasmine had *healthy* men in mind, not these desperate, puny leftovers who often doubled up their eleven-hour shifts and had virtually to be carried out of the cars.

The phones were all going as she watched Goran walk round the bin-bags and out into the light at the end of the alleyway.

They had arranged to call Luke when they needed to get back in. Luke searched for his phone, found it lodged in a trainer under his bed and charged it. He had not listened to his voicemail for a week. There were twelve new messages.

The first few were from 'Jules at Videonation' about an overdue DVD called *Task Force*, which Luke couldn't even remember hiring. Then there was one from a girl who had handed him her number on a napkin a while ago, and who had now, somehow, managed to get hold of his. The desire in her voice was repulsive; he felt violated by it. Then there were some from old rugby friends asking him out for brunch at a gastropub in Pimlico, then telling him how to get there, then wondering where he was. There was a series of messages from Ludo. The first said he needed to get the hell out of London, the second that he had wangled an invite to 'a hot party' in Nice and that Luke should definitely come with him for the weekend. After a few hang-ups there was one from Nice, laughter and music and clinking glasses in the background: 'You are missing the *hottest* party,' Ludo said. Luke wondered what he was doing on the phone if it was such a great party. Before Ludo hung up, there was a sudden explosion of oohs, as if someone had brought out a cake.

Jessica had also called a few times. 'Me again', 'Just me again', she said each time. The last one said, 'Hey, me again, re*lent*lessly checking up on you. You see, Luke, I'm trying to exhaust you into a state of submission so you'll do what I *tell* you. Oh, for goodness' sake, have a *shave*. Go back to *work*, babe.' Luke always smiled at the affection and humour in her voice, but the words meant nothing.

Message number ten was a guilty-sounding one from his friend James, who plainly felt he ought to have called when the story about Luke's father came out in the papers. Luke thought how glad he was that his friends had all missed this opportunity and that even Ludo had resigned himself to not knowing what to say.

263

Then, unexpectedly, there was a message from his sister, Sophie. 'Hey, Lulu,' she said, 'just thought I'd say hi and how are you.' She was ringing from an outside telephone. He could hear birds in the background, the sound of a two-stroke engine sputtering, male voices egging it on. 'You should be out here, you know,' Sophie said. 'There are water buffaloes, Lulu. When I woke up this morning I was thinking you could take one of your beautiful photos. Do you take pictures any more? You should. You were really good at it, you know? Anyway, take care of yourself. And . . . thanks for being around for Mum.'

Her voice sounded different to Luke; it sounded gentler. He was amazed she had thanked him for something. He sat still briefly with the various answerphone options playing into his ear: 'To repeat this message, press *one*, to delete it press *two*, to save it, press *three* . . .'

He deleted it out of habit, and then he found himself wishing he hadn't. It had felt like throwing away a letter.

For some reason, a memory had been triggered, of a time when Sophie had come to an open day at his boarding-school and asked to be shown round. He had suspected that she just wanted the other boys to get a look at her in her miniskirt, but he set off on the tour they gave prospective parents just in case she was actually interested in his life.

In fact, if she had wanted to show off, Luke had been glad to note she was out of luck as the inside of the school was deserted. All the boys were out receiving music prizes or doing judo demonstrations or poetry recitals for their proud parents. Enjoying the thought of her disappointed vanity, he continued an efficient tour, until they walked along the main corridor and passed a nasty little scene. Jonas Gully, a boy from Luke's year, was bullying a first-former. The older boy pushed the younger one against the wall and slapped him hard enough to make his nose bleed. Knowing the etiquette, Luke had continued to walk and Sophie followed him, her head twisted round to stare.

'Who's he?' she said, 'that huge boy?'

'What? Oh, that's just Gully. Anyway . . . so, these are the science labs,' Luke said, trying to continue as normal.

Sophie put her hand on his arm and stopped him. 'Can I see your bedrooms?'

'Well . . . sure. OK. They're nothing special, though. Like yours but stinkier, I imagine.'

'I'd *really* like to see,' she said, 'so I can picture where you sleep, Lulu.'

Impressed, he took her up to them. Each room had a boy's name slotted on the door. When she saw the name 'Jonas Gully', she pushed her way in. Before Luke understood what was happening, she had climbed on to the creaking single bed and urinated, holding her skirt clear. She had not even been wearing knickers underneath it, Luke noticed with alarm.

'What the *fuck* are you doing, Soph?' he said.

Sophie wiped herself with some of Jonas's tissues and stepped lightly back on to the floor. Luke grabbed her wrist and closed the door behind them in silence. He took her straight back down to the picnic, abandoned her to his mother and his aunt and went off to get changed for the tennis tournament.

Later that night, when he was on his own, looking at the little gold medal with crossed tennis rackets on it, he felt thrilled by what Sophie had done. Everyone thought Jonas was a horrible, vicious person and there would be endless gossip about this 'anonymous revenge'. Luke couldn't help being elated at the idea of his part in it, even if it was only accidental. Fundamentally, he thought Sophie was crazy but that she did have a sense of justice which was superior to his own. He admired her, even if her protests always seemed brutal or mad or *specifically designed* to get her into trouble. Secretly, he understood why she got so angry with him for 'conforming' all the time.

While he relived this memory he laid the phone in his lap. It was a shame to have deleted Sophie's message and he looked at the phone and found himself thinking he would quite like to have called his sister. Where had she gone? His crazy sister! She had so little common sense . . . and yet part of him felt sure that because he had not learnt to play *four* musical instruments to grade eight, or done five A levels, one a year early, that as usual he was just missing the point.

With a distinct physical ache, he missed the 'us against them' sensation they had occasionally shared as children, when they weren't allowed more chocolate or were made to swim the lilo back depressingly close to the shore. Perhaps Sophie would have known what he should do about Arianne. At any rate, she would have approved of his helping Goran and Mila. Her approval mattered enormously to him – even though it infuriated him that this was the case.

He imagined standing on a mudbank, taking a photograph of a water buffalo. He had not had the faintest idea Sophie knew he took photographs. Suddenly he wondered what he had done with all the ones he took in Peru and why he had never shown them to anyone except Ludo, who had only said they would look cool as album covers, which had not felt like the right sort of compliment at all.

Luke redialled his voicemail to hear the last message. With suitable dramatic emphasis, it was his boss, asking how he was, hoping he was 'absolutely fine now' and 'just querying' when he might come back to work. Luke pressed 'three' right away and felt physically safer when it had been deleted. Behind the smooth voice, the insulated hush of Sebastian's office had signified stifled instincts, thwarted love, to his racing heart.

He tossed the phone on to his bed and scrabbled his fingers wildly through his hair. It would simply not be possible for him to go back to work now. Obviously not. But he must think of a way to delay his return without actually getting sacked. He decided to call James.

He had not seen James since that evening at Noise, when they had both been struck by an extraordinary sight: a tall, sexy girl standing on a table. It was almost impossible to think that his friend had continued existing – calmly eating breakfast and taking showers, reading the paper – while the great drama of Luke's life played out in other rooms. Fortunately, he and James had developed an easy, casual friendship, which had learnt to admit long absences for James's surgeon's exams.

'Oh, OK – you're alive, are you?' James said. 'I'm a bit disappointed you haven't run off with a religious cult actually. I got the highest points for my story. There was half an ounce of weed in it for me, Luke. Couldn't you at least *consider* it?'

Luke saw what was required and attempted a laugh. 'No religious cult,' he said. And then he changed the subject. 'Listen, James, I'm basically calling to ask you a favour. I've got a kind of medical question for you.'

'Oh, yuck,' James said. 'You little *tart*. Go to your bloody GP.'

'No, no. Nothing like that. I just need an excuse for work.'

'Go on.'

'Basically, if you wanted to get off work for a month, what would be the best way of doing it?'

'Mmm. It's a long time, a month. You'd need a proper medical certificate. What d'you want a whole bloody month off for, you skiver?'

'Well, I might not really need a whole month, but I'd just like to think it's there. You know what I mean – I basically don't want work hanging over me.'

James laughed. 'Interesting way of looking at it. Didn't we use to

266

have to drag you off your laptop? You were like the media whiz-kid. I was just waiting for you to get a pair of those National Health glasses and wear them with withering irony and a pair of Prada trainers, like all the whiz-kids do.'

'I know. No, I know,' Luke said, trying to conceal his impatience. 'Funny ha-ha,' he said. Suddenly he was worried James would think he was acting bizarrely and would tell Jessica and Ludo. He dreaded compassionate interference because he was beginning to realize that it saw no hope for him and Arianne. But the voice sounded amused, rather than concerned: 'OK, Mr Langford. What you're saying is, you need to get yourself a medical certificate and you want the good doctor to tell you how.'

'Exactly. But the problem is, there isn't anything wrong with me.'

James snorted. 'Nothing *wrong* with you? In *this* day and age? Don't be ridiculous.'

Luke could hear him typing as he spoke. It sounded as though he was instant-messaging someone. James 'multi-tasked': he said he had learnt to maximize his extra-curricular hours.

'Listen, all you need is an invisible ailment,' James said. 'I'm told back pain's *de rigueur* among skivers, but you'd be unlikely to get a whole month out of it. In your shoes, I'd go with depression.'

'*Depression?*' Luke felt a thud of dismay. Depression was Sophie's problem. Must he sink to *that*?

'Yeah, depression rocks,' James said. 'Doctors are shit scared of people topping themselves if they don't take it seriously. It's your best bet – and your boss will assume it's all to do with the thing about your dad, so that works nicely. Yeah, sorry if that's unbelievably tactless, but you know what I mean. I'm just trying to help.'

'Oh, that's fine. Forget it. It's a good idea.'

'Look, I really am sorry, Luke – about your parents. It must be a tough time for their marriage and stuff . . .'

Luke could not think what to say.

'. . . and I know I should have called you earlier. Shit, I just want you to know I'm here if ever you need a mate to have a drink with or whatever . . .'

James listened to the dead silence.

'OK,' he said. 'I'm getting the impression you'd rather not talk about it.'

'Kind of,' said Luke.

'Okey-dokey. Completely understood.'

Luke heard James hit 'return' and a paranoid thought formed: what if this supposed friend was instant-messaging *Jessica* or *Ludo*, outlining the necessity for compassionate interference in *real time*?

James said, 'So, what's the skiving about, then, Luke?'

'Skiving? Oh, it's nothing, really. It's really nothing. I just want some me-time or whatever. I'm just having a rethink.'

'A "me-time rethink"? Sounds in*cred*ibly fashionable. Will it involve a yoga mat?'

The phone cut out momentarily.

'Whoopsy-daisy,' James said. 'Call waiting. Might be a *girl*. Look, I'll email you some symptoms, OK?'

Luke was relieved to avoid further questioning. 'Thanks, James. Owe you one.'

'I suspect it might be more than *one* by now,' James said.

Luke made an appointment to see one of the local doctors that afternoon. He read James's email several times until he was sure he knew exactly what to complain of. Actually, he was surprised to find that, other than the 'suicidal ideation', he seemed to fit the profile for 'clinical depression'. When he wondered what a 'clinically depressed' person ought to look like as he stared into the bathroom mirror, he decided that his unwashed hair and dirty T-shirt were probably about right. This was lucky, he thought, because he really didn't have the energy to change.

Dr Crawford had a small whitewashed room with a smell of new carpet and plastic seating. On her desk, in front of the monitor, was a picture of a little boy in a cowboy outfit. Along the walls was a series of government warning posters urging people to wear condoms, give up smoking, get a flu jab, cut down on fat. It was a basement room and the window faced out on dingy steps that led up to the street. In a bright strip at the top of the window, shoes walked past the railings.

The doctor studied him, nodding slowly with her eyebrows drawn together. Luke shifted his weight in the plastic chair. 'Basically I have thoughts about suicide,' he said.

'I see. OK,' said Dr Crawford.

'That's as well as the insomnia, and the appetite loss. I've lost about a stone and a half,' he said, again wondering if this was actually true. 'And I used to find lots of things fun and now . . . now they just seem totally meaningless,' he said.

The doctor was typing something. 'And how long have you been feeling like this?' she said.

'Oh, quite a long time. Months, really.'

'Months. OK. And do you have any idea what brought it on? Any tragic event or mishap?'

'Oh, yes. Yes, I know exactly. It's *work stress*,' Luke said carefully, as if he was spelling out his name for the completion of a form.

'I see.'

'Basically I've been under all this pressure and my boss bullies me. I just can't cope with it any more. I need a rest or I'll – you know – I'll *crack*.'

The doctor gave him a prescription for something called Zylamaprone™, which she said would 'lift' his mood and help him to sleep. She also gave him a medical certificate which would secure him a month off work.

When, out of curiosity, he looked it up on the Internet later, Luke found hundreds of Zylamaprone™ sites. There were a lot of postings from people in bits of America he had never heard of. 'Kayla' from 'Paoli, Pennsylvania', said: 'I gained forty pounds!!! Add to this I wanted to kill my husband with a knife'. 'Lolitaboy' from 'Ybor City, Florida', said: 'Pharmo-friends! Zylie just gets BETTER. Crush it up and you can totally smoke it, too . . .'

Luke wondered if he would try this and he put the pills in his desk drawer, inside his old school pencil case.

Then he put on a clean shirt and went out in search of Arianne.

Chapter 17

Once, when he was eight, Luke had 'watched' a boy called Carlos Navarro, who was two years older than him. Carlos was the best at their prep school at tennis and swimming. Luke was the second best. They were both singled out for extra sports tuition, better to represent the school, and often raced or played against each other. Had it not been for the classes, Carlos would not have dreamt of talking to such a junior boy, but during these extra-curricular hours, they fought and dived and laughed together in private. Afterwards, in the echoing changing rooms, they passionately discussed the teachers – who was 'decent' and who was 'a complete bastard' – while they pulled on their uniforms, their eyes red with chlorine, their hair still streaming wet on to their school shirts.

It was still embarrassing and unsettling for Luke to remember the obsession he had developed for this dark-haired, prematurely muscular child. He could still recall the exotic refinement he had perceived in Carlos's habits: eating a plate of dressed green salad at school lunch (the way parents and teachers did); reading comics in Spanish, and punching anyone 'for my family honour' if they said his sister was fat. Carlos was as mysterious and beautiful as his name: a Spanish king's name, which made you think of golden palaces and scuttling footmen. Even now Luke could picture the thrilling contrast of the white school shirt against the strong, caramel-brown neck.

And it had been Carlos who had delivered the first ever knife wound to Luke's heart. One Saturday afternoon, when Rosalind had left Luke waiting outside Peter Jones while she popped in for Sophie's new hockey skirt, he had spotted Carlos out with a few other older boys. They appeared to be heading away from the cinema – perhaps they had seen the new kung-fu film because they were doing karate kicks at one another.

In a rush of surprise and joy, Luke called out, 'Hey! Carlos! Did you see McEnroe win the semi-finals?'

But, after an outraged flash from those fierce brown eyes, he found himself ignored. For a moment, he stood waving idiotically across the road at thin air while the laughing group moved on.

The darkness was warm and loving; it was velvety and jasmine-scented. The lights in restaurants and cafés gave the dark streets a twinkly, roguish look. People were eating late suppers at outdoor tables – salade Niçoise and fruit sorbets. It might have been a scene in a city in France or Spain or Italy. The faces were sunburnt and laughing, cultur- ally altered by the good weather. There were tall glasses of rosé and of iced water; waiters carried small bowls of olives and of oil and balsamic vinegar.

To Luke, just walking out into this soft night with his secret purpose was erotic. Just setting off to visit some of Arianne's favourite places – Noise, Shanghai Sam's, Zaza's, Blue Monkey, even Lanton's, where Dan had wanted to take her, made him happier than he had been for weeks.

He drank and he watched and he waited for her to come in. Why shouldn't it happen? No one could ever have predicted that he should lose the vision of the girl on the table – only to find the woman herself in the back of his best friend's car. By ten, after three apple martinis, he had reached a state of luxurious submission to Fate. He settled at the long white bar in Zaza's and lit a cigarette. There was an empty glass a few places along from him, pink lipstick on the rim. Was it hers? A jolt of lust passed through him. Perhaps she had set it down and left, giggling, swinging her bag behind her, just seconds before he arrived. And at Lanton's, was that a faint trace of her perfume outside the ladies' loo? Women jostled past him, soused in Chanel and Dior, confusing the whispering air. And later still, in the red room at Blue Monkey, perhaps the characteristically half-smoked cigarette butt, still sending up a wisp of smoke from the ashtray, was still slightly damp from her lips. When he got home at five a.m., he could not sleep for cocktails and sexual excitement.

Searching the Internet, trailing the street, interpreting signs was a slow striptease in the mind, and each titillating clue brought him closer

271

to Arianne. It was pornography for the sixth sense and it became his full-time occupation. It was a night shift and he kept the same hours as Goran.

To Luke there seemed to be no reason why Goran and Mila could not live secretly in the annexe for just a little longer. They were invisible and soundless, and his parents had no reason to go down there since, as Jessica had rightly observed, they would hardly be doing the famous Langford garden party this year.

Luke had the key copied and a way of life – parallel to the life of the house – established itself. In the mornings at around six, Luke would go down the side passage (even at this hour he took the precaution in case a sleepless parent should happen to look out at the lawn as he crossed it) and give a beer to Goran, who had just got in from work. The men would have a cigarette together. Mila had found work at a cleaning agency. She woke up around then, finished dressing in the little shower room, and then she would sit and watch them for a while before she went out to clean.

She had become healthier, prettier. Her face had lost its endangered look and sometimes, when she laughed uncontrollably at Goran, whom she apparently found ridiculous in almost every way, Luke could see why he had thought her attractive. It was hard not to laugh when she did – particularly when it irritated Goran so much. He could be terribly proud and serious in a way that Luke thought foreign and rather comical in itself.

He had asked Goran if he and Mila found it difficult to see so little of each other, what with their different working hours, but Goran refused even to address the subject. He waved it off. 'In few weeks we will have enough money for buying one passport and one National Insurance number. Then I will take a bank loan and then we will begin. You know I will be Spanish man?' he said.

'Really?'

'Spanish and Italian passports are cheapest. I think maybe I will be called Juan. Do you like it? *Juan,*' Goran repeated, trying out his new name, excited by its novelty. He sighed. 'Luke, can you believe we will rent a flat in *London*? And you will come and eat with us!'

'That would be great,' Luke said, clinking his beer bottle against Goran's. 'I just hope you won't mind if I bring someone with me.' He smiled secretively. From the bar across the street he had caught sight of Arianne getting into a taxi outside the theatre the night before.

272

She had been talking – or, rather, shouting – into a mobile phone: 'I *know*. He's a possessive *bastard*, Georgie,' he had heard her say before she slammed the door. (He had time to note a tight white T-shirt, a mossy green suede skirt and beige leather ankle boots. Legs: bare and brown and long and long and . . . Also, there was something sparkly on her wrist, which he had tried to put out of his mind.) He had decided then that he was almost ready to go and see her play. Two and a half hours of watching her from the anonymous darkness: would it really be allowed? He could hardly believe he would not be arrested for it. UN troops would escort him out, as they did in his dreams. As it transpired, it was sold out.

Goran shook his head. 'Oh, Luke. You talk about her always. You know what I think of this girl. I do not understand you.'

'I know. Look, it's complicated,' Luke said.

Goran did an impression of Luke: 'It's *terribly complicated*,' he said. 'It's just so *comp*licated with my *comp*licated French girl.'

Luke laughed self-deprecatingly.

'*Goran*,' Mila snapped unexpectedly. 'You do not know *all* what he feels.' She glared at him and then laid her hand on Luke's arm. Her fingers were soft and warm. Luke smiled back at her, mystified by this act of defiance, and by her sudden fluency. She was powerful even though she looked so frail, he thought. It felt good to be taken seriously.

The next day it was decided that Goran and Mila would stay in the annexe until the end of the month. When Luke told them this, Mila began to cry. She stood up and sat down again three times, then rushed over and kissed him, laughing at her tears and saying, 'Thank you. Thank you, Luke. Thank you sin*cerely*.'

He felt both embarrassed and proud. It was lovely to have a girl's arms round him again, though, because his loneliness was a bodily ache.

'Really, Mila, it's OK,' he said, leaning forward so she could kiss his other cheek. 'It's nothing. I'm glad I can help.'

'*Kind man.* You are *kind man*,' she said, rushing away into the little shower room to compose herself, tugging the door shut behind her.

There was silence between the two men for a moment. They listened to Mila's crying subside and then water started running into the basin. Luke said, 'D'you want another cigarette?'

Goran shook his head and turned away. 'No.'

Luke lit one for himself. It did not occur to him that this was

Goran and Mila's only time alone together. He was afraid of going back to the house and to the broadband connection, which brought news of Jamie Turnbull and Arianne at an unmanageable 500 kbps. At least the bad news he risked learning on his nightly crusades had human proportions, human faces. His web searches felt spiritually dangerous, like consulting a ouija board, and they left him haunted for hours afterwards.

Even so, the fear was worth it: how else would he have learnt that Arianne's name meant 'very holy one', or that she had (implausibly) played the trombone in the school orchestra, or that she had won a county-level triathlon at the age of twelve *just as he had*? What a picture that was – even printed out on creased A4 paper! The twelve-year-old Arianne, pink and glossy, crossing the finish line, her hair bouncing up behind her and the grin of victory on her lips.

Luke took a deep drag on his cigarette and gestured at the shower-room door. 'You think she's OK, Goran?'

'Mila? Yes. Of course.'

'She seems very upset.'

'No. She is not. Thank you, Luke. She is just crazy.'

Goran stood up suddenly and began to tidy the sheets on the pink sofa, his back to Luke.

'Oh,' Luke said. 'OK. Well . . . good.'

Goran and Mila worked hard for their money. The more they learnt about the cost of living in England, the more shocked they were by the näivety of their arriving with just fifty pounds to begin their new lives. They thought about the dreams they had worked themselves up on, in Goran's bedroom in Priština, their friend Vasko supplying endless stories: 'This guy in London, man, Andjela's cousin, he has *three* houses now. No joke. Seriously, Goran, the *money's* there, the *music's* there. You two are doing the right thing.'

Now that they were in England, they did not communicate their doubts to each other as this might have sabotaged the will it took to work so hard, or perhaps it would have constituted a betrayal of their former selves. When they left Priština, Vasko had taken his stories with him to a new life in Belgrade.

So, all there was to do was work hard and make money, buy a passport and follow their plan. Goran told himself he must remember how lucky they had been to find Luke. Without him, their earnings would have been wasted on rent – and he had seen the place Rajan the Kurdish driver rented from Bogdan's brother, Vuk. It was a stinking bed in a three-room flat converted into a dormitory. Rajan got the bed at night and another guy rented it by the day. Goran knew he would never have taken Mila to a place like that. Not his little Mila.

Mila's work was lonelier than Goran's. She rarely saw or spoke to anyone throughout the day, except to the occasional delivery person who rang the bell while she cleaned one of her apartments. Often the deliveries were flowers and she would sign an imaginary name for these amazing, rustling confections and put them in the kitchen in some water. Pink roses a foot high – in the city!

They were all childless homes. Some belonged to single men, some to single women and some to young couples. She looked at the photographs as she dusted them, wondering about the lives she saw depicted. There were sailing-boats and ski-slopes and pretty, laughing girls who held up their hands at the camera to protest at being photographed in their bikinis. She thought it odd that none of the couples seemed to be married – unless English people didn't take photographs at weddings – except one, who had pictures of some kind of barefoot ceremony on a beach, the bride wearing a purple sarong and white flowers in her hair.

The girl in the sarong was the most beautiful one. There were photographs of her doing modelling shoots in black frames along the corridor. Above the king-size bed, her foot-wide face smiled down, a felt hat pulled over one eye. Mila had never seen so many bottles and pots of cream and powder and perfume. Along the marble shelf in the bathroom there was a Chanel nail varnish in almost every colour of the rainbow. Often there were smashed glasses in the kitchen, their contents splashed against the wall at the point of impact and, as she cleaned them up, Mila wondered what this girl and her husband argued about.

You could learn a lot about English people from their mess. They drank a lot, that was for sure. They ate takeaway meals and expensive little portions of things out of foil packets and they never used their saucepans – except suddenly on a Friday night when they used every single one and the whole flat would be strewn with napkins and ashtrays and plates and dirty little espresso cups. They had a lot of different medicines in their bathrooms – hundreds of packets of coloured capsules: blue and green and red, bright orange and pale yellow. They were obviously unhealthy people.

Some of the men kept weights in their wardrobes. One woman

had hundreds of chocolate bars in a bag behind her shoes. Mila thought she deserved to look like a fat pig if she ate all that sweet stuff, but in her photograph she was terribly thin.

Often there were joint butts as well as cigarettes in the ashtrays. There were bottles of champagne and packets of coffee in the fridges. Huge piles of every fruit you could imagine went rotten in glass bowls and there was always a shocking quantity of bread and cheese and good fish and meat to throw away because, even through the wrappers, it had started to stink out the fridge.

Sometimes when she saw three packets of the same cheese and knew that she would throw them all out, mouldy, in a fortnight's time, she felt tempted to put one into her bag. But stealing was a sin – in an immediate and a long-term sense. Mila had been brought up, in the tradition of the Serbian Orthodox Church, to believe that if you did something wrong you were punished in the next life, but she had also decided for herself that you were cursed with bad luck in this one.

The second part of this formulation had been added since the UN strikes in Kosovo, since she had watched her family and friends driven out of Priština by the Albanians they had all oppressed for so many years. She felt almost insane as she remembered how differently life had been structured when she was a child, when Albanian children were not allowed to go to her school. It had not occurred to her then that there was anything wrong in this. Albanians were dirty animals who were always breeding – just as her father, as all the fathers, said. She had thought this along with all of her classmates. She had seen the Serb police bullying Albanians on street corners for years. During the ethnic cleansing, she had watched Albanians forced out of their homes, processions of them going off to the trains, turning the road under her window into a writhing snake . . . And now here she was, cleaning a toilet.

Sometimes there were porno films in the DVD players. In one of the bachelors' flats, the one just off Sloane Square with all the beautiful paintings on the walls, Mila found a stack of magazines with pictures of black men wearing leather jockstraps and thongs. It shocked her but it also made her laugh excitedly about this crazy country they were in, which was not at all formal and reserved as she had been led to expect. She thought about the demonstration in Dover and decided that English people were mostly angry and sex mad.

On the tube she often got on at the same stop as a person whose gender she couldn't guess – he or she had long, pink hair and a face covered in rings and bolts and studs. This person had a favourite carriage, just like Mila. Invariably, the other people on the tube just continued reading their newspapers as if someone with pink hair and metal all over them like a robot was perfectly normal. It was hard not to giggle; the one time she did, the person caught her eye and smiled at her. She found herself smiling back.

The houses Mila cleaned were all in Kensington and Chelsea and Mayfair. She could not believe how wealthy English people were and it was with a sense of moral indignation that she threw open the women's wardrobes to put in the ironed shirts and saw beauty – such riches and beauty! – and wondered why everyone in her life had concealed it from her. She picked up bracelets and rings and laughed bitterly at the idea that Goran would ever buy her something like this or this or this or this. It was so depressing! She was only twenty-two and she had no jewellery at all now, because Goran had gone and sold it all to a fat Albanian woman.

Unlike some of the drivers, who smoked heavily and left rubbish in their cars, Goran kept Bogdan's maroon Ford Mondeo in good order. He always asked the customers if they minded him putting the radio on or smoking with the window open. They never cared about any of it: there are few questions of taste that have not been answered definitively by four in the morning.

He was surprised by how many unaccompanied women he was asked to collect. They were mostly in their late twenties or early thirties, smartly dressed, wealthy-looking, with toned, slim bodies. Often they were terribly drunk and Goran had to help them out of the car or stop so that they could be sick. They said 'fuck' and 'shit' all the time – when they couldn't find their change, when he told them the fare, when they forgot to tap their cigarettes out of the window and dropped ash down their fronts. On two occasions, women like this had run after his car in their crazy high heels, waving and shouting, having left a handbag or phone in the back. He was amazed women would behave like that in a quiet street – a street where they lived and their neighbours might see them and talk.

Sometimes he collected couples and he was equally amazed that they thought it was fine almost to have sex in the back of the car. Goran fixed his eyes dead ahead and wondered why the women weren't ashamed, why the men didn't have more respect in front of another man. And yet it was fascinating and exciting, particularly since Mila was often too exhausted from cleaning to make love. Sometimes he couldn't help looking. He saw a fragment of a scene in the rear-view mirror: a tangle of legs, a male hand unbuttoning, unhooking, a more precise female hand helping it out. On one of these occasions, Goran had been deeply embarrassed. A boy of about seventeen had caught him watching and said, 'Hi there,' into the mirror. There was lipstick smeared on his face. Goran's eyes darted back to the road. The boy said, 'That's OK, keep looking, friend. It's the closest you'll ever get to a girl like this.'

The girl giggled, pulling her top down to cover her bra. 'Oh, shut up, Gus, you wanker.'

Gus pulled up her top again. 'Come on, baby, share a little with the poor,' he said.

On one of his shifts, quite unexpectedly, Goran saw Luke. It was peculiar to discover him in his real life. Zigana had just radioed a pickup from outside a bar called Blue Monkey, off Kensington Church Street, at the Notting Hill end. Goran was just round the corner. He said he would do the job and he took the relevant left turn. He drove along the empty street, past the darkened restaurants, their tables all neatly laid for the next day's lunch, their windows flashing his reflection back at him. He looked at it – now higher, now lower, now stretched across two long windowpanes. Who are you? he asked this picture of himself. He was a man in a maroon car, wondering if he had made a mistake. Should they have stayed in their own country?

Then he saw Luke standing – or, rather, supporting himself – against the wall beneath the huge neon monkey sign. Goran was starting to worry about him when a girl rushed up and tapped on the car window, giving him a shock. 'Kwik-Kabs?' she said. 'For *Claire*?'

'Yes,' Goran told her. 'I am Kwik-Kabs.'

'Cool. Just be a sec.'

As she got into the back, first giving repeated kisses to one of her friends ('No, *seriously*, we *will*, we'll do it again *soon*, sweetheart'), Goran asked himself whether he should call out to Luke. But there was something humiliated about the way Luke was standing, not just the indignity of his drunkenness but something deeper. It occurred to Goran then that Luke had developed the comical snarl of a kicked dog, a dog that cowers and growls at the same time, convincing no one.

A group of laughing friends were all kissing one another goodbye on the pavement and a black cab pulled up in front of them. An astonishingly tall, good-looking couple separated themselves from the rest and got into it. As the cab set off, the girl leant out of the window and waved at Luke. It was then that Goran decided he must drive away: these glimpses of private trouble were not meant for his eyes.

'Just off the Old Brompton Road, please,' the girl in the back said.

Goran drove in silence, longing to get back to Mila and to the reassurance of her sleep-warm arms. He checked the clock. She would be off out to clean in three and a half hours.

Cleaning and *driving, cleaning* and *driving*, he thought. The days rolled over into one another. Perhaps Luke would be too drunk to come today and they would have time alone to make love. With horror and concern, he remembered Luke's face as the beautiful girl in the taxi waved.

Goran wished he could go straight back to Mila now. But there were more than two hours of the night still to go.

Almost a month had passed before Luke had any real news of Arianne. And when it came he did not learn it from a friend in one of the bars where she went, or from the hairdresser's he had watched her go into; nor did he learn it from the usher he never dared to approach at the theatre. He didn't learn it from the maître d' he had not yet spoken to at Lanton's, or from the bar girl at Noise, or even from the flirty gay man on reception at her gym. He learnt it at the breakfast table with his parents.

An unquestioned routine had now established itself in the main house. His parents had now resigned themselves to their son's need for 'a bit of time off' and his father was plainly too afraid of self-incrimination to question it. And, in a way that Luke did not recognize, Rosalind was too self-absorbed to do more than worry about his food. Although this parental negligence shocked him, he knew it worked in his favour. He wanted to be left alone. Let them be cowardly and selfish, he thought, only don't make me go back to the flat without her.

In fact, all three wanted nothing more than to be left alone. They risked only the most superficial interaction: 'Has anyone seen my glasses?' or 'I don't suppose anyone's interested in wine, are they?' or 'Anyone mind if I turn on the news?'

Life functioned, life continued, and Luke became used to the way his mother left a room almost as soon as his father walked into it. This was precisely what had just happened when Luke put his hand into the pile of Sunday papers on the breakfast table, not knowing they contained a shard of glass. He picked up one of the magazines. 'You don't want this, do you, Dad?'

'Please, go ahead,' Alistair said, without looking up from his book review.

On the magazine cover, Luke read, 'A-list Eating, Drinking and Partying'. The cover shot was of the lower half of a girl's face, her pink tongue licking cream off the corner of her mouth. Luke flicked the pages, taking in the words and pictures in little flashes: 'Vitamin B12 . . . day-patient procedure . . . kitten heels . . . ancient Jewish faith . . . scallops with pancetta . . . Palme d'Or . . . Venetian blinds . . . Japanese orchids . . . Lapis-Lazuli.' His fingers stopped at these last two words. Lapis-Lazuli was the name of the bar Jamie Turnbull was planning to open with his footballer friend Liam Bradley. Luke had read about it on the Turnbull and Liam Bradley fan sites. Jamie had told *Stars* magazine, 'I was just fed up with the same old queues at the bar with no exclusive feel. This is going to be strictly members only.'

The photograph in the centre of the article was of Liam and Jamie with their arms round each other's necks like Mafia brothers. In the background, Luke recognized the outline of Arianne's shoulder and arm. She was wearing a dress she had not owned when she was with him: it was high-collared and gold. Luke read,

The opening party for the exclusive members-only club will also celebrate the recent success of Turnbull's girlfriend, Arianne, star of the surprise West End hit *Hotel*. Turnbull, known for his romantic gestures, recently hired disgraced TV gardener Owen Macintosh to replace flower-beds at his Kensington home. The beds had been planted to form the letters of Turnbull's previous girlfriend's name, Elaine Dance, in her favourite orange lilies. Owen Macintosh, 52, who is alleged to have used BBC hardware to download 'adult material', told *Flash* magazine, 'Jamie's dad and I go back a long way. Jamie's a great young guy and should not be criticized for it. There is something wrong with this country. I have no comment to make about the vicious lies said against me. This is all about gardening.'

Plans for the party are said to include a troupe of cabaret dancers to go with the 'All that glitters . . .' theme. There are rumours the couple may also use the event to announce their engagement.

Luke knocked his coffee cup on to the floor.

'Luke!' his father cried out in surprise.

'I – I dropped my cup,' Luke said. 'It was an accident.'

Alistair stood up and reached for the kitchen roll on the sideboard. 'Yes, of course it was,' he said, observing his pale-faced son with concern. 'Not to worry.'

Luke held up a dripping fragment. 'It is totally destroyed,' he said, his voice trembling with sadness.

'Oh, well, never mind, Luke. It really wasn't anything special – just an ordinary cup.' Alistair tried to catch his son's eye and smile at him, but Luke was frantically scraping chairs across the floor – as if he had set fire to something and the blaze might catch.

Rosalind came hurrying in. 'What a *noise!* What on *earth*'s going on?' she said.

The sharp anxiety on her face was a reminder to each of them that fear and mistrust lay just beneath the quiet surface on which they moved. They looked at each other, reluctantly acknowledging this. Then Alistair sighed and said calmly, 'Doesn't matter. An *accident*. Just an *ordinary* cup.'

Rosalind shoved the table further to the side and fell to her knees with tears coming down her face. She began to place the fragments into her left hand. Through gritted teeth, she said, 'Actually it wasn't *just an ordinary cup*, Alistair. It was one of the ones *I* made in my pottery class.'

She snatched the front page of his newspaper, wrapped the pieces in it and dropped the package into the bin under the sink. Then she went out into the garden, closing the door hard behind her.

Luke spent the rest of the day on his bed. Just before six, when Goran usually woke and dressed for work, Luke went out of the front door and down the side passage to see him. He glanced back through the foliage of the tree peony at the empty-looking house. Then he did the special knock so Goran would know it was safe to answer.

'Hello Luke,' came the call – as usual.

Luke pushed his way in.

Goran was standing in the doorway of the little shower room. 'I am washing myself. Be there in a tick,' he said. He was proud of his English idioms.

Luke sat down on the sofa where Goran slept and put his head in his hands. He sat like this for a few minutes, unaware of the amount of time that had passed, or that he was being watched from behind. Goran stood with the yellow beach towel wrapped round his neck; his hair was wet and black and shiny as crude oil. He pushed it back with one hand, then rubbed it with the towel, still watching Luke. There was a feeling of deep anger in him and he would have preferred not to have had a visit today, no matter how lonely and desperate Luke was.

'How are you, Luke?' he said.

Luke started. 'Oh, you're there. You made me jump.'

'I am sorry.'

'Actually, I need your help.'

Goran could not help but be struck by the unmasked pain on Luke's face. He dropped the towel and put on his shirt. 'OK, Luke, I owe you many favours.'

'I only want one,' Luke said. 'Goran, I thought you might know where I could get hold of a gun.'

Instinctively, Goran wanted to pull up a chair, clasp the back of Luke's neck and ask him what the hell he was talking about, tell him not to be so stupid. But the anger inside him told him to wait, out of a kind of spiteful curiosity, and see what the stupid idea was. 'What kind of a gun?'

'Pistol,' Luke said simply. 'I don't know the names. One about this big. I'll pay. I've got plenty of money. Do you know who to ask?'

'Yes,' Goran said truthfully. 'I know.'

'Well . . . will you do it?'

Here Goran's resolve broke. 'No,' he said. 'Luke, are you *crazy*?'

'No?' Luke repeated.

'*No*, I will not find your gun.'

Luke stood up. 'Then I'll ask someone else.'

Goran laughed at him. 'Yes? Who else you will ask? Nice rich English boy – you know so many people who can find you a gun, Luke?'

'You said you would help me, Goran, because I helped *you*.'

'Help you to become *killer*? *Criminal*?'

'Why do you care?'

They heard the door open. It was Mila. She was eating an apple and she smiled at both of them.

'Hello, Goran. How are you, Luke?' she said. 'It is a beautiful evening.'

Luke and Goran both stared at her. She was still smiling at Luke. She had tied her hair back in some new way.

'Hi, Mila,' Luke said.

Goran walked over to her and put his arms round her, but she pushed him away. 'Eeuch. You are *wet*!' she cried. 'Like *big wet dog*!' She laughed with her eyes trained on Luke, inviting him to share the joke. Out of politeness, Luke smiled with her.

Goran moved away and controlled his anger as he laced up his shoes. They were old trainers of Luke's. Suddenly he wanted to tear them off his feet. He wanted to walk out into the garden barefoot and wave his arms at the rich people in the big house.

'OK. I go to take a shower,' Mila said. 'I do five flats today. Everybody have *dinner parties*,' she said, wrinkling her nose in disgust.

When they heard the water start, Goran sat down on the arm of the sofa. 'Why do you want this gun, Luke?'

'To kill him,' he said. Then he lowered his eyes, 'Or to scare him. I don't know yet. I just need the gun, Goran.'

Goran wanted to laugh because it seemed like a joke: a gun, here in Holland Park, where the houses were so tall and white; a gun in this beautiful boy's hands. But Luke's face was pale and sweaty, his teeth were gritted – it was a look Goran had seen often before in Priština. 'You talk about this man who is with your French girl?'

'Yes. Jamie Turnbull. You see, I know where they're going to be. He's having a party next week.'

'You really think she loves you, she will come back to you, Luke?'

'Yes.'

Goran was not sure why, but he felt distinctly irritated by this response. '*Why* do you think this?' he said.

'Because – because I *believe* it.' Luke clenched his fists. 'I *really*, *really* believe it. You know?'

'No, I do not know.'

Luke scrutinized him briefly with a sickly smile. 'Well, look, it doesn't matter, Goran, because I *do* know.'

'Yes? What do you know, Luke?'

Luke shrugged. 'I know God won't let this happen to me,' he said – and Goran laughed to see all the egocentric complacency that Western money could buy laid out so prettily before him.

'*God?* Why do you say God, Luke? When I was young child, we had school teacher in Priština. A good teacher. He was maybe fifty years – he was old Communist like my father, always telling us kids

283

about how great is "Mother Russia". I remember one day we talk him about God – we say, "What is he *like*, Teacher, does he *love* us, is he a *nice old man*?" and all this shit.' Goran shook his head and grinned. 'And this teacher said to us, he said, "Children, don't you know that in Russia the scientists have sent *big spaceship* up into the moon?"

'"Yes, Teacher," we say, "we know this."

'"Well," this teacher say, "and don't you know, children, that your uncle Gagarin, he came out of this spaceship, he had a look around . . . and – oh! – children, *there is no God*."

Luke listened to the horribly caricatured voices and began to cry. At that moment, Goran felt pure hatred for him. Mila was flirting with this ridiculous English boy. That was the truth and he might as well acknowledge it.

Could it really be true that like all those grabbing bitches in Priština, like his stupid sister Irena who had married a guy who pimped Albanian prostitutes in Milan *just because he had a BMW*, that even Mila was only interested in money after all? How could he help but notice that she would not even allow him to touch her in Luke's presence? Not that she particularly wanted him to touch her during their few moments alone.

A 'wet dog', he thought. My Mila called me 'a big wet dog'.

'OK, fuck what I tell you,' Goran said. 'I will get you this gun.'

Luke smiled with relief and Goran smiled back, thinking, Yes, get yourself into as much trouble as possible. Go to prison and be locked away from us, away from Mila. If you are so stupid, then you deserve to go to prison. Stupid people are more dangerous than guns, he thought.

Just then, Goran wished they had only stayed two nights in the annexe and then made their own way, even if it had meant sleeping in a stinking bed like Rajan's, rather than accepting charity from this mad rich boy. He hated Luke for his pointless angst, which was the agony of privileged people. He wanted to say, 'Do you know what real pain is?' and to tell him about the Nato bombings, when the noise of death made your teeth hum in their sockets. Or, before that, about the guilt and gut-fear you felt when, out of each bedroom window on Dragodan hill, you could see the Albanian farms burning all the way across the valley like little Christmas candles and, yes, it was silent but you knew that your own countrymen, dressed up in uniforms, were raping in the dark and that the screaming went on and on into the night. He wanted to tell Luke about what it was like to find body parts – a foot, a finger – as you walked down the street. And now, now that it was all supposed to be over, now that the churches and the mosques alike had been bombed, he wanted Luke to know about the thousands of unexploded landmines, all over the countryside, designed by a devil to look like toys.

But he said nothing about any of this, because suddenly all he could think of was Mila's face, doing that shameless grin of hers for this stupid, rich young man.

Luke stared at his own feet and noticed he was wearing odd shoes.

Chapter 18

It had been a lovely dream and Alistair had slept late. He sat up in bed smiling and drank some water. He had dreamt about his mother and Ivy. He could not remember the exact subject matter of the dream, but it had left him with a particular cosy excitement that he could only associate with the rainy afternoons of his early childhood.

At one time there had been no happier circumstances than finding it was too wet to be sent out to play and being given 'a mug of something nice'. He would sit beside Geoff at the kitchen table and Ivy and his mother would lounge against the sideboard or the cooker. Occasionally his mother would wipe a surface or a cupboard door with the dishcloth, as if to justify their place in the room. She had always appeased her household gods in this way, never able to sit without dusting or straightening – or making an offering of some kind.

Life was contained by domestic routine; the adult heart was slowed to acceptance of the way things were. But on those precious rainy days, something wonderful happened. It was as if the gently therapeutic gossip combusted and his mother and Ivy staged impromptu firework displays of all the local characters. They did men and women alike. Their impressions were frantic and absurd but accurate enough to seem deliciously wicked. The hostile tapping of rain on the windows didn't matter a bit.

They all had mugs of cocoa, Alistair remembered: Geoff and his mother and Ivy had 'a little tipple' in theirs and he had marshmallows from Geoff's shop. (This was a treat American children had, Geoff had told him, tipping them into the cup like a wizard.) The marshmallows melted and could be pulled up in long strings and licked off the back of the spoon.

Every time Geoff performed this wizardry, his mother tutted and Geoff would wink at her and every time she would say, oh, all right, just this once – but it was *very* bad manners: small boys, *licking spoons*. This supernatural licence, this *American* privilege only added to the sensation of anarchy. It was so frightening it made you laugh! Geoff would laugh until the tears came down his face: 'I dunno, Al – these two should be on stage,' he used to say, wiping his eyes. His big hand would paw the air for mercy as Ivy put a tea-towel round her head, like a silk scarf, to do the stuck-up vicar's wife. 'Those two could make us all a *fortune* in the West End,' Geoff said.

Alistair was eleven before he realized that this was a fantasy and that the rest of the world had never heard of posh Mrs Nairne or of his mother's star turn, Ben Singer, the mincing, lisping butcher.

Alistair laughed, remembering the risks his mother used to take when she was in one of her 'comical' moods. He had adored and hated her at those times and had giggled and shifted uneasily, strung up between these poles.

But his mother had loved to seduce him into the wicked intimacy of a private joke. He saw now that this had been their most successful and vibrant manner of interaction: laughing together. It was as if his mother had been determined to reassure them that, no matter how remote and different his mind was from hers, they could still share a joke, have a few laughs together.

He remembered an occasion on which they had gone out to buy the meat. For some reason – perhaps she had been left a tip by a guest – she had decided they deserved something special. 'Morning, Mr Singer,' she sang out innocently, tinkling the door shut behind them.

Ben Singer's fat hands lifted a joint of lamb on to his chopping-board. 'Morning,' he said, in his quavering, feminine voice.

'Lovely day out,' his mother observed.

Mr Singer had a habit of repeating the end of other people's sentences, as if he was turning them over in his mind, inspecting them – like lamb chops. 'Lovely day out,' he said, nodding.

Alistair felt his mother squeeze his fingers mischievously. He knew only too well what this meant and his heart began to race with dread and excitement. She leant down and looked through the glass-fronted counter at the various cuts of meat. 'Mmm,' she said casually, 'I came early enough for once, didn't I?'

'Early enough,' he agreed, smiling.

'Spoilt for choice. Would you believe it? Now I can't *decide*, Mr Singer. I think we won't have chicken today . . .' she tailed off.

'*Won't* have chicken today . . .' Mr Singer repeated.

'. . . but the question is, shall I do us a bit of *steak* or a lamb *stew* or good old *sausages* and mash?'

Alistair's heart contracted at the minefield of sibilants.

Mr Singer brought his cleaver down with a bang and turned, 'Ooh, I love a good *mash* . . .' he said unexpectedly. And then he turned back.

Alistair's mother pinched his arm under the counter and rolled her eyes at him. 'Mash?' she said. 'Oh, yes, me too, Mr Singer. But what to put with it, that's the thing. Is it to be—'

And then Mr Singer, smiling placidly, interrupted her: 'Thteak or thtew or thauthageth?' he said. 'I'd do thteak. With a nithe thauthe.'

It was as if a wild band had struck up. Sheer music! His mother gripped his hand. 'Ah,' she said soberly, '*would* you? *Well*, Mr Singer, that's good enough for me,' and Alistair almost fainted with horror at her irreverence. Mr Singer (referred to as 'Thingy' by only the very wickedest boys at school) was a respected adult! Alistair tugged his hand free and knelt down to tie his shoelace. He faked a bout of coughing to cover the helpless laughter. After a Herculean effort to control himself, he stood up.

His mother said, '*Sir*loin or *strip*?'

She was as cruel as a child. And sometimes she was as tender as a lover. When he had done nothing in particular – or nothing at all, having been left alone with his books all day – she would get home and rush up behind him to clasp him in her arms. 'My little *hero*,' she would say. 'You held the fort, didn't you?'

He felt fraudulent for accepting her praise. 'Holding the fort' while she went out on one of her jaunts seemed a strange thing to be asked to do. He couldn't really see what it meant. He just sat with his books and puzzles and the sandwiches she had made for him and, occasionally, touched by the solemnity with which she had placed him in sole responsibility for the empty house, he would patrol it with his toy gun.

'You were gone ages. Did you have a lovely time, Mum? Who were you with?'

'I was with your uncle Ian, love. You remember your uncle Ian?' she said.

Alistair nodded. 'The man with the moustache.'

'The moustache? Who are you thinking of, I wonder? Oh, no, love, that's Bob Kelmarsh. No, he's *married*.'

Alistair could smell beer on her breath. He felt a familiar uneasiness – from an early age he had suspected he was the victim of some kind of trick and that he must keep a note of all the details if he wasn't to be fooled entirely.

His mother leant over, slapped her hands on her knees and did the grin she gave to babies in prams. 'Want to see what your uncle Ian got you?' she said. She fumbled in her bag and dropped it a few times. Her old cigarette case rattled out on to the floor. 'Aren't I the butterfingers?' she said. And then she held out a tiny little toy car, no larger than a stamp, on the palm of her hand. 'What do you think of that?' she asked him.

'Thank you very much.'

'There's a good boy,' she said.

Was *he* my father, Alistair thought, the man who bought the little toy car? It might have been him. It might even have been the man with the moustache. Or it might have been Tony or Ray or . . . He threw off the sheet and went into the bathroom to wash and shave.

It was a glorious day, golden, windy and autumnal; the rush of early brown leaves past the window still contained the perfume of summer. Soon he went out into the garden with his coffee. Rosalind was already on her knees by one of the flower-beds and he raised his cup to her. She looked up, squinting, and pushed the hair off her forehead with her wrist. The gardening glove looked comically large against it. 'Sleep all right?' she said. But before he could answer her, she told him, 'I'm out all day today. We're having a Home From Home meeting at the showroom.'

'Oh, right,' he said. 'All well?'

'Yes. Why? What d'you mean?'

'I just – all well at Home From Home?' Did he imagine it or had Rosalind snorted derisively?

She stood up and brushed off her knees. 'Everything's fine, thank you,' she said. 'We're planning the next catalogue. We always do at this time of year.'

'Oh. Oh, I see.'

She walked past him into the house. Suddenly he felt afraid. He wanted to say something else to her. What else could he say? He couldn't think of anything at all.

He looked up at the clear blue sky. As if to rescue him from this groping loneliness, the pleasant feeling of his dream came back. He heard Rosalind start her car and drive away, but he was smiling again, picturing dear old Ivy with the tea-towel knotted under her chin. She had done brilliant caricatures (which he was able fully to appreciate only now), satirizing the small-mindedness and the hidden lusts of prominent local women. 'A *naked* Easter parade? No, no, no, Mrs Dawson. (What? A third piece of may Battenberg cake? Why, please *do* – it is *very* good, or so I'm told.) No, no, no, Ay'm afraid may husband (whom is the bloody vicar, you know) would *nevaah* stand for nakedness, Mrs Dawson – particularly from me. What's that? *Cream* and *jam*, Mrs Dawson? On *top*? You're *sure*? Well, each to his own, as Ay *orften* say. Call me progressive, if you will . . . er – yes, just finish the jug, Mrs Dawson, *bay all bloody means!*'

He missed Ivy. He had been missing Ivy for a long time now. What did she think of him? he wondered. Disappearing like that. Apparently she forgave him, at least to some degree: her telephone call was testament to that; it had been incredibly generous of her to make it.

He closed his eyes. Why had he not gone to visit her a few weeks ago? Why had he merely sent her and Geoff the spare keys to his mother's old house? And that cowardly little note!

Do feel free to take anything you want from the box of ornaments and photographs I put on the kitchen table. They are all things which I thought you might like because of the memories with which they are associated. If any of the furniture interests you, please do take it too. The same goes for the box of clothing. Anything you don't want will go to charity.

'*Because of the memories with which they are associated*'? What icy tongs he used to handle their shared past, holding it out at arm's length, at the furthermost point of a Latinate ending. How hurtful it must have been to read that note. He ought to have asked them both round, made tea, shown them the things personally. He ought to have dived headlong into collective memory – if only to thank Ivy for preserving that last vestige of her faith in him.

In fact, Ivy had always believed in him. More than his mother ever had. When he had won his state scholarship for Oxford, Ivy said, 'There's a brilliant head on them shoulders of yours, isn't there? Oh, you've made me ever so proud, Al. Me and Geoff *and* your mum, too

– even if she doesn't know how to say it, love.' She had been tearful, he remembered. She had made him a cake: a Victoria sponge with white lemony icing and raspberry jam in the middle. Ivy made wonderful cakes. Hadn't she always done his birthday cakes, too?

Without thinking about what he was doing, he went inside and called for the train times from Charing Cross to Dover Priory station. There was one in an hour. Then he called a mini-cab. After that he went upstairs and packed a small bag with a change of underwear and socks, and a clean shirt and sweater. He put in his shaving kit (it was a beautiful ivory-handled set: a present from Rosalind on his fortieth birthday), a toothbrush, a tube of toothpaste and a comb. Then he went down to the kitchen and, using up some cold sausages, which must have been left over from one of Rosalind's princely breakfasts for Luke, he made sandwiches for the train.

He checked his watch. The taxi would arrive in five minutes. He could hear Luke upstairs, running a bath, padding to and from his old bedroom. Alistair thought of going up to say goodbye, but couldn't face it. His son's unhappiness frightened him; it had become almost audible, like the neutral hum of a loudspeaker that threatens at any moment to screech out feedback. He picked up the pen by the phone notepad to write Luke a note. On the top page was an elaborately patterned 'A' surrounded by hearts and butterflies and flowers. What was going on in his son's mind? he wondered. He had heard Luke come in at four in the morning for the fifth night running. Alistair felt troubled by an emotional response he found unintelligible and faintly undignified.

He didn't know how to advise his son, although that was plainly what the situation required. When he had come quietly down the stairs and caught the end of a conversation between Luke and his mother – 'But I don't *care* about anything else. That's the whole point. I've just got to get her back, Mum' – he had known he couldn't mix himself up in it all just now.

He was also avoiding the issue of his daughter. Occasionally he eyed the two airmail envelopes on his wife's desk, addressed in what looked like his own hand. Rosalind had told him that Sophie had sent a phone number and address as she had promised, but somehow Alistair could not bring himself to ask for them. He was unnerved by the hint of solidarity between his wife and daughter. He had never seen it before. He was not sure why, but it made him feel even less hopeful that Sophie would ever forgive him. It was as if she had changed sides.

The thought that his daughter might not love him again was unbearable. It made him frantic. His brilliant, beautiful daughter, with whom he could laugh and argue as with no one else, who sent him to the edge of despair and confusion with her self-destructiveness and to the dizzy heights of pride with her flamboyant successes. She was all wild contradictions: anorexia, suicide attempts, self-harm, two A levels at sixteen, a sparkling first from his old Oxford college, a star job at the *Telegraph*. All the way to the station, in the back of the mini-cab, he clenched and unclenched his fists, absorbing the full horror of the possibility that Sophie might never talk to him again. No more highs and lows. From now on there would just be time and getting old on a level wasteland of loneliness.

Alistair did not think about Rosalind at all. Tentatively, he had tried to begin a conversation about Karen Jennings, about his idiotic mistake in that hotel room, but as soon as it became obvious to her that this was his subject, she had remembered a phone call she had to make. He had found himself alone in the drawing room, staring at her glass of wine. He wondered if she felt she would have to leave him and was merely trying to delay the inevitable. After that one occasion, he did not formulate this thought again.

When they arrived at Charing Cross, the driver pulled up with a jerk. 'Is fifteen pound, sir,' he said.

Alistair handed him a twenty-pound note and waved his hand at the change. When the car pulled away, he was mildly amused by the vulgarity of this gesture and hoped the driver kept the tips for himself.

It was a familiar bustle at Charing Cross. His work as a barrister often involved his travelling on trains. He would go to Norwich Crown Court, to Chichester or Leeds. He was allowing himself to confront the end of this agreeable way of life by degrees, like a swimmer lowering himself slowly into a cold sea. Never again would he sit on a train, with a blue legal notepad on his knee, his briefcase and robing bag beside him, putting the finishing touches to his speech for the jury. Work had been a good friend to him for many years.

He moved towards the ticket office, still slow on his bad leg, still suspecting violent intentions in the crowd, and still embarrassed by the walking-stick. He wondered if people guessed he was injured or if the stick just made him look like an old man.

Like an old man, he thought. He virtually *was* an old man. While he stood in the queue, he studied a few free brochures and found he might have been given a pensioner's discount for his ticket. He had never once thought to use the card he had been sent on his sixtieth birthday. He had thrust it into a drawer as soon as it arrived in its ascetic brown envelope. He had felt personally insulted by it.

'You really should try to remember your Rail Card if you've got one, sir. It does make you a good saving,' said the benevolent ticket salesman.

'Yes, you're quite right,' Alistair said, too tired to be offended. Why be offended, after all? Wasn't it a pleasant relief to be spoken to in this gentle way?

There was not much gentleness left in the world. As he took his seat on the train, the thought of soft, round, cool-palmed, cake-scented Ivy made him close his eyes with relief. Perhaps Ivy would forgive him for what he had done. As he drifted into a light sleep, he found himself confused about who might forgive him for which of his wrongs. Was it Ivy to whom he had been unfaithful, Rosalind he had abandoned, Luke to whom he had sent an inadequate, hurtful note? And was it Sophie he had hated with such violent passion for laughing and drinking and drinking and laughing, long into the night, with all of those male guests?

All the way to Dover, he dreamt of men with moustaches.

Chapter 19

There were local mini-cabs outside Dover Priory station and Alistair eased himself delicately into the back of one. His leg felt the strain of the journey already and he longed to stretch it out flat for a while. He asked the driver to take him home, to Maison Dieu Road, where he would drop off his bag and rest for a bit, before going to see Ivy.

The new scenery was becoming familiar to him now, even though it bore little resemblance to the Dover of his childhood. There were taller buildings, there was a brisk, industrial atmosphere that had not existed before. The billboards were designed to be viewed from passing cars, the lettering full of that urgent American song, bright as TV screens, in which the whole world was beginning to join. At the site of his lovely old Café de Paris was a roundabout: lorries – right through the little corner table.

But, still, there was the sea on the right and all the seafront hotels, some with different names, but essentially they were their bleached, sun-strained, pastel-coloured selves, serving the same English breakfasts, no doubt. 'The Castle Hotel', he read, 'The Britannia', 'The Queen Elizabeth' and then, 'We take Euros.' There certainly had been a few changes. He smiled out at the old place with the kind of affectionate surrender with which he had greeted Sophie's blue hair. It had become a sunny, blustery afternoon, of the kind that best suited Dover because it brought the smell of the sea into all the streets.

He paid the driver and walked up the old path with his bag in his hand. The work he had arranged had improved the place no end. The missing tiles on the path had been replaced, the weeds had been removed from the front garden, the grass mown and all the tangled rubbish had been taken out of the hedges. The window-frames, rotten as they were, had been repainted. It looked respectable – if a little battle-worn, he thought. Much like himself. In fact, the place now looked much the way it had when he left it, forty years ago.

He glanced along the street at the other boarding-houses, most of which had 'No Vacancies' signs outside. Business was obviously booming. A group of thin, exhausted-looking people stood at the end of the road, talking. The women wore headscarves and long skirts. The men were black-haired, dark-eyed. Were they Roma gypsies, he wondered. There had been an influx, *The Times* said: yet another group of people sick of persecution or just of being held back, in search of a better life even if it must be in a foreign country, even if it must mean starting from scratch. He watched an Englishwoman with a tartan shopping-bag cross the road to avoid passing them.

When the door was unlocked he felt immediate relief. The cleaners had been and the builders had thrown out what was broken – old tables and chairs and so on – so that now it was straightforwardly good to be there, in the freshly scrubbed little house, with its few remaining pieces of furniture. Suddenly it was a huge relief to escape from the accumulated weight of his possessions and the unspoken demands of their elegance. He wanted nothing more than to put his feet up in the front parlour, as they had always called it, and rest his bad leg for a bit.

As he settled in his mum's old chair, he realized he had forgotten to eat his sandwiches on the train. He took them out and unwrapped them, suddenly ravenously hungry. They were quite delicious – sausages, good butter, soft brown bread and a little coarse-grain mustard. What Michelin-starred meal is better than this, he thought. With his bad leg propped up on the old footstool, his weight sunk deep in the sagging green chair, he wondered why he had ever thought he needed so much out of life.

But Alistair had decided not to be easy on himself, to leave no posture unexamined. Was this sudden charming unworldliness merely another luxury of wealth, he wondered. In one sense it was. But in another perhaps it really did constitute an arrival in new territory. Perhaps the conclusion he was beginning to draw was that it wasn't the wealth, the possessions, that mattered, but the necessity to rid oneself of the appetite for them. It seemed there were two ways of doing this: either by wisdom or by slavish accumulation. This moment would come either way.

If only I had been wise, he thought, rather than merely clever. If only I had thought a little more and worked a little less.

But he was not sure what this might have changed. The permutations were too various: they spiralled off uncontrollably, making him sick with possibility. It was very much easier to believe that life was destined to unfold as it did. But even as he thought this, he knew that he was not prepared any more to sit back in resignation and observe the shambles of his emotional life.

When he felt rested and he had unpacked his shaving things in the bathroom and hung up his change of clothes in the empty wardrobe, he went out.

Uncle Geoff and Auntie Ivy had lived just round the corner. And all these years they had gone on living there, at sixty-three Hill Road, still calling on his mother for tea, still asking her over for a glass of sherry, no doubt. On the way into the centre of the town in the taxi, he had read some signs on the town-hall noticeboard: 'Wednesday nights: Bingo!', 'Tuesday afternoons: Knit and Natter!'. This would have been their life. A game of bingo and a half at the pub afterwards, he thought. Would Uncle Geoff still have fetched the drinks for his 'girls'? Of course he would. Alistair could imagine it all.

He reached the front door and rang the little bell. It gave out a resounding 'ding-dong', which seemed to belong to a far larger house than this two-up-two-down. He waited for what felt like a very long time before a shape became visible through the frosted glass in the door. 'Coming quick as I can,' it called.

It was Ivy! That was Ivy's voice! He was surprised to find that his heart was racing, his palms wet. Why, after all these years as himself, had he so little talent for guessing how he was going to feel?

The door opened and there she was: smaller, stouter, her hair now completely white, but it was no other person in the world than Ivy Gilbert who stood in front of him. He took in her familiar smell. 'Hello, Ivy. Remember me?' he said.

She looked at him and shook her head, smiling. 'Well, look what the cat dragged in.'

How typical of her sense of humour, he thought, adoring her, loving her voice, her sweet face, her satirical eyes. 'May I come in?'

'No,' she said. 'Not without a hug first.'

He moved forward awkwardly and, with his nose squashed against her ear, her white hair tickling it, a sob rose up in him and broke like a wave. Her hand patted his back. 'Tears is it now?' Ivy said. 'Silly boy. Where on earth have you been?'

Then she moved away from him and he followed her down the passageway towards the kitchen. She walked very slowly, her hips plainly uncomfortable, her hands distorted by arthritis. 'I'll put the kettle on,' she said.

The kitchen was completely changed. The sink was on the wrong side of the room; the cooker was in the wrong place. It almost made him dizzy. 'This is all new,' he said.

She glanced round at him as she filled the kettle. Her hands were so shaky he wanted to rush over and help her, but he would not have offended her for anything. She had always been independent. 'New? Oh, love, you're going years back. Martin did this for us. You remember Martin? Our nephew?'

Alistair nodded and smiled. Yes, he remembered Martin. Martin with his incredible carpentry skills prized beyond anything Alistair could do; Martin, who was Ivy and Geoff's *real* nephew. Did he still feel jealous? What a petty character I am, he thought.

Ivy went on, 'Yes. Dear Martin came and done all this work for us about – oh, it must have been a good fifteen years back. He died about five years ago, you see. He got cancer and it took him quick.' She tutted as she carried the kettle across the kitchen and plugged it in. 'Where's the sense in that, eh? Old bag like me still going strong and Martin dying not even sixty.' With an attempt to conceal a wince, she reached up for the cupboard door. 'Now, if I know you,' she said, 'you'll be wanting something sweet. You're lucky I've got custard creams in, aren't you?'

She tipped out some of the biscuits and put them on the table in front of him. He could see the faces of the newly married Prince and Princess of Wales smiling on the plate underneath them. Geoff had always been a royalist, he remembered. He got a tear in his eye when he heard the national anthem. Although he never spoke about it, he had been decorated for bravery in the war.

Ivy poured water into the teapot and Alistair brought over the cups and the milk she had put on the side.

'Thank you, dear. Sorry about the bottle,' she said. 'My lovely milk jug I had since I was married, I went and broke it the other day with these useless hands of mine.'

'Couldn't matter less,' Alistair said. He sat down at the table. Had she no money to buy a new jug, he thought, his stomach clenching, just as Luke's did.

He watched Ivy stir the tea in the pot and took in the sweetish perfume. She poured a little milk into the cups – had this been the first of his horrified discoveries, that in polite society one never put the milk in first? – and then she pushed the sugar cubes towards him. So, you could still get cubes of sugar! Custard creams and sugar cubes and milk jugs . . . Ivy seemed to exist in a time capsule, an England that had died long ago. It was wonderful.

'Thank you very much, Ivy. This is lovely,' he said.

'Well, you always loved a custard cream. Anything sweet.'

'Yes. Yes, I did,' he said.

It was Rosalind's Tarte Tatin, these days. He bit into a biscuit. It was the taste of childhood.

'Good. No change there, then,' she said, nodding definitively. She handed him the cup of tea, her hand rattling the little cup on its saucer.

'Thank you. No, no sugar, thanks. Is Geoff around?' he said.

'No, love. I've not got him here any more. He's up at the old fogeys' home near Castle Hill. I visit him, but it was . . . well, it was too much for me to have him here,' she said.

'I'm so sorry.'

'I've been waiting for ever on my old hip, you see. And Geoff, well, he's not been in good sorts for a while and it just got too much for me.' She looked down into her lap and Alistair thought how typical it was of Ivy to feel guilty when these were circumstances entirely beyond her control. This was what he feared most about old age: the loss of control. Suddenly the balance shifted and the body ruled the will.

'Still,' she went on, 'they've pretty young nurses up there and he's settled in nicely. I've no reason to worry.'

'Oh, Ivy, it must be difficult for you not having him around,' Alistair said. And as he spoke he knew what her stoical reply would be.

'Well, we had a good innings. You can't deny that.'

'Yes, that's true,' he said. Ivy and Geoff must have been married for more than sixty years. He and Rosalind had done less than two-thirds of that! They were mere beginners. 'You're all right here on your own, though, are you?'

'Oh, I'm not on my own, love. I've a fantastic girl from the Meals on Wheels comes in every day with a bit of lunch for me. And I've a nurse comes by from time to time for my physio. And then I have my check-ups with Dr Hargreaves. And you might not believe it, love, but I still get out to my bingo every week with those of us who haven't croaked it yet.'

It was just as he had imagined, then.

'Did Mum go? You and Geoff and Mum?'

'Oh, yes, till a year or two back. Yes – off to bingo. And down the pub quiz with old Ben Singer, your mum used to. Oh, yes, love.'

Ivy spoke about everything with nostalgia – even the current or recent facts of her life. There she was, elevated by her years – as if she was literally gazing down from a quiet place a long way above the struggle. It was only her distorted hands that spoke of immediate sensation, of pain. Her hands and the brief allusion to her hips.

Did she need a hip replacement? Damn the National Health Service and its waiting lists, he thought. He hoped she was not in constant pain and then felt certain that she was. How lucky he and Rosalind were that they would never be without their private health insurance, never have trouble buying another milk jug or replacing anything that broke. Whatever happened now, after all the wise investments, they would be well-off until they died.

Ivy was laughing: 'Yes, every Monday, down the George and Dragon, a little glass of sherry or a half, she always had, and her packet of pork scratchings. She had a bad hip like me, but there was no stopping your mum. Never was, though, was there?'

'No,' he said, smiling.

'Well, except when it came to you, love.'

Alistair put down his cup of tea and looked straight at Ivy, knowing this was something he had to face. He was going to have to hear what it had done to them – his disappearing like that.

He remembered Rosalind telling him about giving birth to Sophie. They had been sitting on their bed with their miraculous little girl on the blanket in front of them. He had asked her if the labour had been very painful: 'It's funny,' Rosalind said. 'You start off shouting and crying and everything, but then it's as if you suddenly see that giving birth to your baby is the one thing in life you can't get out of, no matter what. It's the one kind of pain you know you can't get angry about, as if it wasn't fair, because it's more important than your body. It isn't fair or unfair, it's just happening with or without your consent. So you just accept it and get on, I suppose.'

Rosalind's answer had impressed him profoundly and he knew that now he must be as brave as his young wife.

'Oh, Alistair,' Ivy said, 'whatever did you vanish like that for?'

'I was ashamed,' Alistair told her, trying to speak as honestly as possible, no matter how crass it sounded. 'I wanted to be with smart rich people in big houses, far away from Dover.'

'But this is where you were raised. It's where you come from, love.'

'Yes. I know.'

'Couldn't you have written? Visited?'

'I couldn't keep you in my life. I couldn't have explained it. I'm not proud of it, Ivy, but I was making a new life for myself and, well, the people in it, they would have looked down on – on everything. And I couldn't bear it.'

'We wouldn't have cared about a bunch of snooty so-and-sos. *I* wouldn't.'

Alistair laughed sadly. 'No,' he said, 'you were always too wise for that. But *I* cared. I was the one who cared. If you want to know the truth I was scared they wouldn't accept me and I wanted their kind of life so much, Ivy.'

'Dear me,' Ivy said. 'Did you hate us that much, then? Are we that dreadful?'

Alistair reached out and took up her bent, bony little hand. 'No. I've been wrong and very stupid,' he said.

'And with that big brain God gave you . . . What a waste.'

'Yes.'

'She sounded nice, too, your wife. Not the snobbish type, really.'

'Oh, no, Rosalind isn't at all snobbish,' he said confidently. 'She's never looked down on anyone in her life . . .'

And then he thought: It has always been me, hasn't it? I'm the one who needed the cripplingly expensive ski holidays in Val d'Isère, the children at extortionate public schools, which they hated anyway. I'm the one who needed the chandeliers and the damask silk hung on the walls at a hundred pounds a metre in place of ordinary paper. Hadn't Rosalind once said she thought it would be rather lovely if they lived in a little cottage with Alistair writing a history book the way he had said he wanted to when she first met him? He had told her she'd miss her pearls and her fur coat and her seat at Glyndebourne, her tennis at Queens. But perhaps she had been telling the truth.

'Well, it must be quite a feeling, coming home after all this time,' Ivy said.

'It's changed a lot.'

'You're not wrong there. That huge terrible ferry-port making all that racket. Lot of foreign faces, too. There are wars in the world, you see. They come here for safety.'

Trust Ivy to see it this way, he thought. She was a genuine liberal.

'It's still your home, though – your roots are here,' she said, blowing on her hot tea.

He studied her lovely old face and wondered how many people there were left in England who would die in the same street they grew up. She had been born two houses along. 'Ivy, *your* roots are here,' he said. 'I don't think I ever really had roots.'

'Now why d'you say that? Go on with you, Alistair. You had a home and a mum who loved you as best she could, and there was always me and Geoff.'

'I know. I know. I just . . . it was not knowing about my father, I suppose.'

There. He had said it. It was out and now the world seemed quieter – the way it did when you ran all the way up the cliff path with the wind and rain crashing in your ears, and then you saw an alcove and ducked in and it all went peaceful.

'I can understand that, dear,' Ivy said. And then her eyes fixed on his for a long time – perhaps as long as thirty seconds – her eyebrows contracting in response to her thoughts. She was frightening him. He gazed into her old face: here was the impenetrability of another human mind.

He remembered the extraordinary way he had summed up the issue of his father to Karen Jennings, that night at the Ridgeley Hotel. It had been spontaneous – and totally out of character. Over a glass of whisky, he had calmly revealed to this perfect stranger how his mother always told him that she and his father were planning to marry but that his dad had got killed in the war. It was just a sob-story, he explained, which stopped adding up when he was about eight. He had even told her how he had marked this realization by throwing all his toy soldiers into the sea. He said he hadn't seen his mother for nearly forty years, 'possibly to avoid the conversation'.

The formula was so absurd he had known immediately that there was an element of truth in it. He had avoided emotional contact with his mother just as he had avoided physical contact ever after the day he came home unexpectedly from his confirmation class. (Afterwards, he was sure he had known something wrong was happening when he ran up the path – that the house had grown ugly, that the air had seemed to cool and darken as if for rain.)

He had found them there in the hallway, on the carpet, struggling. At first he thought Mr Bisset was attacking her, but as he pulled back Alistair could see she was enjoying it. Then she saw him. 'Oh, Alistair,' she said, 'I thought you were down the church.'

She had always been passionately insistent that he get to Sunday School on time. And now he knew why. 'I forgot my sandwich,' he said. 'I got hungry.'

Even now he found it difficult to go into a church. Rosalind had wanted the children to be Catholic, just as she was, and he had had no problem in leaving it to her. He had washed his hands of the whole filthy business of religion.

'Ivy,' he said, 'do *you* know anything about my father?'

'Yes, love. I do,' she replied.

He stared at her incredulously. After all these years to learn something – *anything* – about this absent figure. What he had dreaded most of all was that no one knew, that his father had been just one of his mother's sunny afternoon 'jaunts', just one of her Sunday treats or her late-night 'talks'. 'Tell me what you know, Ivy. Please?'

'It's Geoff, love,' she said.

That a human voice should reply so simply, that it should provide anything so contained as an answer, was almost as stunning as the answer itself.

'*Geoff? Uncle* Geoff? Your *hus*band? I don't . . . How can that be?'

'Geoff, my husband,' she said, nodding.

'But how can that . . . how can that *be*, Ivy? *How?*'

She sighed. 'It just *is*, love,' she said.

Alistair stared at the objects on the table: biscuits, saucers, cups and spoons – things reduced to mere physical presence, stripped of their significance. They might as well have been pebbles on a shore or leaves on the grass. Briefly, he saw them with the eyes of a patient historian, ten thousand years after this day.

'Alistair?' Ivy said. 'Alistair? Are you all right?'

'I'm not sure,' he said truthfully.

'I always wished he'd tell you – for what it's worth to you now.'

'How long were they . . . *when*, Ivy? *When did it start?*'

'It was no more than a year or two they saw each other in that way,' she said. He watched her pick the biscuit crumbs off the edge of the plate, squashing them under her forefinger and brushing them off into the palm of her hand.

'A year or two? But you must have been *married* by then. She was your closest friend.'

'Yes,' Ivy said. 'It sounds bad. The thing is, you've got to understand, things were different in them days. I was trying for a baby, Al, I wanted nothing more in the world than a little baby. Anyway, I fell pregnant and in them days we all thought you mustn't have . . . well, you mustn't have *relations* with your husband, if you had a baby in you. All in all I had a baby in me for almost two years . . .'

'Ivy, I don't understand.'

'What I mean is, I kept losing them. Three little babies in a row – miscarriages – before we knew I couldn't do it. And . . . well, it was in that time he must've got tempted. She was a very attractive woman, your mum, *June* – all that lovely red hair and that full figure of hers.'

'*Tempted?*' Alistair repeated.

'She and Geoff were sweeties as children, you know.'

'No, I didn't know.'

'Yes. His childhood sweetie, June was. But she was always a will unto herself and she took up with that Nigel Benson whose dad owned the tackle shop out by the Britannia. Anyway, everyone thought they'd tie the knot, but Nigel got killed in the war. Heartbroken, she was. Me and Geoff, we got together a little bit before it happened – when Geoff was home with his shrapnel in his leg. I'd been writing, you see. I'd always had a soft spot for him. I wrote him letters when he was serving.

'Oh, Al, I used to think he was sorry he chose me – you know, I thought he must feel if only he'd waited a bit he might have had June. I can tell you it ate me up for a while, that did. But I know he loved me now. You can't argue with sixty-odd years, can you?'

'No.' He shook his head slowly. 'How can you be so reasonable? Ivy, you say you always wished Geoff would tell me . . .'

Her face seemed to crumple with pain. 'It's true, love. I did *always* wish that. Part of me won't never forgive him.'

'But if you felt it so strongly, why didn't you *make* him? He respected you, Ivy. You'd forgiven him so much. He would have listened to you.'

'*Me?*' she said. 'Oh, no, love. You've got it all wrong. See, your mum and Geoff – they had no idea I knew.'

Alistair leant back in his chair as if a huge blow to the chest had pushed him there. 'What?'

'No, love. Not to this day.'

'I . . . I don't understand,' he said.

But he did understand. She had not wanted to spoil what she had, and her humility was such that she had simply weathered it through and hoped the affair would end.

But to be in her rival's company so much – to continue to be his mother's closest friend? To suffer Geoff referring to them affectionately as his 'girls'?

But once a thing was said it could not be unsaid. He knew the awful truth of this as well as anyone. He took in Ivy's kind old face, the watery eyes still brimming with humour and affection – inexplicable affection – for him, her husband's illegitimate child. 'You loved me like a son,' Alistair said.

'You were the closest I got, love. There was Martin, I suppose, but for me it was always you. My queer little Alistair with his book and his big frown.' She looked at him with heartbreaking tenderness and then she laid her hand on her stomach. 'I couldn't give him a child, you see. I was no good in there.'

'Ivy, you can't blame yourself, surely.'

'No. Not really. Not any more.'

'Geoff could never have blamed you.'

'No. He never did. And, anyway, it's you I owe my sorries to, really.'

'*Me?* Why? You were always wonderful to me. All your encouragement, all those birthday cakes . . .'

'Yes,' she said, laughing, 'you loved a Victoria sponge with lemon icing. Bit of jam and butter cream in the middle.'

'Yes, Ivy, I did,' he said, almost too moved to speak. 'How can you possibly think you owe me an apology?'

'For keeping you from your father, love. You see, I had a choice, and I thought it came down to my marriage or your father. And I chose not to rock the boat. I was scared if it came out in the open he'd leave me, that I'd force it to happen. You'd have *known*, love – d'you understand? But – oh, I don't know, I used to think they'd go off to London. God knows. You think love just disappears when you're young, don't you?, but it lasts for ever, really, like it gets in your bones. Oh, Al, I thought they'd *leave* me and take you away and go and be a family somewhere like I could never give him. I thought I'd lose him and June *and* you if I said anything.'

'Ivy,' he put his arms out and held her frail body, 'it was for them to tell me,' he said. 'It was for *them*. Not *you*.' They moved apart, and as she dabbed her eyes with a handkerchief, which she always had in her sleeve, he said, 'But I don't think I'll ever understand how Mum could keep it secret. Not when I was old enough to keep quiet.' He looked out of the window at the little back garden. '*Would* I have kept quiet? I suppose I would . . . Oh, how could she *live* with all that deception? How could she tell all those stories to her *own child*?'

Ivy had a soft smile on her face. He knew what she was thinking.

'Like mother, like son?' he said. 'I suppose you're right.'

'Al, you was born with a funny lot in life. We never could really understand you. That brain of yours – it was your greatest blessing but it made you ever so different. I was forever saying that to Geoff, and he used to worry over it no end.'

'Did he?'

'Yes! Oh, yes, he did, love. He wasn't much of a reader. He used to say he had nothing for you, that all he had was his sweets. And you grew out of them so quick.'

'Oh, no, Ivy you're wrong. He was *wrong*.'

Alistair thought of the countless times he had gone to 'help' Geoff in the newsagent's on a Saturday or after school. Geoff had let him play at stacking the shelves or laying out the newspapers or the birthday cards. Geoff had been just as tender as Ivy was when he helped her to make a cake, with a little bowl of spare mixture to stir just as she did.

'All those times in his shop,' he said, lost for words, getting none of it across.

'He loved having you there, Al,' Ivy said.

To think Geoff had quietly given him pear drops and ruffled his hair, never mentioned the fact that they were father and son. The portrait of restraint was too agonizing to contemplate.

'Ivy, do you understand why I left? I'm not absolutely sure if I do myself. There was the snobbishness, of course, that was a big part of it, but I think there was anger too. I always knew there were secrets, that Mum was lying to me. My own mother, Ivy. I know I'm no better, but I'm just trying to explain *myself*. I suppose I just – I couldn't forgive her. Maybe I even wanted to punish her. Do you understand that? Do you understand how I got started off on a path and then there was no turning back?'

'Your wife . . .'

'Yes? Her name's Rosalind, Ivy.'

'Rosalind thought your mother had already died, didn't she? That's what I guessed when I telephoned.'

'Yes. You were right. I told her Mum died when we got engaged. It's unforgivable, I know it's unforgivable, but there was just no going back, Ivy. I suppose I made a choice, too: my mother and you and Geoff, or my marriage and my new life.'

'And you chose not to rock the boat,' she said.

'Yes.'

And now I've capsized it, he thought.

He put his head into his hands and began to cry. He could feel her stroking his back the way a mother strokes a little baby with colic. 'There there,' she was saying. 'There there, love.'

His mind was making wild leaps. That evening with Karen Jennings: it had been a gross infidelity to Rosalind, but had it in some way been an act of fidelity to himself? Had he really brought about this crisis deliberately, in the name of uncovering the truth?

But he knew even as he formulated this thought that if only he could believe it, he might have a shred of self-respect. He would have liked to think he had proved, at last, incapable of tolerating lies. He would rather have been anything other than the smooth, impervious creature he had embodied all these years. He wanted to think that, with some weird logic, some manic instinct, in that bedroom with Karen he had committed his body to the destruction of lies, just as he did when he leapt up in court.

But he could not think this. The night with Karen had been a game of Russian roulette. And he had meant to survive – with the joy of recklessness in his blood for a bit, a recklessness he had curbed all his life. He had meant to carry the sensation about as a souvenir, as a little trophy for his ego. He knew that if it hadn't been for Karen's indiscretion, if it hadn't been for the attack, if it hadn't been for Ivy's telephone call, he would never have brought out the truth himself. He was too cowardly and too long accustomed to speaking in half-truths.

It struck him then that he had fed his daughter on an indigestible mixture of adulation, derived in part from self-love, from corrective speeches aimed at his own undernourished ego, and on crudely veiled misogyny to which poor Sophie could hardly mount a defence. It was no wonder her body had wasted away. If anyone was physically reactive to lies, it was his darling daughter. 'I think I need to lie down,' he said.

'You've had a big shock.'

'Yes.'

306

He let Ivy lead him into her sitting room where she kept her bed now to save her hips on the stairs. He let her plump up the pillows behind his head and draw a blanket over him. She laid her hand on his hair. 'I always wished you was my son,' she said. 'Life's like that, isn't it?'

'Yes,' he said, 'it is.'

'I'm not surprised you were angry with us all, Alistair.'

'No, Ivy. I was never angry with you,' he said. 'Never with you.'

He listened to her sit down in her chair and fold her hands in her lap. Quietly, quietly, the early-evening light filled the window and even the sound of the little ticking clock was muffled by the presence of peace.

Chapter 20

Bogdan's brother, Vuk, could get passports, National Insurance numbers, household bills, bachelor's degrees, speed, dope, coke, crack, smack, cars, stereos, mobile phones and guns. He and Bogdan were sitting in the kitchen at Kwik-Kabs, watching the news and eating baked potatoes from SpudWorld.

Goran put three hundred pounds on the table in front of Vuk. They all spoke in Serbian.

Vuk said, 'So, how come you've got the money for this but you can't pay me in full for your passport yet?'

'It's not my money.'

'Isn't that the best kind?'

'No. I'm getting this for a friend. I owe him a favour. He helped me and my girlfriend out.'

'OK. OK. Shit, I don't want to know about your life, really,' Vuk said. He reached into a sports bag on the chair beside him and took out a handgun. 'There you go.'

Goran picked it up and put it into his bag, which said 'Scunthorne School for Girls' on either side. On one side, Sophie, aged twelve, had scratched out what she saw as the superfluous letters in the school name and coloured in the essential four with red nail polish. The eagle on the crest had a huge biro spliff in its mouth. Goran had forgotten to ask Luke for a bag and this was the only one he had been able to find in the annexe.

'Thanks, Vuk,' he said.

'Sure. You have a nice day at school.'

Bogdan swallowed a large mouthful of potato. 'Goran, you're not going to keep that in the car while you do your shift, I hope. I have enough to fucking worry about if one of you lot crash. I don't need guns in the glove compartment, too.'

'No, I'm giving it to the guy now. I'm meeting him right now.'

Bogdan consulted his watch. 'You've got fifteen minutes till your shift starts, man.'

'I'm meeting him just round the corner.'

Bogdan nodded a kind of dismissal to him and turned to his brother. 'I love it that they call this guy a socialist,' he said, pointing his fork at Tony Blair, who smiled amiably in a garden beside President Bush.

Goran met Luke in a side-street off the Goldhawk Road. On either side there were neat, two-storey houses. Their iron gates opened on to little gardens that led to bright front doors. Many of the houses had bicycles chained outside them and some had cats stretched out in the sun on their doorsteps. Luke stood halfway down the road, beside his car. As Goran approached, Luke's face seemed increasingly amazed – as if, half remembering various elaborate school pranks that had never quite come off, he had been certain of failure.

Now, as he watched Goran walk towards him, he was struggling to believe his eyes. 'You got it?' he said.

Goran shrugged. 'Of course.'

'OK. Right. You did.'

'You did not think I can get this? It is like buying a newspaper. Expensive newspaper.'

'No, of course I did. I knew you could get it,' Luke said. He put out his hand – it was shaking a little – and Goran gave him the bag.

Luke stared at it, feeling disoriented and curiously afraid that this was all being filmed for reality TV. But he persisted: 'Did you keep fifty for yourself?'

'Yes.'

'Good. Look, thank you for doing this, Goran.'

There was little to say. On many occasions, Goran had noticed how the presence of a gun brought an end to all conversation. 'Well, I must work now, Luke.'

'OK. So, I'll see you when you get back, then,' Luke said.

Why will you see us? Goran thought. Can't you just leave us in *peace*? Why do you always need to come and visit us? We love each other, we want to be *alone*. Can't you get on with your rich boy's life on your own? He stared at Luke almost hoping these angry thoughts

309

were getting through in spite of the bright smile and gritted teeth behind which he had learnt to catch them.

Luke had also hesitated. He was afraid of going off alone in sole possession of the gun. There was still the sense that he and Goran were 'in it together' as they stood there in the side-street. He tried to think of something to say and then he remembered. 'Mila said she had something for me. A surprise, she said.'

Goran's heart winced, like an oyster under lemon juice. 'Surprise?'

'A present of some kind. I thought you would know.'

'No. I do not know.'

'Oh. Well, see you later, then.'

'Yes,' Goran said.

When he got back, Luke found the house empty. His mother had said she would be away all day at her Home From Home meeting and even his father had gone out. Perhaps he had a physio appointment or something, Luke thought.

He went up to his bedroom and opened the bag. The gun was small and neat, and just the right weight in his hand; it met an unconscious sensual expectation, like the thunk of an expensive car door. He laid it softly on the bed beside him, then relit the joint he had been smoking earlier. The crushed-up Zylamaprone™ gave it a bizarre flavour and seemed to diminish the nice, dozy effect so that, if anything, he felt invigorated. But it wasn't a bad sensation. In fact, it was quietly wonderful. He blew out the smoke in clouds into the sunny air, and found that the more he thought about it, the more he was becoming aware of a structure of certainty behind his anxiety. In a sense it was as if his fears were just a torn flag, poignantly sun-bleached and flapping, perhaps, but none the less fixed to a good, solid post. Perhaps, he thought, there were such things as right and wrong, after all; perhaps good did triumph over evil. And at least he was daring to dream.

He picked up the pistol. Stefan, his aunt Suzannah's first husband, had taught him how to shoot clays so he was not entirely unused to guns. He and Stefan had used large shotguns, though, whereas this one was the size of a man's hand. Luke remembered Goran pointing Mila's hand at him as if he was aiming to fire it. Goran was an angry person, he thought. Mila always wanted to laugh and joke around, doing impressions of him, but Goran had no sense of humour about himself. She so obviously found this boring – she rolled her eyes and made faces – that Luke wondered why Goran didn't make more of an effort. He had become withdrawn over the last week or so and Luke didn't like the way he spoke to Mila sometimes, when Luke and she had been laughing and Mila scruffed up Goran's hair and nudged him – only to help him join in. He could be almost aggressive with her, telling her to shut up and sit down.

Still, there were more important things to think about. Obviously he was not going to kill anyone. Obviously not. He knew that for sure. What he wanted to do was scare Turnbull a bit, to see that bright TV signal interrupted and flickering. This would be a fragment of justice in itself but, more importantly, it would expose Jamie to a few moments of character-forming silence – just like those Luke had experienced when Ludo's car swung gently towards the tree and smashed. Maybe he would appreciate what he had done to Luke's life. Maybe he would cry and beg and Arianne would see what a little coward her new boyfriend was. They needed a shock, because shocks made you re-evaluate – they made you see what was important. Everyone said that. People saw 'the light' and became saints. It had happened all the time in the old days, in his mother's books from school. Everyone knew that St Augustine had been a drunken philanderer, Mary Magdalen was a prostitute, and the good thief – well, he had plainly been a thief.

Luke wondered if he should tidy his room in case Arianne came back with him straight away.

He did not go out that night. Why bother with chance when he had the absolute certainty of seeing her the next night at the opening of Lapis-Lazuli?

Rosalind's car pulled up in front of the house at about a quarter to nine. Her meeting must have gone on longer than she had expected. Shortly after she came in and called up to him, 'I'm back, darling,' the doorbell rang and Luke heard his aunt Suzannah's voice in the hallway. Hadn't his aunt come round for supper just a few days ago? He did not relish the idea of another helping of the weird tension between Suzannah and his father, but he was so ravenously hungry that he was already running down the stairs.

He could hear his aunt and mother in the kitchen: 'I don't know, I'm *excited* about it, Suze. I really am. I know it's not exactly world peace, but everyone said it's our best brochure so far and it was all my work.'

'Well, good.'

'Thank you.'

'No, I really mean it,' Suzannah said.

Luke went in. They had opened a bottle of white wine and a large packet of crisps was spilling out on the table. He thought it was very unlike his mother not to have put them into a bowl. 'What's going on?' he said.

'Nothing, darling. Suzannah and I are having a gossip. Do you want some wine?'

'Yes, please.'

'Grab a glass, then,' she said.

He went over to the cupboard. 'What's for supper?'

'Good old traditional Indian takeaway,' Suzannah told him. 'I have forbidden your mother to cook.'

'I didn't take much persuading. I'm whacked.'

'But . . . Dad doesn't like curry,' Luke said, a little frightened.

'Well, it's lucky he's not here, then, isn't it?' Suzannah said.

'Why? Where is he?'

Rosalind put a handful of crisps into her mouth. 'Dover again,' she said, crunching. 'Some loose end at the house.'

'It was all done, I thought. What else was there?'

The doorbell rang and Rosalind stood up. 'God knows, darling. He sounded absolutely fine on the phone, though. Anyway, that'll be supper. I'm starving – Jocelyn's dieting so we were all given little salads.'

While Luke poured himself a glass of wine, his mother unpacked a plastic bag full of foil boxes. She spread them out on the table. 'OK, apart from the prawn biryani, everything else is up for grabs,' she said. She put out three forks. 'Shall we not even bother with plates? It's rather wonderful out of the boxes, isn't it?'

Luke stared at her. 'D'you mind if I have a plate?'

Suzannah giggled as she tipped half a packet of boiled rice into the lamb jalfrezi. 'Oh, go on, then, youth of today – show us up.'

Luke got his plate. He was not sure he had ever been so hungry – even after rowing or tennis. It was true that he had forgotten to eat lunch again, and he had smoked a joint, but even so, this was a disproportionate hunger and he wondered if it was caused by the Zylamaprone™. Perhaps the tablets had actually done something. The more he thought about it, the more worried he became that his hunger might never be satisfied, that there might simply not be enough chicken tikka.

312

'Goodness! Do chew, darling,' Suzannah told him.

'Sorry,' he said. Gradually, he began to feel better. The panic seemed to pass with a third glass of wine. 'But how did he get there?' he said suddenly.

Rosalind put down the ring Suzannah had been showing her. 'Who? Dad, you mean?'

'Yes. Because I had to drive him last time. I thought – you know – his leg and everything.'

'He caught cabs to and from the train. The physio won't be pleased. Still, it's Dad's choice.'

'He obviously wanted to go on his own,' Luke said.

'Oh, darling, you didn't want to take him last time. Surely you aren't wishing he'd asked you again.'

'I didn't mind taking him,' Luke said. 'It was OK.'

'Well, I personally think that's disloyal of you,' said Suzannah. 'I wouldn't do him any favours at all after what he's done to your mother.'

'Oh, Suzannah, let's not,' said Rosalind. 'I'm feeling so good.'

'Why are you feeling good?' Luke said.

Rosalind laughed. 'Aren't I allowed to?'

'Yes, of course.'

'Well, thank you, darling.'

Luke thought the best thing to do was ignore her extraordinary tone. He said, 'Actually, Mum, I'm still hungry. Can I put some toast on?'

'Of course you can. We can have toast and butter and honey for pudding.'

'Have you ever had it with a scoop of vanilla ice-cream on top, Roz?' Suzannah said.

'No.'

'Neither have I.' She giggled

'Well, it sounds quite revolting. Let's try it,' said Rosalind.

Luke watched them laughing like schoolgirls, chopping up bananas and nuts and putting ice-cream in the microwave so it went 'a bit scloopy'.

Suzannah went into the storecupboard in search of more ingredients. She called, 'How about dried mango pieces?'

'Too exotic,' Rosalind called back.

'Pears in Calvados?'

'*Far* too grand.'

'OK . . . OK . . . Ah, now who could refuse *this*? Packet of white chocolate bunnies – still in date if you don't look hard?'

'Pre*cise*ly what was missing,' Rosalind said. She popped up another piece of toast and glanced back at her son. 'You all right, darling?'

'Yes, Mum. Are *you*?'

Rosalind walked over to him and gave him a kiss on his forehead. 'I just want to see you happy, darling. You know that, don't you? That's what I want most of all.'

'Yes,' he said.

'I'm sorry we haven't had a chat for a while.'

'That's OK, Mum.'

He gazed into her gentle, pretty face, and it seemed to her that he was about to say something, when Suzannah came out of the store-cupboard. 'Right,' she said, striding across the kitchen. 'I shall smash up these bunnies with a rolling-pin.'

They all laughed at this and Rosalind squeezed her son's arm in encouragement.

While Luke threw away the empty foil boxes and fetched spoons and bowls, Suzannah and his mother spread butter and cloudy honey on the slices of hot toast; onto this they dropped scoops of rich vanilla ice-cream, chunks of white chocolate, chopped walnuts, and bananas and almonds. Rosalind held up a bowl and said, 'Oh, *scrum-o*.'

'God, this takes me back,' said Suzannah.

'Doesn't it just? Remember after Daddy's fortieth birthday bash, when we had the midnight feast after the grown-ups went to bed?'

'I have never felt able to eat gooseberry fool since.'

'No, neither have I,' laughed Rosalind.

'Did they *ever* feed us?'

'Can't have been enough. We were always hungry, weren't we?'

'As *horses*. Mean old things, weren't they? Were they?'

'Well, not to Luke, at any rate. They loved him,' Rosalind said, smiling.

'*That's* because Luke is the son Daddy always wanted, Roz.'

It surprised Rosalind to hear her sister say this: 'Daddy *adored* you, you know he did.'

'He did sometimes, but he really wanted a son and heir. He even told me he'd been devastated when he saw I was a girl.'

'He told you *that*?'

'Mmm,' Suzannah said, licking her spoon. '*Always* longed for a son. Mummy too. And, of course, they were going to call me Luke.'

'*No*, not *really*,' Rosalind said.

'Didn't you know? I assumed that was what put it into your mind.'

'I had no idea at all. It was Alistair's idea. What an odd coincidence. Well,' Rosalind said, 'bad luck them, because *I* got him.'

Luke smiled back at his mother, and embarked on the extraordinary concoction he had been given. Their hilarity was making him uneasy and he ate as quickly as he could, wanting nothing more now than to get back to his laptop and the portable TV.

When he had gone upstairs, Suzannah said, 'So, have you decided what to do?'

Rosalind studied her sister's excited face and thought: OK, I forgive you for asking me, but I don't want to discuss it. She decided to change the subject, knowing the best way to do this was to ask her sister about herself. 'Wait a minute, Suze. I can't be*lieve* I forgot to ask,' she said. 'Did you write to Stefan? You said you were going to send him a sort of "can we put the past behind us" letter.'

'Mmm. The plan was to do one ex-husband at a time. I did send it, yes.'

Rosalind was amazed. Her sister had never said sorry to anyone in her life. The letter she had decided to write to her first husband had sounded rather moving.

'Well, and what happened?' Rosalind asked.

'Actually, he never replied.'

'Oh.' This seemed terribly brutal to Rosalind. 'Oh, I'm sorry, Suze.'

'No, it's all right. It's what I deserve, really – the way I treated him.'

'Oh, come on. Were you *so* bad?'

'God, yes. I'm afraid I was a terrible slut. I was only twenty-two and far too young to be married and so on, but I really did make a fool of the poor man. No,' she went on, 'I'm glad I sent the letter but, on reflection, I'm not *at all* surprised he didn't reply.'

Rosalind was still indignant on her sister's behalf. 'But it was basically a huge long apology,' she said. 'Are you absolutely *sure* he got it?'

'Yes, I am. I'm ashamed to admit it, Roz, but I watched him pick it up as he went in through the door after work.'

'What? How? From the *street*, you mean?'

'God, you make it sound so scandalous. From my *car*, darling. Oh, I don't know – in a funny sort of way I've never really got over him, you see. First love and all that.'

'Goodness. Do you believe in that stuff?'

'Yes. I think I do.'

'I *don't*,' Rosalind said. 'I think you just choose *someone* and you make it run as smoothly as possible but it could just as easily have been somebody else.'

'*Really?*' Suzannah laughed. 'Isn't it odd? The cynic has been married for nearly forty years, while the romantic can't stop getting divorced.'

'Oh, it's not so odd, is it? People always come unstuck if they ask for perfection from life.'

When Suzannah had gone, Rosalind loaded the dishwasher, wiped the surfaces and poured herself a small glass of Cognac. She only allowed herself Cognac in private as it made her hiccup. She had another pile of letters to get through and, not feeling at all tired, she picked them up and took them through to the drawing room.

As she sifted through them, she noticed with horror that one envelope – not the usual airmail envelope that she watched out for – was addressed in Sophie's handwriting. She had looked forward to her daughter's next letter for over a week. The last one had described some of the pupils in her class and the things she was teaching them. Apparently her youngest pupils had all dutifully learnt 'S' is for 'snowman' before Sophie realized they had no idea what she was talking about. It sounded like such an interesting experience for Sophie, such a fascinating place to be. And how lovely to be with all those sweet children.

Thankfully, this latest letter had only been delivered that morning. Rosalind took a sip of brandy and opened the envelope.

It was an amazing sight: Sophie had written in every colour of the rainbow.

> *Dear Mum,*
> *Can you read this? I'm using all the children's crayons. Also, I'm writing on real paper this time because the other stuff just wasn't grand enough for writing something amazing. Want to know something amazing, Mum? I'm going to have a baby.*

Rosalind read the line again – it was so hard to see clearly in pink and yellow and orange and green but—

> *I'm going to have a baby* [she saw again. She read on.]
> *The father is a lovely man called Kwame Okantas. He's British, but his family are from Ghana originally. I met him in London and*

316

he was the person who gave me the idea of coming out here. We only slept together once before he left, the night we met – and though I know you'll disapprove of that, you have to admit it's pretty incredible that it happened first time!

Mum, I love him and he says he loves me too and the best thing of all is that I believe him.

When I look at all my friends I wonder if it does anyone any good taking things slowly and living together and so on. They all just break up anyway and after you've said 'I love you' and 'for ever' too many times, the words don't mean anything any more. It seems to me that the only thing to do is stop thinking and if you find someone you can respect, then just invest everything you've got – invest your DNA – and do the very best you can. Whatever happens, I'll be a mother. I'm crying with happiness as I write this.

Kwame's fantastic, Mum. He read history at Oxford and he's been a barrister but he wants to work out here for a year where his parents grew up. I admire him in so many ways. He sees the whole picture where I get lost in the detail. And he sees through all my tricks.

I got your card with the cats on it. It made me miss you so much, Mum! Your roses sound even better than ever and I can't wait to see your new catalogue – I know how hard you'll have worked on it. You do choose such beautiful things. You know you've always made every-thing beautiful, Mum – even when we rented a villa, you put different flowers by each of our beds, you made the fruit look like a painting in the fruit bowl. It always mattered, you know? It really did.

I'm so relieved you're able to be strong through all this. And I suppose it is good to hear Dad's coping, really. Poor Dad.

Do write again, but I've put my phone number at the bottom in case you feel like calling after what I've told you. I'm away until late tomorrow, but I'd love to speak to you the day after.

Mum, I'm so happy I've got nothing else to say. I'm going to go and look at the sunset and put my hand on my tummy and shut up for a while.

All my love,

Sophie

PS Kwame's just reminded me the school's been given a new fax machine, so you can send me a fax if you'd like me to see it as soon as I get back home tomorrow night. OK, you've probably guessed I'm longing to hear what you think!

'Home', Rosalind thought. Sophie would see a fax when she got *home* – to a village in Africa. Her daughter had so much more imagination than she did. Could it now be used to make happiness? She smiled with deep joy at the thought and picked up a piece of A4 paper. She wrote,

Darling Sophie,
I have just got your news. I've never had such a wonderful letter before – a rainbow letter.
When I think about it, I suppose you always had all those colours in you, but they used to come out angrily, when you dyed your hair green or pink or when you did your bedroom dark red, or when you started wearing that blue lipstick Daddy got so cross about. I think it used to make me a bit dizzy – all those colours in one girl. You always did laugh at me for wearing nothing but dark blue and cream.
Darling, your news has made me as happy as I was on the day you were born. Please send my love to Kwame and tell him I can't wait to meet him. I hope all this comes through clearly on your new fax machine. Of course I'll call you tomorrow. I'm so glad you feel you want to speak. XxxMummy

Rosalind took another sip of brandy, then she clapped her hand over her mouth and laughed with excitement and shock: a little black grandchild! She knew you weren't supposed to think in that way, but all that carefulness was so boring. It tried to make everyone shut up and pretend to be the same. It was stupid. What was wrong with being excited about someone being different? A little black grandchild – or half black, anyway. It would have different colour skin from Sophie or Luke or her and it would have different hair. Perhaps, if it was a little girl, Rosalind thought happily, she could have the plaits with all the little beads at the end. She imagined learning how to do them.

All her life, Rosalind had stifled her sensuality. It had always disturbed and secretly amused her that, had it been socially acceptable, she would probably have liked to squish her fingers into the lovely rolls that spilt over her friend Jocelyn's belt; she would probably have liked to rub her cheek on Julian's little scratchy beard, or to have sunk her face deep into Elise's thick, straw blonde hair, which gave off a scent of blossom when she tossed it and laughed. Most of all, though, she would have liked to go back up to bed with her husband sometimes on a Sunday morning and make love slowly and simply and gently, the way they once had, looking right into his eyes, sharing the breath from his beautiful mouth.

Regularly, over the papers and the orange juice, she would catch his eye and wonder if he was thinking the same thing – until he gave her one of his devastating pecks on the cheek, and she knew he was not. There was nothing more isolating than one of those kisses of Alistair's – they were bland and utterly passionless, they were literally boring her to death. And so, instead of a giggling return to the warm sheets, she would watch him go off alone to his study and in turn she would get on with the garden and the roast. She had become quite famous among their friends for her exquisite Sunday lunches: wine, meat, rich sauces, creamy puddings and honeyed liqueurs – every flavour in mouthwatering communion.

She finished the Cognac and stood in the doorway of the drawing room with her finger on the light switch. A great deal had happened in that room in the last twenty years. The important conversations had all taken place there – when Sophie got expelled from Scunthorne, or when, bizarrely, Luke got caught stealing another boy's tennis shorts when he had perfectly good ones of his own. She had been glad to have Alistair at every time of family crisis. Very often she couldn't help crying, but he always spoke so reasonably and thought so clearly. Most impressively, he had always understood and remembered everything the doctors said about Sophie and the anorexia and depression. It was in this room that they had quietly discussed their daughter, Alistair imploring her to be rational, laying out the brochures for the different clinics on the coffee-table.

Suddenly, Rosalind felt frightened they had done some things wrong, been very unimaginative. And why had she not insisted that Alistair come to a few more of Luke's rugby matches? She would never forgive herself for that.

With increasing fatigue, she thought of all the other events the room had witnessed. All those dinner parties, all those barristers and judges and their polite enquiries about the children, whose names they had plainly forgotten, each of them just sticking it out until they could talk to the other men, really. And, invariably, as the women talked alone over coffee, the room had heard how they had all been to the same places on holiday or for curtain material or party canapés at one time or another. It was interesting how, during these conversations, they had continued to smile at their coffee cups, a little tensely perhaps, as if *their* lives were arranged with some kind of insider knowledge, as if only *they* knew the best florists or the best piano teacher. Of course, in reality, all their lives were the same.

Had this made the other women uncomfortable? She thought about the triumphant faces and decided it had not. It had not particularly bothered her until the children went away to school and at once she had felt terribly lonely. Alistair had worked so hard and they never spent any time together as other couples undoubtedly did. It was not that she had ever wanted to be 'adored' and covered with sparkly baubles or to go on crazy trips to Antigua or Jamaica, as her sister and her various husbands had – that was not her dream at all. But she would have liked to put a few things in a bag and gone off to stay in a bed-and-breakfast in the countryside, visited a few pretty churches with Alistair telling her about the history. They could have gone for a country walk hand in hand, smelt the smoke and rain and grass and had a pub lunch, a lovely glass of wine under an apple tree.

But Alistair had *always* been working because their life was so unbelievably expensive. Once, disgusted by the bill for the silk wall hangings – on top of the school fees and the rented villa in Tuscany – she had asked him how dustmen or taxi drivers managed to support a family. He had laughed at her and had stroked her hair and not even bothered to reply. The trouble was, he loved things to be done in such an old-fashioned English way – just as her parents had done them, really, and she had always wanted to please him. He was so happy, so excited when she produced a huge Sunday roast for twelve people, just like those she had eaten every single weekend as a child.

She switched off the lamps and noticed the moonlight pooling on the wood floor, glinting on the club fender, curving softly over the vase on the mantelpiece. The drawing room never felt empty – it gave you the feeling that your children were hiding behind the curtains, shaking with laughter, or that one of them was crying piteously under the writing desk. It was always crowded with family – like every room in the house.

As she walked upstairs and along the corridor towards her bedroom, she could hear Luke watching TV and tapping away on his computer. She had stopped hoping he was working now when she heard the tapping going on. She wondered if he had actually been sacked. She was going to have to talk to him. He went out until God only knew when every night. He drank – you could smell it under the door from his room – and he had polished off almost a bottle at supper.

What was going on in his mind? She felt such a deep sympathy for Luke that sometimes it was as if she was him. She felt all of Alistair's little slights to him – particularly the way he never remembered exactly what Luke did for a living, so that Luke got into a terrible muddle and started boasting about his salary in a truly disgraceful way. But Alistair knew this, surely, and if he had thought about it for a moment, he might have seen that each one of these slights was like a razor nick to Luke, like death by a thousand cuts.

She went into her room and closed the door.

Luke stayed in front of his computer, drifting out of sleep into a DVD, then back into sleep, and then into a computer game until six thirty. Then he put on a sweater and went out – straight across the lawn – to the annexe for his beer with Goran. It was cool and misty and a little darker than usual. There was a smell of wet leaves in the air. He knocked on the door. It was Mila that answered. 'Hello, Luke,' she said. She had obviously been crying. 'Goran says we want be alone for talk. I am sorry.'

'Oh. Is everything . . . ?'

She looked away.

'No, that's fine. Just give him this, then,' Luke said, handing her the bottle of beer he always brought for Goran. Mila closed her eyes as she accepted it. She seemed agonized. 'I am very sorry, Luke,' she said softly, as if she was trying to speak out of earshot.

Luke was mystified.

'That's OK, Mila,' he said. 'I'll – you know – I'll see you tomorrow or something.'

She nodded, but both of them knew that the routine had now been broken for good.

Chapter 21

After his rest, Alistair had left Ivy with the lovely Meals on Wheels girl and the much-anticipated shepherd's pie, and pears with custard. He kissed her fondly, thanked the girl, whose name was Rebecca, for looking after her so well, and walked back to his old home. His leg was very painful now, but it was not a long journey. After all, his father had lived two streets along all Alistair's life.

Ivy had told him that the visiting times at Rosewood Lodge were between nine thirty and twelve, two thirty and six. When he woke up in his mother's old bed the next morning, he decided to visit Geoff in the afternoon. He wanted to think a little first, he told himself. He needed to work out what to say.

But, as the morning progressed, he realized that the scene was impossible to imagine. He heard the words 'Geoff, Ivy told me,' or 'Geoff, I've come because I know,' and then he was struck by what seemed like a deeply inappropriate amusement. He laughed out loud a couple of times and, imagining he was hysterical, took himself out into the garden for some fresh air.

At around one, he went out to the local shop and bought some crisps, chocolate and a microwaveable sausage roll, which he hoped did not absolutely insist on being microwaved. He ate this peculiar meal without tasting it at all and then he spent the early part of the afternoon attempting to read a history of the Ottoman Empire. He had brought it with him out of a long habit of making sure he always had something to read and he smiled sardonically as it occurred to him that this had proved an effective way of preventing all personal reflection.

The book had been given to him some years ago, rather

unexpectedly, by Luke as a Christmas present. The shaky biro inscription said, 'Dear Dad, I hope I've got this right. I think this was what you said you would have studied if you hadn't been a barrister. Anyway, it's a very good book by all accounts. Happy Christmas, from Luke.' He was not conscious of having mentioned to Luke his interest in the Ottoman Empire. He would hardly have discussed something like that with his son. Perhaps Sophie had told him.

The book had turned out to be by one of Alistair's Oxford contemporaries. He distinctly remembered a rather plump, scathing man, and a defining argument, during one of Philip's tea-parties, about who would 'be a darling' and go and get some more butter for the crumpets. They had decided to draw straws, but Henry Downing had refused to take part, saying he had been invited for tea and it was all very bad manners and Philip, as host, ought to go himself. Alistair could also remember seeing Henry waiting around, trying to corner the dons after their lectures with one of those elaborate questions that are really designed to showcase the scope of the enquirer's mind.

Of course, Professor Downing, as he was now, had been a huge academic success and the book on the Ottoman Empire was probably his life's great achievement. Alistair weighed it in his hand. Suddenly the cruelty and utter senselessness of this gesture struck him and he put the book down.

A local cab driver rang the bell at four and Alistair gave him the address of Rosewood Grange. 'Oh, yes, I know Rosewood,' the driver said. 'Visiting, are you?'

'Yes, I am.'

They got into the car.

'Your old mum, is it? Your dad?'

'My father,' Alistair told him.

The man calmly accepted this incredible information and flicked his indicator switch.

It was only a five-minute drive. Rosewood Grange was an ivy-softened modern building at the end of a short avenue of trees. Outside, in the small parking area, there were a good twelve or fifteen cars belonging to staff and relatives. As they pulled in, two little children came running out of the front door, straight into the path of the car. Fortunately they were driving slowly enough to stop. A frantic mother grabbed the children's sleeves and halted them. She mouthed, 'Sorry,' through the windscreen and the children looked ashamed.

Youthful energy curbed just a little too long, Alistair thought. They could hardly be blamed for finding Grandma or Grandpa slow and boring. He watched them getting into their family car. He could remember being five or six, running like that for no reason at all, merely to expend energy, to express life.

In front of the main entrance, there was a stretch of neat lawn. An implied route, from the bottom to the top, had been marked out on the grass by stepping-stones to the last few metres of the tarmac drive, over a paved forecourt and inside the main entrance. On the forecourt, which was bordered by two perfectly symmetrical beds of bright flowers, were parked three rather ghostly-looking wheelchairs for transportation of residents to and from their relatives' cars.

It was by no means a beautiful place in which to end your days, but it was not merely functional either. The overall effect implied that the designer's heart was in the right place, but that there had not been enough money for anything but the most basic ornamentation.

Alistair paid the cab driver and went up the forecourt, which had a slope, rather than steps, and through the open door into the reception area. He was greeted by a beaming young man, whose name, Dave Pelham, was written on a badge on his chest. 'Hello, sir, can I help in any way at all?'

Alistair explained he had come to see one of the residents, a Geoff Gilbert. As he said the name, the momentousness of what was about to happen thumped into his heart like a fist.

'I see,' the man said, narrowing his eyes. 'We've not seen you before, have we? We mostly just get dear old Ivy coming for Geoff.'

'Actually, Mrs Gilbert said she'd call and leave my name with you,' Alistair said.

'Ah, did she? Right.' The efficient young man flicked through a notebook. His nails were polished and he turned the pages delicately, occasionally licking his fingertips. 'Oh, yes. Here we are. Are you Alistair Langford, then?'

'That's me,' Alistair said, smiling, amazed once again by his exterior calm. He really was an incredible actor.

'That's fine, then.' The young man called out to a passing nurse, 'Um, Julia, would you mind taking this gentleman, Mr *Lang*ford, to see Geoff Gilbert?'

'Not a problem at all,' she said. 'How d'you do? I'm Julia.'

Alistair attempted to say hello but found that his mouth was too dry to speak. He managed to nod and they set off.

The interior of Rosewood Grange also maintained the designer's stand against the institutional look, but somehow less successfully than the exterior. Perhaps it was merely the presence of so much medical equipment, or perhaps it was the residents themselves, whom Alistair glimpsed through doorways as he passed, seeing them slumped in chairs with TVs playing softly in the background.

They walked down a long corridor. 'Geoff doesn't get many visits,' Julia said. 'His wife comes regularly, though.'

'Yes,' Alistair said.

'She's sharp as anything, isn't she? It's Ivy, isn't it?'

'Yes, Ivy.'

'I thought that was it. Lovely woman. She's not here so often now, but you can't blame her – she's no spring chicken herself.'

'No. She comes when she can,' Alistair said, speaking mechanically, and then feeling fraudulent for implying an intimacy with the facts of Ivy's life.

As they turned a last corner, past a desk with a dispensary, a receptionist and a few attendant nurses, Julia said, 'I do hope I haven't rushed you. We're brisk walkers, nurses. What have you done to your poor leg?'

'Me? I . . . The kneecap and shin are injured,' Alistair said.

He watched her wait for a moment, and then, having seen that no further explanation was coming, she said sympathetically, 'Dear me. How painful. Well, here we are. This is Geoff's room. Just come out if there are any problems and one of the nurses at the desk will assist you right away.'

'Yes. Thank you.'

She was still looking at him. 'Mr Langford, you seem a little . . . Are you OK?'

'Oh, perfectly. Thank you very much,' he said.

She took her hand off his arm and he watched her walk away to the desk. She leant over the counter, playfully tilting back her lower leg, and took a sweet out of a bag by the phone.

'Oy, you – get your own!' The receptionist laughed, snatching the packet away.

Alistair turned away from them and knocked. He got no reply, but as he leant towards the door, he thought he could hear voices and wondered if Geoff already had a visitor. He glanced back at the laughing nurses, hating them for their obliviousness. He was appalled at the casual way he had been abandoned at the door, subject to such profound uncertainties. *Were* there other people in the room? Why had the dreadful impropriety of this not occurred to the nurse?

He pushed the door open anyway, and immediately opposite him sat Geoff. In the first few moments of sensory comprehension, Alistair saw that he had become a very old man. He was much more drastically aged than Ivy, though there could only have been a few years between them. A portable radio was playing on the bedside table, which accounted for the voices he had heard in the room.

Geoff looked up at him and, divided by a deep cleft between his brows, his face appeared to crack with anguish. 'Oh, no,' he said simply.

Why was the fist always aimed so accurately at Alistair's heart? He cleared his throat and said, 'Geoff, I'm so sorry this is unexpected.'

Geoff shook his head and glanced down. 'Oh, no,' he said again.

Alistair felt unable to support his own weight any more and sat down on the end of the bed. 'Look, I'm sorry. I've obviously shocked you. I knew I would, really. How does one break a silence quietly? You know why I'm here, of course, I went to see Ivy yesterday and we had a long talk. I—' He broke off. From the window there was a view of the edge of the forecourt and one side of the lawn. It lay beyond a corridor formed by two walls. A car passed through this sunny gap, and the woman driver waved at someone who must have been on the forecourt, waving back. At the end of the lawn, the chestnut trees were moving in the wind.

'I'm finding it hard to know what to say,' Alistair said. He was aware that Geoff was still intermittently shaking his head. Had he been imaginatively equipped to picture this scene, Geoff's reaction would have been the realization of a nightmare.

'Oh, God, you must understand why I needed to come. Don't you?' Alistair said desperately. 'I'm getting old now too, but it's – well, it's never too late. Please, Geoff,' he said, 'are you angry? For God's sake, please don't be angry with Ivy.'

At last Geoff looked at him. He pointed at the radio. 'The cricket,' he said sadly, 'and it looks like rain.'

Alistair listened to the radio voices for a moment. It was not a cricket match at all – it was some kind of cookery programme. 'Then beat the egg whites until they're stiff,' said a brisk, female voice.

'Oh, no,' Geoff said. 'He says it looks like rain.'

Alistair put his head in his hands. In the background, the female voice went on, 'Take an orange and grate the zest, being careful not to cut into the white pith underneath. Orange zest is very high in vitamin C, so you can feel you're looking after yourself as well as making a lovely pudding.'

When Alistair took his hands from his face, he saw that Geoff had fallen asleep. Very gently, and with a kind of ceremonial reverence destined only to be noticed by himself, Alistair switched off the radio.

Why had Ivy not warned him? When she told him Geoff had become 'too much' for her, he had not imagined this. How could he have imagined this? He looked at the old man's peaceful, sleeping face: the anxiety about the cricket had fallen away and the deep cleft between the brows had softened. 'Well,' Alistair said gently, 'I'm your son. And that makes you my father.'

He glanced around him for a moment – at a photograph of Ivy on the chest of drawers, which, without anyone noticing it, had slipped sideways in its frame, half obscuring her face; he looked at Geoff's comb and toothbrush and at the little crucifix standing beside them. Alistair imagined Ivy had probably brought the crucifix in. He walked over to it and picked it up, taking in the effeminate little figure with the down-hanging head.

Growing older had brought a paradoxical understanding to Alistair. On the one hand, on peaceful Sunday afternoons, when he remembered his youthful arrogance and the elaborate means by which it had been schooled out of him, he was aware of a composition, of an artist whose sense of proportion lay far beyond the bounds of his own self-pity and desire. But, on the other hand, when he went over recent events, so many of them acquiring their narrative significance only by weird fluke, they seemed to him to have been generated by chance, by a computer, perhaps, spewing mathematical possibilities.

He turned back to the sleeping old man in the chair. Dear old Geoff. Dear 'tempted' Geoff with his corner shop and his piles of coloured pencils and his sugary fingers and his shoulders for riding on and his paper aeroplanes and his pint of bitter and his 'girls' . . .

And it had been too late, after all.

This did not suggest an eye for composition! At best the whole idea was recklessly unfinished, tossed out at humanity as if to solve an amusing after-dinner conundrum. If God existed, Alistair thought, He was not a great artist: He was a brandy-swilling dilettante with a comical frame of mind.

Alistair ran his fingers over the little arms and legs, the tiny wrists nailed to the cross. A faint memory stirred in him. Instantly he was sure he had seen this figure of Jesus often before. Wasn't it the one that had once stood by his mother's bed? Surely it was the one he had learnt to say his prayers in front of as a child?

What on earth was it doing here? He could not recall its having been in the box of his mother's possessions, which he had left for Ivy to go through. And, in fact, when he thought about it, he knew Ivy had never been much of a believer, so it was unlikely she had either been given it by her friend before death or chosen it afterwards as a memento. No, Ivy would have chosen a brooch, a headscarf, one of the little china dogs to remember her old friend June.

There was only one explanation. His mother had given her little crucifix to Geoff herself. This act, with its implied slow music of shared guilt and sympathy, and of enduring attachment, moved Alistair deeply.

Chapter 22

Luke's own beauty came as a surprise to him. He had not shaved or washed his hair for two weeks. He stood in a bath towel in front of the mirror and studied his sharp, handsome face for a moment, the dark-blond hair with its platinum streaks, the lightly tanned flawless skin, the neat symmetrical mouth and large grey eyes he had inherited from his mother. Losing weight had made his cheekbones stand out and he looked supernaturally lean as a film star. His stomach was flat and smooth and muscular. He took no personal satisfaction in these observations – except in the sense that they made him feel well prepared, well armed.

He patted on some aftershave, then he went into the bedroom and put on a sky blue cotton shirt and a pair of cream linen trousers. He chose a brown leather belt, his white gold and opal cufflinks and a pair of worn tan loafers. He looked at his reflection – Eurotrash to a T; effortless elegance achieved only with much idle consideration and at great expense. He would fit in perfectly. In fact, he would look better than Jamie Turnbull who had rather vulgar taste in clothes, who wore designer labels and silk shirts and indulged in celebrity-style caprices, like flip-flops and Nehru collars and diamond pinkie rings. Well-brought-up people who had been to good schools wouldn't dream of dressing like that, he thought.

He took the gun out of his desk drawer along with the last of the Zylamaprone™. The party didn't start until eight thirty, and since he hardly wanted to arrive on the dot, he had plenty of time for a joint. There was only a tiny bit of stale marijuana left, so along with it he crumbled almost a whole cigarette into a king size Rizla and, having crushed up the Zylie with the back of his hairbrush, sprinkled the powder on top. He was still not sure it really did anything – there was no raised heartbeat or chomping of the teeth or other obvious signs of euphoria, but he had been encouraged by the large number of 'Zylie-face' addiction-support sites: 'www.yourkidsandzylamaprone. com' had contained an incredible list of warnings, and people were not idiots after all – they must be doing it for something.

On the desk was the gold invitation to the Lapis-Lazuli opening party. He had managed to get it through Caroline Selwyn, the plain, brainy friend of Jessica's, who had worked with his sister at the *Telegraph*. They had bumped into each other at Zaza's. The brilliant idea that Caroline, who had never been popular or fashionable while they were at university, might have access to party invitations because of her work had occurred to Luke as he watched her come through the rotating doors.

He knew Caroline had always been interested in him. She used to visit Jessica when he and Ludo shared a house with her and it had been obvious she was always hoping to see him, too. Caroline had gone silent whenever he walked into the kitchen, which had made him uncomfortable. She was one of those girls who had crushes rather than boyfriends, and he knew Jessica was always trying to persuade her to see this made her unhappy. It must be difficult for ugly people, he thought, with a genuine twitch of compassion in his heart. It wasn't as if being ugly made you fancy other ugly people.

He waved at Caroline from his vantage-point at the bar at Zaza's. So, she still had the acne, he noticed, which was just bad luck at twenty-eight.

Having enacted his side of the reunion and suavely bought her a Cosmopolitan, he said, 'So, do you, like, get invitations to all the big parties and stuff?'

'Why would . . . Oh, what, through the *Telegraph*, you mean? Because I'm a journalist?'

He nodded and she watched him take a creamy gulp of his cock-tail and lick his lips.

'Oh. Well, you see, I'm actually not that sort of journalist. I write features – um, you know, the commenty bits – and I do this column. Political stuff, really. Not very *showbiz*, I'm afraid.'

'Oh. Oh, right,' Luke said, making it clear she had disappointed him. He knew Caroline thought he was thick, but he also knew she wanted him anyway – for his eyes and his mouth and his legs. He thought he could probably have asked her to come home with him now. 'Oh, that's a shame,' he said.

He lit a cigarette and blew the smoke away from her over his shoulder. Surely she could use a little initiative on his behalf, he thought. In the corner of his eye, he saw Caroline's hand move unconsciously across the bar counter, as if to draw him back.

'No, but I mean I can *get* them,' she said. 'I can *get* invitations – *easy*. Tash, the girl who does the diary, she's always got loads. Actually, it might be Sash – I should find out. Why? Where d'you want to go?'

'Oh, it's just this bar opening.' He turned back to her and smiled shyly. Then he shrugged, letting his hair fall into his eyes. He eyed her through it, then pushed it back with both hands, turning the gesture into a stretch that lifted his shirt an inch or two above his leather belt.

His stomach was boyishly smooth and brown and her mouth watered at the sight of it. She would have liked to pour the creamy cocktail over it and lick up the sweet rivers as they ran over that chest, round that sculpted back . . . 'A bar opening? Well, I'm sure it's no problem. I can just ask Tash – or Sash – if you want me to . . .' she said.

'Really? Do you really think so? *God*, that's cool of you.'

It had always been easy for Luke to get girls to do things for him. The ones he went out with at university had often done his washing and come by to cook supper. There had been a group. Sophie referred to them as Sweetie, Darling, Poppet and Dumb-Sloane, his four 'intellectual dwarfs'. He was aware that his father thought the girls he saw were idiots, too. It gave Luke immense pleasure to think the old bastard would have been sick with jealousy if he had met Arianne.

The invitation to the party had arrived in the post a week ago, with a note from Caroline giving him her phone number and suggesting they 'try not to lose touch again'. It seemed an odd phrase – they never had been 'in touch'. He hadn't been aware of the existence of Caroline Selwyn even once since bumping into her eight years ago when she had been revising for finals with Jessica in the Duke of Clarence.

Luke put down the invitation. It was still only nine o'clock and he went to the kitchen, took a beer from the fridge and stood on the garden steps to smoke the Zylie joint. He looked over at the annexe and thought Mila was probably sleeping deeply after another

331

hard day's vacuuming and ironing. He wondered what her surprise had been. And what had she and Goran been arguing about? Was it really so important they couldn't even let him in? It was his annexe, after all.

But he was not really upset about that – possessions, ownership had a limited value to him at the moment. It was just that it had seemed so unfair to have nothing but that weird glimpse through the doorway at what had become a sanctuary for him. He needed access to these other young people because a sleepless night was like solitary confinement. And it was always particularly hard after he had admitted that Arianne could only be in bed and that there was no chance of bumping into her somewhere. Goran and Mila were his only effective distraction from pain. For a second, he wondered if he actually needed them more than they needed him.

He kicked the heel of his shoe indignantly against the step. He was not going to stand around reliving bad sensations – what was the point? It was a habit to be consigned to the past, because this evening was going to be unlike any other in his life. He felt passionately that he had never truly done justice to himself before and that now was the time to begin. No matter how much he had felt condemned to genial mediocrity by Sophie or his dad, or by the teachers at school, he had always been conscious of a huge emotional and imaginative potential inside himself. In a sense, he had always been waiting to be discovered. He was sure that other people didn't feel like that; that people wouldn't *feel* unique, if they weren't.

Arianne was unique – and he had told her he loved her and expected it to be enough! How could that ordinary phrase have satisfied a girl like her? She had gone off in search of more because she deserved more – more drama, more glamour, greater depths of expression. She deserved technicolour, not the restrained palette of upper-middle-class English emotion he had offered her.

The irony was, if she had understood what he felt, who he really was, beneath these misrepresentations, she would never have left him! He had everything she needed. He knew he did.

Now he must show her how passionate he really was. Not words: action. She would be convinced by his determination – because it was really the only language she respected. She had played games with him when they had sex – 'Why don't you just *do what you want*, Luke? It doesn't matter what *I* want all the time, just please your*self* – *even if it hurts me*,' – and he had not understood that she was being serious.

The point hadn't got through until now. He had always thought you were meant to be careful with girls and to keep checking you were doing it right, asking them if it felt nice, because all the men's magazines told you how easy it was to get it catastrophically wrong. And girls wanted it just as much as men – he had learnt that very quickly at university: you only had to sit with a group of them and a bottle of vodka to discover that. And, of course, girls could fake it, too, which was terrifying – and he had always found it impossible not to worry that they were.

It was no wonder Arianne had got bored. It was as if he had not had any idea how to be a man! Until he was in possession of the gun, he had guiltily wished, every so often, that her injury after the crash had been far more serious than a few broken bones in her foot. If she had broken a leg and an arm, say, she might have stood still long enough for him to learn how to be a man.

But these were undignified thoughts. He had gone through this self-pitying stage and had come out certain that he had needed to lose her. He had been tested and now he was worthy of her. He would win her back simply by showing her the strength of his love.

He finished the joint, feeling almost painfully elated, and stubbed it out on the sole of his shoe. His heart pounded and he felt a little dizzy. Rosalind was watching him from the door to the hallway and she came into the kitchen. 'Oh, you look so *hand*some, darling,' she said. 'Honestly, why d'you have to go and ruin it all with those smelly cigarettes?'

He turned and smiled and her son's beauty hit her straight on. 'Oh, Luke, you really do look wonderful. I see the beard's gone. I can't say I'm sorry, darling.'

'Shaved,' he explained. He had suspected when he saw her standing there that he might find interaction quite difficult – he told himself he was simply too 'psyched up' – and he knew now that he must get away from the kitchen.

Rosalind put a glass in the sink. 'Did you eat the bits and bobs I left you? The chicken salad?'

'Yes, thanks.'

'Good. Where are you off to, darling?'

'Birthday party,' he said.

'Oh, how *lovely*. Whose? Do I know them?'

'It's Arianne's, actually.'

Her voice dropped with concern. 'Oh. You've been in touch, then?'

He walked over to the bin and put the empty bottle into it, concealing the untouched chicken salad he had scraped into it earlier. 'Yup. Been in touch,' he said.

Rosalind watched him tucking in his shirt. 'Where's the party?'

'It's this new bar. Place called Lapis-Lazuli.'

'What an unusual name. It's rather lovely.'

'D'you think so? I hate it. I think it's really vulgar,' he said, with a tense smile.

'Oh. Do you?' She laughed at the vehemence of his reaction. 'Well, I'm sure the name won't matter when you're in there. You'll all be dancing and listening to awful music on top volume, no doubt.'

'Exactly, Mum,' he said, kissing her cheek.

As Luke ran upstairs – he'd told her he had to get his wallet – Rosalind wondered if she ought to call her husband. Alistair had left a message on the answerphone (having carefully chosen a time at which she would be out), saying little other than that he was all right.

What on earth was her husband *doing*? she wondered. She supposed he probably was 'all right' and it was certainly doing her no harm to be without him for a bit: he was a heavy presence in the house and she did not want to cook for him. For his own part, Alistair must be glad to have his mother's old house to escape to. So be it, she thought.

The trouble was that she was genuinely worried about Luke and she felt it was time to address their son's eccentric night-time habits, his lack of interest in his work. Was he ever going to go back to his flat? These things had to be discussed at some point.

But must it be right away? She had no desire at all to hear Alistair's stupid voice. All that fear and guilt – it was revolting; she had detected a note of self-indulgence in it, and recoiled. Also, more essentially, she did not want to be 'the wife' just now. In fact, when she thought about it, she didn't particularly feel like being 'the mother' either.

No, it was a lovely evening and she wanted a drink and – for goodness' sake, she had worried about Luke for twenty-eight years and he would still be around for her to worry about tomorrow.

''Bye, then, Mum,' called Luke from the hall. She leant back on one foot to catch sight of him. He appeared to be wearing a jacket, which seemed crazy on such a mild evening, but she let it go. Let him wear a jumper in the sunshine and short sleeves in the snow, let him swim right after lunch and fill the machine with a mixture of darks and whites. This would be her temporary attitude – he was on his own this evening. Anyway, he sounded bright enough, she told

334

herself. For God's sake, he was going to a *party* – he was probably in danger of *having fun*. She switched on the radio for the gardening programme,

''Bye, darling. Have a lovely party,' she sang out, but Luke had already closed the front door.

Lapis-Lazuli was near the Portobello Road, just under a flyover covered with ragged posters. Jamie Turnbull and Liam Bradley had chosen a venue in the last remaining 'authentic' patch of the area, not far from the market-place. It would soon become expensive and fashionable like the rest of Notting Hill – and the flats overlooking the littered road would all be standardized with parquet floors and wet rooms, but for now there were still dealers on the corners, still kids on skate-boards, still the sharp, savoury smell of marijuana drifting out at the bus stops.

It was a warm evening, but Luke kept his jacket on, his fingers holding the barrel of the gun in the right-hand pocket. He felt strangely cold and was not sorry to be forced to wear the extra layer to conceal the gun. He decided to walk to Lapis-Lazuli as he was already in danger of arriving too early. In fact, it would be necessary to waste time dawdling in a large circle before he could reasonably think of arriving.

First he went up Holland Park Avenue, along Notting Hill, and then he took a right, down Kensington Church Street. At the bottom he walked slowly up and down the high street, gazing into the bright shop windows. There were shoes and blazers, bras and knickers, vases, cushions, négligées, salad bowls, bath oils, scents and hats. There were silk wraps and bikinis, earrings and trainers, CDs and stereos and surf-boards and books.

After half an hour or so, as the last shops closed, he made his way back in the direction of Portobello.

When he arrived, there were around thirty people waiting outside the entrance to the bar. Luke had assumed it would mostly be women who complied with the 'All that glitters . . .' theme, but the queue was so decked out with costumes it was almost too bright to look at. Men wore sequinned Stetsons, pale gold shirts, diamond cufflinks, gold leather trousers; girls wore sparkly high heels, gold satin dresses, glittering bracelets, metallic hot-pants. One girl had sprayed-gold skin. Everyone had a golden brown tan. Thankfully, there were just enough people in smart-casual to mean that Luke did not look painfully out of place, but he was, none the less, on the precarious boundary between 'too cool' to dress up and 'too boring' to make an effort.

While the queue moved slowly up the carpet, the golden invitations batted out light in aggressive backhands at the passers-by. By the entrance stood an enormous bouncer and beside him a girl in gold jeans who chewed gum frantically and flipped pages of names on a clipboard. Luke surveyed the crowd. These were people who would not ordinarily dream of queuing for a club. They were VIP guest-list people, they were 'So-where's-our-complimentary-champagne?' people: women who never made eye-contact, men who had perfected the nod of authority so the entry rope was up before they had even stepped out of the cab.

But all of them waited in line. It was obviously considered to be a very special occasion.

Ahead, Luke recognized a couple from the society pages in magazines. He knew that the girl was a model, one of the thin, ugly kind who always turn out to have billionaire fathers. Her boyfriend had gold dreadlocks, and Luke wondered if he had ever seen anyone so coked up.

The couple didn't speak to each other, except when they wanted to find or light cigarettes. As they waited, they stared at the road. Luke pulled his jacket round him, feeling sick with excitement and horror at the thought of what was concealed inside it: a little pocketful of darkness in the glare.

Gradually, the couple reached the head of the queue and, quite suddenly, they came to life. The man made a face at the doorgirl. Then he turned to his girlfriend and put on a voice – whining, camp, with an American accent: 'Oh, *man*, we have to, like, say our *names* for the *guest list*? This is *so* fucking *weird*. What's Jamie *doing*, the silly boy?'

His girlfriend searched for something in her bag. He sighed, pushed back his gold dreadlocks and, in what was probably his natural voice, he said, 'OK, so this is *Lay-dee Ann-er-bel Tun-der* and you probably have me down as *Si-mon An-der-son*?'

'Yeah, of course,' the doorgirl said, sounding embarrassed. 'I know who you both are.'

He grabbed Lady Annabel's arm. '*Honey!* We're *faymouth!*'

The doorgirl smiled at him apologetically, 'It's just the system we use.' Then she looked down. 'Um, Slick, this is *so* cheesy, but I just wanted to, like, take this opportunity to tell you that I *loved* your last album. What you did with the Brazilian peasant guy's voice was *so*—'

Lady Annabel interrupted, 'My tits are freezing off?'

Slick moved aside for her. 'You liked that? Did you really? You really did?' Then he followed Lady Annabel, lamenting in the voice again, 'Hey! She thayth she loveth what I did with my *mew*thik, and you don't even *cayer*. She was a nice girl. Nice kitty. Bring Slicky another.'

They disappeared inside and the doorgirl put her hand on her chest and closed her eyes for a second. Then she looked at Luke, blushing, and said, 'Fuck, I can't believe I was just *this* fucking far from *Slick*.'

'Yeah,' said Luke, vaguely. He had realized a few months ago that there were musicians you had only heard of if you were under twenty-seven.

'Oh, my God, *breathe*, Tanya,' the doorgirl told herself. Then she began to chew her gum again and, composure regained, raised her eyebrows at Luke. 'Name?'

Caroline had told him to say his name was Mike Cecil. The girl searched the list of Cs three times.

'Sorry, you're not down,' she said dully.

'What? But I have this invitation. They sent it to my newspaper. To the *Telegraph*, I mean. For *me*.'

'Oh, what, you're *press*?'

'Yeah. Press.'

'You didn't need to *queue*, then. Press can just go straight in. Yeah, you're on the *press list*. Mike Cecil.' She spoke to him as though he was insane, as though he had broken the natural order of things.

Luke slapped his forehead. 'Busy day,' he said.

The girl gave a thumbs-up to the bouncer. The cord was raised and he went in.

And, quite suddenly, he had the sensation of pushing off from a rock through cool, blue water, a cascade of ripples and fizzing bubbles by his ears. It was impossible to relate the interior of the bar to the hot, dusty stream of traffic on the road outside, to the filthy pavement or the gum-chewing passers-by. There were no windows in the room and consequently there was no time of day, no weather. It might have been early evening in New York or three a.m. in Saigon. The electric lighting was gentle and flattering, the music seemed to come from all directions at once, but also, by virtue of some clever device, to run off in streams around quiet areas where there were deep velvet seats and low tables. Access to this room seemed as privileged as a glimpse of the deep sea, or as an image of a distant planet.

The main room was not enormous, but the ceiling was incredibly high and there was a mezzanine gallery around it with matt glass in place of a railing, so it appeared that people were standing on the edge of a drop right into the centre of the floor. The ceiling itself was covered with a vast, apparently single mirror, and the crowd beneath daubed it with a gaudy, living fresco. The bar – as if to avoid design cliché – was unadorned black granite. Beside it, the DJ stand was elevated and glowing and behind the glass a girl in a pink Gap T-shirt was mixing house tunes, oblivious to the crowd.

There were a great many beautiful people in the room. Luke took them in. None of the girls looked older than twenty-four, though some had a fixed expression that suggested surgery or injections. They were all sleek, toned, compact, sizes eight to twelve, depending on their height. The men had all paid due homage to biceps, triceps, deltoid and latissimus dorsi, tastefully avoiding overdevelopment of the trapezius, which gave a man a thick-necked, rather useful look. Luke imagined with envy that these men all had developed pectorals, too – his were rather sadly deflated, these days. It was an incredible party to look at: a room full of narcissists, many of whom were paid to indulge their obsession.

Again, Luke tightened his hand around the gun in his jacket pocket. As his fingers touched it, he told himself that if he wanted to, he could, at any moment, make the whole beautiful room stand still. All he had to do was take it out of his pocket! He did not have to hurt anyone, he did not have to kill anyone; it would be enough simply to raise his arm.

He felt an inexplicable pang of sexual arousal – an image of Arianne, upright in front of him, pressed against a wall, her legs wrapped behind his. Her cheek and her hair scraped up and down the wall, up and down, up and down, her eyes were closed, her mouth slightly open; her weight was surrendered to the strength of his arms . . .

'Hey, Luke,' said a voice behind him.

He spun round. '*Caroline?* How come you're here?' he said.

'I just . . . well, I came after all. Sometimes I do,' she said, shrugging, 'for work.'

She was rather drunk. The alcohol had made her more confident and she smiled flirtatiously at him. Suddenly Luke was incredibly glad to see her. Actually, he decided, it was unbearable to imagine what might have happened if she hadn't been there. He felt himself beginning to panic. What had he been thinking? He didn't know a single person at the party! If Caroline *hadn't* been there, he would have been forced to stand all alone, dry-mouthed with fear, building himself up to some kind of action he had not even fully visualized. The impending moment of confrontation burned a hole in his mind.

He attempted to smile warmly at her.

She said, 'So, I've *already* had too much to drink. Dreadfully unhip. Letting a penniless hack near free booze is a very bad idea. I've been drinking champagne cocktails with the *Hello!* photographer, actually. Now *there's* a man who's seen all humanity.'

Luke knew he ought to respond, to comment, to expand, but all he could muster was, 'Shall we go to the bar?' He was desperate for the burn of alcohol at the back of his throat and could not stomach the rise and fall of this female voice any longer. He knew he must have a drink in the next few seconds or he would lose control of himself in some fundamental way, and although he couldn't say exactly which, it was frightening, none the less.

Caroline giggled. 'To the *bar*? . . . Oh, my God, Luke, I may keel over shortly, but OK. *You have been warned.*'

Luke knew perfectly well that she would have done anything he suggested and, as she followed him to the bar, the thought calmed him. While they waited for the drinks, he lit her cigarette and tried to remember he was good-looking and that he was the person everyone called to find out if there was a plan for Saturday night.

Caroline said, 'So it's a bit of a weird theme, don't you think? I mean, hel*lo*, is anyone aware of the *connotations* of this theme, the *irony*?'

The gun banged against his hip as he raised his cigarette. 'Irony?' he said.

'*Exactly*, Caroline laughed. 'I mean, that's what they must fucking be like at home – *Liam* and the one with the hair. *Jamie*, is it? *Christ.*'

Luke pretended to have understood her and laughed contemptuously too. He had no problem showing contempt.

She gasped. 'OK. Oh, my God, is that *Slick* over there? It fucking *is*. My little sister will completely hyperventilate when I tell her.'

Luke followed her gaze. Slick was standing with his arm draped over none other than Arianne. The gold dreadlocks snaked over her bare shoulder. She was wearing a plain white vest top and some denim shorts with a pair of pale gold stilettos. She had no jewellery on at all. She was like a sexually explicit remark among a thousand coquettish evasions.

'Oh, my God, that girl is *so* gorgeous. Not like your typical small-features, little-hips model, like *properly* fifties-screen-goddess-gorgeous. Look at those tits. How fucking long are her legs? She must be six foot.'

Thankfully the drinks arrived before Luke was forced to reply.

'Oh, I really, really, *really* shouldn't be doing this,' Caroline said, lifting the glass.

The taste of the drink was immediately reassuring to Luke. It was a strong Cosmopolitan, both bitter and sour at once and it made a hot path down his throat. 'So, have you been drinking all day, or what?' he said.

'No, no – just in the pub, after work. You know.'

He knew. He imagined a colleague or two had got her tipsy on pub Chardonnay and told her to go to the party and take a chance with him. With a bit of drink inside her it must have seemed like a good idea. He was intensely grateful to her friends.

Handling Caroline was going to be delicate, though. He would have to give her enough encouragement to make her stay, but not so much that there was a scene, he thought. How appalling if there was a scene and he had to admit he didn't fancy her and she left him on his own.

Anxiety drove him to put his hand into his pocket again. A gun had an unmistakable shape: it felt like nothing else in the world.

Then it struck him that he was a twenty-eight-year-old man at a party with a gun in his pocket and he wondered if he had ever been so lonely. He watched Caroline light another cigarette and blow out the smoke, playing a woman with nothing to care about but the warm air on her skin. She tossed her hair. 'So, Luke, why did you want to come to this thing so much, anyway?'

'This? Oh, I just know someone here, that's all.'

She waited. Then she giggled. 'Right. That's *it*, is it? Thanks for clearing that up. You're a man of few words, aren't you?'

Just then several kilos of tiny gold stars were jet-piped in streams out of tubes at each corner of the ceiling. Fans at floor level whipped them up in the turbulence so that everywhere you looked there were falling stars tumbling and sparkling in the lights. Caroline got some in her mouth and Luke shook them off his hair and brushed them out of the inside of his collar. People laughed and cheered and the DJ put on a new tune so that a huge group began to dance. It was all expertly choreographed.

340

'Fucking hell,' Caroline said, laughing and spitting and wiping her mouth. 'I'm deeply sorry if this is, like, your best friend's party or something, but this is the most pretentious place I've ever been to.'

'It's not my best friend's party,' Luke said.

'No, well, it couldn't be – or you wouldn't have needed me for an invitation,' she said, looking at him quizzically. Then her eye spotted something over his shoulder and she tugged his sleeve and pointed into the room. 'Oooh, hang on, *speech*. Jamie Wotsit's going to say a few words. This should be witty and incisive.'

Jamie Turnbull stood on the nearest available chair as if this saying-a-few-words thing was unplanned, but as soon as he spoke it was apparent he had been carefully wired up with a microphone. He did a little Japanese bow, with his hands pressed together, and then he raised his arms like a marathon winner. '*This* is a fan*tas*tic night for me. A fucking *dream come true!*' he shouted.

The crowd cheered and many people lifted their glasses.

'So *humble*, so *natural*,' Caroline whispered sarcastically, pursing her lips. Again, Luke was relieved that she was there. She was, in fact, the only voice of reason in the room and a deeply hidden part of him was aware of it.

Jamie went on, 'OK, so this crazy idea was born about two years ago – if my memory serves, it was over a Tequila Sunrise at Club Santo in Ibiza.' He saluted the DJ. 'Great night that, Layla. Anyway, I think my buddy Liam will agree it's been *quite a ride*.'

There was polite laughter as Jamie and Liam did a little pantomime of exhaustion together.

Caroline said, 'Didn't he just use his daddy's money?'

'So, what I need,' Jamie went on, 'is to see everyone with a wicked little cocktail in their hand because I want all of you beautiful people – and you are *beautiful* people, if I may say so –' There were more cheers, people raised lit matches or lighters, as if they were at a concert, hearing a real classic. '– I want all of you to drink a big fat toast with me on my – sorry, *our* – opening night.'

Caroline tipped a little of Luke's drink into her own nearly empty glass. 'Don't let me *do* things like that, Luke,' she said. '*Really*.'

'But before we all raise our glasses, I want someone to join me up here – if her heels will allow it. Arianne?' he said.

Involuntarily Luke darted forward, and Caroline glanced at him, surprised. Arianne reached an elegant brown arm up to the outstretched hand. The muscles in her long legs flexed as she climbed on to the chair. She kissed Jamie's cheek. He turned to the crowd and said, 'OK, so this girl right here is the *love of my fucking life* and I want you all to know it.' There were more cheers. 'So, it's, like, one afternoon we're walking around a little market and she mentions lapis-lazuli is her favourite semi-precious stone.' He shrugged, 'So I buy her the little pendant she likes and the kiss she gives me to say thank you – well, I name my bar after it. But the way I see it, there's nothing *semi*-precious about this lady, so I thought I'd get her something a little more fitting to mark the occasion.' Casually hidden in his shirt pocket was a diamond choker. He held it out to her, live and electric, on the palm of his hand. Then he motioned for her to turn so that he could fasten it.

It looked exquisite. Suddenly her neck was elongated and her face sat like a rare flower above it. There was more cheering and wolf-whistling from the crowd, and then the microphone grotesquely magnified the sound of their kiss all round the room. When Luke closed his eyes to block out the reality, he saw two vast mouths, two sets of giant, rubbery lips. After the kiss, one whispered something to the other and the sound was duly broadcast – the word '*love*', was it? Luke's mind fluttered in terrified circles. Was that Jamie's voice or hers? Was it 'love' or could it possibly – just possibly – have been 'shouldn't *have*'. He was trembling.

'Hey, are you OK, Luke?' Caroline said.

He realized he was shaking quite violently and he tried to stop, but it made no difference.

Caroline took the drink out of his hand and put it on the bar. He could hear her saying, 'Oh, no, you've got it on your trousers. They're such *wonderful* trousers, too. Look, I'm sure it'll come out if you use stain-remover.'

Jamie shouted, 'To *Lapis-Lazuli*!' and then there was a deafening roar from the whole ham-acting crowd and arms holding cocktail glasses were raised in every direction. The room had become a forest of waving trees, bearing strange fruit.

'Luke, shall we sit down?' Caroline was saying. 'Hey, we can sit over there. Let's get out of this fucking *mob* a minute. Yeah?'

She took his arm and he let the gun swing against her elbow as they walked. She pushed people aside. 'Excuse me? Hel*lo*? Ex*cuse* me? *Mind out the bloody way*.' By the time they sat down, there was a frenzy of dancing everywhere. They were in one of the miraculous oases of quiet.

'Shit, Luke, you look a bit ill, to be honest,' Caroline said. 'Are you on something? Should I get you some water or something?'

'I'm OK,' he said. Then a particularly violent bout of shaking took over his body.

'D'you know what?' Caroline said. 'I really don't think you are OK. I think I'm going to go and get someone. You've gone really pale and I just . . . I think you might need a doctor.'

She stood up and he put his hand on her arm. 'Don't. *Please* don't. There's no need for a doctor. It's just seeing my ex-girlfriend, that's all. OK? It's just the shock.'

'Oh,' Caroline said. She took this in, and then sat down a little despondently, the chair meeting her bottom sooner than she had expected it to. She pushed back her hair. 'Oh, right. So . . . so, who's your ex-girlfriend, then?'

He said nothing, but she caught on. 'Oh, God, it's not *her*, is it? The incredible girl?'

Luke nodded. 'That's why you wanted to come? To see her?'

He blinked for 'yes'.

'Oh,' Caroline said, 'right.' Actually, more than any disappointment, she felt a kind of relief. It had been petrifying to contemplate taking her clothes off in front of this perfect man. She felt glad to be unburdened of her libido, to be unsexed by his focus on another woman. It was easier, after all, to be the sympathetic friend rather than to suffer all that sharp hope and physical longing. She put her hand on his knee. 'So, how long ago did it end?'

'I'm not sure,' Luke told her. 'I've lost track.'

Caroline watched him for a moment. At her most bitter, when her acne had been at its worst, she had often wished one of the beautiful, popular set at university would suffer like this. Emily, Alex, Richard, Ludo, Georgie – she had hated them all for their effortless beauty, their perfect skin and their huge clothing allowances. Did they actually feel pain in clothes like that?

She had never been able to understand how her friend Jessica had existed so calmly, so normally, in the midst of it all, sharing a house with Ludo and Luke. Caroline had always been torn up with love and hatred of them. She remembered hanging round in Jessica's kitchen, tortured with self-disgust, hoping for a sexy glimpse of Luke after a football match or tennis or rowing.

Over the years since university, she had frequently enjoyed rerunning a delicious bit of mental footage. Once, Luke had come into the kitchen in very short cotton shorts. He did not bother to say hello, but pulled off his grass-stained T-shirt and, with a mesmerizing ripple of his abdominal muscles, threw it into the washing-machine. Then he walked over to the fridge and gulped down a half-litre of strawberry milk before he said, '*Beat* the wankers, three–nil.' Then he grinned and wiped his mouth on his arm. Caroline had thought she might faint, and after he left, she spilt hot chocolate on her Schopenhauer essay.

Now she took in his pale, sweating face. 'Oh, you look so ill, Luke. Normally it's your picture they have in the dictionary beside the word "health".'

'I just haven't been sleeping that well. I think I've been a bit depressed.'

'Hey, I know what it feels like,' Caroline said, nodding. 'I mean the whole nightmare of getting over someone and all that.'

Luke made eye-contact with her, his eyes searching her face. 'Do you?'

She was oddly moved by his interest in her feelings. 'Yes, of *course*. Fuck, I've had to get through it before. It's horrible. It's the worst pain in the world. You're all, like, "Does nobody *know* I'm in this terrible anguish? How can *God* let this happen?"' She shook her fist at the mirrored ceiling. '"*Is there anybody out there at all?*" You question everything, don't you? No, it's awful.'

Luke stared at her, sickened and afraid. To hear his private emotions parodied as if they were common to everyone – to people with acne! What did this unpopular girl know about the way he and Arianne loved? 'No,' he said, 'no, it's not like that.'

She recoiled. 'Oh. Well, look, I'm sorry. Obviously I have no idea what happened. Maybe you hate her. It's really none of my business.'

She looked away and Luke realized then and there that genuine loneliness was worse than humiliation. He said, 'No, I don't hate her. It *is* like you said. The only person I hate is him.'

'Him? What?' She crossed her eyes and prodded Luke's arm. '*Jamie-with-the-hair*?'

'Yes.'

'Why the hell's *she* going out with *him*, anyway? Other than the diamonds and so on, I mean.'

'No, no, she's really not like that,' Luke said. But as he spoke, he realized he wasn't sure if that was true.

'So maybe they're a real couple, then? Look, I don't want to rub it in – believe me, I sympathize – but maybe you just have to let go or whatever. You know what I'm saying?'

'No.'

'But if she's not in it for the wrong reasons, there must be something . . .'

He struggled to speak. He regretted placing his faith in Caroline, opening himself to this onslaught. 'No. All I wish is that he could just . . . just *die*.'

Caroline smiled gently. 'Oh, Luke,' she said, 'but you know you've got to forgive and forget, really. Though I have no idea if there is anyone mature enough to actually wish their ex well. Actually, if there is I really don't think we'd get on.' She frowned in sympathy. 'God, life's tough, isn't it?'

Luke said, 'I've got a gun.'

She scrunched up her face as if he had told a disgusting joke. '*Sorry?*'

He lifted the butt a little way out of his pocket.

'Yes, but it's not *real* though?' she blurted out without thinking. When she went over it later, she realized that even if it had been a replica it would still have been bizarre of him to bring it to a party.

'It's real,' he told her.

She glanced around nervously and spoke in a level, quiet voice, with a false smile on her face. 'Come on. Not really, though. *Really*, Luke?'

'I said it is. It's real.'

She was plainly frightened. He noticed the way her pallor made all the spots stand out. He felt terribly sorry for her. How could he have been so viciously superior about someone like Caroline? Who the hell did he think he was? He took a sip of his drink to give his mouth a little moisture. He could see her eyes flicking round the room. 'You're scaring me,' she said. 'Is that what you want to do? I don't understand.'

'No, I don't want to scare you, Caroline, I promise. I only want to scare him.'

'But why? What's the point? What's the point of scaring people? They'll just be *scared*, that's all, they won't *change*. Why would that stop them loving each other? What has a gun got to do with that?'

Caroline waited a moment. 'Luke, you're not crazy and this is *crazy-person* behaviour. You're *so* far from crazy, you're the most—'

'*Dull, conventional*. Go on,' he said.

'*No!*'

'Yes. That's what I am.'

'No, you're not. You're gorgeous, OK? I've been completely mad about you since we were at university – I'm amazed you never guessed. Well, *there – now you know.*'

What was he supposed to say to this? Because, of course, he had known and he really didn't care. This irrelevance, couched in such significant words, only added to the sense of madness. He stood up as if he might shake it off and restore order, but Caroline jumped up with him. 'Luke!' she cried out, then she clapped a hand over her mouth.

An image came into his mind of what she must imagine he was about to do. He saw himself slowly take the gun out of his pocket and fire it – just once – into the air. Cracks forked across the mirrored ceiling and several fragments dropped. He saw the crowds parted, backed against the wall, the music turned off and everyone motionless, as if they were expecting to be in a photograph, waiting for the flash to go off.

How could he make both the sense of madness and this image of Caroline's disappear? He thought about running – the sound of running, the way his breath would be jarred out with each footfall. But he stood still.

And then, suddenly, with a mouthwatering scent of peaches and jasmine, Arianne walked up beside them. She said, 'Hey, Luke, I *thought* I spotted you. How funny you're here. Isn't it an amazing party? Did you like the falling stars? They were my idea.' Before he had answered her, which did not seem to be part of her objective, she turned to Caroline and leant over to kiss her on either cheek. 'Hi, we haven't met,' she said.

'Hello,' Caroline said, stuttering her name abruptly, less out of awkward loyalty to Luke than because of the stunning effect of the presence of this girl. To be next to her was like standing too close to the edge of a platform as an express train roared past: sheer force of personality, rattling your teeth.

'Caroline Selwyn? Why do I know your name? Are you on TV or something? Oh, God, are you *incredibly* famous?'

'No, I'm not.'

'Thank God for that. Oh, no, *I know* – Jamie reads your column in the Saturday *Telegraph*. Is that right?'

Caroline looked surprised. 'Um, yes. Yes, it is.'

The two girls stared at each other, and it occurred to Caroline that Arianne might think she was the new girlfriend. *Luke Langford*'s new girlfriend — and after this amazing creature: it was delectable!

'Oh, *wow*, you're a *really good writer*,' Arianne said. 'Jamie's *always* saying so. I'll have to read it too, now I've met you. Make me feel *very* important over my morning cappuccino to actually *know* the columnist.' Arianne smiled so beautifully — it was such a prime example of a smile — that it would have required great spiritual poverty not to return it.

'Oh. Well, thanks very much. I hope he keeps reading it,' Caroline said. She was wildly flattered, in spite of herself. She loved the thought of the words she edited meticulously late into the night, with an uncouth tub of ice-cream and a bag of nachos beside her, finding their way into such glamorous hands. Just to picture it: her spotty face in the byline photograph on this girl's breakfast table — by the natural yoghurt, the honeydew melon, the serene green tea!

Then she remembered that Luke had a real gun in his pocket and she watched, in paralysed agony, as Arianne turned to talk to him.

Luke's face was so pale now as to make the grey of his eyes appear lurid and fake. He seemed to have become thinner in the last few minutes — his cheekbones stood out sharply. He was clenching both fists and smiling tightly.

Arianne said, 'You look . . . you look thinner, I think.'

'You look beautiful.'

'Oh, God — thank you. It's really just the necklace.'

Caroline said, 'It's an amazing present. I wish a boyfriend of mine would give me a present like that.'

'Yes, I'm so lucky,' Arianne said vaguely, as her fingers touched the little diamonds at her throat. 'I had absolutely no idea he was going to get me anything at all.'

Jamie appeared behind her. 'You showing off, baby?' he said, tousling her hair. 'Is she flaunting her jewels?'

Shamefaced, Arianne lowered herself so that he could drape his arm over her shoulder. Jamie laughed at her. 'You do what you like, sweetheart. I just want you to be happy.'

She smiled at him, then turned back to Caroline, who, she knew perfectly well, would be the only girl in the room self-effacing enough to grant her an opportunity to boast. 'You can see it if you like,' she said. 'It's Victorian. The clasp's a bit tricky so you might have to help. Here, I'll turn round and you can take it off.'

'Oh, sure, OK. No problem,' Caroline said. 'I'd completely love to see it.'

Jamie grinned at Luke. 'Women.' He shook his head, but there was little life in the sarcasm. 'So,' he paused for a sip of his cocktail – it was something pale orange in a martini glass, 'so, Arianne pointed you out to me. You had a brief thing before she met me, she said. You're not press, right? Are you?'

'No.'

'I didn't think so. What do you do, Luke?'

'I'm an account . . . I'm in advertising.'

'Right. Got it. You're a creative?'

'No, I—'

'Oh, OK, no, I get it. You're one of the guys who . . . What do you call it?'

'An account manager.'

'Jeeze. Sounds like a bank manager.'

'It's not. And you're a soap actor?'

'For now. I have a Hollywood film coming up.' Jamie smiled and took another sip of his drink. 'So, I'm wondering something, Luke—'

Arianne squealed. 'Oh, my *God*, you're so right! It does actually work fantastically as a bracelet. Do you think you could do that in the day, you know, with jeans and a sweatshirt or whatever? Or is it just too, like, HELLO, DIAMONDS?' She was talking to a campy, high-fashion gay man, who had joined her and Caroline.

Jamie observed them for a moment and then continued, 'Yeah . . . So, Luke, I'm wondering how you managed to get in, man.'

'Through the door,' Luke said. He could feel his mouth attempting to twitch out a smile and all the while he thought: Shoot him in the heart. He thought: This man is the thief of happiness.

Jamie was laughing. '*Through the door.* Oh, that's very funny. You're very funny. Do you have a light?'

Luke took the lighter out of his pocket and flicked up the flame in front of Jamie's cigarette. Jamie leant towards it. '*Boom*,' he said, widening his eyes. He puffed out smoke as he moved back. 'Oh, look, I don't mean to be a wanker. I'm actually a decent bloke, mate, I really am.'

Shoot him in the heart, Luke thought. In the heart. His fingers tensed round the gun.

'But it's, like, you *follow* her,' Jamie said. 'I mean, why do you do that?'

'I don't.'

348

'Come on, now. You sit on your own in the clubs she goes to, mate. I've seen you myself. We've all seen you. We make bets. In fact, I've won three hundred quid tonight. I *said* you'd find a way. I've got fucking *faith* in you, man.' He pointed at Luke with his head tilted affectionately on one side, then he lowered his arm. 'Look, you have two choices. One is that I can get Steve on the door to throw you out. Now, I'm totally happy for you to go with this option because it'll get more coverage: "Gatecrasher thrown out of exclusive new club, Lapis-Lazuli". You get the idea. That's a lot of free publicity, so you should definitely feel free to go with that option.' Then he put his hand on Luke's shoulder. '*Or*,' he said, 'or you can *just leave*. OK? Because I don't want to fuck you up any more than you obviously are already. Shit – you need to get some *self-respect*, mate. No woman is going to want you like this. You're *good-looking*. Be a *man*, yeah?'

Luke stared at the tanned face, the polished teeth through the fierce smile, the smooth black hair. This was a man. Jamie Turnbull was telling him how to be a man.

'OK,' Arianne said, 'finished the tedious girly stuff.' She smiled up at Jamie, who kissed her forehead. When he had his arm round her she looked calm, rather than angry or insatiable. Without those qualities, she appeared to be – happy. A little less sexy, perhaps, but happy. She glanced at Luke and he saw a brief burst of genuine pity in her eyes. Then Jamie lifted her off the ground and she giggled like a child as he tickled her ribs and swung her long legs out to one side, then the other. 'Put me *down*!' she said.

'Now, why would I do that? Give me eight hundred good reasons and I'll think it over.'

The giggling and the tickling and the swinging went on and on. Luke watched it as helplessly as a man in his pyjamas before a blazing building. At last two other friends came up to say hello to Jamie and he was forced to put Arianne down and greet them. One of them was a man in a showgirl costume with gold feathers on his head and bright red stiletto boots.

Luke's fingers let go of the gun and it swung freely in his blazer pocket, knocking against his leg, like a pendulum. Out of the corner of his eye, he could see Caroline. There she cowered, hating him, fearing him. He said her name and, reluctantly, she raised her eyes. She looked nauseous with terror.

'Caroline?' he said, as if he was not sure she had really acknowledged him behind the fog of terror.

'What, Luke?'

'It's not a real gun.'

'*What?*'

'It's a joke gun,' he said.

For a moment there was only shock, then every feature of her face wrinkled up in abject disgust. 'This was – what? Your idea of a *joke*? This was a *joke gun*? I mean, *what*?'

He had never been gaped at like that before. Never in his life. It was the kind of look you gave to people who shouted at themselves on the street, people who bit their own hands, people who spat and screamed at dustbins. He felt the various glossy layers between himself and these lost souls begin to dissolve. Off they came: class, education, wealth, schooling, blazer, loafers, cufflinks.

Just then, there was another huge shower of stars. He gazed up and watched them fall – into his hair, onto his eyelids; they slid weightlessly across his face. He could hear Arianne laughing with excitement. Waiters in white gold shirts were taking champagne cocktails around on trays. It was hard to see for a moment, through the strobe light and the tumbling stars.

'*Caroline?*' he said desperately. He reached out for her wrist and caught it. 'I – I've given you the wrong impression of myself.'

She laughed bitterly into his face. 'Oh, my God, Luke, that is just such a – such a *weird* way of putting it.' She tugged her wrist free, and as she did so he flinched and looked at her as if she had walked up and silently shot him in the stomach.

He said, 'Yes. No, I see what you mean.'

Then he turned away and she watched him slowly jostle out through the last snowfall of stars and the bouncing, golden crowd.

Chapter 23

Mila had thought the banging sound was in her dream, but gradually she realized it was coming from the annexe door. She called out sleepily, 'Goran?'

There was no reply. Right away she sat bolt upright and snatched the sheet up against her throat. She was afraid that they had been discovered, that she or Goran had been loud and the people had come over from the big house. They would be sent back to Kosovo – their whole journey was wasted – and there would be nothing but fighting and Albanians hating them for the rest of her life. There would be no joy, just evil graffiti on all the ruined beauty of her childhood; just foreign soldiers with their blank, impartial faces, queuing beside you at the market with their guns.

'Goran?' she said again, pleadingly, her voice weak with fear.

'No, it's Luke,' came the answer.

'Oh, *Luke*!' she cried out. And suddenly she felt that abundance of vitality, of joyous good health that only comes after a lucky escape. She thanked God as she hurried about the room, looking for her clothes. Hanging on the old hat-stand, she found her T-shirt and her long cotton skirt and pulled them on quickly, knocking over the children's globe beside the pile of tennis rackets. The globe lay, spinning on the floor for a moment and she muttered in irritation as she picked it up and set it back on its stand. 'I am just one minute, Luke,' she called nervously. 'Very sorry.'

Luke pressed his ear to the door so that he could hear everything Mila was doing: she went into the shower room, water ran briefly, she came out, a metal hanger was knocked clanging on to the floor, then the camp bed was shifted and the two halves were folded and locked together. At last he heard her footsteps coming to the door.

Her hair was all fluffed up from brushing. She was slightly hysterical. 'I'm sorry I am long time. I sleep,' she explained. 'Luke, you know Goran is drive in cab now?'

'Yes,' he said.

She gazed at him, puzzled at first, and then, with a plummeting acknowledgement of her own capacity for self-delusion, it occurred to her that Luke was going to throw them out of the annexe himself. Why not? Goran had been so rude when Luke came round early the morning before – it had been unforgivable to make her tell him to go away. She and Goran had been arguing anyway, but after that she had been too angry to speak to him. She had hissed at him what an idiot he was to show disrespect to Luke in that way – that Luke had virtually saved their lives, *where the hell would they be without him*? – and then she had locked herself in the shower room until he gave up on tapping at the door like a little brother. He took ages to go away – he just kept telling her to 'relax', asking her, 'Why do you care so much, Mila? Just *relax*.'

It was perfectly obvious why she cared so much! *Relax?* How could she, when they were beggars, nobodies, who had to guard what little they had with their lives or they would end up in one of those bunk-bed boarding-houses with cockroaches and thieves. Did he have a *relaxing* solution to that? After half an hour or so she came out of the shower room to find Goran in a dead sleep of physical exhaustion. His hand still gripped the unopened beer Luke had passed her through the doorway. She eased the bottle out of his fingers and, as she did so, she thought about how it had been those very hands that had sold all her jewellery to an Albanian woman. She had cried and cried when he did that.

'But we agreed. It's for our bus fares. Our *future*,' Goran had told her, stroking her hair. 'It's worth so much more than a few rings and necklaces, little one. You're too beautiful to need jewellery, anyway.'

He snored a little on the sofa and her mouth curled in disgust. She longed for her pretty things. All other girls had pretty things, but not her. And now, to top it all, Goran had been unforgivably rude to Luke, the one source of comfort and beauty in their lives.

And now here Luke was, about to throw them out. She could see that he wanted to come in and she let him pass, remaining in the doorway, utterly stiff with despair. She looked out into the garden for a second or two at the place where Luke had been standing. The temperature had dropped a little and it felt as though it was going to rain. For a second or two, she missed her mother desperately.

Why had she come to this country to work like a slave, anyhow? To be spat at by those angry pink faces at the port with their weird signs and their chanting? Had it been her life's ambition to scrub and clean luxurious houses, to be tortured by the sight of other women's beautiful clothes, by other women's unused kitchens? Why had she ever listened to Goran? She could have gone somewhere else, on her own, somewhere life was much easier . . .

She heard Luke's shoe scuff the floor and knew she must turn round. She closed her eyes tightly, and, with the little energy she had left in her tired body, she decided to work a miracle. Mila had been born with a natural talent for optimism. She was deeply grateful for it: it was all that had got her and her brothers through a childhood punctuated by air strikes and bombs, and by doubt in what the adults were doing. She summoned it up in a kind of prayer, or perhaps it was a spell, really, since it was not on God but on her own body that she called for help.

The familiar sensation spread through her: hope. Perhaps, she told herself, Luke was not going to throw them out, but merely wanted to make sure they had not damaged anything. Immediately, the thought took hold – just as hope always did, no matter how bad things were; it was like a desert plant. Yes, she told herself, of course that was it! Goran was so big and clumsy – he ate in such a disgusting, dog-like way – she was not surprised if someone as elegant as Luke was simply *concerned for his family property*.

Luke stood beside the old pink sofa, running his fingers over a few of his county sports medals, which were piled on the table. He noticed Mila smiling at him and watched her shut the door. He said, 'What happened yesterday? You didn't want me to come in. Were you having an argument?'

Mila was confused. Luke always spoke so quickly. It infuriated her that she needed Goran to translate.

'You and Goran?' he prompted. He shook his fist for anger. '*Yesterday?* When I came with the beer?'

She knew the word 'beer' and immediately she understood. OK, so he was offended, she told herself. But she would stay calm because she would simply apologize and Luke would forget all about it. That was what was going to happen. She laughed tensely. 'Oh, I am understand. Argument is fight of words, yes? Yes, it is argument. Please I am sorry, Luke. Very sorry. Goran also is very sorry.'

'Forget it,' Luke said. He was not sure why he had mentioned it.

'Please, Luke. He speak bad to you. I know this. Please.'

'Look, I said it's OK. Forget it.'

Mila thought her heart might break with gratitude. 'Thank you.' She blushed, and then she said passionately, 'Goran is angry man sometimes. He is *stupid* man.'

Luke was shocked by this assertion. He was used to seeing Mila tease Goran, but fundamentally she always seemed rather afraid and obedient. Goran only had to tell her to stop joking around and open his beer and she did. It amazed Luke. He had often wondered if women were simply more respectful where they came from – if Serbian women, unlike English ones, thought men had a purpose, a real place in society – or if Mila's respect for him was due to some special power of Goran's. Luke would mull this over as they shared an early-morning beer, while he tried to banish his latest memory of Arianne: her bright shape whisked past obliviously to a table, or flickering by in a cab, or waving at him in a strobe flash from a crowded dance-floor.

He would observe Goran and wonder what this tall, rather awkward-looking man had that he so obviously didn't. How did Goran command female respect? Luke had been forced to admit he was jealous – jealous of a man who drove a taxi all night and had to wear someone else's old trainers because he had no shoes of his own.

But perhaps he had been deceived in this, as in so much else.

'You think Goran's stupid, Mila?' he asked.

She sat on the edge of the sofa and brought her knees up to her chest, her bare toes curling under the hem of her skirt. 'Sometimes I think. Yes. Sometimes I hate. Sometimes I . . .' She gripped the sides of her face hard, shaking it in her hands.

Through the darkness, Luke studied this display. After a while, he said, 'So why string him along, then? Why don't you just dump him?'

It was a maze of colloquial English. 'Again I do not understand you, Luke.' Mila sighed. 'I am sorry.'

'It's OK. I didn't think you would.'

'I am sorry, Luke.'

He wished with all his heart that she would stop saying sorry to him. Why did he deserve her apologies? Was she so low that she must apologize to a fool with a gun in his pocket, which he was too scared to fire? He felt a pulse of hatred. But hate could not be maintained:

354

it involved too direct an acknowledgement of another person, of the world outside, and his focus returned quickly to the narrow corridor of despair.

There was silence, and then came the sound of the neighbour's cat thudding off the fence on to its pads. It leapt on to the windowsill in front of them. Because it was not possible to turn on lights at night without drawing attention, the only means of visibility in the annexe were the moon and the enduring London glow. The cat seated itself, blocking out the fragmented view of the lawn, and around its soft body there bristled a halo of silverish-orange light.

Mila watched Luke staring at the cat. She decided he looked reassured that they had not broken anything or wrecked the place and she began to relax. Her shoulders sank and she crossed her legs; she leant back a little on her elbows. She enjoyed staring at him – he was so handsome you always wished you could take a photograph. She remembered pretending to sleep in the back of the car on the way here from Dover and hearing Goran ask Luke if all English men were as handsome as he was. Luke had said they were all far *more* handsome! She had not been able to believe her ears at the time. And, of course, she had been right not to – Luke was just being modest and good. He had done so much for them – saved them from the horrors of boarding-houses and extortionate rent – out of the goodness in his heart. She hated this French girl he spoke to Goran about for hurting him so much. How could a woman undervalue a man like Luke?

Then Mila had an idea and she clapped her hands. 'Oh, I am forget everything! I am *stu*pid girl! Luke, I tell to you I have present for you – yes? Not *big* present, but . . . I tell this, yes?'

He looked at her blankly and then he recalled that she had told him she had some kind of surprise for him. He had mentioned it to Goran when he collected the gun and Goran had not known anything about it.

'Oh . . . yes,' Luke said. He felt exhausted by her enthusiasm, pummelled by her smile. 'You really don't have to do anything, Mila. Really.'

She dismissed this with a flap of her hand. '*Yes!* Is not *big* present. I just – I say thank you, sincerely,' she said. 'I get it?'

He felt he would be incapable of a show of gratitude and wished she would drop the subject, but her bright, pressing manner told him she would not. It would be easier to give in. 'Yes, OK,' he said.

He flopped down on to the sofa despondently, and she rushed behind him to the back of the room where there was a chest of drawers. He heard a drawer open and something removed from a paper bag. It was a faintly nostalgic sound . . . a Christmassy sound . . . his mother depositing a stocking packed with little parcels at the foot of his bed in the early hours of Christmas Day. But no pleasant thought could long have survived the atmosphere in his mind.

Mila was humming a tune. Her vitality was so senseless it began to make Luke angry. What was there to be so excited about, for God's sake?

She held out a small brown cake on the palms of her hands. 'Is Serbian cake,' she said. 'Is for you. I make in Mr Hugo Johnson apartment. It is easy. Luke, no people they do not use these good kitchens and everything it is *beautiful*! I just quickly do' – she mimed mixing in a bowl – 'and I put the cake inside there,' she opened an invisible oven door, 'and why nobody is care? Then I iron all shirts and then it is ready!' Suddenly a thought jolted through her thin body and she looked afraid. 'Luke, I pay money the eggs and all this – I *buy* it. You understand this? Is not take it from Mr Hugo Johnson. I pay *money*.'

'No, of course,' said Luke. 'Of course you did.' So, she had spent her hard-earned pennies on ingredients for a *cake*. For *him*. It was pitiful and somehow sickening. He said, 'Thank you, Mila. It's lovely.'

'No, you do not know! Is just to look. You try? You think crazy, but I tell to you cakes it is good in late night! *Yes?*'

'Yes,' he said, smiling with her, wondering how life could be so menacingly strange, experience so diverse. The truth was, though, he had eaten nothing that day, having thrown away each of the meals his mother had left for him in the fridge while she was out at work, and his stomach rumbled at the sight of the cake. He could smell almonds . . . honey, was it?

Mila spoke in a sing-song voice as she unwrapped the clingfilm: 'You think, *Mila she is crazy*, but is *very good* . . .' she said. She giggled as if they were being very wicked together. '*Cakes in late night!*'

Experience was diverse and yet it was connected. He grinned back at her and remembered Arianne, wearing nothing but a fluorescent yellow G-string that was almost blinding against her deep tan, sitting brazenly in a room full of people after a dip in Ludo's pool. Water streamed off her hair and quietly ruined the silk cushions. She was cutting up lines of coke on the coffee-table. He remembered her swivelling round to admire a compact, muscular man walking across the

356

room. Then she had tossed over the rolled fifty. 'Baby? Have a sniffle? It's *very good* . . .'

Mila handed him a slice of the cake. He looked at her face. Was this innocence? He would not have trusted himself to know. He tightened his fist and said, 'Thank you. It's lovely.'

'First you *eat*, Luke. Maybe you are . . .' She mimed cartoon sickness, goggle-eyed, tongue lolling, throttling herself. It was slightly obscene.

'No, no,' he said, wanting her to stop.

He began to eat. The cake was delicious – it was moist and heavy with almonds; it compacted in sweet, dense pieces between the fingers and poured honey into the mouth. Mila watched him with an expression of insuperable pride. 'More?' she said, before he had even finished the last piece.

Luke had realized that the intense sensation racking his body had in truth been nothing more than simple hunger. He was a little dismayed by this as he had thought his heart was breaking. Actually, he wanted more cake. 'Um, OK. Yes, please,' he said. 'It's delicious.'

Mila giggled with pleasure and hurried to cut him another slice. Her bare feet danced, swaying the hem of her skirt, and she was singing a song in her own language, which he had sometimes heard Goran sing.

'*Samo nebo sna, koliko te volim ja* . . .'

The act of eating had returned Luke to his body. As Mila came back with the cake, her face so astonished and dumbly grateful, he was instantly overwhelmed with sexual desire. He touched her cheek and, before he could withdraw his fingers in astonishment at this behaviour, she had turned towards him and closed her eyes. He studied the face: was this innocence?

Then he pulled her down on to the sofa beside him and undid his belt.

He had never treated a girl like that before and disgust made him unable to ejaculate. She did not seem to notice. He rolled off beside her and she pulled him close, then kissed his hair and his hot forehead. He wanted to run away from her, but she clung to him, her skinny arms and legs holding him down like a baby monkey on its mother's back. He waited in agony, watching a cloud of flies circling and circling in the light outside the window.

Though it felt like very much longer, it was just ten minutes later that he said, 'Mila, I have to go now.'

She tightened her whole-body grip for a second and pressed her cheek against his. She sighed. 'Yes. You must to go in your house.'

He did not understand her implication. 'Yes,' he said.

'It is beautiful in there?'

He watched her dreamy face, feeling irritated. What did she want? He only wanted to get away. 'I have to go, Mila,' he told her, lifting her skinny arm off his chest.

'Yes, Luke,' she said, moving aside. Then she smiled at him sweetly and he felt his stomach churn with fear.

He knew immediately that this was not just ordinary, physical fear. He remembered the time Sophie's ouija board had spelt out 'D-I-E-S-O-O-N-L-U-K-E'. Ludo had been so convincingly afraid that Luke had believed him when he swore he hadn't pushed the glass.

He felt himself beginning to shake again, just as he had in front of Caroline at Lapis-Lazuli. He pulled up his trousers but was unable to fasten the belt. As he leant down for his jacket, he allowed Mila to catch him in her arms and kiss his impassive mouth. Then he went out into the dark garden and closed the door behind him.

Mila lay still for a minute or two, smiling in the darkness, embellishing the short, brutal experience with all she knew about hope. Mixed into the rough action of Luke's arms and hips were thoughts of huge boxes of earrings and bracelets, of pots of nail varnish in every colour of the rainbow and of big, white houses in Holland Park from which you never heard guns. She laughed with excitement at the possibilities her body had received.

She knew she was being silly, but she couldn't help it. What was wrong with getting a little carried away? Was it better to be like Goran and think everyone was a liar and that even your mother would betray you? The world wasn't like that. If Luke married her one day – not straight away but one day, when everything was different – then she might have a cleaner herself. Goran would always be her best friend, of course.

She cut herself a slice of the cake and ate it hungrily. It really was one of the best she had ever made and it was almost half gone now. And why had so much of it gone? Because Luke had *adored* it! She had known he would. She could not believe Goran had been so against her giving it to him. He was just jealous, though, she knew that. But she really didn't want to think about that right now. She told herself she was far too excited and happy to think about arguments with Goran. And yet she found that this was exactly what she was doing . . .

One of their most recurrent arguments – in fact, it had contained the essence of all the others – had been triggered by a picture of the Virgin that her mother had on the kitchen wall. Goran had wanted to know *why*, if you please, were Mary and Jesus always *beautiful*, always *cutie-pies* like Hollywood stars? When he had first brought it up, he said, 'You Bible-bashers are so simplistic! It's dangerous!' and she had to put her hand over his mouth to make him shut up because her mother might easily have heard and she already disliked Goran.

He had never been able to leave her parents' faith alone. Pick, pick, pick. It was typical of him. Nothing could be beautiful in his world, could it? There was just work and sleep and stupid pride and the big, empty sky at night, waiting to swallow you up.

Now she laughed secretly as she tipped cake crumbs off the palm of her hand into her open mouth, her arm pressed lovingly against her stomach. Goran had been wrong about the Virgin, as he had been about so many things. Of course goodness and beauty went together – you only needed to meet Luke to see that.

Chapter 24

Are we really so separate from one another that in spite of all we say about the great nuclear forces of love and hate we actually forget one another's existence from time to time? The truth is, great tracts of experience are taken up in breathing and blinking, in sweating and digesting and not in loving or hating at all. No one who loved Luke – Ludo, Jess, Rosalind, Sophie, Alistair, even Suzannah – had any idea how unhappy he was. And not one of them was thinking of him at three in the morning. He might as well have not existed, so far as the rest of the world was concerned.

Outside the house, neatly parked cars shone in the streetlight. Dustbins had been lined up for collection the next morning. A light went on and then off again in a window and there was a distant hiss of air-brakes from the main road. Inside, the house was dark and warm. The window from the drawing room on to the garden was slightly open, but the air was so still that the sky seemed to be holding its breath. The spiny tree that tapped incessantly against the glass if there was a storm, was entirely motionless. In the hallway, an umbrella, which had not been touched for months, slipped and rotated in the umbrella stand, knocking against the hall table. A few rose petals drifted off the huge blooms Rosalind had put in a vase.

The house was at peace. There was linen folded in the airing-cupboard, bottles of milk lay cool in the fridge, houseplants budded in the conservatory, and in the pantry were new jars of strawberry jam, which Carol made each summer and gave out to each of her friends. Rosalind had never had the heart to tell her that Alistair always took marmalade and that she would never get through more than a jar a

360

year on her own. But the huge jars stacked up, bright red and jewel-like, the sweetest of each year's strawberries and a proof of friendship.

The church clock at St Ignatius, which went unheard in the noise of the day, carefully struck the wrong hour. Rosalind turned in her sleep and muttered the words 'In a minute'. On her bedside table was the pile of newspaper clippings about Alistair, which she had put into an envelope. A car skidded by the traffic-lights on Holland Park Avenue and raced off towards Shepherd's Bush. It was still dark.

Luke sat in his bedroom with the gun in his lap. In his hand was a cigarette, and although he did not often remember to raise it to his mouth, he watched the way the smoke was drawn helplessly through the open chink in the window, only to be lost in the trees.

It had not occurred to him before to kill himself. Of course, he had always enjoyed the notion of how sorry everyone would be as much as the next man; he had made mental drafts of suicide notes during melancholy bus journeys or rainy afternoons, and he had even imagined what music should play at his funeral. But he knew perfectly well that his fantasies lacked authenticity, because when it came to the actual dying bit, he always imagined being safely discovered.

What would it *feel* like actually to *mean* it?

His sister had almost meant it. She had meant it to the extent of effectively demonstrating how not to do it. Starving yourself was obviously extremely slow and painful. With painkillers the nurses just pumped out your stomach and then you were still alive and there was kidney damage on top of the rest of it.

But Sophie always overcomplicated things. That poetic, artistic side of her nature, which Luke knew she blamed for all the trouble she had in accepting the harsh world, was, in fact, what saved her from it. To kill yourself you did not need poetry or art, you needed one of two charmless gods: the Great Height or the Loud Bang.

He wondered dispassionately what exactly was wrong with him and his sister. People met them and thought they had everything. Once, someone had said precisely that. Who? Luke thought for a moment, while he exhaled smoke, and then he remembered that it had been Ludo, when they were about twelve. Rosalind had just put out some ham sandwiches and orange squash for them. They were playing ping-pong in the cellar, or 'The Cave', as it came to be known. There were James Bond posters down there and a chemistry set and a dartboard and Sophie thought it stank of 'boys' smelly trainers' and never intruded. It was a haven.

Ludo flopped on to a beanbag and said, 'You know what?'

'Nope.'

'OK. So what I think is, basically my family might have better cars and the swimming-pool and all that, but I think you don't really need all that stuff. I've worked out you only actually *need* to have a Gamesman and a decent colour TV and a nice house like this.'

Luke stared at his friend while he crammed a ham sandwich into his mouth. He wondered if Ludo was going to eat his, because it didn't look like it.

Ludo took a philosophical mouthful and spoke through it: 'Basically, Luke, why you're really lucky is because you've got all the stuff you *need* and also you all live here together. And plus your mum *cooks well* and everything.' Ludo held up the sandwich, which was cut in neat triangles, crusts off, to add undeniable weight to his point.

Luke had always known Ludo mythologized the happiness of the Langford family. Ludo's parents – Sandro and Isabella – were engaged in a long and acrimonious divorce, which dragged on from Ludo's tenth birthday to well past his fifteenth. At Ludo's house in Knightsbridge there were always telephone arguments to overhear – 'No, no, no, darling. That is *my* fucking villa, Sandro, you *hijo de puta madre*' – while you played on the Gamesman and ate duty-free jelly babies for dinner. Luke was sometimes embarrassed by these phone calls, but Ludo appeared not to notice. It was as if rows were just the background music of his childhood and he continued to be his usual mischievous self, always the daredevil at school. For a while the daredevilry bordered on kleptomania – until a pillowcase of stolen pop-music cassettes and chocolate was discovered in his room and Isabella sent him to a Harley Street psychiatrist.

Luke adored Ludo and found nothing but charm in his friend's childish psychoses. The ruleless paradise of Ludo's home life only added to his glamour, so when he went and said something about how he wished his family could be just like Luke's it was very unsettling. Luke's entirely reasonable envy was interrupted. The BMX bike, the video-player in Ludo's bedroom, being allowed to order takeaway pizza whenever you wanted it and to watch 18-rated films – these were the things that mattered, weren't they?

Luke felt unhappy and asked if he could have Ludo's last bit of ham sandwich – if he wasn't going to eat it, of course. The sandwich was duly chucked into his lap.

'You've got everything, really, you and Sophie,' Ludo said. 'Sometimes I wish I *was* you.'

As he got older, Luke realized that this was unquestionably the way it seemed to an outsider. You pulled up outside the gleaming white house in Holland Park, you saw the sun on the bright red door and you thought safety. You thought family Christmas, birthday suppers, a mother who remembered to ask about your doctor's appointment. It was ten million miles away from the wars on the news; there were no stinging flies, no monsoons, no bombs, not even any volatile Continental-style emotions and divorces.

So, in that case, what was wrong with him and Sophie? It was as if there was a ghost in the house, stealing joy. Why had Sophie starved herself rather than eat her mother's meals and laugh and be happy? Why, after Sunday lunches, had he always sentenced himself to feminine exile in the garden with Rosalind while Alistair and Sophie debated at the table, like father and son?

It was mysterious. Family life was intricate. And he was tired of it now.

Rosalind had always been a passionate, all-weather gardener and Luke had stood out there with her in all kinds of conditions. He had consumed mugs of tea while the cool spring breeze rustled the forsythia; he had clinked ice in a glass of Pimm's while the sun beat on a honeysuckle vibrating with bees. But, just then, it was a memory of standing in the snow with her, tying clematis to sticks before a storm that strangely intermingled with the cold feel of the gun against his temple.

Of course, he had never had any interest in gardening, but he hoped his mother imagined he had. Then he gritted his teeth against the blow.

It is beautiful and terrifying at once to acknowledge that the circumstances that alter our lives are often dependent on the slightest chance. A tiny flashing light and a single high-pitched, electronic beep saved Luke's life. Had he put his phone on silent, he would have died. Rosalind would have rushed into the room to find her son's blood, bone and brain dispersed over the wallpaper.

Slowly, Luke's eyes found the mobile phone, which continued to flash on the desk where it had been sitting for days on its charger. His finger moved off the trigger. It was not that he was interested in who was calling, but he wondered why the phone was going flash-flash — almost as if he had never seen this phenomenon before. The curiosity he felt was bodily, basic as the sense of smell. He picked it up and read the words 'Dad MOB' on the screen.

At that moment Luke could not have evaluated the oddness of this. It was three in the morning, but the middle of the night might as well have been the middle of the black ocean for all the sense he had left of civilization. And now here came a little bottle bobbing towards him from nowhere. He touched it curiously, expecting nothing and yet feeling instinctive dread. His was the motiveless enquiry of a sniffing animal.

'Luke?' the voice said. 'Luke? Can you hear me? Luke?'

'Yes?' It was a curious, hollow sound.

'Oh, you are there. Luke, it's me. It's Dad. I – look, it's the *middle of the night*,' Alistair said firmly, as if it was Luke who had called him, 'but I just . . . look, you'll think I'm crazy, but I couldn't sleep and even though it's an *entirely inappropriate* time, I thought – perhaps wrongly – I thought that, well, you're so often up, and I thought that I might not disturb you if I called. I didn't wake you, did I, Luke? I *do* hope not. Did I?'

'No,' Luke said.

'Oh, good. Oh, I *am* glad. I would *hate* to have woken you. You sleep so badly, don't you? I'd never have forgiven myself if I'd woken you . . .' Alistair let his voice trail off and Luke heard his own breathing echo in the phone. 'I suppose you thought I hadn't noticed you aren't sleeping,' Alistair said, 'didn't you?'

There was a silence.

'*Did* you think that, Luke? God, we haven't exactly talked things over. So I suppose you thought I just hadn't *noticed* what's been happening, how unhappy you are. Did you think that?'

Luke knew he must answer or the questioning would continue. 'Yes,' he said.

'Well, you were wrong.'

Yes, wrong. Of course he was wrong. He was wrong about everything. Luke wanted to put the phone down and thought how nice it would be to quieten the voice and then, with one loud bang, to quieten the whole world. The party at Lapis-Lazuli would go silent after all.

He longed for the quiet he had been exposed to in the seconds after the car crash with Arianne and Ludo and Jessica, before they had all remembered themselves, when his mind had been quiet as snow falling in the night.

The voice went on in his ear – irritatingly, persistently: 'Look, of course I know this is highly eccentric but, God knows, I've had a pretty unusual day and I thought – well, I might as well carry on in the same vein. The truth is, Luke, there are rather a lot of things I want to say to you. They're things I strongly believe you deserve to hear.'

Luke felt his chin jerk back in surprise. It was an emotionless surprise – that of a scientist handed anomalous data. He said nothing, but continued to listen to the voice, to the breath, to this other person whom he had grown used to calling his father but who went to hotel rooms with unknown girls and was really just another load of chaos, like everyone else.

A week ago, when the party invitation arrived, he had stared at the envelope for a while. It said, 'Luke Langford'. He had appreciated the fact that this was a person's name. And yet how could anyone ever hope to know who that person was, if even the man who tore open the envelope could not predict what 'Luke Langford' might do or feel?

But a belief that it was at least possible to know and understand was essential. Why would anyone bother to speak, or to act, for that matter, if other lives – if even your own life – amounted only to a sort of puzzling display? Surely he must have been understood by someone, *known* by someone? At a simpler stage of life, perhaps. Was it just possible his mother had known all there was to know about him when he had still worn nappies?

But even then he had acted without her knowledge; he had loved and detested for secret reasons.

He remembered on one occasion dragging a purple crayon across each of the walls of the newly decorated guest bedroom. It had been wonderful to see the wicked dark line growing over those civilized beige walls. When Rosalind found him, she clapped her hand over her mouth in an extremely satisfying expression of amazement. She still mentioned this incident as the exception that proved her son's sweet nature.

But it was no exception. There had been plenty of incidents she had simply not discovered – the day he had torn the head off the largest rose in the garden, for example, just to see if she would cry.

Stranger still were the dim recollections he had of acting in spite of his mother for reasons he had not even understood himself. His earliest memory was of slamming his fist down in his high chair and refusing to eat his mashed potato. He had been starving hungry – he could actually remember the hunger in his little bare stomach. Why had he refused to eat the mashed potato when he was *hungry*?

He had reached the conclusion that nobody had known him then and nobody would ever know him. The only thing that could have disproved this theory would have been Arianne coming back to him. This would have amounted to benediction, to the fulfilment of promises the world had seemed to make him when he was a child – or during the first week of love.

There was rustling on the line and Luke listened for a bit. Alistair had no idea that his son had gone this far out, almost too far out for human contact to be possible, into the realm where the desire for death overwhelms both the vast horizon and the heartbreaking, heart-broadening desire to be understood.

But, of course, it was only *almost* too far – Luke's wrist had been caught just in time. Gradually he realized that the rustling on the line was the sound of human breath. His father was crying into the phone.

'Luke, I owe you an apology,' Alistair said. 'I'm calling to say I'm sorry.'

As surely as if it had been administered by a paramedic, this 50,000-volt dose, aimed right at the cardiac muscle, resuscitated him. Luke's consciousness came spluttering and choking into life and his first feeling was anger – rage that he had been returned to prison.

'Why?' he demanded, with enormous resentment that his father had, yet again, stolen peace from him. 'Why are you *sorry*?'

There was a long pause, and then Alistair said, 'For never coming to your rugby matches.'

What kind of a joke was that? Luke said nothing. He asked himself what on earth his father meant, what new trick to demonstrate his inferior intellect was contained in this riddle. Sophie would under-stand it, no doubt. But even as these thoughts flashed through his mind he knew there was no deception here. He knew, as we all know it when it so rarely confronts us, that he was in the presence of humility. It was impossible to ignore.

He felt his body growing calm and pliant again, as if it was recu-perating in a gentle climate. He glanced down and the gun had become an object in his grasp now, rather than a part of his hand, which he had merely to point towards a kind of freedom. He put it on the table.

'You are there, aren't you, Luke? *Luke?*' Alistair was saying.

'Yes, I'm here,' he said.

Alistair spoke urgently, almost breathlessly, repeating his son's name as if he was chasing after him down a corridor: 'Luke, I've been a bad father to you. I got it all wrong. I can see that now, I really can. I had no instinct for how to be a father.'

And, as if his father had caught up and thrown his arms around him from behind, stopping him, Luke felt his whole body jerk with emotion. Like Rosalind, he was essentially a kind person and his jovial smile concealed greater depths of compassion and mercy than there are in most people.

Alistair repeated, 'I've been going through it all. I did every single thing wrong.'

And Luke said, 'No, Dad. That's not true.'

'It is, Luke. Not school fees and so on, not clothes and doctors, but . . . the things that matter internally to a child. All wrong. Not even *wrong* in your case – just not done at all.'

'No. No, I can think of things. You used to read to us,' Luke said. 'You remember? You used to tell us all the Greek myths and stuff.'

'But they were to go with Sophie's Greek classes, weren't they? Bless you, Luke. Thank you. There was never anything just for you, was there? I know that. Why?'

Luke said, 'I don't know.' He really didn't know. He had puzzled it out in The Cave a lot, over the years, when Alistair forgot to say well done for being the youngest boy ever to win the Stanton swimming medal, or even when Luke had worked like a maniac, enduring endless teasing from classmates, not to mention Sophie's impatience as a tutor, to get a 'B++' in Latin translation. Hiding in the hall outside the kitchen he had heard Rosalind say, 'Alistair, darling, do make a fuss of Luke about his Latin exam, won't you? He was longing to tell you and you didn't really seem to care.'

'What? I . . . Oh, Rosalind, I've got a big case on and you're telling me about prep-school tests.'

Sophie padded across the kitchen in her socks, carrying the place mats. 'Anyway, they're easy-peasy, Luke's exams – "*amo, amas, amat*" stuff.'

'I'm bound to say I agree with you, Soph,' Alistair said. 'It's a bloody expensive school for the amount of education they give, Rosalind. I know you think the world of it, but it's just sport, really. Brainless stuff at great expense.'

Luke ran away to cry hot tears in The Cave, until he was called for supper.

Now Alistair cleared his throat and spoke clearly into the phone, 'You never once complained, did you? Why?'

'I don't know,' Luke said.

'And you wrote me all those letters from school. All those letters with descriptions of tennis matches and swimming and so on, didn't you?'

'Yes.'

'And it was always Mummy who wrote back. God, I just . . . I just *signed my name*.'

Luke could not have answered this because he was unable to speak.

Alistair went on, 'I want to apologize. I want you to know that I'm more sorry than I can really say, because I'm suddenly finding my vocabulary very limited. The best I can manage is to tell you I had no idea what I was doing – it *amazes* me how little idea I had of what I was doing – and to say I'm very sorry.' It occurred then to Alistair that he had spent his whole life longing to know who his father was, but all that had mattered in the end was that he should be a good father himself. He said, 'Do you think . . . do you think you can forgive me for what I've done – for all the things I've done and all the things I haven't done?' Then he laughed sadly. 'It's absurd to ask! Why on earth would you? How can we ask things like this of one another? But we have to. Oh, think about it, perhaps. Mull it over for a while. Let it sink in.'

'No, I don't need to,' Luke said. 'I already know I can forgive you. I already have.'

But it was not in Alistair's nature to accept love as the arbitrary miracle it is. He had always treated it as a philosophical proposition, subject to the laws of logic and therefore intelligible to the human mind. And in this way he corrupted all blessings. 'Why?' he said, still helplessly at the mercy of this trait.

Luke answered him simply, 'Because you're my father.'

Alistair glanced around at the newly whitewashed walls of his mother's bedroom. Then he put his head into his hands and acknowledged the full force of this reply. He saw that the love one has for one's parents is, essentially, the one love affair we never give up on. It is a pathological love but it is love none the less, regardless of whether it even appears to the rest of the world to be hatred.

Luke heard his own certainty too. In a silent drift, the horrifying discoveries of the last few hours fell away. His eye rested on the gun and he started with fright. What had he been about to do? His mind forgot. His thoughts hurried away from the unmentionable now and

368

the gun was as grotesque to the touch as a human bone. He gave a deep sigh and accepted his life.

He said, 'Dad, are you coming back home?'

Alistair sighed and pressed the bridge of his nose. 'Yes.'

'Then why don't you bring some of her things with you?'

Alistair saw and was touched by the sentiment behind this, but this quickly gave way to shame, which lay beneath all his emotions. He said desperately, 'But *china dogs*, Luke? Such tasteless things, really. Where on earth would Mummy *put* them?'

'For God's sake, Dad, she'd put them on the mantelpiece. It's you that cares so much about things being smart all the time. Mum would put them on the mantelpiece to be respectful.'

Alistair let his eyes close. 'Luke, I wish I had had the benefit of your advice a long time ago,' he said.

They did not speak for much longer. Some conversations are so heavy with matter that the imagination cannot bear them for long and must find rest. When they said goodbye to each other a few moments later, it was with a sense of peace that neither of them had ever known before.

Alistair got back into bed and folded the covers over himself.

Luke took off his clothes and got under the duvet.

Each put his phone on the bedside table with a kind of reverence, a shared amazement at what power so small a machine had contained. Then, both father and son fell into a deep sleep.

Chapter 25

Early the next morning, Alistair walked round to Ivy's house with an envelope in his hand. Inside it was a note. It read,

> *Dear Ivy,*
> *I would like to do some things for you and I hope you will accept my help, because it comes with much love and it would give me great pleasure to think I might be of use to you after all these years.*
>
> *If you agree, I would like to arrange for your house to be converted properly, so that you have a separate bedroom and sitting room and a downstairs bathroom. I would also like to fix for you to see a specialist about your hip because I am sure life could be a good deal more comfortable for you.*
>
> *For now, here is a bit of money for a new milk jug – or whatever you choose to spend it on.*
>
> *I must hurry back to London, but I will call you in the next few days after you have had time to think over my ideas.*
> *With love,*
> *Al.*

It had seemed right to make no reference to Geoff. There would be time for all of that. His immediate concern was to improve Ivy's life. Her poverty had shocked him. If he couldn't renovate her house with his own hands, as the incomparable Martin would undoubtedly have done, then he could at least pay for it with the money his brain had earned him. He remembered then that Martin had died of cancer and he felt sorry: Martin had been an easy-going, friendly man and

370

would never have suspected he was the subject of Alistair's paranoid rivalry.

Having slipped the envelope under the door, Alistair limped back round the corner to a breakfast of crackers and lime cordial, which was all there was in the kitchen. Then he called for a cab to take him to the station.

The driver was the same one who had taken him to Rosewood the day before. 'Morning, boss. Up to see your old dad again, is it?'

'No. Not today. I must get back to London,' Alistair told him.

'Right you are.'

Alistair laid his bag on the back seat and eased in his bad leg. 'Actually,' he said, 'I wonder – would you mind doing a slight detour before we go to the station? It's such a clear day I'd rather like to look out at the view,' he explained shyly, telling himself there was no need to justify his actions to a cab driver.

'Up the cliff, is it? No trouble at all,' came the reply.

They drove up to the car park at the foot of the path. Alistair got out and said, 'I'll leave my bag, if that's all right. Listen, I won't be long – and I'll pay you for waiting, of course.'

The driver wound down the front window and began to roll a cigarette. 'Don't you hurry, boss – my sort of day's work, this,' he said, winking.

Alistair smiled and made his way off.

As he climbed, looking out at the sea, with the soft chalk crunching under his shoes, he was surprised to find he had no sense of occasion at all. He had almost expected – perhaps he had actually wanted – to be filled with a portentous gloom by the sight of this view. It was, after all, hyper-charged with memories of his childhood. But as he reached his favourite spot, he was merely aware of a gentle smile on his face. Just as it had on the bizarre day of his sixty-third birthday, the view brought back a sense of himself, aged twenty-three, on the cliff one last time before he started his shining new life in London. How fiercely he had stared out at the waves, certain he was on the edge of making a grand, indelible gesture to the world. Alistair shook his head affectionately at his silly young self.

Now he saw that all our actions are less final than we insist. He saw, above all, that we are eternal optimists when it comes to love. Our minds entertain strange, secret attachments, long after they ought to. Perhaps only death is blunt enough to convince the human imagination that it is too late to make amends.

He knew perfectly well that he had spent his life in avoidance of reflection and confrontation. He had defeated every impulse to think about his past, or to sit down and confide in his wife, with a relentless emphasis on his work or other practical concerns. He had even put elaborate research about health care or financial security long before an afternoon with his children – a very long way before time with his son. Somehow, for the last thirty-nine years, there had always been a letter to write immediately after supper, or a million bills and a new brief to go through over the weekend.

But, of course, it had recently turned out that even resolute pragmatism requires a particular kind of faith. And it was as if, in return for his long worship, he had been granted a pardon, so long as he went quietly, from the humiliation of disciplinary proceedings. But he had lost the faith itself. Now that it had gone, Alistair found that the manifold little acts of will or of self-denial that account for the steady outline of a personality no longer felt 'natural'.

Here he was again, after all, on the cliff – *thinking*.

He watched the waves curling up and over and back in on themselves. After a while he began to wonder if he hadn't always had the wrong idea about the sea and its display of supreme indifference. The disappearing waves had reminded him of all that is transient and uncontrollable in the world and he had literally dared himself to look at them. But now it was as if, quite suddenly, his perspective altered. He saw that with absolute consistency, with every breaking wave, the sea was repeating the point: nothing lasts and that is why it is beautiful. Just then this seemed to be the unexpected secret of happiness, which he had made it his life's purpose to destroy.

He was conscious that the driver was waiting, but he stayed on for a few more minutes, calmly aware that he would see the view again, that this was in no sense a final gesture of farewell, but that he simply did not want to go just yet. As he stood there, he did not ask for or receive any grand philosophical insight, but every so often there was a kind of sensual satisfaction, when he seemed literally to hold the idea of time, like cupping a marble egg in the palm of the hand. There was weight and there was smoothness and then these qualities dissipated, and perhaps it was time that he saw reflected back at him by the cool and empty horizon.

When he went back to the cab, he found the driver doing the crossword and they discussed clues all the way to the station. It gave Alistair enormous satisfaction to find that he was able to supply all the answers and to receive such enraptured gratitude. 'Oh, well, you're very kind. I'm afraid I'm not much good for anything else, though,' he said, as they arrived, feeling unworthy of such praise although it meant so much to him.

'*Sharpness*, though,' the driver said, refusing to hear anything of the sort. '*Brains* – they'll get you a long way in life.'

Alistair smiled and paid him.

The first train was going to Charing Cross, rather than to the more convenient Victoria. It did not matter very much. On the platform, he took out his book on the Ottoman Empire by his old acquaintance Henry Downing and a coincidence in his mind caused him to remember a particularly touching description Henry had written in a *Times* book review in connection with Charing Cross. He had described how Edward I, distraught at the death of his wife Eleanor of Castile, had brought her body from Scotland to London and placed a cross at each point where her body and retinue had rested. Alistair felt moved all over again by this gesture – particularly when Edward I was only ever remembered for his cruelty to the Scots. There had been good in him, after all – there had been love. Alistair felt tears coming and wondered what on earth was the matter with him. He bought a paper to see if there was another crossword he could do.

But the crossword was of no interest. Neither was the news. Sitting in the train carriage, with his bag tucked rather spinsterishly behind his feet, his thoughts turned to Rosalind – inevitably to Rosalind. His hands folded and unfolded the edge of his ticket. He knew that it was not to an address that he was going back, not to a white house in Holland Park with a number on the door, but to a woman with brown hair and graceful hands and an abject disillusionment in her eyes. He was deeply afraid.

He looked out in amazement as the train pulled in at its first stop, Folkestone Central. Surely this was the fastest train in the world.

Alistair might, as ever, have made a success of avoiding the issue of his marriage, but his mind had none the less been prey to nervous tics. He was curiously plagued by the uncharacteristic phrase that Rosalind had used on the night of the attack: 'But how could you not have *heard* them, Alistair? They must have been . . . silent as *dogs*.'

His immediate reaction had been to wonder if she had ever had an affair. A few little words had caused this big doubt! But his wife's imagination had roamed flagrantly beyond its usual parameters and he had felt threatened. If that, then why not sex, too? Why not one of his friends? Julian, perhaps? Julian had always been in love with her, and Elise knew it and behaved impeccably. How fitting, then, that it should have been Julian who had secured Alistair's disgrace with his upstanding neighbourly spirit.

Yes, Rosalind and Julian – an odd couple, but who knew what women found attractive? Or Henry Sanderson, perhaps – with his broad hands and the thick head of hair he was plainly never going to lose. Or Anthony Crichton, with that smarmy way he had of offering to help with the plates and the way he called her Rozzy, which *no one* did, except her *sister*, for God's sake – 'Oh, Rozzy, you're being an angel as ever. Do let some of us mere mortals lend a hand.'

Alistair heard Rosalind's giggle. Yes, his wife and Anthony Crichton. They were not implausible, physically. Anthony would kiss her neck as he undid her shirt and ran his blunt-ended fingers between her breasts.

There was sweat on Alistair's forehead and his fist gripped the train ticket. The image of Rosalind and Anthony was replaced by one of an early horror in his life: it was the one of his mother, the time he came back unexpectedly from his confirmation class at the church hall. There she was, struggling under Mr Bisset's fat body on the floor in the hall. He remembered thinking at the time, *Can you kill a man with an umbrella? Would they hang you if you were saving your mother's life?* But before these questions were relevant, the huge shoulder moved back to reveal his mother's smiling face. She was enjoying the attack. She was *urging on* her aggressor. What did it mean? What horrible mystery was being played out in front of him on the grubby hall carpet?

'Oh, Alistair, I thought you were down the church.'

'I forgot my sandwich. I got hungry.'

The train burst, obliviously, through a station, past men reading papers, mothers holding children, a man with a dog, two teenagers kissing. It all flashed curiously by, and Alistair found himself wondering if he had ever satisfied Rosalind sexually. He was not sure. They had always made love fairly regularly, but in the back of his mind had been the suspicion that she was always elsewhere, that he might have had possession of her soft, pale arms and legs, but that her mind was closed to him. On one occasion – and this was excruciating to remember – she had fallen asleep. It had been just for a few seconds – a few heartbeats, in effect – but she had undeniably been asleep.

374

OK, it had been after a few very hard months with Sophie in and out of a clinic, Luke with tonsillitis and Suzannah getting divorced, but the sleep had somehow not seemed like tiredness so much as escape. He had stopped moving and stared down at the blind female body, which, though it was heavy in his arms, had left him completely empty-handed and foolish. He remembered thinking: What I am looking at now is the very opposite of desire – not boredom, but isolation, loneliness. And after she woke and he pretended not to have noticed, he had tidied the thought away, so as to survive.

It was fair to say that they had both suffered a good deal of sexual frustration.

He had blamed her for this, of course. (He had done such a lot of blaming over the years.) And yet now he was beginning to wonder if the fault lay primarily with him. Now he could hardly bear to remember the poignancy with which, in their early days, she had put up her face to be kissed, or unbuttoned her dress so that he could lay his weight on top of her, against her pale skin. It had been like leaning towards light to make love to Rosalind. She had been so tender, so trusting of him, her one and only lover. And at first it had been beautiful. He had felt blessed with her body, and when she stood by the window wrapped in her dressing-gown, gazing out over the little garden at their first house, he knew she had been blessed by his. There was a mutual satisfaction that fed on itself; a pleasure in what they gave to each other and of what they created in combination.

But it had not lasted. He couldn't help associating its disappearance with the disappointment he knew Rosalind had suffered shortly after they were married. They had agreed not to have a child for a few years. Rosalind's parents had insisted that Alistair did not make enough money. Her mother said, 'To speak with brutal frankness, Alistair,' he had found himself wondering when she had ever spoken otherwise to him, 'you do not yet have a *secure* environment in which to bring up a child *safely*. You can't *afford* to do it *properly* – in a *civilized* way.'

Chastened and spiritually ashamed as ever, he had spoken firmly to Rosalind about the grave dangers of their attempting to be parents yet. They had followed the advice to the letter. They had not even tried for a baby until Rosalind was twenty-eight, when he could afford the nannies and prams and cashmere shawls that Rosalind herself had been given. Alistair had made certain that all the mystical charms that would bring happiness and order were in place.

He knew that his young wife had found it painful to see all her friends give birth before her. She was made a godmother twice and he wondered now if he had ever acknowledged the humility with which she undertook this role. He remembered how she had spent long evenings embroidering smocking dresses for Laura and Harriet, her two goddaughters. She must have minded so much!

Rosalind's pleasure in her unusually clever husband had always been apparent to him but, as she cradled her friend Camilla's son, Rory, Alistair thought he could hear her thoughts roam: a husband with enormous potential was very nice, but even a dull insurance broker had his appeal if he could give you a life to adore. Alistair would pat the baby's head awkwardly, and then he would wander off and talk to the men.

Why *had* they listened to her parents? Or, rather, why had *he*, because Rosalind had in fact listened to him? He recalled, with horror, how frequently she had hinted to him that she wouldn't mind doing *absolutely everything* for a baby herself, that in fact she would *love* to and that she would be more than happy to use Camilla's hand-me-downs rather than buy expensive new Babygros and so on. But he, knowing better, had shaken off this romantic folly. He had merely placed an empty kiss on her forehead like a full stop and gone back up to his desk. He had treated her as if she was a child swearing to care for a guinea-pig – if only she could have one for Christmas.

How patronizing he had been to Rosalind! It was no wonder that her resentment had been physical at times. His own kisses had become a subtle form of violence – she got a little blow to her cheek or forehead or mouth if ever she seemed to be on the verge of questioning his methods. It was no great surprise that she had learnt to close her eyelids, avoiding him, even as they made love. He had insulted her in many ways.

Over the years, he had begun to view the loneliness of his own body as 'normal'. So there was, after all, he told himself, no transportation in the act of sex, no mystical communion. Afterwards, he loped clumsily from the bed to the bathroom on feet of clay. And, of course, he saw other couples settle into filial indifference to each other's presence; he noted affable shoulder squeezes batted off in irritation. From these observations he derived a mixture of reassurance and heart-freeze.

But neither feeling persisted because there was always an important discrepancy when it came to himself and Rosalind: their attraction to one another remained far stronger than their sex life might have suggested. She walked quietly past him in the hallway and he caught that light, lemonish scent of hers and felt weak – as weak as he had when he helped her into the punt at his college ball. He saw the hips, the waist still slim and smooth beneath her dressing-gown, and his mouth watered quite automatically – just as it did for the taste of raspberries and cream or a good single malt, or venison in a pungent, red-wine sauce. And if her hair brushed his cheek when she reached past him for her toothbrush, he could find his eyes closing as if to contain the sensation.

One could not entirely confuse the body – no matter how scrambled the mind.

These moments did not occur all the time, of course – habit and schedules and the practicalities of caring for children saw to that. But they did happen *sometimes* and when they did he could only draw the conclusion that his attraction to her was timeless, intact beneath the landslide of life, and that this was greatly to be envied.

But Alistair had never known what to do with any of his blessings. His self-consciousness spoilt everything. He thought of catching her wrist, of shouting her name after her down the hall, but every gesture seemed contrived or embarrassing in some way and he rejected it.

And yet when his friends began to be unfaithful to their wives, he knew he would always be the odd one out. He was unable to add his part to the wicked titillation they afforded one another at their men-only suppers. The others shared their descriptions of trysts with nubile secretaries or plump au-pair girls the way boys at boarding-school pass round dirty pictures. But he could only remain silent. It was soon thought that he 'disapproved' and the stories were censored around him.

The truth was, he didn't understand. He genuinely didn't desire other women because Rosalind was the woman he had always wanted and that was why she was his wife.

This last assertion caused him to laugh now – with deep bitterness. If this charmingly monogamous notion was the truth, then what had happened recently – on that night at the Ridgeley Hotel?

Strange as it was, though, he hadn't particularly lusted after Karen. Of course, she had possessed her textbook sex appeal, and her attraction to him, though blatantly Freudian in origin, had still been flattering to a man in his sixties. But he had not made love to her as he had made love to the young Rosalind. And this was not merely a subtle distinction between making love and having sex, but the more brutal one between making love and masturbation. In fact, what he had done in that huge white bed, with the weird images flickering on the screen beside them, had not even amounted to masturbation. The primary thrill had not even been sexual.

He felt perplexed and scared by the mystery of himself. What had he been doing – after almost forty years of fidelity – having sex with an unknown girl, with a witness in a trial he was prosecuting? A girl who had inspired only the bare minimum of physical reaction?

Suddenly he remembered something Rosalind's cousin Philip had shown him, during his last weeks. Poor Philip had gone through a repentant, pious stage, languishing in his four-poster, surrounded by lilies and peonies. His frail, shaking hands and yellowish skin had been at such painful odds with the vibrancy of the flowers and all the hand-painted cards. And it was awful to see how even against all the colour in the room, against the good wishes so superstitiously accumulated, cirrhosis of the liver still won hands down.

After a life of constant activity, whether it was sex or eating or dancing or travel – and, sadly, it was *always* drinking – Philip had taken to reading and meditating a great deal. He began to read the Bible, which, at the time, Alistair had found wildly hypocritical. Philip had always spoken of his Catholic upbringing with nothing but vitriol (it had been the subject of all his most wicked and brilliant jokes) and his promiscuous, homosexual lifestyle had seemed no less of a refutation.

Hypocrisy had always been, in Alistair's mind, profoundly irritating as a split infinitive. But in this case he was unnerved – even emotion-ally disturbed – by it. Philip was a bright, possibly even brilliant, man and there he was, contradicting himself at the essential moment. Why?

Alistair left this unsaid, of course, because it was hardly the time for intellectual debate, and Philip died at last with no idea that he had lodged a thorn in the mind of his finicky old chum, Al.

Alistair gazed out of the train window at the light rain falling on the glass, at the trees pulsing by. Of course, he could see now what had got him so worked up about Philip's change in reading habits. It had not been a fixation with logical consistency (and had this ever *really* been his concern? Had it not always been a preoccupation with honesty, rather than with that mere surface detail, clarity?). The sight of Philip's Bible had contained the terrifying idea that the past might lie in wait, intact, despite the beatings it had taken.

Had he always been quite so transparent?

It had been a passage in St Augustine's *Confessions* that Philip held out to him with such difficult passion in his eyes. Augustine described the pleasure he had taken as a boy in stealing pears – unripe pears, which were inedible anyway, only to toss them away. He confessed to God, 'I loved my own undoing. I loved my error – not that for which I erred, but the error itself.'

Alistair had read it, politely acknowledged the beauty of the passage and put down the book as quickly as he could. Thankfully, Philip's boyfriend Jake had arrived at that point with yet more flowers and a load of photographs of friends unknown to Alistair and there had been an excuse to leave. As he left, Philip was humming a tune and it had seemed so peculiar and undignified to do this after being so solemn that Alistair attributed it to alcoholic dementia.

But, of course, he had merely misunderstood. Over his St Augustine, Philip was humming Frank Sinatra's 'My Way'. Alistair's sense of the sacred had never incorporated resigned laughter before. He smiled and shook his head. Dear old Philip, he thought.

But it was a mystery, really. Why would anyone steal unripe pears, or, as Alistair had, a custard tart from Ivy's kitchen only to thrust it into a coat pocket where it was bound to be covered in fluff and spoilt? St Augustine had tossed away the pears; Alistair had thrown the custard tart to a dog on the way up the cliff path. Much later, he had deposited almost forty years of fidelity with a girl in a hotel room, before going home to his wife. He repeated St Augustine's words to himself: 'I loved my own undoing . . . not that for which I erred, but the error itself.'

At once, Alistair felt conscious that he had arrived somewhere dramatic – just like the cliff top, only internal – and that again there was no sense of occasion. Perhaps, he thought, we are all silently at odds with the life we have chosen. Perhaps these moments of wilful immorality really were, in a terrible and violent way, necessary. They were not righteous in any sense (no, they could not be compared to leaping up in court to object!), they were simply destructive. But how else might we recognize and even bear a kind of witness to the sacrifices we make in attempting to be a consistent personality? Consistency is, after all, a constant creative effort and Alistair had made so many sacrifices for this end.

But it was outrageous to compare in any way the disposal of nearly forty years of fidelity to the toss and thud of unripe pears! Still, the comparison enclosed an important truth; and it seemed there was rarely anything fair or dignified that went under that name. Pears or fidelity – to destroy the value of either involved the same show of power. Loving your own undoing was actually a form of self-expression; it was a desire to expose the crude self behind the artifice of belief, even if it meant losing everything.

And if this loss should happen to prove that our beliefs and ambitions were all artificial, he thought, then it is important to remember they are not therefore worthless. They are natural, just as a spider's web is natural. And they are amazing in the same way. Just as one might pause in a garden to watch the sun making seed pearls of the dew on an intricate pattern of silk, so the structure of our lives is worthy of contemplation.

Alistair put his hand into his overnight bag to check his mother's ornaments. He had taken three – two china boxes and a porcelain shepherdess; each one was wrapped carefully in an item of his clothing. What fierce judgement he had inflicted on a lonely and frightened woman. Perhaps she had really loved Geoff. Who knew? Either way, if she had taken what joy she could from her questionable admirers, from her sunny jaunts with their ordinary treats, her occasional bit of pleasure from a male guest, who was he to blame her? These ornaments, with their kitsch sentimentality, contained a life of unrealized passion.

How was it that he had continued to judge her so harshly as he grew older and gained perspective, as he told his own lies? Had he not noticed how much England had changed? In the 1940s, an unmarried woman with a child had no choice but to be 'a widow' so far as the enquiring stranger was concerned. It was a testament to her local popularity that this polite fiction had been maintained. But there had, of course, been no question of anyone wanting to marry her.

And so, much later, she had brought her son a little toy car on the palm of her hand when all he wanted was his father. But could he be sure that this had not devastated her, too? Could he truly be certain that her increasingly frequent drunkenness, her fearful insecurity about his reading books she couldn't understand, about his going away to Oxford, had not been born of a deep guilt that she was powerless to resolve? After all, she had been right to think that his books and his place at Oxford would teach him how to abandon her.

The very least he could do was put her ornaments on his mantelpiece. At once he knew that his inability to do this was intimately connected with a lifetime of erotic disappointment.

★   ★   ★

He arrived back a little before ten. Luke's bedroom curtains were closed and Alistair hoped his son was still resting peacefully after their late telephone conversation. The house smelt of toast and of furniture polish and he could hear the dishwasher running in the kitchen. These were the sounds and smells of domestic peace and contentment. But the essential element was missing.

He wanted Rosalind desperately. He wondered where she was, but he remained standing in the hallway as if he was not at liberty to walk around the house. And then he saw, unobtrusively tucked in by the umbrella stand, the leather holdall that he had given her last Christmas. It was open, and inside it he saw neatly folded clothes.

It was as if, in one moment, his hopes fell away and showed him just how important they had been. It seemed they had literally supported his body. There was a little chair in the hall, which nobody ever used, and he sank down on to it and pushed his hands through his hair.

So, he had left it too late. Rosalind was leaving him and he had no right to be surprised.

Just a few moments later she came out of the kitchen, dropping something into her handbag and clicking it shut.

'Oh!' she said, putting her hand on her chest. 'I didn't hear you.'

He looked up at her and smiled. 'Sorry – I should have called before I barged in like this.'

'Well . . . hardly. It's your own house.'

'No, exactly.'

'Actually, I was just . . . I was just writing you a note, Alistair.'

'Ah,' he said. 'Yes.'

He had come long before she had expected him to. She had intended to be gone by the time he got back and his wilful presence had shocked her. She lost hold of the determination with which she had made all of her arrangements. She was too stunned to speak for a while and she resented the power his presence had over her. She simply stood in the kitchen doorway, looking at him, and after a while she stuttered impatiently, 'Well, I needn't have. Written a note, I mean. I mean, I could have spoken to you directly. I just had no idea when you were coming back.'

'No, I've been extraordinarily self-centred,' he said, with disarming frankness.

She looked down at the carpet. 'Yes,' she consented.

Then he said, rather vaguely, 'I'm afraid I've been putting my past before my future.'

This irritated her — it was no time for poetical-sounding language. She said, 'Alistair, I'd so much rather not talk about it. You've never made it my business before.'

'Yes, I know,' he said, 'but I ought to have done.'

She turned angrily to the hall mirror and feigned an interest in her hair. 'Oh, "*ought.*"' She snorted.

'Aren't I allowed to *wish* I had done better? To *wish* I had been a better husband?'

'Not in front of me. It's in poor taste.'

He let his head drop into his hands again and, seeing him reflected in the mirror, Rosalind's body fought contrasting impulses both to hit him and to put her arms round him. She hated him, but he had never looked so dejected before — and yet it was not her job to protect him and it never had been, really. She had done him no favours by protecting him.

Just beyond his right shoe she noticed the edge of her suitcase and the folded jacket and realized that he must have seen these things.

He raised his head. 'Rosalind, will you at least let me say a few things? About the girl? I would like at the very least to offer you an explanation . . . of sorts.'

She laughed bitterly. 'Oh, Alistair, what could there possibly be that isn't glaringly obvious to everyone? You think you're an extraordinary case, that's your problem.'

'You might be right,' he said. 'But perhaps there is more to it.'

'No. Everyone's complicated. It's just that you think it's OK for you to do things other people wouldn't dream of doing, simply because you're Alistair Langford — as if somehow you didn't get what you deserved at birth. What do any of us deserve? You think the bad things you do are somehow more . . . I don't know . . . intellectually sophisticated — that you're guilty of a better class of wrong. But I can tell you, a lie is a bloody lie!' she said, becoming angry now, 'and you have told *so many.*'

'Yes, I've told lies.'

'Yes, you have. And I've *helped* you!'

'No, Rosalind — you can't blame yourself for a second.'

'Why not? *Oh* — do they make *allowances* in heaven for people like me? People who need *extra help*?'

'I . . . no.'

'Then I'll blame myself, thank you. We started this marriage in an atmosphere of pretence. I thought you weren't telling me the whole

382

truth. I thought something didn't add up about your complete lack of interest in your past, or the fact that on our wedding day there wasn't a single person there you hadn't met in the past four years. And I thought it when Mummy said how sad it was that we hadn't even been shown a photograph of your mother. Sometimes I wonder if she knew too.'

'Yes, I wondered that.'

Rosalind shook her head in disgust. 'Oh, *did* you? You're *so* clever, aren't you?'

'No,' he said.

'Honestly, what on *earth* had your mother done, Alistair? How could she possibly have deserved to be rejected like that? Was it murder? Kidnap? *Torture?*' Her cheeks were flushed with anger.

'It was because she didn't know who my father was,' he said quietly.

'What? But your father was killed in—' She stopped herself. 'Oh. *Another* lie?'

'It was *her* lie, Rosalind. Well, to start with, anyway. Oh, please – look, I can see that doesn't matter. Obviously I can. The fact is, she never told me a thing about him – except that. I had to tell your parents *something!* The trouble was, I always knew it wasn't true, I don't know how but I just knew.'

'Yes, well, one does. We all know if we're being lied to. You can *smell* it.'

He braced himself against the rage he had never once seen in her before. 'But, Rosalind, I sort of went on hoping it *might* be true and . . . well, I knew better than to bring it up and be certain it wasn't. I held my tongue and, during the course of my childhood, my mother and I developed a sort of agreement not to address the issue. But you can't *have* that in a family. It's all right between friends or work colleagues, but you can't have lies in a family.'

'No, you *can't.*'

'I'm so incredibly . . . Rosalind, I . . . She was lying about my *father.*'

'But she was your *mother.* Wasn't that worth anything?'

He looked at her miserably, asking for understanding, but she did not want him to feel understood. She wanted him to feel exiled, because it was what he deserved.

'You must have hated her so much to do what you did. To say she had *died.* It was like killing. Do you know that?'

'Yes.'

'You actually *hated* her – your own mother.'

'I hated her, yes.'

'And *such* hate.'

'Yes, with my whole heart.'

'But you promised that to me,' she said.

She pressed her temples to stop herself crying. The simple pain her fingers inflicted was a rest from betrayal. The blood pulsed under her fingertips and she suddenly understood why Sophie had made those little cuts on her arm – she saw what her daughter had meant when she attempted to explain by saying it was like changing the channel on the TV for a while – if the film got too scary or sad.

Alistair said, 'Rosalind, I see it's too late, I really do – it's been too late for a good many years, really, but I do want you to know I did the best I could, in some respects, at least. May I say anything in my defence? There were other, more practical reasons for cutting her out of the picture. Yes – a euphemism, I *know*. But please listen to me. All I'm saying is, don't forget how much England has changed, how much attitudes have changed.'

He saw that she was listening. He went on, 'When you and I got engaged your father and mother already saw me as a great disappointment. They wanted you to marry someone with money and land, someone with a title, I imagine—'

'Oh, they were just snobs.'

'Yes, they were. And so was I for playing along with it, but I was young and stupid and they – well, they were from a different age. Do you have any idea how hard it was to convince your father I wasn't a total dead loss?'

Rosalind leant back against the wall beside the mirror and sighed. 'No. I suppose I don't.'

'I can't *tell* you what those intimate little drinks of ours were like, Rosalind. They were *soul-destroying*. They left me in no doubt at all that I was not good enough and the way I saw it was that this was their opinion *without* the addition of my mother. Had they met her, then that load of sentimental rubbish I palmed off about her being a translator and so on—'

'Sentimental rubbish?'

He could not look at her because he had 'palmed off' this 'rubbish' on her, too. He went on, because it was all he could do. 'Rosalind, you have to understand my mother had barely been to school. She was almost illiterate. She was from a completely different background. She was vulgar – yes.'

'*Vulgar?* So, naturally, you thought the best thing to do was never see her again? This was a fitting punishment?'

'Not a *punishment*. Why do you say that? I had no desire to punish her.' But as he said this he knew that it wasn't true. He had wanted her to suffer her son's absence, just as he had suffered his father's absence. If she could withhold, then so could he. 'Look, perhaps you're right,' he said. 'No, you *are* right. But there were many reasons. And one of them – a very important reason – was that I wanted to marry you. I desperately wanted to marry you, darling, and I couldn't risk offending your father's . . . sensibilities.'

Rosalind knew that her father's 'sensibilities', as Alistair so delicately described his vile snobbishness, had been terminally offended anyway. James Blunt had swiftly established that Alistair would not be inheriting a stately home – or even a manor house. There had been an appalling conversation before a drinks party in which he had come into the room and said offhandedly, 'He does have a decent blazer and everything, doesn't he, Roz? It's just that Lady Seddon's going to be here.'

'Well, he'll probably wear the one he wore last weekend, Daddy.'

'Yes, I imagine he probably will. Oh, darling, you must do what makes you happy, I know that – but do take care.'

Their relationship had never really recovered. The implications of this simple question were too vast and too blatant. A decent blazer meant the right sort of background, the right sort of values, the right sort of future.

Rosalind felt a twinge of pity for her husband, 'But you could have told *me*, Alistair. Surely. And if not right away then at some point in *nearly forty years of marriage!*'

He shifted frantically in his chair as if he had received an electric shock. 'I know! Rosalind, I'm an idiot – *please!*'

'If only you *were* an idiot one could defend it. But you're a *clever man*. I always believed you were a clever man.'

'Until now, I suppose,' he said self-pityingly.

'Don't,' she said.

'I'm sorry. I haven't much dignity. I've realized I have nothing left.' He watched her for a moment as she blinked and breathed and let her eyes move about the hallway. This was the woman who had given him two children, who had endured hours of loneliness while he worked at weekends when she might have demanded his attention. This was the woman who had been father and mother to their children at times, facing the other parents at the sports days with no husband on her arm. And in spite of all this she had been faithful to him – he knew that, really – and on the day he was made a QC she had put on a new pale blue suit with pride that had made her tremble. What was the value of anything if he did not bring it to her? No, she had never caught his allusions to Homer or Pope, but she had cared for his happiness more than any other human being. He could not bear to be exiled from her sympathy. 'Rosalind, may I tell you something?'

Aware immediately that he was asking her to do something for him, to be available to him in some way, her face contracted in a frown. 'What? What about?'

'About my father.'

He saw the frown relax and he continued, 'Do you remember the woman who called about my mother's death?'

'Ivy?'

'Yes, Ivy.' Of course Rosalind remembered her name, he thought – this was his considerate wife. 'Well, my father was – is – Ivy's husband. His name is Geoff Gilbert. I went to see him yesterday.'

Rosalind walked over to the stairs and sat down. 'Goodness.'

'He's in a retirement home in Dover. But the thing is, Rosalind, it turns out his mind's completely gone. He had absolutely no idea who I was.'

She shook her head in disbelief.

Alistair smiled. 'D'you know, it's rather funny, really – in a pathetic sort of way? I mean, he was just two streets away. I just never knew he was my father. And then, at long last, when I finally do . . .'

'It's too late,' Rosalind said. She put her hand over her mouth and drew her eyebrows together in that expression of deep compassion he had always admired. He loved her for the way she loved other people – for the depths of emotion she had suffered for the sake of her children, even if this had made him jealous at times.

'Yes, too late,' he said, shrugging.

This phrase plainly had resonance and she looked at him, certain now that as soon as he had seen her packed bag he had assumed she was leaving him. The right thing to do was to tell him she had not yet decided to do this, but something prevented her speaking. Of course, this was in part merely a desire to keep control of a situation in which she had felt utterly helpless, but it was also curiosity about what Alistair would say with no fictions to bolster him.

'Well,' he said, 'somehow I can't quite believe this is what happened in my life — that this was the story, if you know what I mean. But there it is. Your parents were right — I wasn't good enough for you.'

'You talk as though you were dead.'

'I suppose I might as well be when all I have to offer my wife is the supremely useless word, "sorry".' He looked at her. 'I won't insult you with a whole load of rhetoric. You have always spoken plainly to me. I merely want you to know that I regret what happened, that I regret what *I* did — *me, myself* — with that girl, in every cell in my body. I'm always afraid to speak simply,' he said.

'Oh, all your stupid fear,' she replied bitterly.

'Yes. *God* — all my stupid fear.'

She stared at him for a while and eventually she folded her hands in her lap in the way she always did when she had reached a conclusion. 'It seems to me,' she said, 'that loving someone is all about fear, really.'

He looked confused. 'I don't think I . . . I'm sorry, I don't understand.'

'It seems to me it's all about seeing the fear — the *stupid* fear — on another person's face and somehow loving them anyway. If only you had trusted me to love you *anyway*.'

He glanced up at her hopelessly. 'Yes, I see,' he said.

'And if only I had been able to do it in spite of you. You've assumed I'm leaving you, haven't you?'

His eyes flicked to the packed case and then back to her, his face in total confusion. She turned away from him and knew that she was more relieved than sorry to be surrendering her moment of power. 'Well, I'm not. I'm just going away,' she told him.

When at last she turned back he was still staring at her, and she realized that this was because he did not dare to speak — or even to move. She was not designed for revenge, and because she had long been in the habit of caring for him, she felt pity and wanted to end his pain immediately. She put out her hand to him, but rather than accepting the cool pressure of her fingers, he clasped her wrist with both of his hands — almost as if he was drowning and she was standing on dry land. She was reminded of the way Luke had thrown himself on to her when she collected him from his flat. She was shocked, but she adjusted herself to the desperation on his face and knew that she could tolerate it. 'Alistair, don't push me too quickly. There is a very great deal to live through.'

'I know,' he said, 'I know, but I can't help it. I love you and I want

to be a better husband. There is so much of life left! I've retired somewhat earlier than I intended, and there is a completely different existence to be had now.'

'Why? Not just because *your* life has changed. You may remember
I have a business.'

Alistair was ashamed of himself. It seemed the habit of egocen-
tricity was hard to beat. 'Yes, of course you have. Then I want to learn
about it.'

'Tables and chairs and rugs, Alistair? You'll hate it. It'll bore you
senseless.'

'No. No, it won't. I want to learn about it all. God — it's as if I
want to get to know you. I want to learn who you are.'

There was no hostility in the gesture but Rosalind gently removed
her hand from his. 'To learn who I am?' she said. 'You always want
knowledge, don't you? More knowledge. But I don't think you get
knowledge from other people, no matter how hard you try. What *you*
want is facts, but people are like pieces of music just playing for themselves and other people can listen if they want. You don't learn facts
from listening to music, do you?'

'You don't think I can know you?'

'I honestly think only God's mind could do that.'

The grandfather clock in the hall chimed its endless eleven.

'Oh! My plane,' she said.

'Your *plane*?'

'Yes. I'm going to Ghana, to visit Sophie and her boyfriend.'

'Sophie has a boyfriend?'

'There's a lot you don't know, Alistair. I probably — no, I *certainly*
ought to have told you, but I — well, somehow I didn't.'

'Tell me what?'

'That she's pregnant.'

She watched him attempt to comprehend this. She felt it was
entirely inappropriate to produce this sacred information as if she was
raising the stakes in a game of surprises and she regretted the fact that
she had not told him sooner, if only for this reason.

'His name is Kwame Okantas and they've decided to have a child
together. I suppose I didn't tell you because it was all I had to be
happy about and you didn't bloody well deserve a share. I'm sorry.'

'My God, please, Rosalind, don't apologize to *me*,' he said.

'No, I had no right to keep it secret — whatever you've done wrong.
She's your daughter too.'

She watched him taking in her words. He shook his head with the sheer strain of accepting this new reality: a baby, a new life. His little daughter with a child in her stomach.

Rosalind said, 'He grew up in England, but his parents are from Ghana.'

'So he's . . .'

'Yes, he is, Alistair. And they love each other and she is happier than she has ever been and she's going to have a baby. I spoke to him and he's charming. He's a barrister, just like you.'

Alistair nodded in acceptance.

'Sophie and he are collecting me from Kotoka airport.'

It seemed that these physical details gave him some kind of impetus. He stood up, and putting his hand on the banister, he said, 'Rosalind, I'll come *with* you. It's *easy* to buy a ticket at the airport and I'll pack my bag in no time.' He started to limp up the stairs. 'There couldn't be a *better* time to go away and I can talk to Sophie and *explain* everything and—'

'Alistair,' she said softly, before he had made it halfway, 'would you understand if I told you that I want to go on my own?'

He stopped and turned to face her. 'Yes,' he said. 'I would understand entirely.'

He reached his hand out over the banister for reassurance, but this time she gestured for him to come down because she felt able to put herself into his arms. He folded her against himself and she felt his breath on her neck; it was as familiar to her body as the flow of water is to pebbles worn smooth over time.

A floorboard creaked in Luke's bedroom and they moved apart, smiling at each other. Rosalind glanced at her watch and said, '*Hon*estly, what time is this to get up?' But their gentle laughter had nothing to do with their son or with the time – these merely supplied a vocabulary to two lovers as awkward as they were sincere.

Rosalind picked up her handbag and lifted out a piece of paper with her passport. She said excitedly, 'Sophie *emailed* this to Suzannah, Alistair. Isn't it amazing? She got it up on your computer. I would have thought you had to be at home – but it doesn't matter where you are any more.'

'Yes, it's clever, isn't it?'

'And you don't even need a ticket. You just give them a code at the airport and they whisk you off to Africa!' Her eyes narrowed dreamily. 'Not like when we were young at all. Gosh, I don't even feel as though I *paid* for it – I just typed in some letters and numbers. Isn't the world barmy?'

Alistair smiled at her, loving the nervous excitement in her fingers, seeing and hearing in her the girl of twenty with whom he had fallen so painfully in love. He said, 'Rosalind? Will you let me drop you at the airport?'

Her smile fell. 'Oh. Well, I've already called a cab.'

'I could always telephone the firm and tell him not to come.'

'But your leg, Alistair.'

He knew it was he who was asking the favour, really, and he understood her reluctance to let him encroach on her plans. He said, 'My leg would survive in your automatic, it really would. It's nothing like as painful as it was. Please let me take you to the airport, Rosalind.'

She looked down at her cases, at the things she had assembled in such a hurry late last night after Sophie had called and the plan was hatched and Suzannah had booked the ticket online. Of course, she could have done all the packing in the morning, but it had seemed urgent to do it that instant. She had given in to the excitement.

She leant down and zipped up her bag. When she straightened and looked at Alistair again, she found that her heart moved with love for him – just as it always had, just as it had even in the terrible blank time after the papers came out, when her friends asked her if she wanted a divorce. If Jocelyn thought marriage was 'self-limiting' then that was fine with Rosalind, because surely the self needed limits. Loving Alistair was one of the things she had decided to do with her life and, knowing that her anger would pass, she knew she wanted to learn to love him better.

How could anyone really make up for the wrongs they had done to another person? You had merely to forgive them and decide to go on. Love set this limitation, and if you accepted it, your reward was – love.

'All right,' she said. 'You take me to the airport.'

Chapter 26

Luke woke up with an intense thirst and stumbled into the bathroom to gulp water from the tap. For the first time in weeks he had slept for seven hours straight and he felt blank and dazed. He drank for a long time and then stood, panting, over the basin, wondering if there was anyone in the house. He felt certain there was not.

He stood under the shower for a while, dried himself carefully, then dressed and went downstairs. In the hallway, he saw his father's bag. Beside it was the history book he had given Alistair for Christmas a long time ago. Not having seen it read, Luke had always assumed the book was wrong in some intangible way – that it was the poor choice of someone who knew nothing about history, or about books, or about his father. But there was the Dover to London ticket stub lodged two-thirds of the way through. It pleased him to see this. He picked up Alistair's jacket and hung it carefully over the back of the chair.

Sitting on the hall table were the little ornaments Alistair had brought back. Luke recognized them immediately and was again touched that his opinion had genuinely been respected. He picked up one of the boxes. Inside was a lock of baby hair and his heart jumped with tenderness at the thought that it might once have belonged to his father. He lifted out the little curl in its blue ribbon and then, as if there might at any moment be a savage gust of wind, he put it safely back in the box. Rosalind had kept locks of his and Sophie's hair in just the same way.

Behind the hall table was a mirror. It was with a sudden kind of inspiration that Luke turned to it and looked himself in the eye. He did not speak out loud, but the voice in his head was firm and clear:

'You've lost her,' it said, 'and you know you'll never meet anyone like her again. When it comes to love, the rest of your life is going to be a series of compromises. But the truth is she did not love you. There is nothing anyone can do about this.'

He felt as if he had poured iodine on a cut. Blinking back tears, he went into the kitchen to distract himself by making coffee. He took cereal out of the cupboard and fetched a bowl. Then he got milk and orange juice out of the fridge. Wasn't there, after all, a simple satisfaction in these daily rituals? They were quietly absorbing. He wondered whether to have sugar or chopped fruit on his cereal. Chopped fruit was healthier, he decided. But should it be apple or banana? He gazed at the fruit bowl. On the other hand, though, muesli was healthy enough already, without the addition of fruit. Perhaps he would have sugar, after all. He was sure he had read somewhere that if you were going to have refined carbohydrates it was best to have them in the morning because you burnt them off most effectively that way. Best to have sugar now, then – if he was going to have it at all, that was. He wondered, with a faint anxiety, when he had last taken a good multivitamin.

It was not until he splashed milk on to the floor and leant down to wipe it up that his thoughts were interrupted. There, through the kitchen window, was the annexe, solid and terrible somehow, behind the foliage of the tree peony. Luke put down the cloth and gripped the edge of the sideboard. He listened to the lawnmower running next door: up and down, up and down. It was a horrifying sound. Then he rushed out of the kitchen and into the drawing room.

But there were windows everywhere. There was no escape. Even in the drawing room, where all was peace and stillness – the light mellow on the chandelier, the bottles and glasses ready on the tray, the clock ticking dustily on the mantelpiece – he could still see the top of the annexe roof. He thought about getting into his car and driving away, but immediately rejected the idea. He thought about taking the bicycle out of the cellar and racing off as he had done when he was a little boy.

But instead he paced up and down for a while, his heart pounding. There was a dreadful weight on his brain, which he had not yet allowed to take on logical form. It was a monolith of ice and it was melting inexorably, seeping life into reluctant synapses.

As yet he was aware only that he had done something terribly wrong, but this position could not last and he was beginning to realize it. His mouth was dry and there was sweat on his forehead. He began to whisper, 'I'm so sorry. I'm so sorry.' But who was he talking to? He rushed to the mirror and watched his lips muttering. There was no reassurance in this!

He turned to the window and immediately he saw something: the flash of a human shape through the bushes. It had looked like someone heading for the side passage. But it was far too early for Goran and far too late for Mila. His mind felt vulnerable to illusions.

He shook his head as if he was clearing water out of his ears and then he went over to his mother's desk. Again, he was seeking distraction. In the letter rack, there were a few airmail letters written in his sister's hand. It was odd, he thought, that Sophie had just the same handwriting as their father. Luke's was childish and messy. He supposed that this was yet another thing that separated him from them – but the thought failed to convey the usual slight to his heart and he abandoned it. He wondered what the letters said, but it was not in his nature to read another person's mail.

He remembered hearing Sophie's unexpected message on his voicemail – about the water buffaloes, about how she had been thinking he might have taken a beautiful photograph of them. He had felt touched, of course, but also indignant, because she had never said before that she liked his photographs or that she cared about anything he did. How much this disdain had hurt him over the years! He had always felt summed up and casually discarded by his clever sister.

As he relived this awful feeling, it occurred to him that Sophie had actually bought him books of photographs for Christmases and birthdays for as long as he could remember. Huge, beautiful, expensive books of photographs – of animals or cities or spectacles of nature. He had assumed she was implying that he couldn't read. Was it possible he had been mistaken?

With shame he remembered they were all resentfully stacked, unopened, in his wardrobe.

He looked at the airmail letters. Where *was* his sister? The envelopes, which might have supplied the answer, had been thrown away. He knew his mother had occasionally mentioned Sophie over the past few weeks but he hadn't really been listening. His sister might be anywhere in the world: China, India, Africa. Did they have water buffaloes in China? His body ached with concern. He was also plagued by the sense that he had excluded himself from something important and exciting, just as he had once as a child, after long-jump on the lawn at Suzannah's old villa in Spain.

Suzannah's second husband's son, Jean-Pierre, had plainly landed a full centimetre behind Luke's footprints, but Sophie had denied the evidence of her eyes and said it was a draw. That afternoon Luke had refused to go swimming, as planned, with 'filthy cheats'. He had expected an apology, some kind of justice as a response to this enormous gesture. But Sophie, Jean-Pierre and Gabriel, the local boy they had befriended, had grabbed their towels and run off to the pool without him. In the full knowledge that he was by far the best swimmer anyway, Luke endured splashes and screams of laughter all afternoon while he studied the footprints and snapped dry twigs.

He hoped with all his heart that those photography books were still in the hall cupboard. It would be just like his mother to have packed them up cheerily and given them to a hospital or a charity shop.

He bit his lip as he appreciated, for the first time, the absence of that scrawny sister of his, with whom he had fought so passionately all his life. Really, where *was* she? He thought of all those interminable car journeys through France when they were children – the mutual eye-rolling at the vineyards and churches their father had got so worked up about; he remembered sharing headphones on the back seat as if the pop music was their only hope for salvation. They had communicated with each other in pinches or by sticking out their tongues. She had always swapped her blackcurrant fruit gums for his lime ones and, though it had made him feel corrupt to accept them, he had done so none the less. He smiled at the memory of her bony legs kicking against his in the bath when she refused to have her hair washed. Half a life of constant proximity – and yet now she might be anywhere in the world.

Water buffaloes? What did it all *mean*? And yet he knew exactly. All Sophie's fantasies had involved distant travel; each one had embodied her fervent belief that if only she could remind herself of the sheer size of the world, her problems would seem unimportant.

Suddenly Luke was afraid that his sister was wrong about this, that it was nothing more than a lovely idea. For the first time in his life, he did not think he would take pleasure in contradicting her. She was just plain horrible sometimes and she could be sarcastic and intellectually snobbish, but in spite of all this he knew he loved her and that she loved him just as much.

Poor Sophie – she had hardly been happy and it was not as if he had ever really tried to help or even to understand. He had just watched her getting skinnier and skinnier and told her no one would fancy her if she looked like that. It was terrible to think that he had not talked to her, never genuinely asked her about her life – not once! Somehow he had always been too tired or hung-over or stressed out. She was so dramatic, so loud. He had preferred to block his ears with TV if ever they were alone together, rather than listen to her piercing doubts about their parents' marriage, or her belief that she and Luke were incurably selfish, self-pitying children. She never let up!

And what of all those wounds she had inflicted on him, which he had so carefully enumerated, which he had tended in raptures of martyrdom and brought out to shock the crowd at Easter or Christmas or on their mother's birthday?

It seemed that, in spite of it all, love was going to persist. His attachment to Sophie was illogical but undeniable – almost as if it was hard-wired into his genes. Perhaps it was. This thought gave him a feeling of deep peace.

But how could the violent machinery of Luke's mind have accommodated peace for more than a second? It shattered there like spun glass and his head jerked round to the window again.

Had there been someone in the garden a moment before? He walked over and put his face close enough to the windowpane to feel the coolness coming off the glass. The spiny tree tapped against it and startled him and, as if he had now woken by another vital degree, he unlocked the french windows and walked out across the lawn.

He could see from a distance that the annexe door was ajar. His immediate fear – horrible as it seemed to him straight afterwards – was that Goran and Mila had stolen everything and left. He knew then and there that, no matter what he had told himself when he longed for companions in his suffering, Goran and Mila's desperation was essentially foreign. They had nothing – and he could not even imagine what that would be like. He thought: I have let desperate strangers on to my family property. For a moment, he was appalled and tried to reassure himself that there was nothing of value in the annexe.

From the gap in the doorway he saw that Mila was sitting on the table by the window. Her back was to him and her heels banged the table leg with that brisk, military rhythm she sometimes clicked out with her tongue or tapped with her fingers. He studied her for a moment and then said her name quietly: 'Mila?'

She turned round a little way and smiled.

He pushed the door open and glanced round the room. Nothing had been stolen; everything was as he had last seen it. And yet he was aware that something was wrong, that something had taken place.

'Mila? Where is Goran?' he said.

She did not answer him and, after a second or two, he walked over to the table. The light from the window illuminated her face and as he saw it, front on, he gasped. The right cheek and eye were deep red and swelling. He said, 'Your face!' Then he realized he was standing on something strange and sticky. When he looked down at the floor he saw that he was treading on the remains of the Serbian cake. The plate was broken beneath it. He looked up at her and again he said, 'Your face!'

Mila shrugged. 'Is nothing pain for me. I tell to him this but is hit only one time.'

'Who? Who hit you?' Luke said, in increasing panic. 'Mila, he didn't do this to you. Not *Goran*. I don't believe he did this to you.'

She shrugged. 'Is the cake.'

Luke saw no meaning in this ominous riddle. '*What?*' he said.

As if she was recounting a funny anecdote, Mila laughed and said, 'He say to me, "*Mila! You do not eat half cake!*"' She held up her hands in conclusive surrender.

'What? I don't understand,' Luke said, understanding only too well.

'He is *look* and *look* at this cake,' Mila said, 'and he is say to me, "*I know you!*" And it is right, Luke, because Goran he know me from I am thirteen. Always I eat *only little*.' She repeated her impression, deepening her voice and wagging her finger like a schoolmaster. '"*Mila! You do not eat half cake!*"'

She thought for a moment and touched her face. Then she glanced up at Luke and smiled shyly. 'You know it is go this red? It is go and then I am nice again?"'

He stared back at her in amazement.

'Is ugly today but I am nice again,' she insisted. Then she screwed her eyes shut and clenched her fists and said, 'You believe I am think hard maybe is go quick?'

Luke's voice was almost a whisper: 'Mila, where is Goran?'

Beside her was a Kwik-Kabs card. A few seconds passed until she opened her eyes and noticed him staring at it. She said, 'Yes. Is give to me this for maybe I need some money. Goran is not work Kwik-Kabs now.'

'Why? What happened?' Immediately Luke thought of the gun. Of course: Goran had been sacked, arrested even, in connection with the gun. The police would now come for him.

'Is nothing what is bad. Is only for work in kitchen of hotel now because is shift of day time so is *like me*.' She shook her head at the foolishness of this. 'Is *present* for me. But now is not. *Now* he do not want I know where he is live. He says he go like is dead it is better. He tell to me he is put money with friend in Kwik-Kabs. Is Kurd man also drive cab. He say it is "Mila bank".' She laughed sarcastically. 'Dead man is put money in there for I can buy passport.'

She narrowed her eyes. 'But I tell to him I *do not want money of dead man*.'

Luke remembered Goran's plan to buy a National Insurance number and passport and – fake phone bills, was it? He was going to open a bank account in his newly adopted name, using the documents as proof. He would be in possession of some or possibly all of them by now and the job in the kitchen was probably 'legal'. He and Mila had been planning to get her documents after his, because this was the way his mind had organized their future: with him as the provider. Luke had the impression that the whole plan to come to England had been Goran's. Where on earth would Mila go now? In spite of all she had seen in Kosovo, she was innocent of the ways of a large city like London. She had been amazed by a car slowing down as she came home from work, an electric window lowering, a male voice: *How much?* She had wanted Goran and Luke to explain: what had he thought she was selling?

But she could not stay in the annexe any longer. That would be impossible after what had happened. Surely Goran had not just gone – as if, in Mila's words, he was 'dead'? Luke told himself he must be jumping to conclusions. They had argued, certainly, but surely Mila would have explained the half-eaten cake in some innocent way. Surely this would have been her instinct.

'I don't understand. What did you *say* to him, Mila?'

She looked away. 'I tell to him all, Luke.'

He stared at her, feeling fear and rage. 'What *all*?' he said.

'I tell to him what is happen in late night is so beautiful for us.' She lowered her eyes. 'I know is wrong for God but is beautiful for us. And I tell to him I love you now.'

When she returned her eyes to him, it was as if having said these precious words had only increased their truth. She loved him. In a mist of happiness, she listened to Luke telling her he must go out for

397

a bit and sighed tenderly at the thought of his gracious life. 'Yes, Luke. You must go again in your house.'

He nodded at her and said yes.

Mila shivered and drew her knees up to her chest. 'Luke, I ask question? You say I am bad this? I think I do not clean in Tessa Campbell-Sutcliffe apartment today. I tell to you is *million* and *million* clothes for iron and all time she shout to me.' Mila did a high-pitched, rasping voice: '"Be *care*ful. Is *cou-ture*. You *know* what this *mean*?" I think is better Hugo Johnson but is tomorrow. Today is tired for Tessa Campbell-Sutcliffe. You think I am bad this?'

'No,' Luke told her. '*No.*'

Dear, good Luke, she thought. *Ljubavi* – my love. He wouldn't hear of her working!

He watched her getting into the little camp bed and she watched him, taking in the light gold hair and the most beautiful grey eyes she had ever seen. Her love for him mingled with her slight concussion. After a while she became aware that his whole face had gone pale, even his mouth. He was plainly terrified with concern for her. She couldn't bear to see it – he ought not to feel a moment's worry! Her face was painful, but she forced a huge smile across it. 'Ah, Luke,' she sighed, 'you know I am happy and I lie in this bed and it is beautiful. Is not pain. You know this? You know this, Luke?'

'Yes,' he said, hurrying towards the door.

'I am sleep and is *not pain*,' she called after him.

'No,' he said. He shut the door behind him.

Is it possible to desire physical punishment as much as physical pleasure? As fervently as he had ever longed to make love to Arianne, Luke now wanted Goran to punch him, to break his nose and his ribs. Could he go and see Goran and tell him it had all been his fault, that he had seduced Mila and that she was so upset she was gibbering? Would this matter? Surely his being brave enough to own up, his being sorry, would count for something?

He remembered Goran laughing at him for saying he would forgive Arianne and take her back so long as she was 'really sorry'. Luke pictured the sardonic face, the cheeks contorted by the chewing of a hunk of cheese. Then, with a wince, he remembered how Goran had raised Mila's hand and pointed the fingers at him, as if they were the barrel of a gun. 'I kill you,' he said, 'and now I am "*really sorry*"?'

Goran's mind did not make an ideal out of justice, or out of anything, really. He just had his tight-lipped nod of respect for survival against the odds, for adaptation. Luke had wondered what it would be like to see things in this way – as if human beings didn't *mean* any more than cows or bats or other things that ate and reproduced. He had been stunned by the vehemence with which Goran held his stark principles: expecting no heaven, no long-awaited explanation, no acknowledgement, just that the dark would come at the end of the day.

And yet, on the afternoon they met, on their drive from Dover to London together, Goran had countered the vast embarrassment of all Luke's riches, with the words, 'I am lucky, too. I have Mila.'

He might have lashed out at Mila for hurting him, swiping at her like one of the struggling animals in his vision of the world, but what of the tenderly named 'Mila Bank'? The contradiction was heart-breaking.

Slowly, Luke forced himself to accept that there was no point in going over these thoughts because they only added to the desire for punishment and it might take months to seek out Goran. After all, who knew where he was? He had told Mila he did not want to be found. Undoubtedly the Kurdish friend at Kwik-Kabs would have been told to say he knew nothing. Goran had disappeared without a trace, without a single record of his presence in the country. His new job might be in any one of hundreds of hotels in London and he might have left the city. He even had a new name! Perhaps a message could be sent to him one way or another, through the friend, but it would all take time.

For now, when it was so urgently needed, there would be no conclusive punch. Instead there was a pale blue sky and a breeze and birds twittering in the chestnut tree. It was a beautiful, English autumn morning with the scent of bonfires in the air. Luke gazed up at the elegant white house and suddenly he wanted to smash it down.

Had meeting Arianne taught him the tremendous importance of his heart? But it was not important *above all else*!

He put his hand over his face as he thought of his ex-girlfriend, Lucy, and of the ten-line email he had written to her as a note of dismissal. He recalled the countless messages she had left on his voice-mail, like little fistfuls of flowers on a grave. He and Lucy had been boyfriend and girlfriend for two whole years! How many hundreds of times they had made love! They had learnt to sleep peacefully together, she had looked after him when he had a hangover, she had massaged his neck when he was tired; she had kept note of allergies, passions, loathings. She had always remembered to wish him luck or to congratulate him. She had done things to please him in bed that he knew she had found embarrassing.

And the awful thing was that she had done all this while enduring his constant uncertainty about whether she was the right girl for him. And, in the end, he had abandoned her in the course of just one evening for the sake of someone with a more beautiful face, longer arms and legs, a more vibrant personality. And in turn, just as Jessica had implied, the same had been done to him.

All this talk of the 'right' girl or the 'right' man, with its romantic astrological implications. It sounded much more practical when you told the truth: people went for clear eyes, thick hair, height, IQ. And yet love did come out of all the bartering. He had truly loved Arianne. But it was as if love was the design fault in an otherwise effective genetic machine.

Whatever the truth of this idea, it was certain that the question had not been whether Lucy was the 'right girl' for him but whether he was simply the 'wrong man' – for anyone.

And it was also certain that as much as his guilt over Lucy was genuine, he was dwelling on it because what he had done to Mila was worse. What he had done to Mila was *unthinkable*. When the memory of it threatened to overwhelm the horizon, he could think of nothing to do but run. First he ran up the steps, slamming and locking the door behind him. Then he snatched up his wallet and keys from the hall table and ran out on to the street.

With infinite gentleness, Alistair carried Rosalind's bag across the check-in hall. He had insisted on doing this – even though she was plainly far fitter than he, what with his ridiculous limp. He nodded to her – '*Yes, yes, of course, you go on*' – and she rushed off ahead in search of the right desk. When she found it, she waved and smiled at him and he lurched off in her direction, feeling ungainly. He was in more pain than he would have admitted.

'You all right? Leg OK?' she said as he arrived, but she was fiddling with her bag and not really waiting for his reply. He saw that she had asked after him out of habit – and, just then, he could only find this beautiful.

'Fine, thanks,' he said, knowing she would not hear. She was so excited – it was rather amazing to see. There was a thrilling breath-lessness in her voice.

There were two couples and a man ahead of them. They shuffled along as the man went up to the desk with his bag and ticket.

'Shouldn't be long,' Rosalind said.

'No,' he agreed, 'no time at all.'

As he watched her make sure, for the umpteenth time, that she had her passport and reference number, he remembered an odd thing about the circumstances in which they had got engaged. They had re-met after a long gap. He had resigned ninety-nine per cent of himself to the fact that she was beyond his expectations and had allowed himself to drift out of touch. But Rosalind had appeared unexpectedly at the Christmas party of an old St Hilda's friend of his. This friend, whose name he had now forgotten, had known Suzannah, who had brought her little sister along.

As far as Alistair could remember, the party had taken place around the time he was taken on by Alan Campbell's chambers. He had been astonished by Rosalind's being in London. With a smile, he remembered proposing they raise their glasses of eggnog to St Jude, the patron saint of lost causes.

But where had he imagined she would be if not in London? He could clearly recall his own relief that she was there. It had involved the realization that he would not now have to endure a long period of attempting simultaneously to put her out of his mind and also, in the hope of astonishing her one day, of drearily beginning to *make something of himself*. Yes, he remembered the relief clearly, but not where she had been going or why she had not gone.

The check-in queue shuffled forwards and he racked his mind. Suddenly it struck him. Of course: 'The Big Adventure'! She and Lara Siskin had been planning to go off on a tour of Italy and then Lara was injured or ill so the trip was called off. Suzannah had often brought it up bitchily at the beginning of their marriage when she whinged about not going on holiday enough. She would mention the *wasted* tickets and say what a *waste* it was that Rozzy hadn't had the guts to go on her own.

He had been furious with Suzannah for being so rude to her sister, who merely shrugged and called herself 'a silly sausage'. But also, less flatteringly to himself, he remembered being glad that Rosalind hadn't had 'the guts' to go on her own. He had been glad in a practical sense, because she had been at the party, but also in an emotional sense, because he hadn't really wanted his wife to have 'guts'. He had always relied on her dependence on him more than he cared to admit. Had he ensured it by patronizing her, by dismissing her interests as trivial, by implying that she was only qualified to express an opinion on household matters? He had undervalued her, that was for certain, but it had never dawned on him that this negligence might have been a subtle form of domestic violence.

The ground steward fixed labels on to Rosalind's luggage and shunted it on to the conveyor-belt. 'Well, there it goes,' Rosalind said, plainly stunned that this was really happening.

'Yes. There it goes,' Alistair said, smiling at her. Apparently he could only repeat variations of her words back to her. As if he had none of his own. He knew he must try to stay calm.

They moved off towards the 'DEPARTURES' sign and arrived a few feet in front of a row of desks and Passport officials. Rosalind stood in front of this view, embarrassed by the literalness of the barriers. She thought Alistair looked so sad and left out. 'Well, thank you very much for bringing me,' she said.

'Have a wonderful time, darling. A *really wonderful* time.'

She faced him. 'You will be all right, won't you, Alistair?'

'Me? I'll be fine. I shall miss you. But I'll be fine. Well,' he said awkwardly, pressing his lips to her cheek, knowing he had no right to kiss her mouth, 'well, you'd better go.'

But as he moved back, he found he could not let go of her and his hands gripped her arms, just as they had in the hallway at home a little while before. His heart leapt with fear that she might change her mind and leave him after all. Space . . . independence . . . perspective . . . She would see how stupid she had always been to love him!

As ever, Rosalind had understood his fears. She said, 'I suppose you'd like me to bring you back some photographs?'

Only she would have thought to say that, he thought. It was the perfect, most moderate kind of reassurance – a cool hand on his brow. She intended to come back with photographs. 'I'd like that so much, darling,' he said.

Alistair wondered how, throughout the course of their marriage, he had ever ceased to be amazed by the depths of Rosalind's generosity towards him. It was as if he had been unable to acknowledge its significance precisely because it was being wasted on him. Suddenly he felt that he might cry but he knew that this would be deeply inappropriate – mere self-indulgence.

She smiled at him and he knew they understood each other. She was not promising that they would be happy immediately – as she had so reasonably put it, there was 'a lot to live through' – but she was at least promising to come back. This was more than good enough, far better than he deserved.

None the less, it was still his instinctive desire to push for more, to cross-examine her until he understood her intentions precisely, until he had forced out of her some kind of legally binding guarantee. His heart jolted again, but he stopped himself. He knew that this was meaningless.

All his life he had applied standards to himself that no human being could have met. It struck him then that if he had always had cause to despair, this was a fitting punishment for spending his time so foolishly. Of course, all he had wanted was to hold something completely still – his own image in the pool at the very least – in defiance of the constant flow of doubt, the fear of being discovered. But how lonely he had been in his own exacting company!

And now here were his worst fears. Here were change and uncertainty, in the most intimate area of his life: Rosalind. He simply let them be. And it was with a sense of the beautiful and mystifying injustice in the world that he acknowledged that, after all he had done wrong, he felt blessed with – hope.

Perhaps there are two kinds of people in the world: those who make life their subject and those who are the subject themselves. One act of violence had knocked Alistair Langford from the first category into the second. He watched his dignified wife hand her passport to the official and he waved and smiled at her as she went through.

Luke was out of breath. He had spent a frantic hour and a half, having to return once to the house for proof of identity, and to visit several branches of his bank. Now he ran back home from the high street. In his pocket was a wad of fifty-pound notes, which amounted to two thousand pounds. It was all he had had left in his account.

He had not been outside in the morning for a few weeks now. All was bright and busy on the high street and although the noise was an assault on his funeral mood, he was glad that other people were happy. In the queue at the bank, he had even attempted to count blessings: just to be white and male, to have no inherited deformities, to have an ordinary blood type – these things gave you an enormous head start.

Of course, he had been born into far more than this. But even with all that he had, Arianne had not loved him – had not even acknowledged him as a recipient of love. He had merely been, as she said, 'a temporary thing'. Her heart had not stopped at Luke Langford because the exchange had not seemed fair to her. His heart and mind and body for *hers*? No, not a good deal. He had aspired to her, but she had not aspired to him.

Why the hell had Rosalind promised him he was perfect? How *could* she have done that?

In self-disgust, he literally spat these last two thoughts out of his head. He knew perfectly well that his mother had always shown him unconditional support and had always done her best to prevent him falling through the gaps in Alistair's love. And on the one occasion his mother had needed his protection, after all that had happened to her marriage, to her heart essentially, which, in spite of her age, was *no less real than his own*, he had not really been listening. He had let her do his scrambled eggs the way he liked them and thought about himself.

When he went down to the annexe, he found Mila awake. She looked at him in puzzlement and said, 'I do not sleep. But I am so tired.'

He adopted the calm voice he had designed for the occasion. 'Well, you've been through a lot,' he told her. 'You're upset.'

'We are so *like*,' she said, smiling at him. 'You also do not sleep if upset.'

Luke gritted his teeth and put the wad of money on the arm of the sofa. But just as he did so, Mila turned and ran to the mirror in the shower room. For a moment he was unsure if she had seen it, but when she spoke he knew she had not.

'Oh, is so ugly my face!' she cried. 'I think is bad for children see me!'

She was visible through the doorway. She tried to arrange her hair so that it covered some of the swelling, but it would not stay in place. She called out to him, 'Luke? How you say place in sea where is no one? Is *little little* country – very little.'

'Island?' Luke suggested. He wished she would just turn round, but who was he to interrupt the flow of her happiness?

'Yes, is right. Always you know! It is so clever.'

'But it's my own language,' he said.

Mila ignored this. 'Yes, I go in island for my face is nice again. Is nobody in there look me.' She giggled. 'But I think I like you also come. We are two people only in whole island. There is passport control: "*Only Luke and Mila*"! Yes?'

404

He said nothing in reply and to an onlooker he might even have appeared not to be listening, but with each high note of her joy, he could feel himself collapsing inside. Very slowly, he began the business of folding and tidying away illusions about his own essential goodness, which he had long carried in his mind. Here they would remain, assuming their place among the other souvenirs of his childhood – his old sports medals and school photographs, his first-aid certificates.

Oblivious to all this, Mila went on, 'And also we eat fruit of trees and we go to the sea for wash and is beautiful sun!'

She came out of the shower room, and as she did so, she allowed the hair she had been piling on top of her head to tumble down around her shoulders. She was smiling and as her eyes caught sight of the wad of banknotes, she thought for one extraordinary moment that Luke had anticipated her dream. He had brought money for a holiday! They would go away together – not out of England, of course, because she had no passport – but somewhere as quiet as an island.

But the look in his eyes could not have allowed this to last. She understood immediately. Her body visibly shrank – her shoulders hunched, her head lowered, she drew her arms in against herself. She cowered. Luke said, 'Look, Mila, everything is going to be *OK*. I've called my friend Jess. OK? You can stay with her for a few days until you find somewhere. You just *can't* stay here now, that's all. I'm sorry. But Jess is lovely and . . . I'll put you in a cab,' he said. 'I've called you a cab.'

She seemed unable to raise her face to look at him. He saw this, but he had decided what to say and he would doggedly say it. He continued, 'This money – this is two thousand pounds, Mila. You can get your passport and your National Insurance and the phone bills – everything you need for opening a bank account. Remember Goran said they're Serbs at Kwik-Kabs? I think it's the boss's brother who gets the passports. You know all this anyway. What I mean is, it's lucky because they'll explain it all in your language, won't they? So, all you really need,' he said, 'is the money. And here it is.'

His voice had built to a tinkling crescendo of optimism. When it had rung out and faded on the air like the sound of a bell, she found she could look at him. She found she could stare. She stared and stared at him until he turned away to an imaginary point of interest in the corner.

After a minute or so, she began to collect her possessions. He could hear her stuffing them into a plastic bag. He remembered Arianne finding the bag of Lucy's things under the sink when she was packing.

She had said, 'It's all a trail of plastic bags, really, isn't it?' She had asked him to remember that this was not her fault.

It was not Arianne's fault. But why had he assumed he had any more control than she did over such wild phenomena? Just as he had when he kicked walls in self-loathing if his team didn't win the tournament, he had blamed himself for the temporary nature of love. Perhaps all along this had been a kind of egotism.

Luke's mobile rang and he answered it, knowing it would be the cab firm. 'Oh, OK. Thank you very much,' he said. 'Your cab's outside,' he told Mila, 'but there's no hurry. No rush.'

She snatched up her bag and when he looked at her tormented face he wondered how any of this had happened. What landslides of consequences were set off at the significant moments in life. A few months ago he had caught sight of a sexy girl on a table. And now? Now he wanted to press money into Mila's hand. But there it lay, filthily inadequate, on the arm of the pink sofa. After a while, her hand reached out for it and, with an expression of disappointment that her face would never quite lose after that moment, she said, 'I take money. What else I have?'

There was no answer to this. In silence, Luke watched her walk out of the annexe. In an image he would never forget, her face was caught, framed for an instant: a lost girl crying, passing a window on to a beautiful garden.

As the aeroplane climbed, Rosalind noticed the way the fields became patches of rich colour in an abstract painting. England was going brown and yellow for autumn. It was incredible to think that in everyday existence, while she was down there, believing reality was the mess of people and the tangled details of life, this view was here for all who cared to see it. To the passenger on a plane that passed over her garden, she was merely a part of the blurry earth. But, to her, they were merely part of the blurry sky. Who was right? The answer was no one – or everyone, of course.

She remembered a programme she had once watched with Sophie about the beginning of the universe. It had been listed in the paper as *The Story of the Earth* and they had wondered how this could possibly be told in forty-five minutes, with commercial breaks. Sophie had been amused by the voiceover, which made the over-simplified physics sound like a trailer for a horror film. She had imitated it later for Alistair, wriggling her fingers at him as he poured a whisky: '"*Toxic gases swirled and temperatures swerved between violent extremes."* But silly as the programme undoubtedly was to educated people, Rosalind had been deeply struck by one piece of information. Apparently energy was indestructible. It couldn't be created or destroyed, it merely took on different forms throughout the never-ending ages of its existence. It might become a gas or a rock or a person or an orange on a tree, or even a very loud bang. This meant everything on earth was made of energy that had always been around, just changing over time.

This idea still struck Rosalind as rather lovely somehow. She remembered the peaceful voice of Sister Margaret, reading to them at school from Ecclesiastes: '"What has been will be, and what has been done is what will be done; and there is nothing new under the sun. Is there a thing of which it is said, 'See, this is new?' It has been already, in the ages before us."'

The biblical words were unquestionably more beautiful, but it did sound like the same story.

It occurred to her then that perhaps, just like energy, emotion is indestructible. Even if it seems to have disappeared or to have arrived unexpectedly, it has only taken on a new shape. Perhaps, she thought, each family has its combined store of love and pain. And if people don't live out their share, then the most sensitive take it upon themselves to suffer.

She thought of all those battles she and Alistair had avoided – or Luke and Alistair, who had always been a disaster together, really. Perhaps Sophie had become a kind of family scapegoat, fighting it all out against her own starved body, her own scarred arms.

Oh, she had done such damage to herself over the years – and they had each privately blamed her for spoiling the peace in the house! Had Sophie in fact been acting, in some mysterious way, on their behalf?

Emotion must go somewhere, after all, she thought, if it can never be destroyed.

Both Rosalind and Alistair had often been seized with terror that their daughter's body would not fully recover and that she would never be able to have children. They had not voiced this concern, but Rosalind knew her husband shared it. She knew he shared it very painfully in the night. And she was also aware that if this had turned out to be the case, they would both have held him personally responsible. One way or another, he was the one who had brought hatred into the house; Rosalind had never hated anyone in her life.

But was this a cause for self-congratulation? She might not have hated, she might not have contributed so unmanageable a blast of emotion to the family store, but she had never loved enough, she told herself. Her love had stopped in the face of fear – her daughter's fear, her husband's fear, certainly. But even her sister's alcoholism and divorces had been impossible to confront. Suzannah could not forgive Rosalind for her emotionally hygienic mind – and quite rightly, Rosalind thought. After the split with her first husband, Suzannah had been devastated and her own sister, long in the habit of survival by restraint and pretence, had suggested they go to Kew Gardens for tea! Suzannah, being herself, had politely declined the invitation and drunk enough gin to kill a horse.

Only Luke had been easy to love because, until recently, he had spoken the same moderate emotional language as she did. He had been easy to love because he was so like her.

But this was simply not good enough! One had to love outside oneself. It was easy to be captivated by similarity, but to learn to love *difference* – frightening and mysterious as it might be – this was the second and the greater act of love.

Who, she thought, could such unwise parents thank but God Himself for the fact that their daughter was pregnant, for the fact that hatred had burnt off under the African sun? She had never felt closer to Sophie than she did now, at this precious time, when her own child was becoming a mother.

Just then she was aware of an absence, of something missing, and she looked at the empty seat beside her. Immediately her body told her to go and check that Alistair was all right because he seemed to have been gone a terribly long time.

Rosalind leant forward, but her hand stopped before it had reached the seatbelt.

As she sat back, a picture came into her mind – of the tickets for her trip round Italy, which, long ago, she had been afraid to use, which she had left suffocating behind the clock on her bedroom mantelpiece. Just then, her fears seemed curiously irrelevant: they were primitive and faintly sinister, like Aztec figurines.

Beneath her, she watched as the land gave way to sea and, gradually, sea was lost to clouds.